WITHIN THE DARKNESS

L. ROSE

Before I was born, the world changed.

When monsters stepped into the light to rule, most humans were forced into servitude.

My family was one of many.

But I hold a secret inside me.

One I don't dare share.

Until I meet my new vampire master—who wears cold and angry like a second skin—and his shifter friends. While he can't compel me, I long to share every part of me with them.
Only fear holds me back.

I need courage to move from within the darkness to the light. But maybe with the support of the three men, I can embrace my true self. And if I bring change to humanity along the way, that will be an even bigger win.

To those readers who love a fantasy romance where she doesn't have to choose between her guys. Sometimes its good to be greedy!

One

TWENTY-SEVEN YEARS AGO, the world changed. The monsters who lived in the dark walked out into the light, and things for humans weren't the same. Actually, that was wrong. Things were the same for the wealthy, but those who didn't have money to back them, their lives altered in a way no one would have seen coming.

Not for me, though, since I was born into the world already changed. It was my parents' existence that had been altered in a blink of an eye, as had the lives of most of the human race.

The vampires, shifters, and enchanters led the uprising before I was conceived. But it was drilled into me from a young age that the monsters were stronger, faster, and deadlier than us. It was inevitable that, after years of war against the humans, they won and took control.

To try and create some semblance of peace in this new world, a council was formed after battles for land control continued, as well as a whole bunch of other dramas that created even more chaos. Leaders were selected to ensure order. The council contained three members of each species, and they oversaw everyone. However, after holding a fifteen-year-long position, the council members were switched out with newer monsters.

The council also appointed house leaders in various parts of the world—those who stood above the rest and governed, policed, and controlled their assigned areas, only seeking the help from the council when needed.

It was the monsters time to reign, and they relished the control.

Equality only existed for humans with money or skills.

Those who didn't have the riches to stand by the monsters and live a regular life were forced into servitude with no rights and a pittance of a wage. The monsters refused to supply us with anything other than a room, uniform, and food. Our contract could be bought and sold without our input, and, like the poor humans we were, we had to obey our masters.

Needless to say, life as I knew it was pretty damn unfair.

"We've stepped up in the world, Amara. Make sure you don't ruin this for us," Mom said from behind me. She was excited because the family who bought us was one of those governing families. They were vampires, and their family ruled over a large clan.

A shudder swept over me, and my fear rose, but I still caught her gaze in the mirror and nodded. Drawing in a calming breath, not that it helped much, I finished braiding my long raven hair and then ran my hands down the front of my uniform. Double-checking there wasn't a weapon in sight, I exhaled, confident my blades were hidden under the god-awful maid outfit.

Mom went on. "If I was glad for anything, it was when that old codger died, and we were bought by the Prince family."

Sorrow stabbed through me. How could she be so crass? Mr. Langley, a wolf shifter who had lost his mate, may have been old, but he was a good master. He was gentle, kind, and had been my friend and teacher. He'd taught at a local school and allowed me to attend there with him as an "assistant," but really, he'd let me sit in class like the other students. He'd taken over the role of father figure when I lost my real father at a very young age.

I missed Mr. Langley terribly.

"Do not use this power around someone, Amara, and never tell anyone what you can do. No one." Words Mr. Langley had used one afternoon a year ago, when he'd caught me using my power to help in the garden, rang through my mind once more. *"People will want to use you if they find out, and believe me when I say it won't be good for you, my dear."* The urgent tone had struck fear within me. Since the day he'd caught me, he had insisted training me to fight with weapons. It was all for "my own protection." Because one day, I would need to use everything I had to keep myself safe. But from whom, he didn't know, and neither did I.

Always have a weapon on you, even when you sleep.

I did. Always.

Everything Mr. Langley told me to do, I did. He didn't have to teach me. He didn't have to give me the chance to continue school or treat us kindly, but he did. Never once did he treat me like a slave.

"Oh, stop looking like that," Mom demanded, bringing me from my thoughts. "Look where we are." She giggled, and I barely contained my eye roll. "You know, Olivia won't believe the luck we've gained. Why, our rooms are enormous compared to the one we shared at that old man's cottage." She hummed under her breath and straightened the bed I had already made.

"Mr. Langley," I said.

Her cool gaze swung to me. "You dare to correct me?"

I ground my teeth together and shook my head. My gaze went to the floor in front of me. Anger burned inside me. I hadn't despised my mom my whole life. Mr. Langley had told me she used to be good and caring when I was younger, when my father had been around, and I remembered glimpses of her smiling face and sweet words. However, now it was hard to recall those moments.

After my father passed and as I grew older, she turned bitter—telling me she wouldn't have become a slave if it wasn't for me. She would have had the money to be seen as an equal if it wasn't for me. Thankfully, whenever she started ranting, Mr. Langley had always been there to distract her or had pulled me out of the situation.

"I wish you had a different mother, Amara. You deserve so much more."

It had been sweet of him to say, but I couldn't change what I had been dealt. I was stuck in this miserable existence with her.

"Come on. We can't be late when they give the job details out," Mom said as she made her way to the door and glanced over her shoulder to make sure I followed. I had no choice but to do so. "If we're lucky, we'll get jobs in the garden or kitchen. Anything is better than cleaning. My hands just can't take it anymore." She was vain. So very vain. To the point that she thought Mr. Langley would have taken her on as a wife if she flirted with him enough.

It didn't work, of course.

But I had a feeling she would try it here as well. She'd be a fool if she did. I didn't think she understood just how dangerous vampires were.

There was also one job she didn't mention.

A blood slave.

A person who sat around and waited to be called to their master to satisfy their thirst. I prayed to the gods above I didn't get that job, even though I wasn't even sure the gods were real. How could they be? Why would they give the monsters control?

"Straighten your shoulders," Mom snapped when she stopped at the end of the hall. She shook her head. "You should have put on makeup." I'd always refused to use the items she'd stolen from the late Mrs. Langley.

Besides that, there was no point. I didn't want to impress anyone. Mom had caked her face in the stuff, hoping to look younger than her forty-eight years.

She made me sick.

"I swear, if you ruin this for me somehow, I will make your life hell."

I bit my tongue to keep the snort at bay. I was already living in hell, more so after Mr. Langley passed away and he could no longer be the filter between Mom and her controlling ways. Nodding, I waited for her to move around the corner. When she did, I started forward, slouching while shooting her a middle finger.

I stopped when my bottom lip trembled, and hopelessness washed through me. Closing my eyes, I took a deep breath and quickly opened my eyes again. Resting my hand against my uneasy stomach, I drew in another breath.

I was stronger than this. I could do this. I could live and hope to one day have a time in life when I wouldn't have to follow.

I am strong.

A noise escaped my lips when I saw someone standing in the shadows at the other end of the hall. Had the person seen what I did behind my mom's back?

Maybe I wasn't so strong after all, because dread pumped through my veins, causing my hands to shake. I tucked them behind me and gripped them together. With a frantic heart, I thought of the dagger at my thigh, and I swiftly made my way down the hall, then into the room Mom had just walked through.

Mom smiled coldly at me. Anger only I was able to see burned in her eyes. She put on the show for the other new slaves and the head butler who stood off to the side where another door lay. Mom.... Actually, I was sick of calling her my mom. She hadn't been one for many years. In my head I could at least fight back. *Charlotte* pointed to the spot beside her. I shifted over there, and as soon as I stopped next to her, she gave the room a fake smile but pinched my side hard.

"Where did you go?"

I pointed toward the door. "Nowhere. A painting caught my attention outside the room."

She laughed. "You were always easily distracted by things. Simpleminded."

I didn't respond, but I did thank my luck that I remembered the hallway we'd come from had been lined with paintings. The mansion was something like a museum with plates of armor, cased documents, sculptures, and such placed all over. They were mainly in the Prince family's living quarters; the servant's quarters weren't so extravagant. Not that it bothered me. I didn't see the need to show things off for other people's sake. Unless Mrs. Prince enjoyed seeing those things herself.

As I adjusted from one foot to the other, Charlotte pinched me again. I ground my teeth together and busied my mind with the people around us. There were two women my age, or a little older, who giggled with each other; the fools were excited. A man and his son, from what I gathered by the way he had a hand on the young boy's shoulder. The boy, who looked about twelve, seemed scared, the father uneasy. There were two other men. One appeared close to twenty-five and glancing around the room as if waiting for someone to jump out. He was ready to take them on, judging by the way his fists were clenched at his sides. The other seemed to be in his thirties. He stood in a military pose, like nothing fazed him. I'd wondered how they'd come to be bought or why there were so many positions available, but knew I probably wouldn't find the answers.

Then there was one other woman, around the same age as Charlotte, with a weird polite smile on her face. I didn't know this group's story, but they all would have been in the same boat as Charlotte and me.

Poor. Destined for a life of servitude.

All of the women were dressed in black-and-white maids' outfits that went from collarbone to ankle. The men and the boy wore black trousers and shirts with gold ties.

The twentysomething man bounced on his feet, obviously hating waiting for the Prince family to give us details on our assignments.

The Prince family.

Everyone knew who they were.

The head of the family, Kane, was the clan leader, age unknown, but old enough to rule over a thousand vampires and a large part of the city we resided in. I'd heard he was cruel and would kill anyone who went against him. The wife, Crista, was beautiful and cherished among her people. But everyone knew not to cross her or she'd be just as mean as her husband. Then there was—

"Attention. Line up into one line," Bennet, the butler we'd previously met, called. The others scuttled to stand on either side of Charlotte and me. Bennett's head tilted toward the door, and he cleared his throat. "The Prince family has arrived."

The doors behind him opened, and in glided our masters, Kane and Crista Prince.

Their son was Kincaid. He was twenty-three, a couple of years older than myself, and I'd known of him from high school when Mr. Langley had taken a new position there, bringing me with him.

There was no way Kincaid knew who I was, since I was younger and beneath his status. Also, I'd only ever seen him from afar. I made sure to keep out of any alpha's sight and off their radar. Their power intimidated me. Usually, a vampire with Mr. Prince's status would be classed as a master vampire, but the title had changed over time, and all family heads were now referred to as alphas. It simply meant they were more dominant than others. Though, from what Mom had told me, we were only allowed to call our owners "master." The alpha title was used when or *if* a servant had to greet another alpha of a different line, and the monsters also utilized the title among themselves.

I hadn't needed to worry about any type of title with Mr. Langley. He had preferred for us to use his first name, but I had always called him Mr. Langley to show the respect I had for him.

Charlotte tugged on my dress. I quickly slipped into a curtsey and stayed down until either the people around me stood or someone said something. My knees shook as time went by. I wanted to yell for them to hurry up but would only be punished for it.

"Rise," Mr. Prince ordered crisply.

We straightened, but I kept my eyes downcast. The less attention I got, the better chance I had at a half-decent job within the house. I would even take cleaning. *Please, anything but blood donor.*

"You understand that your servitude is with this house, and you will follow the rules?"

"Yes, master," everyone echoed.

"Everyone, stand tall," Bennett called. "The master

will walk the line, stop in front of you, and bestow on you a position within the family."

I wanted to gag, but I quickly swallowed and lifted my gaze to stare straight ahead. My body tingled with an urge to run, and I fought the need by digging my nails into my palms behind my back. I could feel eyes on me, but I didn't dare look away from the wall. I worried who it might be, since the only others off to my right were the Prince family. They were speaking so low that no one could have heard them, and I was surprised they heard each other, but then again, they had abilities they could use.

I sensed movement and heard Bennett say, "This is Camila and Zoe. Both are twenty-three. They worked as housekeepers for the Solaris family."

Mr. Prince hummed. "They would have sold them because of their money situation." When no one said anything, Mr. Prince ordered, "Blood donors."

My stomach bottomed out for the two of them.

"This is Lyall and his son, Elliot. Lyall is forty-one, his son twelve. They were grounds assistants, also with the Solaris family."

"Keep the same positions here."

"We have here Charlotte and her daughter, Amara. Charlotte is forty-eight, Amara twenty-one. They were with Waylon Langley until he passed on."

Mr. Prince grunted. "Waylon was a well-respected man even from within our faction. Previous positions?"

Mom preened beside me.

"Cooking and housekeeping," Bennett informed him.

Mr. Prince stepped closer my way. The sensation of him studying me made my skin crawl.

"The older woman in the kitchens, cleaning when she's not," Mr. Prince announced. Charlotte made a noise in the back of her throat. She thought her looks would have impressed him in some way. When my lips twitched, I quickly thinned them, holding back the laughter desperate to escape.

"Amara will be servant to Kincaid."

No!

My eyes widened, but I quickly blanked my expression and clenched my teeth so hard, I was surprised they didn't shatter.

I would have taken a position as a blood donor over being servant to Kincaid. He scared me, and I wasn't sure why that was. Maybe his hard expression, his cold, dark eyes. Maybe his snappish tone, or the hatred he had in his heart, which bled out through his words and actions.

It didn't matter that our paths had never crossed. I knew all of that to be true.

Whatever it was that terrified me, I feared him more than the father. Quite a feat, since I'd heard terrible things about Mr. Prince.

Mr. Prince stepped along the line, while Bennett stopped in front of me. "Do you understand your position?"

Nodding, I bit on the inside of my lip so I didn't beg for something, anything else. If I did, there was no doubt I would be killed for insolence.

"Are you sure?" Bennett asked.

"Yes," I uttered. I had heard everything about a

servant's role. Mr. Langley had informed me of many things in case I was ever in need. Maybe he knew he wouldn't always be around. A servant was to be at their master's beck and call, day and night. I would have to follow Kincaid around like a lost puppy and do anything he wished for me to do.

My stomach rolled, and I swallowed, taking a shuddering breath. Bennett saw my reaction and offered a sad smile before he moved back to Mr. Prince's side. I didn't hear where the others were assigned; the blood rushed to my head too much and my ears started to ring.

What I needed was to calm down. I needed to stop my racing heart, or I would gain the attention of all the Princes. I dug my nails into my palms again, the pain lessening the panic attack. I dropped my gaze to the floor and emptied my mind.

Rolling back my shoulders, I straightened again.

"Someone will be along to take you to your new positions shortly. Thank your masters," Bennett said.

I dipped into a curtsey like the other women as the men bowed. Even Elliot, the youngest. We always had to show respect for the masters, no matter who had control over us within the family.

As soon as the Prince family left with Bennett following and closing the door after them, the two giggling idiots approached me. I tried to recall their names, but I couldn't remember.

"Oh my God, you are so lucky to serve Kincaid. I wish I was working so close to him. Then again, we're just as excited to be blood donors for any of them." She beamed.

The other nodded beside her. "I wouldn't worry about the rumors, though. I'm sure that's all they are."

Confusion dipped my brows. "Rumors?"

"That Kincaid killed his last few servants."

Blood drained from my face.

Charlotte stepped closer. "Please excuse us for a moment." She gripped my arm and dragged me to a corner. Once there, she got in my face and snarled, "How did you get a job like that over me?"

Did she not hear what that woman said about Kincaid? Yet, she was still peeved I got a better-standing position than her. I shook my head, appalled. "I don't know."

Her hold tightened. Nails dug into my skin as she shook my arm. "Don't fucking lie to me."

"I had nothing to do with *their* choice."

"Tell them you won't do it. Tell them you want me to."

They would kill me.

As I stared at her, I saw she knew this, yet she didn't care.

She didn't care about her own daughter's safety. My life.

How utterly disgusting. The knowledge had my stomach churning, hatred rising, and I snapped in a low tone, "No."

Her eyes widened, then quickly narrowed. "No?"

I tugged my arm from her grasp and shook my head. I couldn't hold back any longer. Not when I now knew that what she felt for me was beyond hatred. I was at a loss with the woman who birthed me.

Shaking my head again, I said, "I knew you hated me, but to sentence me to death because you want to... what? Be known as a Prince servant? So you can brag? Or is it because you find the young Prince handsome and want to—"

My head rocked to the side from the slap she delivered. The noise echoed around the room.

Rage uncurled inside me, and I slowly turned my head back and caught her gaze. Whatever she saw in my expression had her stepping back. For the first time, I wanted to ignore Mr. Langley's warning.

I wanted to hurt her.

Bennett appeared beside us. I hadn't even heard him enter the room again. "What is the meaning of this?"

Charlotte straightened and smiled sweetly. "Oh, just a misunderstanding. But my daughter wishes to ask you something."

Bennett faced me. I glared at Charlotte and said nothing.

Bennett sniffed and hummed under his breath. "Amara?"

"I can't seem to remember what it was, sir. Sorry."

"*Amara*," Charlotte scolded.

"Yes?"

"You wanted to ask him if you could switch—"

"No, *Mother*, it was you who wanted to switch positions with me. But when I refused, you hit me." She gaped like a fish as I turned to Bennett. "I am honored to be a servant to Master Kincaid." The lie tasted disgusting, but I would not follow the woman before me ever again.

"Amara." Fake tears clouded her eyes.

It wouldn't work, not when I had seen the wolf behind the sheep's clothing. I was done.

"Very well, Amara." Bennett nodded. "Please follow me, and I will take you to your new room."

"She gets a new room?" Charlotte cried, only to quickly clamp her lips closed.

Bennett sneered at her before spinning and walking away. "Come, Amara. The rest of you, stay until someone else arrives to show you where to go."

I didn't look back as I followed Bennett, closing the door behind me. Even if I was walking into a new danger, I was glad to see the end of Charlotte, my so-called mother.

Two

MY PULSE RACED and my hands wouldn't quit shaking, so I rested one against my thigh where I had a dagger strapped and kept moving. Knowing I was armed helped. Somewhat at least. Bennett took us through the house to where the Prince family's living quarters were.

"I could speak with Mr. Prince and inform him about your *mother*," he snarled, "hitting you."

My wide gaze rose. He didn't stop, didn't turn when he spoke, but tension radiated off him. He definitely didn't approve of Charlotte's behavior.

"No. Thank you, though."

He hummed under his breath. "You are kindhearted. Be sure to steel that heart when it comes to your new position."

My throat thickened. "I will," I uttered. "She will get her own," I added, just as softly. I had to believe that. I just didn't want it to be from my own hand. She would do something to jeopardize her life, though, and I couldn't bring myself to care. Maybe when it happened, I would feel differently, but I doubted it. Did that make me cold? Probably, but she'd driven me to be this way.

"I believe you are right. Especially when one of the masters or the mistress sees the mark on your cheek."

I raised a hand and covered said cheek. It was tender, but I pushed the pain down to deal with later… if I ever got a chance to have time to myself again. I dragged my top teeth over my bottom lip while hoping no one in the Prince family concerned themselves with a slave's family dispute. Though, I couldn't do anything to stop them if they did. I also couldn't have it play on my mind when I had more pressing matters to deal with.

Like staying alive.

Had that woman been right? Had Kincaid killed his last few servants?

No. I wouldn't let that thought settle and fester inside my mind. Doing so would make me vulnerable in my new position.

Pushing my shoulders back, I lifted my gaze from the floor to Bennett's back just in time to see him stop in front of a door. He turned his head my way. "This is Master Kincaid's suite. Your room is next door. He will be getting ready for his college classes; you are to accompany him and do anything he asks of you. Some days he stays in the dorms at college and some he comes home. Wherever he goes, so will you."

"I understand." My calm voice surprised me, since on the inside I was a mess.

Bennett knocked on the door. I bit down on my tongue to keep from screaming, "Stop" while my heart hammered in my chest. It was too late to do anything, though, because next I heard a gruff "Enter."

The butler twisted the handle and stepped through. I froze for a second, then forced myself to walk in after him. It didn't prevent me from hiding behind Bennett, though, with my eyes on the floor.

"Master Kincaid, I have brought the servant Amara."

Kincaid grunted. Apparently, that was answer enough for Bennett. He turned and jolted a little at seeing me behind him, but I caught his small smile before he shifted around me. I slid my gaze down once more. My heart skipped a beat when I heard the door shut behind Bennett.

Something dropped to the floor, a chair squeaked, and my pulse raced as footsteps approached me. Two sock-covered feet stopped close.

"Do I scare you?"

Was I supposed to be honest? Lie? No, he could probably tell a lie with his hearing. I swallowed. "A little."

"Look at me," he clipped. My stomach swooshed as I lifted my gaze all the way up and met his dark eyes. A soft tingle started in my lower belly, and even though I had a tight hold on my power, the darkness gave off a tiny trill inside me. Mentally, I scolded it until it settled once more.

He was taller and broader compared to most vampires I'd seen. I wondered, and not for the first time, how he got the jagged scar that ran from his left temple, over his eye, and down across the bridge of his nose to his right cheek. Vampires healed without scarring. Why hadn't he?

"What about now?" he said with a sneer.

Kincaid was asking if I feared him more because of the

mark on his face. I searched myself for the answer and found it, but I also thought it strange when I realized that the scar didn't bother me. He must have gone through a terrible ordeal to have it upon his skin, and for some reason, that didn't sit right with me.

I made sure to keep his gaze. "Still the same."

His jaw clenched as he drew in a deep breath through his nose. His upper lip rose. I guessed whatever he scented, he didn't like. Most of me wanted to flee, but I steeled my body and pressed my palm against my dagger. Then there was the very small part of me that wanted to reach out to him. I brushed that side away quickly.

His eyes zeroed in on my bruise. "Who hit you?"

"No one," I answered.

He studied me a moment longer. "Get my bag."

I nodded once. "Yes, master." I walked around him and spotted his bag on the floor at the end of a couch. I picked up the heavy backpack and slipped my arms through the straps. I nearly tilted backward from the weight but locked my legs and used my hands under the bag to help hold it up.

Glancing at Kincaid, I found him waiting and watching with his boots on by the door. "Let's go." He stormed out the living area in his suite. I quickly followed him but stayed a couple of paces back.

Cleaners scuttled by or quickly fled the area as soon as they saw Kincaid. People were fearful of him. I hoped I grew out of mine quickly, or else working for him would be a nightmare.

We continued walking, and once more, gratitude eased through me for the grueling training Mr. Langley had put me through to strengthen my mind and body. If he hadn't, I would have been a huffing and puffing mess. Especially when I had to carry the backpack.

Kincaid stepped out the front door and into the morning sun. The myths about vampires were a lie; they could walk in the daylight and weren't affected by crosses, garlic, or silver. The best way to kill them was to cut off their heads. Much like all monsters.

Closing the front door after myself, I sped down the million steps to catch up with Kincaid as he climbed into the back of a stretch Hummer limousine. I paused at the opened door. Was I supposed to get in or was there another vehicle for the help?

I glanced around and saw no other car. With a final pat to my thigh and a deep breath, I pulled his bag from my shoulders and held it in front of me as I slid onto the seat. I cringed when the door shut with a bang. I shifted to get comfortable, pressing close to the door that was my only escape and gripping the armrest.

"Who do we have here?" a husky male voice asked. I didn't dare look or move. I kept my gaze on the floor, knowing if I brought more attention to myself, it wouldn't be good.

"Servant," Kincaid clipped. "Thanks for grabbing the car, Levi."

Levi.

My heart stumbled.

The vehicle moved. I didn't know what college Kincaid went to, but I hoped it was close by. The pressure from being in a tight space with two alphas was stifling.

"All a part of the job, *master*." It sounded like a taunt.

"Call me that again, Levi, and I'll fucking kick your ass."

Levi snorted. "You could try."

Kincaid was close with only two other people, from what I had seen in high school and what had been reported on the news. Levi Grayson was one of them. He was a twenty-five-year-old co-owner of a warden company. In other words, he was one of the members who provided top security to those who needed it.

As he was the next alpha in line, Kincaid needed it.

What I didn't understand was how Levi—a lion shifter and also the up-and-coming top alpha to the Grayson pride—would run the business when he would be busy being head alpha to his people? Not that I'd spent too much time wasting my thoughts on it.

Then there was Silas Peril, who was also twenty-five and the other owner of the warden company. He was in the same position as Levi when it came to his status, since he was next in line to become alpha of the Peril Weyr family. Dragon shifters.

Silas and Levi didn't currently attend college, having already done the courses for their leadership roles. They were now on their one-year break before they took over. However, neither of them was lazing about in their free year. Instead, they worked as Kincaid's bodyguards. But who guarded them?

Another thing that surprised most people was that Kincaid associated with shifters. The three friends always created a bit of a stir when together, since species tended to stick to their own kind.

While the council ruled together, it didn't mean all species got along.

Sure, it was general knowledge that Silas and Levi's business had a 100-percent success rating at protecting their charges, and Kincaid would want the best. But the men had been close from a young age. Still, no one was foolish enough to question any of them about their friendship.

I could feel Levi's gaze on me. I wanted to look at the boy who I used to admire from afar during high school. His amber eyes were always full of mischief, and he wore a cocky smirk well. But I didn't dare look. The three of them had always flustered me with their good looks. Thankfully, I'd gone unnoticed by being too young and the wrong type of species to get their attention.

"Are you staying on campus tonight?" Levi asked, and I chanced a glance his way. His eyes were already on me, and when ours clashed, a tingle spread through my lower belly. My body wasn't the only part of me that reacted. Like with Kincaid, my darkness took notice of Levi, sparking and then settling when I admonished it.

I quickly looked away.

Kincaid sighed. "Yes." Great. Another new place I knew nothing about. Where did the servants stay? Did I dare ask?

No. No, I didn't.

"Did you hear from Silas last night?"

"No doubt he would have told you the same thing, but he said he would be late due to a meeting with his uncle."

Levi hummed. "And the other issue?"

Kincaid growled in the back of his throat. "I know you believe another attack will happen, but I don't. Not after the message we left last time."

My pulse raced, but other than that, I didn't react.

"It's starting, Kincaid. The closer you get to taking over, the more your life will be at risk."

"I know, and the same goes for you and Silas." My master's tone was sharp.

Levi snorted. "The attacks seem to be intended more for you, Kincaid. Silas and I haven't had one in eight months."

Kincaid sighed. "The sooner we can move in together, the better."

Levi laughed. "Your parents aren't ready for that yet."

"I don't fucking care anymore."

"Once things are worked out, we'll consider it again. For now, we must be vigilant for any type of attack."

What was I suddenly involved in? Why were they being attacked? Did it mean my life wouldn't be safe? My heart thumped so hard with fear, I worried it would crack a rib.

The car slowed. Levi shifted in his seat. "You might have a good one for once."

Kincaid snorted. "I doubt it." They were talking about me. I didn't care. What I did worry about was what they'd been talking about before that.

When the car stopped, I flung the door open and got out. Sliding Kincaid's bag onto my shoulders, I stood by the door, waiting. Kincaid was first out, then Levi. Both received attention from men and women walking around the outside of the main campus building. Closing the door, I quietly followed Kincaid as he and Levi veered off to the east side of the building. They spoke so softly to each other, I couldn't hear what was being said, but I didn't care too much anyway. My heart was already in my throat over what I'd heard. There was something serious and dangerous going on. I needed to know what in case I had to save myself.

After we'd entered a building and stopped just outside a classroom, a sultry voice called, "Kincaid." I glanced to the left. A woman around the same age as Kincaid approached with a wicked smile on her lips. I frowned as a sudden burst of hatred entered me.

I shook the emotion away and watched the small boy, who seemed no older than ten, following her. His back was weighed down by a large backpack and he held a handbag that also seemed heavy, judging from the way he struggled with it.

"Angelica." Kincaid's tone was no different from what he'd used before—tight and gruff. A slight dullness hit Angelica's eyes, but it disappeared quickly.

She flicked her hair over her shoulder. "How have you been?"

"Since I saw you last week? Fine." Kincaid stepped through the door while Levi threw his head back and laughed.

Angelica's expression darkened as she ground her teeth together. The young boy stumbled into her, and she spun, grabbing the back of his shirt and shaking him. "You stupid little runt."

Anger warmed my belly. I stepped closer to her, stretching out a hand to stop her when my other wrist was grasped and I was spun away from the scene. Levi dipped his brows at me and shook his head before nodding at the lecture room.

Even though my skin tingled from his touch, I wanted to fight his silent order. I wanted to do what was right and tell Angelica to not treat her servant like that. I wished I *could* fight her, but if I did, I wouldn't get anywhere.

There was no justice for humans in my position. If the monsters wanted to act like we were the dirt beneath their nails, they could.

It needed to change.

Sorrow washed over me as I gently tugged my wrist free and walked into the room. I could only hope she didn't harm the poor boy. I didn't even know what type of paranormal she was. If I knew, and if she was alone, I could have done something... maybe.

Disgust twisted my stomach. I hated that the fear of losing my own life to protect another had me second-guessing my actions.

Would it ever change?

Would they see us as more than the help?

The only thing I could do was hope that when the time came for the new alphas—the sons or daughters from an alpha or a direct bloodline—to step into their power positions when they reached twenty-six, they would see the injustice and do something about it. If the current alpha didn't have a family member to take over, they would keep their position until they deemed someone worthy or someone challenged him or her for it.

Though, I doubted things would change when the next alphas stepped up.

Not for the first time, I wished I could use my powers to fight. I wished I could help the world, the humans... even though I wasn't sure if I truly was one. My power gave off an excited little peep inside me at the thought of fighting.

I could feel Kincaid's burning gaze on me when I moved by him and stood at his back. He switched it to Levi, who smiled, rolled his eyes, and shook his head slightly.

Angelica entered and relief loosened the tension I'd been holding when I saw the boy was unmarked. I moved my gaze back down to Kincaid and couldn't help but glare at the idiot. If he hadn't brushed Angelica off as if she were nothing, even when she was obviously into him, then she wouldn't have lashed out.

I thinned my lips when Kincaid suddenly faced me, and his gaze seared into mine. I didn't look away. I didn't move. My eyes watered from keeping the stare. Eventually I gave in and blinked, and I was sure I saw a small smirk on Kincaid's lips, but when I glanced at his mouth, it was gone.

"Bag." I slid it off my shoulders and held it out to him. He took it, and thankfully, he then faced the front again.

The professor entered and started speaking about the profits when owning your own business. Levi pulled a paperback out of his back pocket and relaxed back in his seat to read. I had no use for the knowledge, since I would never be so lucky, so I zoned the lecturer out and took in the room around me.

The large classroom was nearly full; only a few empty seats were scattered around. Just under half of the people had a servant standing at their back. Most of those with servants sat in the back pews so their servants didn't obstruct the views of another alpha. If those spots were already taken, I noticed the alphas who sat in the middle or front seats, their servants stood off to the side of the room instead of behind their master.

I didn't know if they were just rich children of humans or others like Kincaid and Levi. Although, where those two were concerned, it was easy to tell they were something other than human. It was the way they moved and acted, but also the power that rolled off them in waves even I could feel. It stated they were some of the strong ones. Alphas.

By the time the hour-long session was over, my feet were killing me from standing in the same spot. I noticed I wasn't the only one when the boy assigned to Angelica bounced on his feet to get the blood flowing once more. *Please don't let her notice his fidgeting.*

The professor had already left the room, but Kincaid and Levi stayed in their seats. Some of the others did as well, while the rest filed out after the professor. I wanted to ask what we were waiting for, but of course, I kept my mouth shut.

When new students swept into the room, I bit down on my tongue to stop the groan from being heard. However, I still managed to make a small noise in the back of my throat, which had both Kincaid and Levi glancing over their shoulders at me.

"I think I like her." Levi grinned.

"Don't," Kincaid said, facing the front again.

Levi winked and shifted his gaze to the door as Silas

entered. My darkness perked up once again as my belly fluttered. Silas made his way toward the other two and slid into the free seat beside Kincaid. A girl about my age, maybe younger, scurried in after him and dropped a bag at Silas's feet before curtseying, and then she stood at his back.

Was I supposed to curtsey when I handed over Kincaid's bag?

Shit.

The woman leaned in and whispered out the corner of her mouth, "Hey."

Glancing at her, I nodded and faced the front, pressing a hand to my lower stomach, since it wasn't settling.

What was it about those three? That they were appealing was undeniable, but my body hadn't reacted this way in the past. Neither had my power. Admittedly, it hadn't fully surfaced until I was sixteen, and by then they'd already left the high school.

Instead of thinking about them, I forced my mind to the fact I was going to have to massage my own feet later on, *if* I got time. It wouldn't surprise me if I fell flat on my face when it was time to move since my feet would be asleep.

"My name's Mary."

Internally, I sighed and ground my teeth together. Didn't she know speaking to me could cause trouble? I dipped my head again but stayed quiet.

She bounced on her feet. "What's yours?"

Shaking my head, I pressed a finger to my lips.

"Come on, tell me—"

"You need to teach your servant better, Silas. They're to be seen, not heard," the professor said as he entered the room. Mary blanched. The professor was some type of paranormal. Even rich humans wouldn't have the confidence to speak to any of the three men in front of me like that.

"Lucky she's not a servant, but our assistant." He thumbed at Levi and himself. "What's also lucky is that I'm not here to take your fucking class but to work. How about we both just do our jobs, yeah?"

The professor glared. "Do not take that tone with me."

"Do not stick your nose in my business and I won't."

Silas was just as intimidating as Kincaid. If I didn't clench my thighs together, there was a chance I would pee myself.

The professor glared at Silas for a moment longer before he addressed the class. Obviously, he wasn't stupid enough to take on more than he could handle when it came to Silas.

Before today, my future had already appeared bleak. Now I wasn't sure I would live another month. Tears brimmed. I quickly clenched my teeth and blinked them away.

AFTER CLASS, I trailed behind the men with Mary at my side. She didn't try and speak with me again until we got through the doors to the lunchroom. It was bigger than I'd expected, with three different eateries. I had never seen a college like this before. Then again, I'd never been to one either. I'd only looked at a couple online when Mr. Langley allowed me access behind my mother's back. But this was nothing like those.

"Come on. Kincaid will want you to get his lunch." Mary made her way toward a place that sold burgers. My stomach growled. I glanced at Kincaid, but he was already headed toward a table with Levi and Silas. I didn't know what he ate, but I hoped Mary had an idea, so I quickly went after her, hiking Kincaid's bag up on my shoulders.

"Grab a tray and pile it with food. I'm sure he'll eat something you pick."

Great, she wasn't certain either. *I better not mess this up.*

Mary side-eyed me as other servants and students stepped into line behind me. "You don't talk much, do you?"

I shook my head, finding it better to say nothing in order to keep myself from getting into any type of trouble.

"That's okay. I understand, since it's your first day. I've been working as Levi and Silas's assistant at their warden business for six months now." She had two trays in front of her and placed a burger, fries, toasted sandwiches, steaks, and fruit on both. Since vampires ate normal food and only ingested blood once a week, I grabbed the same food and added some type of pudding and cookies. Mary spoke some more at the drink station. "You'll get the hang of things, so don't stress. The guys aren't so bad to be around."

Laughter nearly bubbled up, but I swallowed it down. I took a black coffee, a soda, and juice to place on the tray while praying nothing fell off. Mary easily picked up the two trays and glided her way back to the tables. Mine tipped to the side until I righted it while my pulse drummed under my skin.

Mary placed hers down, one in front of Levi, the other in front of Silas, and she stood with her hands folded behind her back, waiting in front of their table. I did the same and watched as Kincaid stared down at the food.

I waited and waited some more as I stood still beside Mary. When my gaze caught on Silas's, yet another strange tingle rolled through my stomach.

Was I coming down with something?

Kincaid flicked his hand. "Go. Eat."

If I was getting sick, I'd worry about it later.

Mary smiled up at me. "Come on. It's our turn to get lunch." She spun and made her way back to the lunch line, which was now longer. As we waited with our own smaller trays, she asked, "How old are you?"

I flicked my gaze around and back to Kincaid, who was speaking with Levi and Silas. "Twenty-one," I whispered.

"Why are you whispering?"

My brows dipped. "Servants are to be seen, not heard. We don't have the right to speak freely."

Her lips thinned and she nodded. "Sorry, I forgot you're a servant, whereas I'm an assistant. I get why you're apprehensive, but I'm sure Kincaid won't rip your head off if you talk. His last servant wouldn't shut up. She babbled on about this and that."

Was that why he killed her?

"Don't get that look. He didn't kill her. I promise," she said, as if reading my mind. "She was sweet, a little younger than you, but Kincaid didn't care that she was chatty when she wasn't around him. I mean, it might be different if there's a heap of people around, but if it's just him, Silas, and Levi, I'm sure they won't care."

I wouldn't risk it, but I offered her a nod.

Mary laughed and shrugged. "I guess you'll see with time. You don't know me, so of course you won't trust me. It's good to be cautious around this place. Don't trust just anyone. No matter who they are, they're all in it for themselves." Her eyes widened. "Not me, though. I already have a job, and my dad owns an electricity company in town, which is how I got such a good job as well. I'm twenty-four, by the way. Though Dad says I act sixteen."

"You look it as well," I uttered.

Mary giggled. "Thanks. I'm happy to look younger than I am."

I paled; I didn't think she would have heard me.

She tapped her ears. "Shifter hearing. I forgot to mention I'm a wolf shifter." Mary grinned. "But my dad's only a beta." She grabbed some food when it was our turn, and I did the same.

Suddenly I didn't feel like eating. I had to, though. I needed sustenance to keep me going.

Mary led us to a table off to the left, but I paused where Angelica's servant sat on his own with a tray that only held an apple. I pulled out the chair next to him and sat down. The young boy gaped up in shock.

"You can't sit here."

"Why?" I asked, still taking the seat.

"She doesn't like me around others so I don't say anything to anyone."

This poor boy.

"What's your name?" I asked.

"Jimmy—I mean Jim."

"What's going on?" Mary placed her food down and took a seat opposite us.

"Mary, this is Jim. Jim, this is Mary, and my name is Amara."

"Pretty name." Mary winked at me, and I realized I hadn't given it to her when she asked in class.

"Sorry," I offered.

"It's okay." She shrugged. "Jim, where's your food?"

He dropped his chin to his chest. "I was only allowed to get an apple because I made a fool of my mistress."

I gripped my fork and wished I could stab Angelica with it.

Mary took a plate of spaghetti off her pile and slid it across the table. "Here, you can have this."

"But—"

"Nope," Mary interrupted with a wave of her hand. "Didn't your mistress say you could only get an apple? She never said you couldn't be given food from someone else."

Jim's face morphed into one of happiness. "She didn't."

Mary winked. "Then eat up."

It was in that moment I knew I would like Mary. I smiled at her softly as Jim tugged the plate his way and dug into the spaghetti like he hadn't eaten in a long time. From the way his stomach growled, I suspected that was the case. I loved my sweets, but I took my two cookies and put them on his tray. He grinned over at me. I picked up the burger and took a big bite. The juices ran down my chin. I quickly wiped them away with a napkin and savored the taste my mouth was having a party with.

"Do you have anyone else from your family with you at the Prince Estate?" Mary asked me.

I nodded, swallowing my food. "My... mother." I near choked on the word.

Mary winced when she noticed. "Not a good one?"

"You could say that." We ate in silence for a while, which I was grateful for so I could use the time to fill my stomach to get me through the afternoon classes.

"What about you, Jim? Do you have anyone at the Roads Estate?" Mary asked.

"I have my momma. She cooks and cleans. She's a great cook." He leaned in. "Always sneaks me food when Mistress is being...."

"A bitch?" Mary offered. Jim's eyes widened and he peeked around to look at where Angelica sat with her friends, oblivious to us and what we spoke of.

"Hormonal," I offered, and Mary laughed.

"Um... yes."

I placed a hand on his arm. "I'm sorry you have to go through that, Jim."

"Thank you, miss."

"Just Amara."

Jim blushed. "Amara."

I picked at some fries and asked Mary, "Do you know... um, what she is?"

"Human. Her family owns banks. They're rich."

Human. How could a human treat another so disgustingly? Rage rang in my ears as I looked over at her again, only she wasn't there.

A shrill voice came from behind Mary. "What is the meaning of this?"

Angelica stood there with another girl, both sneering down at all of us.

Jim pushed the empty plate away from him so fast, it flew across the table and would harve crashed to the floor if it wasn't for Mary snatching it up and putting it back on her tray.

Mary straightened. "We were just eating our lunch, Angelica."

"Mary, I don't want to hear from you. But you." She pointed at me and stalked to my side. She gripped my wrist and went to pull me up, but her strength was nothing compared to mine. I stayed rooted in my seat. "Who do you think you are, giving my servant food?"

Mary tipped her chin up defiantly. "It was me who gave him some."

"No, I saw this one give him food." She pulled at me again, but I fought her grip. Even though I didn't want to cause too much trouble, she wasn't my master, and this woman had really gotten under my skin, since she was willing to treat another person badly.

"Kincaid," she called snappishly.

The room fell silent. I caught Kincaid slowly look our way before I dropped my gaze to the table.

She flung my arm to the side. "Your servant fed mine when I ordered that he couldn't have anything. I hope you will punish her."

"Angelica, no," her friend warned softly.

Angelica paled just before I heard a chair smash to the floor. She made a noise in the back of her throat as pounding footsteps approached, and somehow, they matched with the beat of my pulse.

Then they stopped.

"You think you can order me?" Kincaid snarled low. A shiver raked over me.

"No... I-I didn't mean it like that." I lifted my gaze enough to see Angelica try for a sultry smile. "Come on, Kincaid. You know I meant no disrespect. I spoke out in anger over what happened, that's all."

Levi shifted closer. "Your servant is skin and bones,

Angelica. Maybe you should concern yourself with how *you* treat *yours* than what happens with other people's servants."

It was a slap in the face, but I was glad someone had said something. I could only hope it didn't cause Jim any harm.

Angelica clenched her jaw and somehow kept a smile on her lips. "Of course." She nodded. Her gaze dropped to mine, and I saw retribution in her eyes. All I could think was *Bring it*. If she would come at me alone, I could defend myself, so I hoped she did. Then again, maybe she wouldn't, as it was easy to tell that Kincaid, Levi, and Silas scared her.

Her gaze moved to Jim, and I didn't like it. In fact, I moved an inch forward so she had to stare back at me.

"How much?" Silas asked roughly.

Everyone focused on him, including me, but when I found his gaze already on me, I ignored the flutters in my belly and went back to staring at my plate.

Angelica's face scrunched up in confusion. "Sorry?"

"How much for your servant?"

Shock charged through me as my breath caught in my throat over Silas's words.

"You cannot be serious?" Angelica said with a laugh. I wanted to throttle her, maybe bang her head into the table. Usually I wasn't prone to violence, even where Charlotte was concerned, but Angelica and her attitude stirred my desire to lash out.

"I am," Silas clipped.

Mary cleared her throat. "Jim has a mother who cooks."

The dragon shifter grunted. "I'm in need of a cook."

Out of the corner of my eye, I saw Jim sitting as stiff as a board with his fingers crossed on his lap.

I did the same. Though, I wasn't sure if Jim would be going from one nightmare to another. At that new thought, my stomach clenched, and my lunch threatened to come back up.

"Why would you do this?" Angelica's voice had risen an octave.

Levi laughed. "Because he can." And Levi meant it; it really was that simple. Silas could do anything he wanted for the right price or force.

"How much for the boy and his mom?" Silas barked.

"Twenty thousand dollars," Angelica blurted as her friend gasped.

"Mary" was all Silas said before he turned and walked back over to the table. Kincaid and Levi followed.

Mary stood, pulling a phone from her pocket, and her finger flew over the screen. "The money will be in your account in three, two, one. Done."

Angelica sniffed. "Fine."

"I'll have someone from the Peril Estate come to your home to collect Jim's mother." Mary sat back down. "Jim will stay with us from now on. Please take your things."

There was a pause before Angelica huffed, walked around the table, and picked up her bag. She stomped off with her friend following quickly behind.

"Jim, are you okay?" Mary asked.

Jim's head had dropped during the exchange. I heard a sniffle. "I'm good, miss."

"Jim." Mary smiled gently. "Can you tell me your mom's name?"

"Pearl." He glanced over at the table where Kincaid, Silas, and Levi sat as Levi laughed loudly about something. Jim drew in a shaky breath. "Do you... think I should thank him? My new master?"

"Nah, he won't need it. I have a feeling he did it for another reason. Well, besides the fact they can't stand Angelica since she spread the rumor that Kincaid slept with her." Mary's eyes widened on Jim. "But I probably shouldn't have said that."

Jim snorted even as a blush touched his cheeks. "I know about *that* stuff. Not the rumor, but the... never mind."

Mary and I shared an amused look. Shaking my head, I felt a new lightness inside me at knowing Mary would be around Jim a lot more, and I was sure she would take care of him.

"Yeah, I definitely think he's done it for another reason." Mary gazed over at the other table.

I didn't look. Instead, I picked up my coffee and took a sip as Mary's attention swung back to me. "What do you think it was?" I asked.

She grinned. "Nothing. Anyway, Jim, you'll follow us for the rest of the day until I leave, and I'll take you to the Peril Estate where your mom will already be. You'll work in Silas's quarters. I'm sure you'll be happier there."

"Thank you both," he whispered around a bite of his cookie.

My brows dipped, confused. "For what?" We hadn't done anything.

"If you both hadn't sat here, then things wouldn't have changed."

Well, when he put it like that, I supposed it wouldn't have.

"It's all Amara, really." Mary waved a hand at me. "I would have sat elsewhere if it weren't for her."

I shook my head, uncomfortable with the attention. Still, I reached out and gently squeezed his wrist. "I'm glad we sat here." I never would have thought sitting here would have brought such a turn, but it had, and really, I was happy for the change and for Silas's sudden kind gesture.

Mary's name was called. I glanced over to see Levi nod toward the doors.

Mary sighed. "Time for some more boring classes." We took our trays and rubbish to the appropriate area to discard them and then quickly caught up with Kincaid.

"Anything?" Silas asked. I didn't dare look, since he wasn't speaking to me.

"A few emails to deal with later. Nothing urgent. Though, Donny texted and said he had to call Rivet in because something happened that he had to attend to."

Silas grunted.

Levi curled an arm over Mary's shoulders, and a stab of anger brushed through me, but I quickly stamped it down. My emotions were all over the place since I'd begun my new position.

"Mary, honey, be a dear and inform Kincaid's lovely servant of her nightly duties."

Mary snorted at Levi. "If you stop applying the sugar, I will."

Levi chuckled and winked as he removed his arm. The stories about Levi and his flirting were common knowledge. Apparently, he'd tease anyone to get what he wanted. Though, it didn't seem to work on Mary, and I refused to be swayed by it. I wanted to see what lay beneath his persona. What really made him....

No. I didn't want to see anything from anyone.

I just wanted to survive.

"I'll have your room number this afternoon with a map. Don't worry, it'll be close to Kincaid's dorm," Mary instructed.

I wasn't worried.

"I'll also have a phone that Kincaid can reach you on. After dinner, you'll get to go to your room and rest until whenever Kincaid calls for you. The schedule should be the same until Wednesday, when he'll no doubt be staying at home, since Mr. Prince likes to have family dinners then. Got it?"

I nodded.

Mary smiled playfully. "Back to the silent girl. I get it." She nibbled on her bottom lip and leaned in closer. "I'd advise staying in your room unless being requested. It'll be... safer."

My eyes widened, and I stumbled a little. What did she mean?

Mary winced when she caught my fearful gaze. "Look, I heard not all the servants are great, and you'll be stuck around some of them until the morning. But if you stick to your room, you'll be fine."

The servants?

They would be the ones to cause me problems?

But why? We were all in the same boat. We all suffered from being classed as nothing but the help. I didn't understand.

Tension pressed down on my shoulders. Just when I'd felt lighter, it was taken from me in a moment. Honestly, it was foolish of me to think I could have an afternoon of ease.

"Sorry," Mary whispered.

I shook my head. "I'd prefer to be warned than to go in blind," I told her softly. It was the truth. That way I could guard my back and hope that Mary's information was wrong.

It was doubtful, though.

I wanted to ask her how she knew and exactly *what* she knew, but I couldn't release the words now that we were around Kincaid. Besides, I had been treated badly enough by my own mother. I could handle a few servants with whatever issues they had.

Maybe it was because I worked for the Prince family.

Probably.

Lunch fought its way up once more, but I swallowed quickly.

I would get through this.

I had to.

DINNER WAS the same as lunch. Mary held off leaving to take Jim to the Peril Estate so they could sit with me. Which I appreciated. If they hadn't, I would have been alone and left to my wandering, worried thoughts.

"Okay." Mary pulled out a piece of paper, and another dropped onto the table. She pushed both across to me. "Your room number and a map of the school. Kincaid will be a floor up, but it was the best I could do."

"That's okay, thank you." I didn't mind being away from Kincaid. I was looking forward to my alone time. Although Mary's warning still burned in my brain. I pushed my tray away, suddenly not hungry at the reminder of what could happen tonight. Instead, I pulled the map close and studied it.

"Levi and Silas house with Kincaid in their apartment-slash-dorm suite. If you ever get into any trouble, run to their area. All three of them will help you."

I doubted it, but it was nice of Mary to have that

much faith in them. Then again, she had been around them a lot longer than I had. Maybe she did trust them.

Surprise flickered through me over the three of them being trustworthy.

However, I had to remember that Mary worked as their assistant. She was *needed*, and she was also a *shifter*.

I nodded. "When do I leave him?"

"When he tells you you're dismissed."

Glancing over the table at her, I asked, "Did you help his other servants?"

Mary opened her mouth, closed it, and nodded.

I looked at Jim. He still shoveled food into his mouth. "What happened to them?"

She sank her teeth into her bottom lip and shook her head.

"Mary." I reached across the table for her hand, but she pulled it away.

"Jim and I had better get going." She stood. Jim leaned over his plate and took a few more mouthfuls before standing.

What wasn't she telling me?

What happened to them?

Nodding, I glanced down at the map. "Again, thank you for your help," I said to Mary before looking at Jim and smiling softly. "I hope you love your new residence, Jim. If I don't see you again, take care of yourself."

"I will, miss—Amara." He grinned. "I wish the best for you."

"Come on now, Jim." When I met Mary's gaze, she added, "Good luck." They both walked off. As soon as they were out of sight, fear stabbed at my chest.

I wished Mary hadn't bid me luck. Now I really was worried that I would need it, and I didn't understand why.

Studying the map, I worked out the quick escape routes to reach Kincaid, Levi, and Silas. I still wasn't sure they would help me, but they were the only ones I knew. And since I worked for Kincaid, he might at least want to save me if things did hit the fan.

Unless.... Could they be setting me up? Mary would listen to anything those guys said. All of her warnings could be lies. Honestly, I didn't see a reason why other servants would want to hurt or intimidate me.

"Maid Amara," Kincaid barked from across the way. Maid instead of servant. I wasn't sure why he'd changed the term, but it didn't matter. I quickly stood, hooked his bag over my shoulders, and picked up the pieces of paper before following the three men.

Who could I trust?

I didn't have a clue.

My hands shook with fear of the unknown, but I pressed my palm against my dagger and took a deep breath. I could handle servants and whatever they threw at me... *if* they were going to do something.

The door to their suite was open by the time I got there. I hadn't been far behind, but I did pause just beside the doorway to catch my breath. Kincaid wouldn't have anything more for me to do. Soon I would get time on my own. I would shower and sleep. Then nothing else would happen. I hoped.

Stepping through the door, I placed Kincaid's bag close to it before waiting with my eyes on the floor and hands behind my back.

I heard a sigh. "Dismissed. Be back here at seven."

Curtseying, I spun around and made my way down the hall again. My feet felt like lead, and for some reason, a part of me wanted to stay right where I was, near my master and his guys. That thought surprised me the most because, really, I had no one. I was used to being by myself, so wanting to be around anyone, let alone them, was something new.

When my stomach twisted and my food threatened to rush up and out, I pressed my hands against it.

No. I reminded myself that I knew how to defend myself. I was going to be okay.

On the floor below, servants moved around greeting, smiling, and talking to one another while they stared at me as I made my way to my room. My skin prickled from the amount of attention I got.

Once I'd arrived at the room, I opened the door and quickly stepped in, closing it behind me. I leaned against the wooden barrier and took a shuddering breath. I'd made it without any trouble. Besides the gazes, nothing else had happened.

The small room had no window, only a bed and closet. I walked over to the closet and opened it. A clean maid outfit hung from the one hanger and a toiletry bag was on the shelf inside. Next to it was a towel and clean undergarments. A sticky note was stuck to it.

I thought you'd need some clean clothes. There's shower stalls two doors down. Stay safe. Mary.

Stay safe?

Again, why did she have to say something like that?

Why did she expect something to happen? Had they planned it? Her bosses? Mine?

How was I supposed to get through the night, knowing something was coming?

My eyes snapped open when my head rocked forward. For a second, sleep had taken me under, and I cursed at myself for allowing it. Exhaustion gripped me, but I stayed sitting on the floor in the corner of the room with my eyes on the door. I would stay awake all night if I had to. Even knowing I would be wrecked tomorrow. Mary wouldn't have warned me for no reason. Even if it was something she and the men had planned themselves.

Tension tingled up my spine when I heard shuffling outside my door. This was it.

Something *was* about to happen.

The door flew open, and five bodies were outlined by the light outside the room before the door slammed closed. Two jumped at the bed, ready to grab me. You would have thought they'd have seen I wasn't there before shutting the light out.

Idiots.

This told me these people didn't know what they were doing. They weren't masters at this, unless they only worked with people who didn't know how to defend themselves. Obviously, they didn't know who had taught me.

"She's not there," a male voice snapped low.

"She hasn't left the room," another man whispered.

"Hit the light," a female commanded.

Standing, I locked my legs in a fighting stance, my hands at my sides with a dagger in one. The other weapons remained hidden under my clothing. A light flared to life, and I wanted to laugh at their surprised expressions when they saw me.

"What do you want?" I asked calmly.

The only female in the group stepped forward, gaining my attention. "Do you think since you're ready for us with your little knife that we don't have the situation under control?"

Well, yes, I thought, though I said nothing.

The woman, who appeared to be in her late twenties, glared. "You need to know we're in charge in this section. You *will* follow *our* rules or else you'll have to face the consequences. For your time to stay pleasant, you'll learn to do as we ask."

The men around her shifted uncomfortably. Probably because I didn't cower from their actions or her words.

"Who do you work for?" I asked.

Her chin tipped up, pride shining in her eyes. "The headmaster himself. We all do."

I didn't even know who the headmaster was, nor did I care.

"The Prince family are my masters. I listen to them... and them alone."

Her face scrunched up like she'd sucked on a lemon. "Under this roof, you will listen to us. We control *all* servants here."

I was missing something. Why did they need to come

here and tell me this? There had to be another reason. "What do you want?"

She smiled, satisfied I was listening. Little did she know, I wouldn't follow through with whatever meaningless task she had.

She held out her hand and a guy dropped a vial into it. "You need to give this to your master. If you do, you'll be greatly rewarded. You'll no longer be a slave, and you'll get to attend this magnificent college as a student instead. The headmaster will cherish you in ways you cannot fathom." She either believed her own spiel or she was so in love with the headmaster that it clouded her judgment.

I held back my sigh.

She was either crazy or she really was completely in love with the headmaster. If he could promise these things, why wasn't she free? She could be a student or a teacher, but instead, she stayed a slave.

Lies.

Whatever was in that vial, it would harm Kincaid, and I would be killed for it. Then again, if I denied these people, they could also do some damage to me. However, I would try taking them, as they were a lesser evil than Kincaid.

"Fine." If I pretended that I'd give it to Kincaid, they'd leave.

The woman's smile died. "You're lying." She sighed, and with a nod, the guys advanced toward me.

Two of them were quicker than the others. As they neared, I stabbed toward one and kicked out at the other. Both jumped back and looked at each other. Their jaws clenched right before all five attacked.

I ducked and swept a foot out. One landed with a thud. I rolled back to avoid fists flying at me and sliced at thighs, arms, stomachs. I didn't want to mortally wound them. I just needed them to back off.

They didn't.

Even with blood flowing and soaking their clothes, they kept trying to grab me, harm me, and foolishly on my part, one managed to hit me in the side of my temple. It temporarily stunned me. I dropped my dagger before I got twisted and thrown onto the bed. My dress tore at the sleeve when I tried to stop them from pinning my arms down. I kicked out. Someone groaned. I twisted my hips, swinging my legs to the side and forcing another to the floor.

"Stop," the woman shouted. Everyone stilled. I found her standing on the other side of the bed, looking down at me. "All this will end if you just listen to us. It'll work out for everyone *if* you just listen."

No, it wouldn't.

What I needed to do was get out of here somehow.

I nodded, and like I expected, the fools backed off, their holds on me loosened. I dropped, yanking my arms free to punch the two who'd held my arms down in the balls. Their pain-filled grunts were music to my ears. They clutched their groins, and I used the distraction to crawl on the floor between them. One of the guys grabbed my ankle, but I kicked him in the face. Another launched at me. I brought my foot up and kicked him in the stomach. He fell into the other one trying to take me.

I slipped through them on my hands and knees and bolted for the door. The woman was there.

"Since you're not going to listen, you'll have to die." She uncorked the vial and attempted to grab me. I slapped her hand away with ease and punched her in the face. Blood squirted out of her nose, landing on me as I pushed her out of the way and tugged the door open to run.

The halls were silent except for my footfalls as I made my way up a flight of stairs. Breathing heavily, I paused outside Kincaid's suite. Should I knock or wait until morning, trusting that having their suite at my back was enough of a deterrent if any more trouble found its way to me?

Staying outside sounded better to me, but it meant I wouldn't be able to go back to my assigned room until morning. No doubt they'd be waiting for me.

It also meant I wouldn't be able to shower or change clothes. I glanced down. My temple pounded, but I took in my sleeve where it was torn at the top of my shoulder. There were also a few other little rips in the dress. I knew my clothes weren't the only things damaged. Bruises and scrapes dotted my skin. Mostly in areas I could hide. Although, from the throbbing at the side of my head, I had a feeling a bruise would show there.

How could I explain it?

Should I tell Kincaid the truth? That people, the servants, wanted me to give him poison and the headmaster was behind it all?

Without knowing what to do, I sank to the floor beside the door and leaned against the wall. Since no one had come after me, I doubted anyone would show, because Kincaid was nearby. Not that I trusted him, but many feared him. *That* I believed.

I rested my head back and stared up at the ceiling.

Why would the headmaster want Kincaid dead?

What would he gain?

There would have to be some type of motive for the plan, but what? No doubt the headmaster was another paranormal, so wouldn't his status be high enough already, since he oversaw this college? He'd be well respected for his position. What else could he want?

A gasp escaped me, and I startled when the door beside me opened abruptly.

Kincaid poked his head out and glared down at me. "Up," he ordered and disappeared back into the room.

Clenching my jaw so I didn't moan aloud, I scrambled to my feet and stepped through the door.

"I can smell your blood from here," Kincaid snarled from where he stood half naked at the far wall, staring out a window.

I dropped my gaze to the ground. "Sorry, master." Why did I apologize for bleeding when it was *his* fault in the first place? If I hadn't been working for Kincaid, the attack wouldn't have happened.

My gaze lifted when a door to the left opened, and Silas walked out, running a hand over his face. He was also half naked. My cheeks warmed, and I quickly moved my gaze back to the floor, appalled at the idea of being embarrassed for seeing them without tops on.

Stupid, Amara.

"What's going on?" Silas asked gruffly.

"I scented the servant bleeding outside our rooms," Kincaid explained. He didn't move or look away from the outside. "What are you doing awake?"

"Doesn't matter. What the fuck happened?" Silas stalked over to me, and my heart rate increased. A growl rumbled from deep within his chest as he stopped in front of me. The tingle in my stomach appreciated the sound, but I swallowed and touched my thigh, only my dagger was no longer there. Dammit. I'd dropped it back in my bedroom and forgot to pick it up again. I would have to go back for it. I couldn't lose it; Mr. Langley had it made for me.

I pressed my hand to the dagger on my other thigh; it didn't comfort me like the one I'd dropped, but it still managed to give me a sense of reassurance.

Silas brushed his nose against my throat and drew it up into my hairline, taking in a deep breath. I locked my body down so I wouldn't reach out for him like I wanted to. My power perked its head up and brushed against my insides. I didn't react, knowing it didn't want to come out; it wasn't looking to protect me. It was just curious. All because of these three guys, and I really wanted to know why, but it wasn't like I could ask anyone about it.

A pang of frustration punched me in the chest over my body's reaction to Silas. He shifted around me, pinching at my torn sleeve and poking at the cuts in my clothes. One of the wounds was painful enough that I hissed, then quickly clamped my lips closed.

"Who damaged you?" Silas asked.

I said nothing.

Another door opened. "Are we having a meeting that no one told me about?" A loud yawn dropped from Levi. I didn't turn his way, though. "And look, the lovely Amara is here for it. I knew I woke up for a reason.... Wait, why does she look like she might have a bruise on her face?"

Silas stuck his nose in my hair and sucked in a breath. "All I can smell are other servants."

I lifted my gaze as Kincaid spun to face us, his hands clenched at each side. "Will you tell us what happened?"

It was a question. He didn't order me. He left it up to me to inform them. Surprise raced through me.

Sweat formed on the back of my neck at the thickening tension in the room.

There was no other way. I had to tell the truth.

"Other servants came to my room. They wanted me to feed you a vial of poison at the request of the headmaster. When I refused, they tried to kill me. I made my way up here to... rest." And for safety.

The silence bubbled and grew as they all stared. Fresh goose bumps darted across my skin at the intensity.

Had I said something wrong? God, why did I care if I did say or do something wrong? I would do what I had to do to stay alive. Sure, hearing that people wanted Kincaid dead wasn't the best news, but it was the truth. I hoped to hell I wouldn't be punished or killed for it.

Levi snorted. I caught him sharing a look with the other two. "We knew it was someone."

"But we never got answers before." Kincaid's gaze lasered back on me.

"No, we didn't," Silas added, also staring at me. "Levi, call someone to go to her quarters. See what they can get from the scene." Levi nodded and returned to his room. Silas focused back on me. "Do you know the servants?"

I shook my head. "They didn't give names."

"If you saw them again, would you recognize them?"

"Yes."

Silas nodded. "Good. I may need you to testify—"

Kincaid made a noise. "Silas, I want this handled in-house."

"He needs to be made an example of. Then these other attacks might stop."

Kincaid shook his head. "They won't. You know this."

Silas swore under his breath. "Fine. I'll take a couple of men to see the headmaster now. Do you want me to hold off on...." He glanced at me and back to Kincaid. I had a feeling Silas was about to say, "killing him."

Kincaid rested against the window. "Yes. I want to be there."

Silas tipped his chin up. "Done. Tell Levi to stay with you until I get back." He started in my direction, since I stood near the door.

"Shirt," I blurted, then clamped my lips closed and scanned the floor for nothing. My cheeks flooded with heat, and I wanted to kick myself for that action and for saying something in the first place. It didn't bother me if he wanted to walk around half naked... so why *did* I say something?

Silas grunted. I heard his retreating footsteps.

"Master, should I go back to my room?" *Please say yes.* I needed to get out of this suite and away from the thickening alpha magic. It would also give me a chance to sleep a little, since there were still a few hours until morning.

At least the lack of rest explained my outburst about Silas being shirtless. I was obviously sleep-deprived.

"No. Go to my room. Get some rest. I don't want you

screwing anything up that I'll then have to deal with. Someone will bring you clothes. For now, shower before you lay on my bed. You reek."

Dread, and a tiny amount of excitement, raced through me at the thought of being in his room. Honestly, I didn't want to go into his room, his domain, and I really didn't want to sleep on his bed.

Yes, you do. No. No, I didn't.

There was no choice, though.

Even as my hands shook and my stomach tightened, I made my way across the floor and in through the only door that hadn't been used. I closed it after myself and blew out a breath.

There were two more doors inside the room, one a closet, the other a bathroom. The room was the size of a small apartment. I noticed a chaise lounge off to the side under the window. It would be a better place for me to nap instead of the king-size bed that sat in the middle of the room up against the far wall. The blanket was thrown back, the pillow indented, and even I, a human—well, somewhat—could smell Kincaid's scent.

No, I would *not* rest on that bed.

Instead, I took a quick shower, forgoing washing my hair, but at least I was clean enough to be in Kincaid's rooms. The cuts and scrapes had stopped bleeding. When I felt their fresh sting from the water, I figured they were probably what Kincaid had been complaining about. Why I reeked. My blood.

Kincaid, being a vampire, would have smelled it from far away.

Though, he could have gone without saying it reeked.

Shaking my head, I placed my thigh holsters back on each thigh and slipped the only dagger I had in the left one. Once dressed in my bra, I placed the throwing stars in the pockets that protected me from cuts. I'd blushed profusely when Mr. Langley gifted me the bra, but having the extra weapons helped ease my mind. I then got back into my torn outfit, since I had nothing else to wear, and slipped into my combat boots—another gift from Mr. Langley—which were hidden by the length of my maid outfit. I checked that the knives were still concealed within them by stamping my heels. Nodding to myself, I set the towel in the dirty-laundry basket and moved out of the bathroom.

I eyed the bed as I walked by it.

The urge to lie there crossed my mind for a second before I forcibly pushed it away. That I would think such a thing in the first place didn't make sense.

Sitting on the edge of the chaise lounge, I kicked up my feet and rested back, staring out the window into the still-dark sky.

A pang of longing had me wishing Mr. Langley had never died. He'd missed his mate something fierce, but I didn't think a heart attack would take him from the world. Such a condition in a werewolf was unusual. Though, the coroner confirmed it had been his heart.

I missed him.

So much.

Tears welled. I closed my eyes and took in a shuddering breath. I never expected my life would change so much after I lost Mr. Langley, but it had. He was all I'd been used to. The only master I'd ever known, and he'd been so different from my new one.

No matter. I was stuck where I was, and I couldn't do anything about it but sleep my worries away. Even though they'd be waiting for me when I woke.

Five

THE WORD "WAKE" was barked close, startling me. Sitting, I stretched. Tiredness still tugged at my head and body, and I would have given my left arm to fall back asleep. Only then I noticed the culprit who woke me. Kincaid stood by his bed, fully dressed and ready. I quickly scrambled up until my feet tangled in a blanket, and I dropped to my hands and knees with a gasp.

Wait, a blanket?

Who had put a blanket on me?

Could I ask? No, I wouldn't dare. Levi maybe? Only it meant someone had been in the room while I slept, and I hadn't heard them.

I hadn't *heard* them.

That wasn't good. They could have killed me.

"You done?" Kincaid asked. It wasn't like I meant to trip, and I wouldn't have if I'd known the blanket was there, nor would I have if he hadn't scared me awake.

Straightening, I brushed off nonexistent dust. "Sorry,

master." I caught his sneer before I dropped my gaze to the floor.

"You have a new dress. Get changed and come to the main area."

I tipped my head down and heard him leave, closing the door after himself with a bang. I swiftly changed, but I wasn't sure where I was supposed to put my old torn uniform. Glancing around the room, I spotted the clothes basket in the bathroom and placed it in there.

Just as I opened his door, my stomach roared.

A snort sounded, and my cheeks burned as I pressed a hand over my belly as if that would stop the hunger pains.

"Maid Amara, come sit by me, sweetheart," Levi called from the couch. I'd taken a step his way when I remembered who I was and my position. Stopping, I looked at Kincaid, who sat on a chair opposite Levi, glaring up at me. I noticed there was no sign of Silas.

"Kincaid, don't be a dick," Levi said, and my eyes widened for a fraction of a second.

"Sit." Kincaid pointed to the couch Levi was on.

Biting the corner of my lip, I found myself unsure if I was supposed to curtsey or not. It wouldn't hurt if I did, so I dipped down into one and then moved to the couch. I sat at the opposite end from Levi, who winked. Clenching my jaw, I fought another blush and the same tingle as the day before. Levi flustered me with his looks and charms, like I was sure he did every woman.

My stomach howled again. Levi gestured to the platter on the coffee table in front of us, one I had been ignoring, but the smell of the croissants, muffins, and bagels was obviously getting to my belly.

"Have something," Levi said when I didn't move to take anything.

Again, I looked at Kincaid, and when I did, he nodded. Embarrassingly, I dove forward to take a muffin and bit into it as I sat back. The taste of blueberries exploded in my mouth, and I closed my eyes, chewing slowly to savor it.

The meals at the college were outstanding. Charlotte had done the cooking at Mr. Langley's, and her food had been edible but plain. This tasted like heaven, and I wondered if I could sneak some into my dress pockets.

Levi hummed under his breath. "I never knew a muffin could bring such a reaction from a woman. I feel like I want to be a muffin right now."

My body locked at Levi's words, and I opened my eyes to glare at him, only to realize what I had done, and I dropped my gaze to conceal my instinctive reaction. A blush warmed my cheeks, yet his words wouldn't stop me from finishing the muffin.

Levi chuckled as the door opened, and I glanced over to see Silas step through with my dagger in his hand.

The muffin dropped from my grip. I quickly stood and backed up. All of them watched me.

Silas lifted the dagger and waved it. "I'm guessing this is yours."

If Kincaid knew I had concealed weapons on my body, he would kill me.

I shook my head but couldn't hide the way my heart raced in my chest, aware that those around me had excellent hearing. I cursed myself silently when Levi smirked and leaned forward, resting his elbows on his knees and clasping his hands in front of him. Kincaid gripped the armrests to the point that they groaned.

Levi chuckled softly. "You all know she's lying, right?"

A rumbled growl started in Silas's chest. A snarl dropped from Kincaid's lips when he stood up slowly. Their eyes never strayed from me as I took another step back. Fear like I hadn't felt before ripped through me.

"Why do you have this?" Silas demanded. He placed the dagger on the coffee table and planted his hands on his hips. "How could we not scent it?"

"Is that to try and kill me?" Kincaid clipped.

"No. No, master," I told him.

"Then why would you have a weapon?"

I couldn't explain why without tarnishing Mr. Langley's name. Him teaching a human how to defend themself would do exactly that. Only, they could scent a lie so I couldn't make anything up... unless I told a half-truth.

Just when I was about to talk, a yip fell from my mouth instead when Kincaid was suddenly in front of me. I hadn't even seen him move. He grabbed my arms and shook me.

"Why did you have it?"

"Kincaid," Levi warned, his tone rough for once.

"No," Kincaid roared. "She needs to tell me." His eyes bled from their dark color to red. His scent grew stronger. I clenched my thighs together when pleasure swept over me in a light caress.

"Tell me, why do you have a dagger?"

I licked my suddenly dry lips. He needed to back off because I had a sudden urge to wrap my legs around his waist. Which wasn't good... right?

When I blinked up at him, his eyes washed back to his normal dark color, and he dropped his hold on me, turning to Levi and Silas. "My compulsion didn't work."

Levi snorted. "I don't know." He drew in a deep breath. "It worked in a way."

Kincaid clenched his hands at his sides while I pressed mine to my chest as if to hide the fast beating of my heart.

"I didn't use lust, Levi. I used fear."

"What?" Silas said, shock evident in his tone.

Confusion had me glancing at them all. I didn't understand what was going on, and I wasn't sure I wanted to either. Especially when Levi started laughing loudly.

"Shit, fuck, this is too funny." He slapped his thigh, still chuckling.

"Shut up, Levi," Silas ordered, only Levi didn't listen.

"Fear... *fear*, and she smells like that. God, that's rich."

Smelled like what?

No. No... they could not have smelled my arousal. Nausea twisted my stomach. I wanted to throw up the small amount I'd eaten. I wanted to bury my head in the floor and never show my face again.

Silas threw out a hand. "It doesn't make sense."

I wanted to clap and point at him, yelling, "No, it doesn't." But I didn't. I freaked out on the inside instead, while I chanced a glance at a bedroom door—Levi's. I could hide in there... but if I didn't do my job, I could be punished for it or killed.

Damn my life.

Kincaid ran a hand through his hair.

What did it feel like?

No. I do not need to know. I retreated another step and my back hit the wall. All eyes shot to me. Shit.

"The dagger helps me feel safe," I blurted. "You can't scent it because... because of a dampening spray I have on them."

They all blinked slowly at me. As if they thought I had something wrong with my mind. Maybe I did.

"Is that the only reason you have it, for safety?" Silas asked.

I nodded. "Yes."

Kincaid shifted. "You said *them.* You have others?"

I nodded again.

"Where?" he demanded.

"My thigh."

"Show us." Silas moved my way.

"I want to see," Levi said, grinning as he stood up from the couch.

They... they wanted to see under my dress. My body warmed. I didn't understand why they needed to see it. Unless—did they mean to take it from me? I couldn't let that happen. If I didn't have my weapons to protect myself, it meant I would be more likely to use my powers, and I refused to do so. If I did, it would mean I was more than human. It would mean that I'd allowed the darkness inside me out... showing everyone I was something else.

I stared at Kincaid. "Master, I would never use them on you."

"I can't believe that." He waved a hand my way, wanting me to get on with it.

My stomach twisted.

"I only have them to protect myself."

"Maid Amara." Levi gained my attention with his gentle tone. "We've had trouble trusting the servants that Kincaid had been given before. They've all tried to kill him—"

"And now you know why," I said quickly.

He gave me a sad smile. "Sweetheart, we know you refused their plan. Look, all you have to do is show us this other dagger. We won't take it from you."

Both Kincaid and Silas scowled at Levi. He rolled his eyes. "She's had them on her since yesterday morning. She could have tried to kill you many times, Kincaid, but she hasn't."

He made a good point, and I prayed that Kincaid and Silas listened to him.

"Fuck," Kincaid clipped. His gaze bore into mine. "I do not trust you, though."

"I give you my word I will not use them against you," I tried.

Silas strode back to the coffee table, picked up my other dagger, and walked to me, holding it out. Hesitantly, I took it from him, and with my free hand, I lifted my long dress to place the dagger in its holder on my right thigh. A sense of ease swept through me.

Dropping my dress, I looked at the men before me.

"Who gave them to you?" Silas asked.

"I would rather not say." I bit my bottom lip when Silas's chest rumbled with a growl.

"Who was her master before you, Kincaid?" Levi was smart, and I wished he wasn't.

"Langley."

Levi snorted. "That explains a lot."

Confusion rolled through me and had me scrunching my brows down. How did it explain anything?

"I should have thought of it." Kincaid's jaw clenched. "We'll be keeping an eye on you," he warned.

I nodded.

The door to the suite opened, and within it stood a tall guy with fiery red hair tied back at his neck. Under his uniform, he had a slim waist but the well-formed shoulders of a swimmer. He was handsome, very much so, but my body didn't react at all. Nothing like it did for the other three in the room. Not for the first time, I wondered why I only responded that way to them.

"Cassar?" Kincaid stepped his way.

Cassar tipped his chin down at Kincaid. "The headmaster wishes to speak."

"We should *all* go down there," Silas stated. They turned to look at me.

"What do we do with her?" Kincaid rubbed at his chin.

Did they not realize I was still in the room? I ground my teeth together. My job was to be at Kincaid's beck and call, but he was about to go and speak with the headmaster. I didn't want to see what would happen if the headmaster didn't give them the right answers.

"If I may, master, I could stay here." *Please.*

"No. Follow us," Kincaid clipped and started for the door. Levi gave me a shrug and an awkward smile, but he walked out after Kincaid.

"Go." Silas nodded toward the door.

Closing my eyes for a moment, I drew in a deep breath

and braced myself before I went after them with Silas at my back.

It was quiet in the hallways. Our footsteps echoed, and I imagined the other students were either at breakfast or in class, depending on the time.

We walked and walked, descending step after step into the pits of the college where it was dark and cold. The thin uniform I wore did nothing to help fend off the breeze. Where the fresh air swept in from, I didn't know, and it wasn't like I would open my mouth to ask.

The stairs ended and opened onto a room full of jail cells. I found the cause of the frigid breeze. At the end of the cells, there was a wall of windows. Two were open, and beyond them was the cliff the college stood on.

Shivering, I ground my teeth together to keep them from chattering and wrapped my arms around my waist as the men approached a cell closest to the windows.

The door was already open, which I thought was silly until Silas pushed me to step into the room after the others. Inside, four guards stood around a man chained to the floor where he knelt with his back to the far wall. If I didn't know he was the headmaster who wanted me to kill Kincaid, then I wouldn't have suspected him of anything. He seemed like a regular old man in his sleepwear, with graying dark-blond hair, a trimmed beard, and a pot belly that would have made Santa jealous.

"Leave us." After Kincaid's order, all the guards except Cassar filed out of the cell. Once they were gone, Kincaid turned to the headmaster. "Cassar said you wanted to talk." With his arms crossed over his chest, he stood right in front of the man.

The headmaster's gaze drifted to me standing behind and just to the side of Kincaid. Levi shifted in front of me, blocking off my view, which was probably for the best.

"Talk," Levi growled, his lion showing in his rough tone. Gone was the flirt. Levi was in business mode. Why did I like it? I shook my head slightly, annoyed at myself.

The headmaster beamed. "I'm not the only one who wants you dead."

Kincaid chuckled darkly. "That I already know. Tell me something new."

My stomach twisted tightly before dropping to my feet. Why did people want Kincaid dead? And why did knowing someone wanted to kill him bother me? Why did the knowledge slash at my chest? That I would be in danger as well had to be it.

Seriously, it had to be that and nothing else.

"You will die," the headmaster stated.

Kincaid ignored the words and asked again, "Who is behind this?"

The headmaster laughed. "I guess I am."

Silas shook his head. "Don't play games. You're not smart enough, or you wouldn't have been caught."

The chains rattled as the old man yelled, "I wouldn't have been if it wasn't for her!" I lifted my gaze and caught the headmaster trying to look around Levi and Kincaid to me. "Why? Why couldn't you have been like all the others? Why did you warn him? I would have given you everything." He stopped trying to see me since Kincaid and Levi kept adjusting their position to stop him.

Kincaid snarled at him, "You—"

He stopped as soon as I opened my big, darn mouth. "The others were fools."

Everyone turned to me, and in doing so, the headmaster could finally see me. He snapped, "How so?"

I kept his gaze. "They believed the promise of a better future. I don't. They believed my master could have easily been manipulated. I don't."

"Then you will die alongside him." The headmaster cackled.

The men turned back to him as Silas flashed forward and kicked him in the gut. "Enough of this." He gripped the top of the headmaster's hair and forced his head back. Silas leaned in. "Tell us who you work for."

The headmaster still only laughed.

Something was wrong. Why would the headmaster say he wanted to talk when really, he had nothing to say?

He was stalling. But why? "This isn't right," I said before I thought about keeping my lips closed.

Levi looked at me. "What's that?"

"He's up to something." I turned my gaze back to the headmaster, who was still laughing.

Footsteps pounded down the hallway. We turned toward the doors, but before I did, I caught Kincaid smile wickedly.

"His reinforcements are coming."

Levi cracked his knuckles. "I've been waiting for this."

Silas stretched and then jogged a couple of steps, a maniacal grin on his face.

"Maid Amara, if you please," Cassar said, right before his hands landed on my waist, and I was picked up and deposited behind him.

"Wait, wait—you knew they would come?" The headmaster's cocky look disappeared.

"We did," Kincaid answered.

The headmaster jerked his head back in shock. "But there's only four of you."

Silas snorted. "So?"

Their alpha power saturated the room. I locked my body down and ignored the tingle. I also pushed down the wave of energy rolling inside me from my power.

Surprise filtered through me when I finally tore my gaze from Silas, Levi, and Kincaid to note that the alpha power also vibrated from Cassar, though I wasn't sure what species he was. Still, my body didn't react to him.

More importantly, why wasn't I trembling in fear with what was coming?

Did I trust the men surrounding me to protect me? Maybe. But more so, I knew I could defend myself if necessary.

At least twelve people stopped outside the cell. Twelve to our five.

Bending, I slipped my weapon free from my thigh and welcomed the weight in my hand. My pulse slowed and I straightened with the dagger held up in front of me.

The men stared at me before they turned back to the door. For a better view, I shifted to the side and noticed the servants that had been in my room.

"They're all there." I hoped they understood what I meant.

Kincaid, but Levi smiled, and said, "Good."

It was Kincaid who addressed the newcomers. "For a

chance to live, give yourselves up, or die trying to save your useless leader."

"Let the headmaster go and we won't have to kill you." The same woman who'd been in my room stepped forward. Her nose still looked swollen. I shot her a finger wave, receiving a glare in exchange. How were they so confident when they were humans facing monsters? Unless not all of them were human.

I eyed them quickly and noticed subtle movements, trying to work out who was what. "There's six humans. The woman, then three to her left, two to her right. The rest are some type of shifter. I don't know how strong, though." I couldn't feel their power, since I was surrounded by four alphas who were emitting so much of it already.

Again, the men around me stared as if I'd lost my mind. Didn't they understand I was trying to help? Leave the weak to last. Take out the unknown.

Was I ready to kill?

Yes, if they didn't stop. If they weren't smart enough to run, I would kill to protect myself. I knew more than anything that the men around me were the better evil. A given since they held my life in their hands because I was a servant to Kincaid.

Silas stared at me the longest and nodded once.

"Last chance," Kincaid offered before he put on a show. His fangs grew, along with the nails on his hands that formed into sharp claws. They could easily rip out a throat. I also caught red veins tinting his dark eyes. Kincaid wasn't the only one whose body had changed. A tough, scaly gray skin covered Silas's arms. The whites of his eyes disappeared, altering to a darker green. The pupils were much like a reptile's with their vertical slits. Levi's own claws and fangs were ready in his half-shifted lion form. His eyes shone gold, his nose flattened, and his hair was shaggier with tinges of red rather than his usual dirty blond.

Cassar was yet another shock. He had wings. *Wings.* Long and fluttery translucent wings with pointy tips. I couldn't guess what he was because I had never heard of or seen anything with such wings.

Taking them in, rightness settled in my veins. Sticking by their sides was the right call. Only a fool would go against their type of strength and power. *I* wasn't a fool.

"Know you will die if you try to stop us from protecting the headmaster," the woman said. "He is our master, and we will do anything for him. Nothing you say and do will stop us from protecting him. He has guided us into the light, into a better world, and we will—" She tapered off with a groan and looked down at the dagger protruding from her stomach.

All eyes swung to me. That time, they all shared the same expression of wide-eyed shock and mouths gaping.

My face heated, and I shrugged. "It slipped." No chance could I tell them the truth, which was that I'd grown tired of her words, and the fight was bound to happen because no matter what neither side would back down.

A roar reverberated through the area. I heard clothes being torn and glanced back in time to see six men shift. A servant moved the woman out of the way, helping her to the floor. The other servants rushed while the shifters finished morphing into wolves and a couple of—

"Bears!" I yelled, taking out my other dagger from under my dress. My power wanted out to play, but I forced it down. I could feel its own annoyance over missing the action, but my power knew *I* was in control.

Levi chuckled; it was deeper with his lion showing through. "We're keeping her."

I couldn't take in his words when a servant managed to slip through the others as they slashed, punched, and ripped through the group. He stood before me with knives in each hand.

"You killed her."

What did he expect me to say? Saying nothing, I readied my body instead. He lunged. I twisted out of the way and stabbed back, catching his hip, but he kept moving, so it didn't pierce, just sliced.

I caught Kincaid leaping into the air and landing on the back of a bear, sinking his teeth into its neck. The man I was dealing with tried to knife my back. I crouched and swept my leg out. He jumped it, but I sprang up and lifted my dagger and spun, slicing it across his throat. Blood sprayed before he dropped to the floor, choking. He would be dead quickly.

I moved on.

All the humans were already dead. A gust of wind blew through. Cassar stood with his hands out, controlling the air as it dragged a wolf his way. It looked as if the wolf couldn't breathe, right before its body twisted in the same direction Cassar's hands moved.

Lifeless, the wolf dropped to the floor.

Cassar caught my gaze even as madness surrounded us, and he sent me a friendly smile, but it faded quickly, and his eyes widened. He flew at me. Flew with his beautiful fluttery wings, which seemed to move like a hummingbird's would, which was fast, because he was instantly in front of me.

His arm circled my waist, and he twisted, yelling, "Levi." I was thrown through the air and saw Cassar attacking the wolf that had been behind me.

Arms caught me, and I stared up at Levi with a wildly beating heart. "Hello, sweetheart." He grinned.

"Levi," I breathed. But then a roar had me turning in his arms to see Silas tackling a bear to the ground. "Silas," I screamed when I saw a wolf sneaking up on Silas as he beat the bear with his hands.

"He'll be okay," Levi reassured me just as Kincaid appeared there, picking up the sneaky wolf and snapping its neck.

The room quieted. My ears rang, but I still managed to hear the headmaster's words when he said, "More will come for you. More will fight the battle so you do not become the ruler."

It was Kincaid who answered. "Let them come. We will stop them." He flashed over to the headmaster. "Like the others, you thought you were invincible. Your potions are nothing. *You* are nothing, and you'll be nevermore." He gripped the headmaster's hair, shoved his head to the side, and buried his fangs in the headmaster's neck. The man screamed, cried, and pleaded until he could no more.

Kincaid had drank him dry.

Six

SILAS MADE a phone call and the guards from earlier returned. I stood back while they started to clean. After a moment of hesitation, I recalled my position and made my way out the door of the cell to where the dead woman remained. I pulled my dagger free and cleaned her blood from it on her clothes before I slipped it back into its holder. At least the fight had taken my mind off the chill in the air from the still open windows.

When I grabbed the dead woman by the arms and started to drag her, a rough tone asked, "What are you doing?"

Dropping the body, I turned to face Kincaid. "Cleaning, master."

His scowl deepened. "Stop." He faced the cell. "Levi, Silas, Cassar, with me. The rest of you take care of this." Kincaid about-faced and started stalking down the hall.

For a moment, I stayed right where I was because he hadn't said my name, but then I remembered I was *his* servant and was supposed to follow him everywhere. Sighing, I quickly followed him. Feeling the others join us, I suddenly felt self-conscious. Had I done the right thing by taking their side? By fighting with them?

I'd killed, yet I didn't feel any remorse or turmoil. It had to be done or it would have been *my* life on the line.

Only... Cassar saved me. He saw danger at my back and got me out of it. The throw across the room had been scary and a little painful, but I still couldn't believe one of them had helped me.

And I had no idea why.

I was expendable to them. Not only that, but I also didn't expect they'd believe I was worthy of their help, unless me telling Kincaid the truth and stepping up to battle had changed things.

That had to be it.

At their suite, Kincaid opened the door and stepped through. When I entered, there was a flash, and next, I was being restrained.

My heart skyrocketed. Fear clutched my throat.

This was it.

This would be the end of me.

I was about to call my power, call my darkness forward to protect myself until I heard, "You're alive!"

Sucking in a couple of unsteady breaths, I stared at Mary when she pulled back from... hugging me. I'd expected it was Kincaid attacking. I thought he'd led me to my demise.

How wrong I had been.

I gave Mary a small smile and a nod as my pulse settled. She clutched my hands and glanced down at me.

Her eyes widened. "And you've got blood all over you." Mary turned to Kincaid, who stood over near the window, gazing out once more.

"Our little maid decided to kick some ass," Levi said, walking into the room with Silas and Cassar. All our clothes were covered in dirt and blood. It was lucky the halls were still quiet as we'd made our way back to the suite.

When I moved out of the doorway, Levi shifted with me and placed his arm around my shoulders. My heart thumped hard in my chest.

"Wait, what?" Mary asked.

Cassar and Silas took seats on the couch. They didn't care they were filthy and probably staining the cushions. I guessed they didn't have to. No doubt someone else would clean it. Cassar's gaze snagged on Mary, and I was sure I saw some interest within it.

Kincaid turned from the window and glowered at me. I lowered my gaze, swallowed thickly, and curled my arms around my waist. My fear spiked. Worry gnawed my stomach. It was stupid. So what if I'd upset him.

Anger washed through me. Straightening, I stared back at him with a blank expression. I would not show fear or any other emotion. I'd done the right thing to save my own hide.

"Is someone going to explain?" Mary asked.

Misery tightened my chest as a flash of awareness of my situation slammed into me. I would never belong with these people. I would never be seen as a comrade or anything other than the help.

I had a job to do, and that was it. Maybe I had overstepped with my actions, but I wouldn't take them back. I wouldn't cower. I would accept what had happened and move on... back to what I was supposed to be.

Walking across the room, my legs shook. Deep down, I didn't want to do this. I didn't want to be the maid, the servant, but it was who I was, and I still had to respect my master.

Nearing him, I dropped to my knees in front of Kincaid and bowed my head. "Master, if I've acted in ways you disliked, please forgive me. I shouldn't have been forthright with the situation or with any of you."

"What happened?" I heard Mary whisper.

I waited for Kincaid to say or do something. He didn't.

The pause was deafening, painful.

A moment later, he strode by me into his room, slamming the door after him.

Tears threatened and I didn't know why. Annoyance? Anger? Rejection? Hurt? It could be any one of those, but I refused to accept it was the latter two. I didn't concern myself with those feelings when it came to a man like Kincaid. A man I served and one I didn't truly know.

"Sweetheart." Levi's voice jolted me; I hadn't heard his approach. He laid a hand on my shoulder. "Hop up."

Blanking my expression, I climbed to my feet. "I should attend the master."

"Enough," Silas clipped.

Tension stilled me, and I caught Mary looking from one person to another as her right hand rose to press against her lips and her eyes widened. Her gaze settled on me.

"Mary," Silas barked, and Cassar hit him in the gut. Silas cleared his throat, glaring at Cassar.

Mary turned, missing the action. "Yes, sir?"

"Have you found a substitute headmaster? Have the teachers been informed that the headmaster no longer works here?"

"Yes and yes. Also, everyone is in class and knows nothing that's happened."

"Good. Take the maid to Levi's room. She'll need to shower again, and find her another uniform."

"You got it, boss."

Levi's hand slid from my shoulder to gently squeeze my hand. I didn't understand his support. Why was he so different from the others?

"Come on, Amara." Mary smiled encouragingly.

Levi's hand fell from mine when I started toward his room. Just as I was inside with Mary and the door started closing, I heard Levi say, "She helped us. When are you going to stop being absolute assholes?"

With a hand on my back, Mary guided me toward the bathroom. "I'm nearly dying to know what happened since I left, but are you willing to tell me? Or do you want a shower first? I could get some food and drink and we can talk it over. I think they're staying here another night and—"

"Mary?"

"Hmm?"

I knew Mary was obviously in the fold of those men out there or they wouldn't trust her with so much knowledge in the first place. There'd be no harm in telling her what happened. Maybe by doing so I could sort through it myself.

But first... "I would love to get this blood off me, but then I promise I'll tell you if they haven't already."

She grinned. "Deal." She started toward the door, and I slipped into the bathroom. Turning on the water, I undid my braid while it warmed. It was naïve of me to think fighting beside them, having their backs, changed something. That it could have made them see me differently. As more. Sure, there was Levi, but Silas and Kincaid.... They still saw me as nothing.

It hurt my heart

Made me want to cry.

I wished like hell the disappointment clawing at my chest didn't hurt so much.

Feeling this way was ridiculous. Dangerous.

Shaking my head at my idiocy, I undressed and removed my weapons before slipping under the hot water. The blood ran pink from my skin, and I watched it swirl down the drain while I scrubbed at my hair with Levi's shampoo.

Would my life be the same as it once was?

Probably.

Despair gripped my stomach.

Kincaid and Silas would continue to hate me. Why else would they speak to me in such ways? I wondered if they'd hated Kincaid's previous servants. I scoffed at the thought. Of course they had, especially when they'd all tried to kill him. It made sense that he ended their lives.

Perhaps that was the reason for their indifference. But it felt like more than that. Their mistrust was evident in every interaction. Had I not proved myself enough? I'd fought at their sides. I'd told Kincaid what happened. How could it not be enough?

The reality was, it never would be. Nothing would change.

All I could do was keep living.

After washing out the conditioner, I turned off the water, got out, and dried myself. I placed my holsters on my thighs, daggers back in their spots, and slipped into my underwear before wrapping the towel around myself. I opened the door a little and peeked out. No one was about, and the door was still closed, but I spotted a new maid's dress sitting on the bed for me.

I dropped the towel to the floor and picked up the dress. I had it over my head when I heard the door to the bedroom open. My face heated as I pushed the dress all the way down and faced—*oh shit*—Levi.

He leaned back against the door with a smile playing on his lips. "Looks like I came in at the right time... or wrong. I could have joined you in the shower." He was already clean, so I knew he was teasing.

It didn't stop my body from reacting, though. I pressed my hand to my stomach while it stupidly fluttered. Something inside me wanted to reach out to him, to beckon him closer. A part of it was my darkness, and the other.... I wasn't sure. Staring at him, I locked my body down and stood before him with wet hair, lost for words.

No one could deny Levi was attractive. He was, and the way he flirted dragged everyone's attention toward him. I hated how it seemed I was like every other woman when around the lion shifter.

His head tilted to the side as he pushed off the door and walked my way. I took a step back, but the bed was there, and the backs of my knees hit it.

Levi stopped in front of me and reached out to play with a strand of damp hair. "Let me do your hair?"

"S-Sorry, sir?"

His brows dipped. "Don't do that. Don't call me that."

I had to know. "Why are you kind to me?"

His lips thinned. "Are there people who aren't? Langley?"

"No, never. Mr. Langley was...." I clamped my lips together.

Levi sighed. "One second," he said, and then moved into the bathroom. I heard him shifting things around before he returned, holding a brush and some hair ties. Levi sat on the edge of the bed and grinned up at me. "Sit between my legs and I'll braid your hair."

What?

My body warmed at the thought of being between his legs. Being so close to him. I couldn't be allowed to do such a thing.

I shook my head. "I'll, um, tie it up and see if the master—"

"Amara." His rougher tone elicited something inside me.

"Yes?"

"Sit, please. Kincaid is showering anyway."

The heat within me intensified at the thought of Kincaid in the shower.

Levi's grin grew. "Interesting."

"Sorry?" I chirped.

"Nothing. Come on. Sit down for me." He patted the bed between his legs. I needed to hide my burning face from him, so I quickly moved to sit on the floor and pressed my forehead to my bent knees as I wrapped my arms around my legs.

Levi brushed my hair. He ran his hand over it first before the brush needles slipped through until it reached a knot. Carefully, he worked each of them out.

I had no idea why he was doing this. Questions burned my tongue, but I didn't want to ruin the surreal moment.

My eyes closed as the sensation lulled me into a sense of peace. Who knew having my hair brushed could be so personal... hypnotic.

"Lift your head, sweetheart."

A small noise of complaint slipped from my lips because I really didn't want to move. Levi chuckled. "Glad you're enjoying it."

I stiffened. I wasn't supposed to enjoy it. This was Levi Grayson, lion shifter alpha, and soon, he would take over the pride from his father. He was... beyond being someone who would brush anyone's hair, let alone mine.

"Why are you doing this?" I asked.

"Because I enjoy it," he said simply, as if that was honestly all it was—enjoyment for him. His fingers slid through my strands as he parted it and then started braiding one side.

"How do you know how to braid?"

"I have many sisters in the pride. I like taking care of people."

My back snapped straight. I didn't need to be taken care of.

"Relax. You proved you can take care of yourself." How had he read me so quickly? "It's times like this that are an indulgence for me. I don't get many of them because we're so busy. Let me have this."

Gradually, I relaxed my shoulders and drew in a shaky breath. It dawned on me that I wanted to give him this for no other reason than he enjoyed it. Which was strange.

"You know, Kincaid and Silas don't hate you." I held back my scoff. He waited for a beat for something from me, but when I didn't say anything, he went on, "You have to understand, you're the first servant of many who came to us about the headmaster's plans for Kincaid. We suspected him but didn't have proof. You've shocked us in more ways than one, Amara. It'll take some getting used to."

I had shocked *them*?

That was.... I didn't know what to think.

He ran his hands over my head and leaned in. His breath fanned my skin. "They might not say it, but I will. Thank you, Amara." When his lips pressed against my cheek, a small shock zapped into me, sending my pulse racing. He slid his nose to the back of my ear and took in a breath. A sweet rumble sounded in his chest.

My hands itched to grab him, to hold him close to me.

I wanted....

My chest rose and fell rapidly. My eyes widened at the reality.

I wanted to kiss him.

"Jesus, Amara." Levi's hand slid to my neck, opposite to where his lips teased the side of my throat.

Did I dare turn?

Did I dare take my first kiss?

The door to the bedroom opened with a bang, and Mary said, "Sorry the tray—oh."

Shock had her brows shooting up as I jumped to my feet to Levi's side. My body hummed. I wanted Mary to leave. I wanted to hiss and snap at her or stand in front of Levi so she wouldn't look at him. It was crazy.

I fisted my hands at my side and clenched my jaw, breathing deeply through my nose. I fought the urges and ducked my head down, eyes to the floor. I was mortified. Not only for what my body craved, but for allowing Levi to tarnish himself with a maid. If Kincaid and Silas found out, it wouldn't be good for either of us.

Levi groaned in agitation and stood up. "Talk to you soon, Amara." When I didn't reply or move, Levi cursed under his breath and stalked from the room. Mary moved out of the way just in time.

Sadness dug its way inside me. I hadn't wanted him to leave.

What was going on with me? The more I was around this group of men, the more I felt myself connecting to them, which I didn't understand.

All I knew was that I was in deep shit, since I was stuck with them.

Seven

"GIRL, you have some explaining to do." Mary grinned as she set the tray down on a coffee table. Thankfully, the door had been closed, and I guessed the guys would have soundproofing in their rooms, preventing them from hearing each other's nighttime activities.

My stomach soured and twisted at the thought of them in their rooms with someone.

Which also made me want to punch myself in the belly and knock my head into a wall a few times.

Mary sat opposite me. "Are you okay?"

A little dazed, I blinked and nodded.

"You can talk to me. I can keep a secret like the best of them."

I couldn't.

"Why didn't you warn me about what's been going on with his servants?" I asked softly.

She frowned. "I couldn't. I would have if I hadn't promised them." She nodded toward the living area.

"Amara, there were at least thirty before you, and *all* of them failed Kincaid when they didn't seek him out and tell him what was happening. *We* didn't even know the full extent of it. We thought an outside source was getting to the servants before they joined the Prince family. Then there was also the idea that they wanted to kill him to get out of working for him. The stories about Kincaid—okay, some of them are true, but a lot aren't. He has a heart. He cares. If they had come to him, he would have sorted things out. None of us expected you'd be different from the others. We thought you'd already been bought or promised whatever they had been. I couldn't warn you in case you were against them as well. After I saw how you were with Jim, I *hoped* you would be different."

I understood her reasoning. I did. She was protecting Kincaid and her bosses. I just hated how alone it made me feel. Yet, I probably always would feel this way because I wasn't anything to them.

Then why is Mary in the room talking with me?
Why did Levi sit and brush my hair?
Why did Cassar save me?

There wasn't an easy answer to those niggling questions, though. For now, I would have to continue being who I had been for many years—a servant.

Nodding, I quietly said, "I understand."

Mary smiled brightly and gestured at the tray of food and coffee on the table between two couches. "How about we eat?"

My stomach growled in response. I gave her a grateful small grin and nodded, walking over there. I took the couch closest to the wall with nothing behind me, while Mary sat in the one near the door.

Sandwich in hand, I took a bite and sighed happily at the taste of cheese and meat. I hadn't realized how hungry I'd been, eating one after another until my plate was cleared. Sitting back with a coffee, I patted my stomach and said, "Thank you, I needed that."

Mary grinned. "Kincaid mentioned you've only had a bite or two of a muffin. I could get more if you like?"

"No." I shook my head, still reeling from the thought of Kincaid speaking to Mary about me. Not that I thought he was being considerate. He probably wanted me fed so I could still do my job. "I'm fine, honestly."

Mary shrugged and finished off her plate. "So," she drew out. "What was the scene I walked in on?"

My face burned. "Nothing."

Mary's brows shot up. "Didn't look like nothing." When I didn't reply, Mary gave me a small smile. "How about you tell me everything that's happened since I've been gone?"

I glanced toward the door and reminded myself Mary was close with the men out there. They wouldn't mind me saying anything. She already knew about the headmaster.

I grazed my bottom lip with my top teeth and told her what happened during the night. She didn't interrupt besides a gasp here or there, and I was sure it was the quietest and stillest I'd ever seen her.

After I was done, Mary gaped like a fish out of water for a little while. But then blinked and said, "I can't believe all that went down. Are you okay?"

Instead of answering, I shrugged. Was I? I didn't know, but I had to move on. There wasn't any point in dwelling. That would get me nowhere.

Glancing away from Mary's concerned gaze, my eyes welled up. I clenched my jaw and drew in a shaky breath.

I'd killed.

Ended people's lives.

Shaking my head, I reminded myself that taking their lives had been necessary. It meant I was safe, and I'd assisted in saving those around me. If I hadn't fought back, I would have ended up dead.

The door burst open. I jumped and looked over, quickly wiping away the tears that had managed to fall.

"What did you do?" Silas snarled at Mary while he pointed at me.

Mary rolled her eyes, not even looking at him. "Women cry. Didn't you know that?"

"Why is she crying? What did you say?"

Why does he care why I'm crying?

Mary sighed. "Everything just hit her all of a sudden."

Silas stared at me. I lowered my gaze and wiped at my tears, since it seemed his scowl followed the tracks down my face.

A growl rumbled through the room, and I looked up quickly as Silas took a step forward. His hands fisted at his sides. "You have nothing to be upset about."

I blinked, unsure if it was best if I said something.

His scowl deepened. His jaw clenched and actual smoke billowed from his nostrils when he let out a breath through them.

The dragon was pissed.

"Just stop... that." He waved a hand at my face.

Covering my mouth with my hand, I sank my teeth into my bottom lip to keep the sudden urge to laugh at bay. He really didn't like to see women cry. I nodded.

He glared for a moment longer before stalking from the room. I heard Kincaid ask, "What happened?"

The door closed, so I didn't hear Silas's response, and Mary started laughing.

"What?" I asked, eyes wide in disbelief.

Mary shook her head. "His reaction was priceless."

"How would he have known? This room is sound-proof, right?"

Mary shrugged. "Maybe Kincaid scented the salt in the air."

Shocked, my brows shot up. "His nose is that good?"

"His is the best out of the four of them."

I knew vampires were good with their noses, but not that good.

"Have you ever cried in front of them?" I was curious to see if they acted like that all the time and a bit hopeful that they didn't.

Mary snorted. "Yes, nothing major, though. Just 'that time of month' emotions. But do you know what they've said to me?"

My heart fluttered. "What?"

"Suck it up, buttercup. Well, that was mainly from Silas. At least Levi has a heart and offers me a little bit of sympathy before throwing chocolate at me."

My stomach joined my heart. A smile lifted my lips. "He throws chocolates at you?"

She nodded. "Wait until you get your period around them."

I sobered. It wouldn't matter if I did. They wouldn't care. Except to maybe complain about the smell, which would be mortifying.

Mary mattered because she was different from me. She wasn't human. She was their ally, their assistant. They needed her.

"Hey, what's the frown for?"

Quickly thinning my lips, I shook my head. "Nothing."

Mary gave me sad eyes. "Amara, give this time. They're not the monsters people have painted them as. Even Kincaid and Silas. They care, or else Silas wouldn't have stormed in here, on Kincaid's command probably, to see what was wrong with you."

Hope uncurled in my heart, but I squashed it with an invisible hand.

Trust was hard to come by.

Maybe I could learn to believe Mary's words, but only time would tell.

Mary sighed. "I get it. I do. You'll need time to understand I'm not pulling your chain. But eventually you'll see that they're pains, but good ones." She nodded. "Anyway, Kincaid is staying another night here, and then he'll be going back home tomorrow night for the family dinner."

"Bennett, the Prince family's butler, said the same."

"Good. We'll see if the committee for the college has hired someone else for the headmaster's position and if any gossip has spread. I mean, the men who work for Silas and Levi are amazing, but no one is certain there wasn't a witness lurking. Fingers crossed everyone stays silent."

"Did Kincaid find out who else is behind the attacks? The headmaster mentioned his attacks were to stop Kincaid from becoming the next alpha. Have all the other attacks been the same, for the same reason? Do I still need to be on alert?"

Mary nibbled on her bottom lip. "I'm afraid it's always best to be on alert. We're sure the headmaster's attack was instigated by someone else, but we don't know who, so there's no doubt more will come."

Confusion dipped my brows. "Why don't they want Kincaid ruling?"

"There's always those who believe they'd be best suited for the job. They're power-hungry." She shrugged. "It's hard to give reasons for why the people want to stop Kincaid from becoming alpha. They could think he would be worse than his father or better than Mr. Prince. Not everyone is completely happy when it comes to the alpha leaders. Mr. Prince has had over a hundred attempts on his life. It's not fun being a ruler, but Kincaid, along with Levi and Silas, will form a powerhouse no one will want to go against once they transition into their positions."

Mary did indeed hold a lot of trust in the men.

A knock sounded on the door, startling me.

"Come in," Mary called.

The door opened, and Cassar stepped in, closing it after him. I stood quickly, brushing away any crumbs, and slipped into a curtsey.

"Please, Maid Amara, you do not have to do that for me."

Straightening, I kept my gaze to the floor. "Is there anything I can do for you, sir?"

Mary sighed. "Honey, relax."

It wasn't that simple. I knew and felt Cassar was an alpha. It was my role to serve and treat all alphas honorably.

Cassar walked further into the room, and I tensed when he got closer, but he moved past me and sat on the couch where I had been.

"What's going on, Cassar?" Mary leaned forward.

As I remained standing, I clasped my hands behind my back and kept my gaze to the floor.

"Amara, come sit back down." I peeked to see Mary gesture to the couch before Cassar answered.

"Please, Maid Amara." Cassar's voice was soft. His eyes stayed on Mary, who seemed to blush under his stare. He smirked over at her.

Since it was an alpha asking, I had to listen. There was also the fact that I felt more relaxed around him since he'd saved me, but also his attention was mainly focused on Mary. Something I would have to ask her about. That was another foreign thought. I'd never had the urge to talk with another woman in a friendship way, but Mary made it easy to like her, trust her, and foolishly or not, I wanted to make an effort to get to know her more.

Maybe I could even make a friend.

Cassar shifted down the couch a little. I took the spot right near the armrest, on the edge of the cushion, in case I needed to move quickly when someone else came in and saw I was sitting on the job.

"Well?" Mary rolled her hand in front of her.

Cassar grinned. "Levi has gone out to see to a situation. Silas, on Kincaid's behalf, is in a meeting with the school's board and teachers. He'll know if anything got out about the situation to the school committee or even the council. Now I'm here and bored, since Kincaid is out there, watching television."

It meant Cassar was in the suite to watch over Kincaid... so wasn't he supposed to be out at Kincaid's side to do that?

He needed someone at his side in case someone attacked.

Panic clutched at my heart.

I didn't believe it was for Kincaid. No, I had to believe I was concerned for myself.

I had to.

I didn't care about that man.

Standing, I straightened my dress out. "Someone should be out there in case anything happens." I stalked to the door, flung it open, and paused for only a moment when I saw Kincaid resting on a couch with his attention on the television. He'd never looked so human before.

After closing the door behind me, I kept my eyes on the floor and went over to the couch to stand at the end where his head was. I pressed a hand to my dagger and glanced at the windows. We were on the third level, but it wouldn't stop casters or shifters with wings. I flung my gaze to the door. Was it even locked? I nodded when I saw it was and shifted around to make sure the other bedroom doors were closed. If someone somehow got into one of those rooms, at least I would have enough time to react when the door came open.

"What is she doing?" Kincaid's rough, dark voice snapped.

"Keeping watch over you." Cassar covered a chuckle with a cough. I swung my gaze to the doorway where he stood. I hadn't heard him enter. That wasn't good.

Kincaid grunted while I glared at Cassar, who smiled back.

"Why?" Kincaid asked.

"She doesn't trust your safety when no one is in the room with you."

Kincaid snorted.

I ground my teeth together.

Kincaid's jaw jutted out when he glanced at me. I quickly looked elsewhere.

"It is my job to be by my master's side," I informed both men with a ticked-off tone as annoyance settled inside me.

When Kincaid's upper lip rose in a silent snarl, I didn't balk, and I was proud of myself for not looking away. When Cassar moved over to the chair near the couch that my master relaxed on and sat, I finally focused elsewhere.

Cassar picked at something on his pants. "Silas mentioned Langley trained you for combat."

I didn't reply, since he wasn't in charge of me, and I didn't want to speak of Mr. Langley in case anything tarnished his name.

"Answer him," Kincaid ordered.

Shit.

My gaze shifted to Mary as she walked from the room

with the tray in hand. "I'm just taking this back to the kitchens."

"Please, allow me," I said. Mary wasn't a servant, and the time out would be good. I wouldn't have to speak about Mr. Langley.

I started for her, but she shook her head. "No, no. It's fine. I'll be back soon."

Double shit.

When Mary was out the door, locking it behind her, Cassar, with his pleasant voice, said, "Maid Amara?"

Closing my eyes, I let out a small breath. "Yes. Mr. Langley trained me."

"Why would he think you needed training?" Cassar asked.

My body froze.

He trained me because he feared people would want to use me for my power. I had my power to protect me, but, back in the day, my darkness wasn't a good feeling. I'd been worried it would take me under and I'd never be the same.

When I'd confessed as much to Mr. Langley, sadness had cast his face in shadow, then he'd instructed me on how to not let my power consume me. That was another reason he trained me in combat.

Now I knew different.

My darkness wasn't something to fear. Not for myself anyway.

Yet, there was still the risk of being used, or studied, or controlled.

There wasn't a chance I could confess any of this to

Cassar, though. I couldn't let anyone know about my darkness within.

Once again, I didn't feel like I was a human.

"Don't listen to those thoughts, Amara," Mr. Langley had said. *"You're more human than anyone. Just because this lives inside you doesn't change the person you are. Never doubt who you are."*

Many times, I tried to remind myself of my humanity because I didn't want to be a monster. I didn't want to be different.

Now I wasn't so sure I could hide forever, and I wasn't so sure I wanted to. What happened if I could be the one to help humanity?

"Answer him," Kincaid ordered again.

I jolted. Sudden tears pricked my eyes. "Mr. Langley was a good master. He worried that if anything happened to him, my next job could be unsafe. He wanted to make sure I could protect myself. That's all."

Mr. Langley was the best.

Sorrow gripped my heart.

Kincaid was suddenly in front of me. With a finger under my chin, he lifted it so my gaze clashed with his. "You're holding back something."

"I'm not, master."

His gaze hardened before the white disappeared and red invaded. My legs shook, and my heart thundered in my chest, but I didn't look away.

"Tell me." His tone was soft, like a caress.

"There is nothing, master," I replied with a hard edge. Worry and irritation ran through me.

Kincaid ground his teeth together and turned his back

on me. "I try fear, you get aroused. I try lust, and nothing happens." He spun back my way. "What makes you different?"

I had to stay calm, but I could already feel my pulse increase. "Nothing." We all knew it was a lie, though.

Would he press me on it?

Please don't. Please leave it alone. Please.

His jaw clenched while I waited.

"This is tense," Cassar commented.

Kincaid kept staring, and I matched his gaze, hoping he would see I wouldn't budge on my answer.

The door unlocked. "What's going on?" Silas was back.

"If you ask me, it looks like a lovers' quarrel." Levi was also back.

Kincaid hissed Levi's way but still stared at me.

"Cassar?" Silas said.

"We were speaking of Langley. Apparently, he trained her because he wanted her strong for her next master in case he was an ass."

"And look what happened. She got an ass for a master," Levi teased.

"That can't be all," Silas said.

"Kincaid tried using compulsion on Maid Amara, and it didn't work."

Someone drew in a large breath. "At least we know it wasn't fear this time. I'd hate to have missed that," Levi commented.

Cassar hummed. "It was lust."

"It didn't work?" Levi asked.

Silas grunted. "Obviously. So what did happen?"

"Nothing, she didn't react. Now they're having a standoff."

At least he didn't mention Kincaid not believing me when I said I wasn't different. I couldn't explain why I didn't react normally when Kincaid used compulsion. Maybe it had something to do with what was inside me. I couldn't tell anyone that or how I feared for my life.

The door closed, and I sensed Silas and Levi move further into the room.

I could have backed down and taken my gaze away from Kincaid's, but I didn't. Even when everything inside me screamed at me to submit, to look away.

"I know you're hiding something," Kincaid said darkly.

I was, and I hated that I had this secret. I didn't understand what was inside me in the first place. I had no clue where it came from—obviously not Charlotte, or she would have foolishly used it for her own gain. Charlotte never mentioned that Dad had power, and I was young when he died, so I didn't know enough about him. It must have been him, right? How else would I explain my power manifesting when I was fourteen?

"I don't know how to answer you, master."

Kincaid's fist hit his chest. "Tell *me* what it is."

No. No way in hell. I wouldn't be used. I wouldn't be experimented on. There was little doubt in my mind that would happen when no one understood this thing inside me. I had never heard of another like me.

Swallowing the lump in my throat, I tried again. "There is nothing to tell you."

Kincaid snarled out a breath. "Lies. One day I will find out, and if I don't like it, I will kill you."

"Kincaid," Levi bit out.

Kincaid glowered at me some more and then headed for his room, slamming the door after him. It was my job to follow him, to stay at his side, but my feet wouldn't move.

I didn't want this secret.

I didn't want this power.

And I definitely didn't want to be different.

Anger and worry stabbed inside me.

Why couldn't I just be normal?

I shook my head, dropping my attention from his door to the floor.

What I wanted most of all was to really believe I was still human.

"Amara." Levi's soft voice ran over my shoulder before he rested his hands on them both. "He'll come around."

I didn't understand what he meant. Come around how?

Silas snorted. "I doubt it when we know Langley wouldn't have trained her just in case her master was an ass. There's another reason, and not knowing it pisses him, and me, off."

"*I can't tell you*," I wanted to scream. If I told them, my life would surely end faster than if I remained mute. Of course, there was the danger of working as Kincaid's servant, considering his death threats. That was proof enough that my time would be shortened.

Either way, I was screwed.

Eight

KINCAID

Anger churned inside me. I wanted to shake her. Demand she tell me all her secrets. I had to be sure she wouldn't be a liability. That my friends would be safe with her around. I wanted to get in her face and....

Fuck.

I wanted to kiss her, taste her, take her.

I ground my teeth, refusing those urges. I *didn't* like her. I *didn't* trust her. She could be poison to the group, and there wasn't a chance in hell I would risk anything for a woman.

No matter what Levi said.

My door opened and I faced it, ready to yell if she'd dared come in here. It wasn't her, though.

Why did a breeze of disappointment run over me?

Clenching my hands, I ignored the pang of frustration and instead summoned my anger toward her.

Silas closed the door and leaned against it. "What are we going to do about her?"

Nothing came to mind, which irritated me. In most situations, I knew what to do and how to handle people.

With Ama—the *maid*—I was out of my element. She was different from any of my other servants. Her actions were new to me, and I didn't know how to react, especially knowing she still hid something from us.

There was also how she assisted us in fighting. Not that she had to, but she put herself in harm's way to help *us*.

Sighing, I scrubbed a hand over my face and groaned. "I don't know."

Silas nodded, a rare half smile on his lips. "I know what you mean. She's a conundrum."

"What's that smile about?" I asked a little too roughly.

Silas rolled his eyes and shrugged. "I get why it's hard to trust her, but... I don't know. I liked how she had our backs in that fight. Kincaid, she threw a dagger at that woman before the fight even broke out because she knew it would happen in the end anyway. She's also smart. Knew the headmaster was stalling. She could tell who was human."

"I know," I snarled and stomped to the window seat to sit. But the scent of the maid still lingered. My damn cock throbbed. I wanted to bury my face into the seat and draw in a lungful. Instead, a growl slipped from my lips, and I stood, walking to the other side of my bed.

"She didn't have to help us," Silas mentioned. Was he softening toward her?

"Get to your point before I break something."

Silas snorted. "Fine. She may be hiding something, but I don't think it has anything to do with you or us. It's something about her."

"That's still worrisome."

He nodded. "It is. However, I say we keep her around, keep an eye on her. It'd save you finding another maid."

My upper lip rose. "I wish Father would quit throwing maids at me when I don't need one."

"I'm not saying I like her. She's annoying in how she switches from timid to fierce instantly. But she's the best one you've had, and it's good that Langley had her first. He was always trustworthy. If it wasn't for him, none of us would be friends or where we are now."

That was true.

Mother had hired Langley, behind Father's back, to teach me self-defense. At the time, he was also teaching Silas and Levi. I used to hate shifters; my father had drilled into me at a very young age that shifters were below us and were scum. Yet, Mother had organized the lessons anyway, knowing I would need to be able to protect myself against many evils. My father included.

And Langley was an excellent teacher.

The first few classes were tense because I let my father's hate consume me. It wasn't until I saw the fun Silas and Levi were having—and how I'd hated that I missed out—that I joined in, and we soon became fast friends.

Of course, when Father found out, he was furious. I'd been six at the time, and my punishment was beyond what any child should have to endure.

Reaching up, I touched my scar. A caster had spelled

my father's knife as he cut into my skin, preventing it from healing. The lesson had been that I should never make the mistake of listening to my mother.

His torture was supposed to make sure I didn't defy his rules.

At first and for many years, I didn't, but only until I was strong and old enough to stand up for myself.

Thinking of the past, I wished I'd taken a photo of his face when I walked with Silas and Levi at my side into our estate and then informed him they were my hired guards. Of course, Father had tried to stop me. That was the last time he took his anger out on me, since I won the hand-to-hand combat, only to be beaten later by his guards. Though, I hadn't cared. How could I when I won against *him* and got to keep Silas and Levi at my side.

"Hey." Silas grabbed my attention with one word, no doubt knowing I was lost in the past. "If your father is behind these attacks, you know he'll be taken care of eventually."

We'd suspected my father from the start. He was high up on the list, not just because of how he treated me. The questions he'd asked were immediate red flags, but we couldn't prove his involvement; he was good at covering his tracks.

One day he would slip up, and until that happened, I would keep going as I was. But when it was my time as alpha leader, things would change. Many things, and the changes would be all for the better. It was only unfortunate that Levi and Silas would inherit their positions before I did. I had to wait until I was of age before we grouped together and enforced some of the planned changes.

We expected retaliation and kickback. But together, we could make a difference.

"I know." I nodded. "Did you get anything from the board meeting?" I needed to change the subject. The less I thought of or spoke about my so-called father, the better.

"Nothing. No one is the wiser on what went down. We're in the clear."

"Good. Did they appoint a new headmaster?"

Silas tipped his chin up. "Mrs. Brownstone."

"Another caster?"

"Yeah, but I've heard good things about her. She cares about her students and doesn't discriminate against any species."

"I guess we'll see if it stays that way if someone gets in her ear."

Silas grunted. "We'll keep an eye on her." After another beat, he chuckled. "How long are you going to glare at the seat?"

I snapped my gaze to his, not realizing I'd been looking at the chaise lounge the maid had slept on. "I was looking out the window," I lied.

"Sure," he drew out. "You know Levi had a moment with her."

"What does that mean?" My tone was rough and harsh. I was annoyed that she'd already weaved her way into Levi's trust.

"They were in the room together, and if Mary hadn't interrupted, he thinks it could have led to a kiss."

I groaned and scrubbed a hand over my face. "He's half

in love with her already. If he gets a taste, she'll have him by the balls." A small tang of jealousy reared its ugly head, but I pushed it aside. There was no way I'd get jealous over her. Nor with Levi or even Silas if she got her claws into him as well. They were my brothers. I didn't care that we were born different from one another; they were family. My only true one, since Mother never protected me from Father.

She didn't even stop him when she knew his punishments were too much for a young child.

"I figured as much. He got all soft talking about it. Do you think what he said could be true?"

I sucked in a sharp breath. "We will not speak of that."

Silas's jaw clenched. As his gaze narrowed on the floor, he nodded. I knew he would agree. There was no way she could be.... I didn't even want to think of it. I'd managed to push it into the far back of my mind and had forgotten Levi's foolish idea.

Silas threw out a hand. "What do we do, then? I can't stop him from developing feelings for her. She's a good actress. I don't want to see him hurt."

"Neither do I." If she did hurt him, I'd kill her. No questions asked.

No, you won't. My mind threw me the challenge. But I knew deep down if that... woman hurt Levi or anyone I cared for, I would end her.

After I sank my fangs into her and drank her dry, that was.

I wanted her blood on my lips and in my mouth.

"Where will she stay tonight? Mary offered to take her back to my estate."

"No," I bit out. I wouldn't let her out of my sight. "She stays here." I threw an arm out toward the hated chaise lounge. "There."

Silas's brows shot up. "In your room?"

"Don't you dare read too much into it."

He held his hands in front of him as a smirk played on his lips. "I wouldn't dare. I know you'll dislike her until you discover what she's hiding."

"Even if I do find out, I still won't like her."

She didn't appeal to me other than her blood. *Yeah right.* I tried to lie to myself that her hair was too black, she was too short, and her body had curves in places she could have done without. Yet still, my mouth watered. I swallowed and thought about what else she lacked.

Her skin was too pale. Her face too plain.

Standing, I glared at Silas as a thought crossed my mind. "You say *you* dislike her, but you always seem to bring her up."

Silas matched my glare. "I have to. It's my job to keep an eye on threats surrounding you."

"Are you sure that's all?"

His upper lip rose. "Yes."

"Fine." I waved a hand his way. "I'm taking a nap. Later, get Mary to organize a donor for me." The headmaster's blood hadn't been sitting well inside me. It happened sometimes with some magical folk—where I had to force it out to settle my stomach—but now I needed to replace it.

"*Fine,*" Silas clipped. He was still annoyed with my question as he left the room. I would rather have him angry with me than thinking of her. I wasn't stupid. I knew she played on all our minds.

She was dangerous until we knew everything.

My gaze had somehow managed to snag on the chaise lounge again. The blanket I'd felt compelled to drape over her still sat on top of it. I could scent her even from where I stood. Not only from the lounge, but from where she was in the living room.

I lied when I told her she reeked.

She didn't.

I hungered for her blood.

It was why I would feed tonight, earlier than my usual intake. I wished I'd been born anything other than a vampire, as I truly hated the act of taking blood. Doing so meant I had to get close to a person, and the thought of them touching me twisted me up inside.

Ever since my skin had been sliced open, not only my face but my back and chest, I couldn't stand a woman's gaze on my body. All I saw in them was fear or pity or a need to give me what I wanted, whether it be blood or other carnal urges in the hope it would bring them some type of fortune.

At first, I'd been fine with the exchange, but I'd soon grown bored and disgusted with them all.

Now, my feedings were a necessity, and that was all. The donors would come, sit, and be instructed to not touch me while I drank. Then they would leave.

Once, I'd hoped to find someone I could spend my life with without sensing those things from them. However, the more days that passed, the more I thought it would be impossible. There were too many users out there—too many who feared me or only looked at me with pity.

Shaking my head, I pulled out some paperwork, sat on the bed, and gave the work my full attention, hoping to contain my wayward thoughts. Too many bad memories had surfaced today.

Time flew by as I worked. I only stopped when a knock on the door interrupted me. "What?" I grouched.

The heavy door opened, revealing the maid standing with her gaze to the floor. I clenched my jaw in irritation, like I always did whenever she did that and when she called me master.

"Master," she called softly. I scowled. "Dinner is on its way. Would you like to eat in here or out in the living room?"

"I won't be eating," I told her coldly.

She hesitated, gnawing on her bottom lip. "Master."

"What?" I clipped.

Her jaw clenched, and she glanced out into the living room before she straightened, looking at me with a glare. "You should eat something."

Some of the things she said didn't make sense. It was like she cared, but as Silas had said, she was a good actress and only doing her job as my maid.

"Leave," I stated. She didn't need to know I would be eating, only it wasn't normal food.

Her nostrils flared. "I'll bring you something—"

"Don't. I order you around. If you don't listen, it just agitates me. You don't want me agitated, servant."

"And this isn't you agitated already?" slipped from her

lips, and her eyes widened. She took steps back out into the living room and closed the door after her.

Surprise flicked through me, my lips wanting to tug up into a smile. Instead, I frowned, but it didn't last. It was times like those, when I saw her fire, that I thought I could handle having her around. Until she fought her attitude and switched back to the good little maid she was meant to be, that was.

Then again, she probably knew no different. I was certain Bennett would have warned her to be seen and not heard. She was doing her job, but out of all the servants I'd had, none of their robotic actions burned my gut the way hers did.

Groaning, I pushed the books aside and went for a long, hot shower. I was thinking too much about her and had started to make excuses for her actions, which only irritated me more.

When I walked back into my room after my shower, it was to find the maid sitting on the lounge by the window with her hands tucked under her thighs, feet as well as her gaze on the ground.

I stilled. "What are you doing in here?"

"The others adjourned to their rooms, master. I was told this is where I would sleep for the night."

Those assholes. I stomped to my phone and picked it up, seeing a text from Levi: **We're all tired. You'll have to take care of your maid and get the door for your dinner :)**

Death would be on their doorstep because I was going to kill them. Slowly. With some torture involved as well.

I glanced at the time to see it was a little after eight.

There was no chance they'd be tired. What were they playing at? I expected this act from Levi, but not Silas. Why would he do this?

My phone cracked under the pressure of my grasp. I dropped it onto the bed and shifted my gaze to the maid again. I did not want her around when I fed.

A knock sounded on my bedroom door. The maid went to get up until I snarled, "I'll get it." If it was the donor, I would kick the maid out to the living room until I finished feeding. When I opened the door, sound hit me. Anger lit inside me.

The woman in front of me squeaked and took a step back. "Stay there," I ordered and swiftly moved over to Cassar. "What's going on?" I spoke louder than I normally would because of the music pounding out of the speakers.

"Levi said we could have a party." He smirked as I glanced around at the men who worked for Silas and Levi. Not all of his men were here, but there were still a lot.

Those... bastards had set this up. Was this a test? Did they not think I would send the maid out into a room full of men? I didn't care what happened to her.

"Clear out," I ordered, and I said it for *their* own safety, not knowing what the maid was capable of. If someone spoke too much, they could end up with a dagger in their gut like the woman had in the cellars.

Cassar started swaying his hips to the beat and grinned. "No can do, sir. The food's on the way, and Levi commanded us to have fun. We have to listen to our boss."

I really was going to murder that lion. I could push Cassar and get my own way, but I also knew how hard these men worked, and it wasn't often Levi gave them a night to relax.

Pointing to the door, I glared. "Do it elsewhere then."

Cassar shook his head. "Can't. Gotta stay close, since Levi and Silas are indisposed. We're also here to keep an eye out for trouble."

My arm dropped. "Indisposed?"

"Yes."

"How?"

Cassar shrugged. "It's not my job to question them." It was a lie. Cassar was Silas and Levi's top man; he knew their every move.

I snarled at Cassar and wanted to wipe that smile away with my fist. Instead, I stalked back to my door and ordered the donor, "In." She quickly stepped through the doorway, and I slammed the door closed.

My narrowed gaze lasered in on the maid, who glanced back with a blank expression. Should I send her out there? Could I trust her around those men?

I moved my attention to the woman who would have seemed timid with her hands clasped in front of her if it wasn't for the sultry smile on her wet lips.

"Sit on the edge of the bed." I pointed there. Not that I wanted her anywhere near my bed, but since the couch I usually fed on was occupied, I had no other choice. I could have stood to drink, but sometimes the women reacted physically to a feeding. It wasn't uncommon for a donor to become shaky, faint, or aroused, no matter what feeling we compelled them with.

With another glare at the maid, I went over to the

woman, sat beside her, and took her arm in my hands. She turned her body my way, lifting a bent leg to the bed.

"Do not touch me," I ordered.

The woman nodded and licked at her lips again. Sneering at her, I warned again, "Do not touch me."

She giggled. "You could enjoy it." She looked over her shoulder at the maid who was watching, but I couldn't read anything from her. "It doesn't seem likes she's done a good enough job to calm you down."

"She does not warm my bed." My tone wavered toward disgust, and I caught the maid wince. I ignored the stab of regret.

The woman winked at me. "Then I'd like to—" I wrapped my hand around her neck in a tight grip. The woman choked and her eyes widened as fear saturated the room. "You'll have heard about me. Do not come into my room and play these games. Whatever you want, I will not give. Now shut up."

She managed a nod, and I released my grip to pick up her arm. I drew her wrist up to my lips and bit. The woman cried out, but I pushed peace into her. On my first pull, she relaxed. The second, she smiled dazedly. I closed my eyes, not wanting to see anything more. Especially not those eyes watching me from across the room.

The maid hadn't reacted in a way I had expected when I'd grabbed the woman's neck. I thought she would have screamed and run from the room. All she did was flinch for a second before she kept watching with a straight face.

I worried that if I stayed looking at her, I would—

A hand touched my thigh before it quickly disappeared. I opened my eyes to see the maid behind the woman with a dagger to her throat and a hand fisted in the woman's hair, tugging her head back.

"He said not to touch him," she warned the woman, her unbraided hair swept around her shoulder, bringing with it a tantalizing scent.

The woman whimpered. "Sorry."

The maid nodded at me, and I took a few more pulls of the woman's blood before sealing the bite with my tongue, using my saliva to heal the wounds. I didn't look away from the maid as I ordered the woman, "Get out."

The maid removed the dagger and her hand. The woman nearly tripped over her own feet in her haste to leave.

When I heard the door close, I asked, "Why did you stop her?"

"To help," she replied simply.

Standing, I stepped into her space and drew in her scent. I locked my body down when her sweet arousal hit my nose.

This woman definitely was a conundrum.

But still, she was a woman I didn't trust. "Go to sleep." I made my way to the bathroom. I needed another shower. A cold one this time because I refused to touch myself over her.

Nine

AMARA

SLEEP WAS GOING to be hard to find after what I'd witnessed. His mouth, his fangs, the way his eyes fluttered closed. I'd wanted it to be me he drank from. I didn't understand why, but I did, and if he hadn't walked to the bathroom, I would have offered myself up because the sight of him with another woman soured my insides.

So much so, I had to hold myself back from slicing open her throat when she touched him and ignore the way my darkness encouraged that thought.

The urge to take her life had burned so brightly, I'd nearly acted on it.

That scared me.

Was it my power trying to take control?

Why would I want to kill a woman because of him?

He was nothing but my master, and not a very nice

one either. He hated me. More so, he didn't trust me, and trust meant a lot to him, but I couldn't tell him the truth.

When I heard the water shut off, I quickly went over to the chaise lounge, lay down, and pulled the blanket over me, facing the window just as the door to the bathroom opened.

He would hear my heart, and earlier, I was certain he'd scented my arousal. I hadn't been able to stop the tingle between my legs from watching him, even when murderous thoughts had overtaken me.

I blinked as I looked out the window, not really seeing, and listened to him get ready for bed. The light went out, yet he still moved around the room. I wanted to roll over to see what he was doing. Instead, I turned my head a little to look out into the dark, starlit sky.

Does he sleep naked?

My pulse increased as my breath caught, and I thinned my lips, pushing that thought from my mind, or else my body would react when I didn't want it to.

Never would I have thought I would see Kincaid as attractive. *Lies.* Where had my fear for the vampire gone?

My eyes widened when I fully thought it out. I didn't fear him. I feared being killed, but not him. How and when had that happened?

Was it when I fought at his side with the others?

The bed groaned under his weight. A sigh escaped his lips.

I slapped a hand over my mouth at the thought of him touching himself.

Where had this wanton hussy come from? Sex or the actions leading up to it had never really crossed my mind. I wasn't interested. So why was I reacting to Kincaid, to his friends? My core throbbed because of the man in his bed.

This was wrong.

So wrong.

I covered my face with my hands and prayed he wasn't breathing so he couldn't scent my arousal. Vampires didn't have to breathe as much as humans; they only did it to make themselves blend in.

Please let this be one of those times he isn't breathing.
Please.

A gasp escaped me when I felt hands sliding under my back and legs. My eyes widened and my mouth gaped when Kincaid picked me up, grumbling under his breath. His hold on me tight, I could feel the comforting warmth of his skin against my side. My body reacted as another throb pulsed. Kincaid hissed, stalked to the door, and opened it. The music I'd heard before when the door had been opened wasn't blasting now as he swiftly crossed the empty room while muttering, "Fucking lion."

Even though I was beyond wanting to kill myself, I had to say something and apologize for my body's reactions. "I-I'm sorry. It's not me, but my.... I don't understand why—"

"Shut it," he clipped roughly.

Arriving at Levi's door, he pushed it forward, looked in, and whatever he saw had him cursing and moving over to Silas's door. All while I stared up at him with a flaming face.

"What the fuck?" Silas called from his bed when Kincaid strode into his room after swinging his door so hard, it hit the wall.

Kincaid said nothing until he was at the side of Silas's bed. He dumped me down on the mattress and I bounced a couple of times. "You watch her" was all Kincaid said harshly before moving toward the door.

Silas climbed out of bed quickly and stood to the side of it with his hands on his hips. My core clenched. There were mountains of soft, yet hard, naked skin on display. His back. Chest. Stomach. All of it must have been carved from someone's fantasy, because he was positively gorgeous. My body reacted. The only material that covered him was black sleep shorts that rode low on his hips.

"Wait," Silas barked. "Why are you—" Silas's gaze dropped to me as he took in a deep breath. His pupils slid into dragon form, then switched back. "No. Fuck no. Kincaid, get back here." He rushed after Kincaid, but Kincaid already had the door closed. It didn't stop Silas grabbing the handle and twisting it this way and that. No matter which way he tried, the door wouldn't open.

"Let go of the damn door, vampire." When there was no reply, Silas kicked the door and tried to wrestle it open. It came back a little, but Kincaid must have pulled it closed again.

If I wasn't humiliated and confused, I would have found this whole situation funny.

Silas eventually gave in with another kick to the door. It seemed their strengths were evenly matched. He turned back to me, scowling.

"You're not sleeping there." He glared and pointed to a couch in the corner of the room.

I quickly stood, brushing my dress down before I

clasped my hands behind my back and dropped my eyes to the ground. "I'm sorry—"

"Don't do that shit." I looked up at him as he approached his wardrobe entryway. "You're not my maid. Don't act all proper like that with me. Hell, I'm sure Kincaid even hates when you do that."

He did?

Did that mean...? Could they possibly want me to be myself? Was Mary right when she told me the previous maids had acted freely, even when they did their job serving Kincaid? Though, they'd never lasted long because they were polluted by other people.

Honestly, I didn't know what was going on.

The night had turned strange, and I was to blame. No, *my body* was to blame for Kincaid kicking me out of his room. Was he so disgusted by my scent that he had to get rid of me? Yet, Silas was being... I didn't know, different, though somewhat normal with me. Didn't I stink to him? Didn't he find my arousal off-putting?

I rubbed at my temples; a headache bloomed. Kincaid had wanted Silas to take me away when he'd scented me. Maybe I was also unappealing in many ways other than my scent.

Not that I cared what they thought. I didn't. If only I could get my heart to understand that. I rubbed at my chest to try and ease the ache.

"Here, put this on." A piece of clothing was thrown at my face. I managed to grab it and hold it out. It was one of his T-shirts. Since he was largely built, it would be long enough to cover everything important. Silas threw a blanket and pillow on the couch. His body moved gracefully, and if I hadn't known he was a dragon, I would have guessed he shifted into a feline form from the way his body moved.

A scar marred his left hip, which made him more perfect.

My nipples pebbled, and my face heated. Silas dragged in a breath before his dragon eyes trained on me. A rumble sounded in his chest.

My heart dropped to my feet when he stalked toward me and picked me up in his arms. They stretched out to hold me away from his body. Just when I thought he was going to throw me onto the couch, he paused.

Panting, I gripped the T-shirt he'd thrown at me to my chest and waited while he stared at me. A noise sounded in the back of his throat. It was almost like a chuffing.

Slowly, he drew me back to him and pressed his nose against my throat. My body quivered when a hot, wet tongue licked up the side of my neck before he sucked in another breath.

The noise grew louder in his throat, and he pulled back, looked at me, and then his lips were on mine. My heart and body exploded with pleasure. I acted on instinct, wrapping my arms and legs around him while he pushed his tongue into my mouth and curled it around mine.

I moaned and gripped him tighter, lost in the passion, lost in his touch.

Never had I experienced anything like this.

Which was not unexpected, since Silas was my first kiss.

Our heads tilted further, deepening the kiss, and my

body was enflamed when he pressed his hardness between my legs.

Pulling back, my eyes widened.

He's hard.

He was aroused because of me.

I did that.

Awe nearly had me smiling until I saw Silas blink slowly. A growl rumbled out of him before he flung me over his shoulder and started for his door.

No!

My heart cracked. My body ached and my soul cried.

Like Kincaid, he was going to kick me out, no doubt because I wasn't worthy. I saw the horror in his eyes when he slipped back into reality and saw who he'd been kissing.

My throat thickened as another crack formed. I slammed my eyes closed when he opened the door, and I willed myself not to cry. Still, a few tears managed to leak out, and I quickly wiped them away.

At Levi's door, Silas opened it with a bang. A roar filled the room but was cut off quickly.

"Silas, what the hell?" Levi demanded.

In the next second, I was airborne, then bouncing on yet another mattress.

"*You* watch her," Silas said roughly. He didn't look at me when he turned and stalked back out, slamming the door behind him.

My chest clenched painfully.

Rejected.

Again.

I wasn't supposed to care. I wasn't supposed to be attracted to any of them. So why was I?

"Amara?" Levi's soft, gentle tone hurt as well.

With watery eyes, I ground my teeth together and looked up at him where he stood beside the bed. My core throbbed. He stood there with a towel around his shoulders and only wore dark blue boxers. The light from the bathroom silhouetted his firm, mouthwatering form.

My bottom lip trembled. I bit down on it hard enough I could taste blood.

"Angel," Levi uttered before he dropped the towel to the floor and sat on the bed, dragging my body to his, where I was perched on his thighs.

Shaking my head, I pushed at his arm and chest.

I couldn't do it. I couldn't have him be kind and sweet, only to reject me.

I was already broken, but I didn't want to be shattered.

"Amara, it's okay, honey. What happened?" He pulled me in again, but I fought him. "Shh, come on, angel. It's all right. Tell me what happened."

Shaking my head again, a sob caught, and I made noises in the back of my throat.

Please, just let me go. I'll leave. I'll... do something.

Levi wasn't giving up, though. His hands kept grabbing me, trying to hold me close. With a frustrated groan, I stopped moving, hoping he would loosen his grip.

He didn't.

He wound his arms around me and pulled me into his chest. He hummed a tune under his breath and glided his hand up and down the back of my hair.

Another sob caught in my throat. Another pathetic noise.

Why was I acting like this? I didn't understand why their rejection hurt so much. Why my heart tugged as if it wanted out of my chest.

Tears dropped, and I knew he would feel them on his shoulder, but I couldn't get them to stop. My darkness released a little sympathetic trill inside my chest.

This was stupid, crazy.... What was happening to me?

"Angel, tell me what happened."

It was too pitiful to say, especially when I didn't understand it myself.

"Please, just let me go," I tried, ashamed that my voice shook a little.

His arms tightened. "I can't do that. I need to know what's wrong. If they did something, I'll kill them."

I snorted lightly. He wouldn't.

"I will." His voice was a low growl.

"They didn't do anything," I told him, because really, they hadn't. It was my own damn responsibility that my body reacted in a way I'd never felt before. It wasn't their fault they didn't want anything to do with a maid. One they didn't know. One who kept secrets from them. One who was below their status.

They did nothing wrong.

Gently, I tried pushing his arms from me. When he relented with a sigh, I slipped from his lap and ignored the feeling of loss from being away from his warmth, his hold.

My stomach twisted, but I pressed my hands against it and moved away from him.

"Amara," he called softly.

"It's not their fault. I-I don't understand why...." Heat hit my cheeks. I didn't want to say anything because it was embarrassing. I moved over to his window and stared out into the darkened sky.

"You can tell me anything."

Closing my eyes, I drew in a deep breath. "My body became aroused in their rooms. They didn't like it, so they got r-rid of me. Please don't ask any more. I-I'll go and sleep in the living room. I'll do my job as I'm supposed to and try to control... myself." Turning, I started for the door.

Levi stepped in front of me, and his hands fell to my waist. I looked to the side. I didn't want to meet his gaze, mortified and angry at myself. Also, I was hurting.

Levi didn't like it, though.

He cupped my cheeks and drew my gaze up to his. I'd expected pity, but I didn't see any, just his hard gaze. "You'll not stay out there."

"Levi," I breathed. "It's for the best."

A snarl ripped from his lips, and my eyes widened. He thinned his lips and shook his head. "Please, stay in here. I have something I need to do, but I'll be back."

"It's not my place to sleep in anyone's room."

He winced, only to have anger drawing his brows down again. "It is your place." He sucked in a breath and slid his fingers through my hair. My eyelids fluttered closed, my lips parted, and a wave of desire pulsed through me. Opening my eyes, fear gripped me, and I went to step away, but Levi's hands pressed into my back, holding me to the spot.

"It's okay." His tone sounded almost like a purr. He leaned in and kissed the tip of my nose. Another wave rolled over me. I rested my hands on his stomach and went to push him back. Levi shook his head, the color of his irises shifting to amber then back. "Stay, please." He dropped his hands and smiled gently. "I'll be back soon." A darker look washed over his face.

As I stood there like a fool, I watched him walk to the door, open it, and exit, closing it after himself.

How was he so different from the others? Did he want something from me?

I couldn't think about it anymore or I'd be a puddle of desire when he came back. I glanced at the bed. Was I supposed to make myself comfortable? I wouldn't sleep there, not now, not after what happened. I had to keep my distance from the three of them. Yes, it would be hard, since I worked for Kincaid, but I could be aloof. Even if I hungered for their touch, for their claim.

Claim?

Where had that come from?

Shaking my head, I walked to the couch and sat, drawing my legs up onto it. My shoes were back in Kincaid's room. I wouldn't get them until I absolutely needed them. Since I was about to sleep, it wouldn't be for a while, which was a relief, as I didn't want to face any of them.

If I died in my sleep, I'd be okay with that also because it meant I wouldn't have to see them. Rolling my eyes, I knew I was being a chicken, but it was better than trying to understand my body's reactions.

Sighing, I rested my back against the armrest and stretched my legs out. Getting comfortable, I lay down on my side, facing the door, and placed my head on my arm. Falling asleep before Levi entered the room again would be a good idea, and luckily exhaustion slipped into my body and mind. It had been a long and eventful day. I was ready to let slumber take me.

Yet, I blinked slowly, looking at the bedroom door.

Waiting.

Watching.

Where had he needed to go?

Why wasn't he back?

Why can't I be enough?

Ten

LEVI

I WAS LIVID. Absolutely furious and gutted from seeing Amara so distraught. Even my lion stalked and roared inside me. He wanted me to kill my two friends for disrespecting our mate.

She belongs to them also, I reminded him.

He wasn't sure, or else they would treat her better. *They're just stubborn and have had bad experiences with people.* My lion huffed and prowled close to the surface. He wouldn't give up on the idea of drawing blood to make up for their treatment of our mate.

I banged on Kincaid's door first and then Silas's before waiting in the middle of the living room for them while trying to rein in my lion's need for revenge. He hated seeing our mate so upset as much as I did.

It took them a moment, but Kincaid opened the door, saw me, and glared before he stepped out of his room.

Silas swung his door open, growled under his breath, and stalked my way.

"You...." I clenched my hands. My claws wanted to come out. "I don't even know what to call either of you because whatever I did, it wouldn't be enough and would probably be still too kind." Disappointment in them had me shaking my head and dropping my hands to my hips.

They were good men. The best I'd ever met, and we'd been close from a very young age, but it didn't stop me from getting exasperated at them.

I had to get them to understand.

To acknowledge that how they'd treated her was wrong.

My lion snarled inside me, wanting me to slice them open for hurting Amara.

Kincaid sat on the couch, leaning back, while Silas stood rigid with his arms crossed over his chest. Both still scowled at me. Anyone lesser than an alpha would have pissed themselves, but I could hold my own against these two dumb shits.

"This is your fault," Kincaid said.

A growl escaped from within. "My fault? I wasn't the one who wanted her in my room in the first place. *You* did that."

He stood in a flash and got in my face. "You were the one who organized a party so I couldn't send her out here for my feeding, knowing my emotions are wired when I drink."

I threw up my hands. "So?" It was obvious my plan had worked, and instead of sending the maid to the living room, around other men, he'd kept her in his room.

"So? So it was too close to becoming *something* because she started scenting.... She became...."

"Aroused?" I swung my gaze to Silas as Kincaid turned away from me. "I guess the same happened with you?" I wished they understood the precious gift they had in their hands, but until they got their heads out of their asses, they wouldn't.

All Silas did was shrug. In fact, as I looked closer at him, he seemed a little frazzled around the edges. Even my lion cocked his head to the side, studying him.

"Did something else happen?" I asked. Kincaid's gaze snapped to Silas.

"No," Silas clipped.

My lion huffed. Neither of us believed him. Still, I wouldn't push just yet.

Instead, I said, "You both know my thoughts already—"

"She is *not* our mate," Kincaid snarled. My lion roared, and I wanted to grip my hair and scream at them. I knew they felt the same connection as I did. She was different, she'd be good for us, yet they didn't understand how lucky we were to have found our mate. They could contradict what it was, but I wouldn't deny or hide what was growing between Amara and us. I refused to be blinded by suspicion. She was kind, charming, shy, and fierce at the same time.

Slash them open. My lion pushed the thought at me. Hell, even I wanted to punch them both for their stupidity. Maybe I would knock some sense into them. However, I tried with words once again. "You cannot deny the connection we all feel for her."

Kincaid snorted. "I can and I will. She is a *maid*—"

"Who is the first to come to you with the headmaster's plan. Who had our backs in a fight. She is *not* an enemy."

"She *is* until I know everything," Kincaid barked.

Shaking my head, I unclenched my jaw. "Only a mate would become aroused like she has with us."

There was nothing but silence from both the peanut brains.

Kincaid replied, "That's not true. I've scented women all the time like I do her."

"Your power of persuasion didn't work on her," I pointed out. It was a clear sign she was a mate for Kincaid.

"That's because *she's* not normal. She's hiding something."

A growl rumbled out of my chest.

Stupid pigheaded bastards.

I glanced at Silas. His hard gaze was on the floor, but I knew he was hiding something. What exactly happened in his room before he brought Amara into mine? I'd heard Kincaid try my room earlier when I'd been in the bathroom. Maybe I should have walked out then, but I'd hoped he would take her back to his room and accept what he was feeling for Amara.

I was an idiot to think these stubborn pricks would accept her right away like I had. Even though she was a maid and presumed human, I couldn't ignore how my soul had connected with hers. I couldn't help the pull I felt whenever she was in a room. I wanted to be beside her, hold her, have her. All. The. Damn. Time.

My lion whined, wanting the same and to claim her.

It sucked she wasn't only mine, but at least Kincaid

and Silas were the *only* idiots I would share anything with. We were connected in a different way. A brotherly way.

Would they see the light in the end? Maybe. But I still worried that, considering how they already treated Amara, they had hurt her too much, and soon the bond between them would rot.

Blowing out a breath, I rubbed a hand over my face. "Look, I had Amara in tears in my arms because she doesn't understand why she's reacting this way toward us. She was in tears because you both rejected her. She sobbed because you both kicked her out without a calming touch, without soft words. You both threw her away, and it crushed her."

Kincaid winced.

Silas looked stricken.

I had finally gotten through to them.

Until both blanked their expressions.

Shaking my head, I said, "All I'm asking is that you treat Amara with respect. No doubt she'll go back to being the perfect maid because she doesn't believe she can be herself around us. She'll refuse to examine this new feeling she has for us because of you two." *And I goddamn despise the both of you for it.* "So if you want to keep peace with *me*, neither of you will be a motherfucking dickhead, asshole, bastard to her because I'm not stupid enough to reject her." With that, I turned and walked back into my room, gently closing the door behind me.

I paused. The light from the bathroom still shone and blanketed Amara where she lay on the couch, her breathing steady as she slept. I was glad she'd relaxed enough to sleep here but was disappointed she hadn't taken my bed to do it in.

I moved over to her side and crouched next to her. I probably looked like a stalker watching her sleep, but it helped cool my anger over those idiots outside. My lion wanted out to lick her, watch over her, and scent mark her. She shivered in her sleep, cold from the room and having no blanket. Immediately, all my animal and I wanted was to take care of her.

Tucking a stray strand of her black hair behind her ear, I smiled happily when she subconsciously pushed up into my touch. Yes, there was definitely a bond between us, and I wouldn't jeopardize it. I didn't understand how I was so lucky as to gain a mate who could become vicious when needed, but who was also gorgeous on the inside and out.

She was hiding something, but she could keep her secret if it meant she would stay at my side. *Our* sides, if those idiots got their heads out of their asses.

I wanted to cherish her, to show her how precious she was to me, but it would take time. I'd have to be patient, knowing all she understood was being a servant.

Sliding my arms under her legs and shoulders, I picked her up and held her close as I walked us over to the bed.

My mate didn't sleep on a couch.

She slept in my bed and stayed protected and warm through the night. What was left of it.

My lion huffed happily in my mind.

The sheet was already pulled back, so I gently rested her down on the bed and draped the blanket over her body. I should have insisted she changed first, since she still wore that god-awful maid outfit. My fierce mate probably still had daggers strapped to her thighs. I hoped she was comfortable with them on. Then again, she wouldn't be sleeping if she wasn't.

Straightening, I stood at her side and couldn't help but think how amazing she looked in my bed. I wanted to climb into the other side and hold her close, but I wasn't sure she would be okay with that.

Because of those douche canoes.

Sighing, I made to move over to the couch until a small hand curled around my wrist, stopping me.

"Amara?" I dropped to my knees.

She blinked tiredly at me. "W-Would... never mind." Her hand released my wrist, but I grabbed it in both of mine.

"What, angel?"

She dragged her top teeth over her bottom lip before whispering, "I don't want to take your bed. You can lie here." A blush coated her cheeks, and the reaction tugged at my heart.

My lion preened inside me. I had to remind him it was just to lie on the bed beside her and nothing else. Not that he cared. He was just as happy to be by her side, as was I.

"Are you sure?" I asked.

"Yes." She nodded.

Since I was already only wearing boxers, I straightened and moved around the bed, sliding under the sheet. I didn't make a move to curl around her and hold her like I wanted. Like I ached to do.

She would have to make the first move, and I would wait an eternity for her if I had to.

When she shifted beside me, I held my breath. I rolled my head to the side and found her facing me.

I wished I could tell her the reason she was... attracted to us. How she was our mate. Only, I wasn't sure she was ready to hear it, especially since she'd been through a lot lately, but also, she could be even more hurt from the rejection the others had given her.

There wasn't a doubt in my mind she was our mate. I hungered for her in a way only a mate should.

"Levi," she whispered.

I rolled onto my side. "Yes, angel?" I tucked another strand of her hair behind her ear, and her eyes shuttered closed at my touch. Her scent changed, became headier, stronger, and sweeter.

God, how had Kincaid and Silas resisted her?

Mate her, my lion pleaded.

I couldn't, and it took everything I had inside me to stay where I was and not kiss her.

Amara cleared her throat—a throat I wanted to lick. I ground my teeth together and slipped my fingers through hers between us on the bed. She eagerly held on to my hand tightly.

"Do you think.... Would it be best if I asked to be removed as Kincaid's maid?"

My lion roared his disapproval. We worried that if she did ask, Mr. Prince would allow it, and then we'd never get to see her again.

"No, Amara. You're right where you should be."

Her lips thinned. She was unsure if she should believe my words. Tears glistened in her eyes. "I don't think I am."

Hearing it broke something in me. My lion snarled

along with me on the inside. I couldn't resist, even if I tried. When I released her hand, her gaze became pained, as if she thought I was rejecting her. But then she let out a gasp when I curled my arms around her and brought her flush against my body with her head on my chest.

"Please don't leave," I said into the top of her hair. I pressed my lips there, and her scent intensified.

"Levi—"

"Amara, you *are* needed here with us. I know you can't see it, but you are. Don't give up on us yet."

Her shaky hand dropped onto my chest. My lion made a noise in the back of my throat, which caused Amara to sigh, her breath brushing across my chest.

I held her tighter to me and kissed the top of her head again.

"No one has told you this, but I'm very good at telling the future." It was a lie, but I was thrilled when a small laugh slipped out of her.

"Really?"

"Yes, and it's telling me that with time, you will rise above your position and step into your own when the moment comes. I know I'll be at your side when it happens, and I won't be the only one."

They had to get their heads out of their asses to see what I held within my arms. The gift they had been given.

She patted my chest and hummed under her breath, not believing me. Instead, she said, "I'm out of my element here, Levi."

"How?" I asked, running my hand up and down her back. Only, it caused her to push her pussy against my hip, and once again, her arousal grew stronger.

"Um" was all she said until I stilled my hand on her shoulder and her train of thought came back. "I-I'm a servant. I shouldn't be here in your bed. I shouldn't have done many things, but I have. I'm at a loss about what to think or do. This is confusing, *especially* being in here with you and you wanting me in here."

Those pricks.

"You may be a servant, Amara, but you deserve all the happiness in the world," I told her sincerely, placing my hand over hers on my chest. "I know this is confusing, but for now, for me, could you try and be yourself even while you do your job? I would like to get to know you. I don't care that you're a maid."

"Is that even allowed?"

"What? Me wanting to know a beautiful, strong, unique, yet shy woman?"

She groaned, burying her face in my chest. "I am none of those things. Except maybe shy."

Had she never been complimented?

I would have to work on that. "It is allowed. I'm an alpha, after all."

She lifted her worried gaze to mine. "That's it exactly. You're an alpha. You shouldn't want to get to know me, to... to become my friend. I'm only a servant. I should be running from the room or making you see sense or leaving altogether. I-I don't understand." She made a move to roll away, but I held strong.

I didn't just want to be her friend, and I expected she knew this but was brushing off what I really wanted because she was scared.

"Our titles don't matter. Do you think you'll be able to overlook my title when we're around each other?"

She was silent, and I feared for her answer. Even my lion prowled inside me, waiting.

"I-I'll try."

Smiling, I kissed the top of her head once more. "That's all I ask. For now, we should get some rest before the new day starts."

"Okay," she uttered.

"Will you be able to sleep like this?" I hoped so, since I wasn't ready to let her go.

"Um, yes."

My lion huffed in pleasure, happy our mate didn't want to move away from us. Closing my eyes, I smiled in contentment, enjoying the weight of Amara pressed into my side. I already knew I couldn't wait to have her close like this again.

Actually, those idiots could take their time coming to the realization she was our mate, because I was more than happy to have all of Amara's attention to myself.

Eleven

AMARA

MY STOMACH FLUTTERED from being close to the men after what happened. I sat as stiff as a board in the back of the limousine with Kincaid on one side and Levi on the other. When I woke, Levi hadn't been in the room, which was a relief, since sleeping beside him had been tough. I'd wanted to... do many things to him. Things that I'd heard about or seen on television but had never done myself.

Levi was an amazing man—one who cared about me and wanted to get to know me. I still couldn't believe my luck after I'd been so crushed by the other two. The reminder of it soured my stomach. I still didn't understand my reaction to their rejection, especially as I really shouldn't have cared, since I'd practically thrown myself at them.

Well, in a way.

It wasn't *their* fault they could scent my desire and

didn't feel something in return... although there was that kiss from Silas.

Heat hit my cheeks, and I had to think of my grueling training with Mr. Langley to get the blush to go away and my heart to stop racing.

My body wasn't supposed to act this way in the first place.

When I woke this morning, I decided to behave exactly as I had before my body shamed me. Except, bravery also fluttered to life within me. I wanted to be more myself and share that part of me with Levi and Mary. If the others were around when I spoke up for myself, then so be it. I would face the consequences when they came—*if* they did come, since I'd already survived yesterday's ordeal without any ramifications.

I understood why Kincaid and Silas remained hesitant, why they didn't trust me. I was keeping something from them. Maybe with time, they'd see I didn't have an ulterior motive to harm anyone from within the group.

Even with all that said and with my new courage, I couldn't even look at Kincaid, or Silas in the eyes, who was sitting up the front of the vehicle with Cassar. My nerves got the best of me when I tried.

Little steps were needed.

Fingers slid over mine on the seat, and I glanced down to see Levi's hand. I quickly peered up and caught his smirk as my face burned once more. A small smile tugged at my lips before I faced forward. Sleeping beside Levi had been.... Honestly, it was tough in an arousing kind of way but absolutely wonderful. I'd never felt special until I was in his arms.

And wasn't that a struggle to get my head around. In a matter of days, so much had changed. I'd changed. Me? Lusting after three men? If it wasn't for the constant flutter in my belly, I would never have believed it possible.

"We're nearly there," Cassar announced.

Kincaid tensed beside me. We were heading back to the Prince Estate, since Mary had called early that morning to say that college classes were postponed until Monday, courtesy of the new headmaster. Kincaid had soured at the news of returning home and hadn't said a word to anyone after hearing it. Which confused me, since we would have returned that night anyway for the family dinner. Did he honestly not like his home? If that was the case, I wanted to know why, but there wasn't a chance I'd ask anyone. Well, not yet.

Little steps, Amara, I reminded myself.

I glanced to my left. Levi would possibly tell me. His gaze captured mine, and he smiled gently. It brought up the image of him lying half naked in bed beside me—how I'd ached to run my hands over him, to kiss him, to lick every inch of him. My face bloomed with a new blush, and I cursed myself before dropping my eyes to my lap. A soft chuckle came from Levi.

After getting through security, the vehicle pulled to a stop in front of the grand concrete staircase. Levi opened the door with a sigh and climbed out. I slid along the seat and followed him, waiting to the side of the car until my master appeared.

"Wait there," Kincaid ordered me.

The men congregated at the front of the limousine and spoke in low voices. Levi rested a hand on Kincaid's shoulder before saying something else, and then Levi moved back my way.

"Is everything okay?" I asked softly before I could stop myself. "Not that it's any of my business," I quickly added. But then I wanted to kick myself for sounding so weak and not listening to my new resolution of being myself.

One day I would get to the point of demanding answers to all the questions I had on my mind.

The problem was, my role required me to behave every bit the weak human so I didn't get into trouble or fired, kicked out, or even killed. There was also the risk of someone figuring out my secret, and that would be worse than anything else.

I would be used beyond my control. I would be weaponized and, in the end, probably lose myself.

Levi's fingers brushed against mine. "It's fine. Silas and I have to see to things, but we won't be far."

My eyes widened. "Kincaid needs protection even here?"

His jaw clenched and he nodded once.

I swallowed thickly at the knowledge and straightened. "Okay, I'll keep an eye out while you're away."

A soft smile crossed his lips, but then it faded quickly. "He's stupid."

My brows shot down in confusion. "Sorry?"

Levi sighed. "Nothing."

Kincaid stopped at our sides, and I dropped my gaze to his chin. There. I at least managed to look at a part of his face, without blushing. "Let's go," he clipped and started up the steps.

When I looked back at Levi, he nodded Kincaid's way. "See you soon."

My heart skipped a beat, and I shared a smile with him before I followed after my *master*. I really hated that title.

Kincaid had been summoned to his father's office as soon as he'd arrived at his bedroom. Bennett, who'd delivered the message, had quickly disappeared. Since Levi and Silas hadn't yet shown up, it would be up to me to guard him within the house, even after he ordered me to stay back in my room.

Kincaid glared at me over his shoulder as he walked down a hallway. "I told you to stay in your room."

I didn't reply. When he kept moving, so did I.

Kincaid snarled, "Stop and go back." I still didn't listen. Even though his voice was scary, it didn't affect me like it should have. I stayed behind him.

Suddenly, he stopped and faced me. "What is it you're doing by ignoring my orders?"

My face flamed to life, since it was the first time I met his gaze after what had happened in his bedroom. Only in this situation, I had to stay strong. I tipped up my chin, crossed my arms over my chest, and glared back at him.

While fear slid into my stomach, my darkness fist pumped the air inside me.

I could do this.

It didn't matter that he was my master; I wouldn't cower. I would stand up to him, especially since it was for his sake in the first place.

"Levi and Silas aren't here."

"I know."

I ground my teeth together, frustrated he didn't understand what I wasn't saying with that one sentence. I glanced to the side, then back at his dark gaze. "I'll be of assistance until they get back."

His brows dipped for a moment and then shot high. Kincaid opened his mouth, closed it, and shook his head. "Are you saying you'll be my guard until they get here?"

His lips twitched.

My gaze dropped to his shin, which I wanted to kick. I'd already proven myself in combat. Lifting my gaze, I swallowed around the lump of fear in my throat and scowled at him.

If he didn't punish me for what I'd already done, I could stand to be braver.

"Yes, I will be." I sniffed, annoyed when his lips twitched again before his stony hardness blanked his face.

Kincaid turned and went on walking. Suddenly I felt lighter, like there was a new spring in my step or beat to my heart when he said no more, obviously relenting. My lips tugged up as I hurried to keep up with him.

The fears that had been twisting my stomach since our arrival eased.

I *could* do this. I *could* be strong and myself.

When Kincaid stopped at a door, I bounced on my feet as happiness spread throughout me. Kincaid turned to face me, and I couldn't wipe the smile off my face before he saw it. He scowled, but did I care? No, I didn't.

Kincaid shook his head. "Stay out here."

My lips thinned. I wanted to argue, but since I'd just

won a small victory, I supposed I could listen to him with this. I nodded, clasping my hands behind my back as I stood beside the door.

Kincaid sighed. He straightened his shoulders and opened the door without knocking. I heard Mr. Prince greet his son before the door closed.

In the first half hour, I stood by the door and relished in my good mood. If I could go back to my first day, I would tell myself not to be scared. I would promise myself that I could speak and not fear death.

By the time another half hour passed, I grew bored and started shifting on my feet while I stared at the same paintings, and the more I looked, the duller they became. They weren't bright and didn't have a story to tell. They were dull and dark and only shared the soulless gazes of past Prince family members.

I tensed when I heard voices before two maids I didn't recognize stepped around a corner. I was surprised that when they saw me, their chattering stopped, and they glared. I hadn't done anything to anyone to deserve hostility.

It couldn't be because I worked under Kincaid. Not when they also worked for the Princes.

They went to pass by, but then one stopped and the other followed suit.

"Hello," I greeted.

The one woman, who appeared to be in her late thirties, sneered. She glanced at the door beside me and back. Her voice was low and sharp when she spouted, "How could you disrespect your own mother like that?"

What in the world?

Shock had me jerking my head back. "I'm sorry? I don't know what you're talking about."

The woman glanced at the other, and they both scoffed. "Charlotte told us all about you." She stepped closer. I tensed, ready to fight. "You'll get no respect from the maids here."

The urge to roll my eyes was strong. "Please, pray tell, what has my mother been telling you?"

The woman squared her shoulders. "You already know because you're the one who treated her the way you did."

This wasn't going anywhere.

"Believe what you want from Charlotte, since you aren't saying what it is and instead are wasting my time."

"Come on, Abigail, let's leave—"

The door beside us suddenly opened. Kincaid's eyes bore into all of us as he stepped out and shut the door behind himself. "What's this?" he asked, his tone rough.

The maids curtseyed. "Master Prince," they said together.

"What were you saying to *my* maid?"

Did *my* sound like it had been emphasized?

No.

No, no, no.

I did not like it when he called me his maid.

I didn't.

As I clenched my fists at my sides, I also silently prayed for my body not to react in case it had a mind of its own like it had the previous night.

"Nothing, Master Prince. We were only greeting her,

since we hadn't yet met." Abigail was quick to lie, and I wondered if Kincaid could tell she was spinning a tale.

Kincaid glanced at me, and since the other women had their eyes to the floor, I shrugged. A stupid blush hit my cheeks. He ignored that reaction and shot daggers at me instead. I would tell him, but not in front of them.

I liked my new resolve. I didn't understand why Kincaid was lenient toward me, but I would take it, since it meant I could relax on the inside. It wouldn't stop me from being cautious when around other people, though.

"Dismissed," Kincaid ordered with a bark. They scuttled off down the hall. Two days ago, I would have done the same. Even the day before, that would have been me. Thankfully, I had changed, and it had a lot to do with Levi.

Kincaid started toward his room. "What happened?"

"They mentioned that I disrespected my mother but wouldn't say how."

Kincaid grunted. "Was it your mother who bruised your cheek?"

Drawing in a breath, I glanced up at him, but his eyes were forward. "Yes, but she knows I won't take... anything from her again."

Kincaid spun on me, and I stepped back when he crowded me. "Where is this coming from?"

My pulse raced, but I met his gaze. "What?"

"You've changed. You're talking more. You're... *different* again." His eyes narrowed accusingly. "Did Levi say anything last night?"

"About what?"

"You tell me," he snapped, dipping his head closer as his hands pressed into the wall behind me.

His breath brushed over my skin, his warmth—yes, vampires were warm, not cold like the myths claimed—caressed my front, and I wanted to press into him.

My eyes widened at the first throb my core produced. *No, no, no.*

Closing my eyes, I dropped my head. "You need to step back."

Kincaid snorted. "Now you try and act the timid maid, but mere moments ago, you looked me in the eyes and refused to leave me unguarded."

Through clenched teeth, I told him, "I'm both." Only I wasn't really timid. That had been an act of necessity, the desire to survive and stay under the radar had been my main goal. Now I was just scared of my reaction to him. I drew in a shaky breath, but he was too close. All I could smell was him, and my body liked it all too much. "Step back."

"No. Not until you tell me why you've changed again."

My hand itched to grab him, to run itself over his body. I raised my head and glowered at him. If he wanted an answer, he was going to get it and probably hate it. "The truth is, I have never been timid. At the start of my job, I worried for my life, but the people around me kept saying I could be myself. I could speak freely. I was trying that, and this is how it turned out."

The color in his eyes swirled to red and back. I held my breath but forgot to hold my hands back as they reached for him, pressing to his stomach.

A low growl sounded from within him.

"Kincaid dear, you have donors. You don't need to feed on your maid."

We both stilled at the cool voice of Mrs. Prince.

However, Kincaid didn't move away from me. His head tilted to the side. "Mother."

Over Kincaid's arm, I saw Mrs. Prince move down the hall as if she were floating and not walking. At her side were two other women. Both ran an appreciative glance over Kincaid, and my blood boiled.

A need so fierce gripped me. I wanted to rip their eyes out and slit their throats.

Kincaid's gaze snapped down to me, and whatever he saw had his eyes widening before he straightened and stepped in front of me. My hands dropped to my thighs, and I sucked in some deep breaths to try and control my urge to murder. My darkness nodded encouragingly inside me.

What was wrong with me?

Why did I have the impulse to kill? And all over other women looking at Kincaid like he was candy they wanted to unwrap. My upper lip rose, a small snarl tearing from me.

"Mother, can I help you with something?"

"No, thank you, dear. You will be at dinner tonight?"

"I will."

"Very good."

Pressing my back to the wall, I stood straight and prayed Mrs. Prince would move on.

"You remember Camila and Jasmine?"

I stiffened. Mrs. Prince wouldn't have brought them

up if they were just workers. It meant there was a high chance they were vampires.

"I do. It's a pleasure, ladies."

Both giggled, and I wanted to gag and tear out their vocal cords.

"Kincaid, it's wonderful to see you. You've definitely grown." I didn't know who spoke, but the purr in her tone annoyed me to the point that I gripped the back of Kincaid's tee so I didn't jump over him and punch her in the face.

What is wrong with me?

"As have you, Camila." At least Kincaid's tone sounded bored.

"Do you have plans this afternoon, Kincaid?"

My nails dug into Kincaid's back because it was either him or Jasmine—the one who asked the question—who'd bear the brunt of my displeasure. A grunt sounded from Kincaid, and he shifted back, forcing me into the wall with his back pressed into my front. His hands moved behind him and gripped my thighs.

I knew it was his way of trying to shut me up, but I still wanted to slice the women open.

"Unfortunately, I already have plans, Jasmine. Maybe another time."

"Perfect," Mrs. Prince said. "I'll give her your number."

"N—"

Kincaid pushed into me again. His back squished my face so I had no choice but to shut my mouth. I pinched at his sides, and a surprised grunt rattled out of him. I didn't know where the bravery had come from for that action.

All I knew was that if I didn't stop these women, my world could end.

How, why, or when, I didn't know.

This is crazy. Calm down, I told myself.

Or hump his leg, then they'll know he's taken.

Oh my God, I did not just think that. I needed to see a doctor immediately.

"Is there something the matter with your maid, Kincaid? We could have her *replaced*."

My upper lip rose in a silent snarl. She wouldn't get rid of me. She couldn't…. Why I suddenly cared bothered me and had me drawing myself up.

"It's nothing I can't handle, Mother." His hand lifted and clasped my wrist. "Ladies, I'll look forward to seeing you both soon."

"See you at dinner, son." Mrs. Prince walked by and caught my gaze. Hers narrowed on me. I quickly looked to the floor…. Well, at her son's back actually, since he still had me pressed to the wall.

As soon as they turned a corner, Kincaid dragged me by the wrist down the hallway, grumbling under his breath. At least I knew why he was frustrated. I was still baffled over my reactions.

Kincaid threw open his door, tugged me through, and shut it behind him. His hand dropped from my wrist, and I faced him, waiting for his lecture. He opened his mouth, closed it, and glowered at me.

Snorting, I shook my head. "I can't explain myself either."

Kincaid strode by me. "Go to your room. I won't leave here, so it's safe. I'll call you when I leave."

He wanted me gone. Again.

Bile rose in my throat. I went to the door that joined our rooms and walked through it, closing the door after me. I didn't stay by it. I stumbled toward the bed and dropped to my knees on the floor, throwing my top half over the mattress to scream into it.

What was wrong with me that caused Kincaid to cast me off quickly and for me to act as I did?

Twelve

SILAS

KINCAID WALKED into the dining room first. Amara soon followed, and I shifted my gaze away from her. My dragon perked up, though, and wanted me to stare at her. To stalk her and fuck her.

That kiss—I couldn't get it off my mind. My hunger for her grew.

Ours to protect. To claim. To mate.

My dragon was insistent that she was ours. Had Levi been right, and the maid was my mate? Not only mine but Levi and Kincaid's as well. My dragon huffed inside, pissed I didn't believe him right away, but I had Levi in one ear and Kincaid in another. There was also the fact the maid was hiding something.

What was Fate playing at?

Why would they pick a human for the three of us? I

knew that was a dickish thought, but I'd always pictured another shifter as my mate.

Instead, she was a *human*. My mind caught on that word and turned it over.

I wasn't sure she was quite human. There was something unique about her, and I had a feeling it had to do with the secret she held close to her chest.

Kincaid nodded to us, and the maid walked over to stand between Levi and me. The heat of her skin radiated my way. Fuck. My dragon and I wanted to rub all over her, make her smell like us so no other would turn their attention toward her.

Levi murmured something to her, and I glanced down at her tiny frame. A blush coated her usually pale cheeks. My dragon chuffed; he liked looking at her. I could also admit she was appealing.

That kiss.

That fucking kiss.

When her body had been wrapped around mine, it was like my own slice of damn heaven. My cock was still half hard from that moment. But when I broke the connection, my angry dragon had thundered inside me. When Levi told us she was in his room confused and crying, my dragon wanted to go to her and comfort her. I had to lock my body down because I would have gone in there and begged for forgiveness. I hadn't wanted to believe she was our mate since... she was so different from others in our world.

But even before then, she'd messed up my resolve to keep her at arm's length by fighting at our sides as if she'd done it a million times over.

When she'd shouted my name in that cell, her voice still echoed in my head. The fear had been like a knife to the gut. My dragon and I had combated harder, stronger, to make sure she wouldn't have to feel that fear again.

I lied to Kincaid when I said I didn't like her. I did. She was too hard to resist, having proven herself when she told Kincaid of the headmaster's plan and when she didn't cower through the fight.

So why was I resisting?

Why couldn't I be like Levi when he was charming and flirty with her?

Fuck that. It just wasn't in me.

Maybe I resisted because *I* was scared she'd reject *me*. I wasn't sweet. I wasn't nice most of the time. She needed someone like Levi and only Levi because Kincaid was just as fucked up as I was.

"Silas," Levi clipped.

"What?" I snapped. It was then I realized I'd been staring down at the maid. Thankfully she hadn't noticed, since she was glaring at the back of Kincaid's head.

Levi's brows rose in question. "Did you hear what Kincaid said?"

Shit. They'd been talking? I hadn't heard anything since she'd entered. That wasn't good.

I ground my teeth together. "What was it again?"

"Amara sweetly had Kincaid's back while we weren't here."

Kincaid snorted as he played with the table knife in his hand. "Sweetly? She wouldn't listen to me."

The doors to the dining room opened again. Bennett stepped through, bowed to Kincaid, and moved to the side of the door, holding it open. Kincaid stiffened in his seat. When Bennett appeared, we knew Mr. Prince wouldn't be far. Kincaid hated his father, and he had good reason to. Hell, I even despised the fucker because of the shit he put Kincaid through.

Mr. Prince stepped into the room. Levi and I dipped our heads, but since we were alphas, we wouldn't bow. The maid dropped into a curtsey. I wanted to haul her up so she didn't have to show respect to the prick.

"Kincaid." Mr. Prince nodded to his son but kept his gaze on the papers in front of him. He took the seat at the head of the table.

"Father." Kincaid glanced over his shoulder and saw the maid still in a curtsey. His eyes narrowed on her, and he looked at me.

I grabbed the top of the maid's arm and tugged her up. Her gaze met mine; a new blush shone on her cheeks. My dragon chuffed when she gave me the smallest of smiles before facing forward again.

Levi caught my gaze over her head; the lion was grinning. He wiggled his eyebrows, and I scratched my forehead with my middle finger.

"What are they doing here?" Mr. Prince placed his papers down on the table to stare at Kincaid.

"They're my guards."

Mr. Prince scoffed. "How many times have I told you that you do not need them in this house?" He waved out a hand. "Make them leave."

"No."

Mr. Prince's gaze narrowed. "You defy me?"

"As I told you earlier, there was another attempt on

my life. I prefer to have them close to deter any others who think they can get to me."

"And as I said, Kincaid, that attempt was foiled like all the others have been. They are not needed under this roof when we have our own guards here."

His guards. They weren't loyal to Kincaid; they followed his father.

"Silas and Levi will be taking rooms down the hall from my bedroom."

Mr. Prince snarled and rose, pounding a fist into the table. "I've already been lenient to allow them their own cottage on the estate. Plus, they have their own estates to take care of."

Kincaid rose also. His chair shot straight back, heading for the maid. Both Levi's and my hands swung out to stop it from hitting her. I could hear the fast beat to her heart. But again, she didn't cower.

"I hired them. I will see fit to place them where I want."

"How do you pay them? With my money—"

"Actually, with the money that I get from *my* business."

Mr. Prince scoffed. "Those apps wouldn't bring you in enough money to hire those people."

Those people. He meant shifters. I gave a small shake of my head at his attitude toward other species. Levi and I were used to his prejudice, but it was obvious from the way the maid had her hands fisted at her sides, she hadn't heard his shit before.

My dragon enjoyed seeing the anger in her eyes. It meant she liked shifters.

Christ. Just another thing to add to her... charm?

Kincaid chuckled darkly. "My apps bring in over one million dollars a year, Father."

Mrs. Prince appeared in the doorway, her maid at her back. "What are we arguing about tonight?"

Again, Levi and I dipped our heads, and she bent in a curtsey. Only that time, she quickly straightened again.

"Your son thinks that because he pays for his guards, they can stay in this house when we already have our own security."

Mrs. Prince sat in the chair opposite Kincaid, which Bennett had pulled out. The butler quickly disappeared through the swinging door into the kitchen. This was the first dinner Levi and I had been in attendance. We'd heard about them—how once they were all seated, Bennett would try and rush through all the courses so they could end this shitshow.

"Come now, Kincaid. You need to trust your father to have the house protected enough that you won't need your guards. Really, they're not far if you are in need of them."

Kincaid turned, took the chair Levi and I slid his way, and sat back down. "Fine, Mother."

Mr. Prince grunted and also sat back down just as the doors to the kitchen opened again, and Bennett walked back in with a tray of food. Two others followed, and they all rested their trays in front of their designated Prince member.

"Camilla and Jasmine were very happy to see you, Kincaid." Mrs. Prince gave him a pleased smile as she picked up her spoon for the soup in front of her.

She tensed beside me, and I glanced down just as she made a move to step forward. I quickly grabbed her wrist, holding her back. Her hard gaze snapped up to mine, and I shook my head. She looked pissed off.

"It was good to see them, Mother."

Her gaze shot back to Kincaid, and she scowled at the back of his head. I glanced at Levi. He was paler than before as he stared down at the tiny female.

"That's grand news. I do hope you'll consider one of them at your event to find a life partner." Even when Kincaid had told his mother he didn't want a damn party to look for a life mate, she hadn't listened. She'd organized one anyway, saying he didn't need to select someone at this event; it was more a gathering to see who was available.

Oh shit.

She opened her mouth as if to say something. I tightened my hold on her wrist and caught Levi taking her other one. It seemed to help her, since she pressed back into the wall, dropped her gaze, and shut her mouth.

She was reacting as a mate to the news of Kincaid with other women. If a person was lucky enough to find their mate, they became possessive over them. Her actions were a clear sign of her discomfort at the mention of Kincaid with someone else.

"There is a chance, Mother."

Mrs. Prince smiled tenderly at her son. "Very good, but I do have some others for you to meet."

"I look forward to it." Kincaid sounded anything but happy about the situation. If it'd been my mother trying to set me up with someone to spend the rest of my life with, I would run for the hills, knowing whoever she picked wouldn't be the right person.

Our tiny mate sneered at the floor.

"Excuse your guards, Kincaid. They're putting me off my food."

Kincaid shot his father a glare. Over his shoulder, he said, "I'll see you both after practice." His father beamed at the word practice. Fucking asshole motherfucker.

Mrs. Prince cleared her throat. "How about we excuse all our help and just enjoy the meal?"

Levi started for the door, taking the maid with him, since he still held her wrist. I didn't realize I still held on to her as well until her movement pulled me into step behind her.

Outside the room, we walked further down the hall and stopped. She started pacing with her hands fisted at her sides. "How can you be around that man and not want to throat punch him?"

An abrupt laugh left me, and I clamped my lips closed when Levi grinned at me.

Levi took hold of her, curling her into his arms. In a hushed tone, he said, "We're used to him, but that doesn't matter. Can you tell me what was going on with you in there?"

She hesitated and glanced at me before looking back at Levi and shrugging. My dragon roared inside me, pissed I'd made her reluctant to speak in front of me.

Sighing, I scrubbed the back of my neck. "Levi." I nodded further down the hall.

"Wait here. We'll walk you back to your rooms and text Kincaid where you'll be."

She shook her head. "I'll wait out here for him."

"Amara, sweetheart. Kincaid will be fine to walk to his room without anything happening." He leaned in closer to her. "We have the estate covered with cameras. Ones that are undetectable to all paranormals."

"I'll wait here if both of you have to leave the house."

Levi smiled affectionately at her, tucking a stray strand of dark hair behind her ear. She leaned into him, and he freely kissed her forehead. "I'll be back in a second."

As I moved down the hall, a stab of jealousy hit me right in the chest. My dragon was pissed we couldn't hold her, kiss her, comfort her, and he was blaming me for it.

Jesus. Was I supposed to give up my doubts and trust her? Let this connection form into the mate bond as it was supposed to be?

With all the signs I'd seen, I couldn't deny she was our mate.

But... I didn't fucking know what to do with the knowledge.

In front of a window, I faced Levi. "She looked beyond pissed about the talk of other women."

Levi lifted a brow, just one condescending brow, which made me want to punch him.

Growling, I clipped, "Fucking fine. I see it. Now what in the hell are we supposed to do?"

The slow, sly grin he shot my way simply made me want to punch him more.

"Amara is ours. Admit it."

"Do you want my dragon to eat you?"

Levi chuckled. "Come on, just this once, say 'Levi, you're right.'"

Crossing my arms over my chest, I stared him down.

"All right, what about 'Levi, Amara is ours, and I was stupid to fight it.'"

"You're wasting my time with this shit. The maid—"

"Amara."

Amara. I tested the word in my mind.

Christ, even her name was perfect for her. As were her hair, her face, her body, even her fucking feet.

Her name in my head shot a thrill right to my dick and had my dragon chuffing. Glaring at Levi, I tried it aloud. "Amara is—" Movement caught my attention.

Down the hall, where *Amara* stood leaning against the wall, a guy was talking to her, smiling at her.

Looking at her.

Kill him. I couldn't agree more with my dragon.

Levi moved toward them first, but I grabbed his arm and pulled him back to overtake him as we strode back to our mate.

The douche stopped speaking when I rested my forearm above her head and leaned into her. "Who's this?" My tone was sharp, just like my claws would be in this guy's throat any second now.

Levi shifted around behind the guy, drawing in a breath, before he stopped on the other side of Amara, taking her hand in his.

Amara panted between us.

A visual of her between us in bed slammed into me.

Now wasn't the fucking time.

Since Amara seemed a little too out of breath to speak, I eyed the guy again. "Who the fuck are you?"

He took a step back. "I-I work in the stables."

"He didn't ask what you do, but your name," Levi told him, his own jaw clenching. I had a feeling his lion wanted to bite this guy's head off. My dragon rumbled his approval.

Kincaid appeared beside us. "What's going on?"

"What happened to dinner?" Levi asked.

"I grew bored." Kincaid nodded toward the stable guy.

Before Levi or I said anything, Amara did. "Trist was just introducing himself."

Trist backed up a couple of steps and bowed. "Master Prince."

"Leave," Kincaid ordered. Trist went to race down the hall, but I grabbed his arm, a little too tightly judging by the way he winced, and I dragged him away from prying ears.

"I didn't do anything."

My hold tightened and he cringed. "Never speak to her again, for your own sake. Actually, don't come in the house at all, and if I see you looking at her when she's outside, I'll burn your eyes out. Got me?"

"I'll also let my lion eat your intestines." Levi's growl was a low hum, but when the fucker turned to see Levi's half form, he whimpered before he turned and ran down the hall.

Levi shifted back, eyes on the hall. "Our job is done." The scent of urine hit me. As we walked back to Kincaid, who was blocking Amara's view from us, Levi swung his arm over my shoulders.

"Good to have you on board."

A grunt dropped from my mouth. I wasn't sure my

"being on board" was good, as all I could think about were the other fuckers who'd try to get her attention and the bloodbath after I dealt with them.

But then I looked at her when Kincaid moved, and my damn breath caught in my throat.

Fuck it.

She was ours.

"What did you say to him?" Amara asked.

Amara.

Using her name had been the last hurdle I needed to accept our connection. As I stopped beside her and looked down, a contented chuff escaped. Her eyes widened.

"It was nothing." I took her hand and gently pulled her stunned self along, following Levi and Kincaid. I chanced a quick glance at Amara and saw her gaze was on our joined hands.

My dragon chuffed even more.

Kincaid looked over his shoulder, brows drawn. He wouldn't like me giving in to the idea of Amara being our mate. He was worse than me when it came to trust. I didn't like upsetting him, but I wouldn't give Amara up if she, our mate, would lead us to a happiness I could only dream about.

Thirteen

AMARA

An hour after we'd returned to Kincaid's room, my hand still tingled from Silas's hold, and my body felt warm where Levi had touched me. More noticeably, something had changed in Silas. He seemed... nicer, content to be in my company, and some would even say sweet.

Okay, that someone was me. But he held *my* hand the whole way back to the room. However, what surprised me over anything was how Silas and Levi acted with Trist. It was as if they'd been jealous.

Rolling my eyes at the floor, I snorted quietly to myself at the outrageous thought.

They couldn't be jealous.

Although, I did wonder why Silas pulled Trist away to have words with him. Not only that, but why Levi shifted into his half form. I wished I'd seen everything that happened, but Kincaid had moved in front of me to block my view and told me to stand still. I thought about arguing, but when he stared down at me, for once without malice, I'd lost all brain activity and instead couldn't look away. Of course, his attention played havoc with my pulse. However, his distraction tactic couldn't have been for any other purpose than to keep my prying eyes away from whatever Silas and Levi said that made Trist run for the hills.

Not that it bothered me. I didn't care for Trist's attention.

In a way, I could say I was grateful for their interference. However, that wasn't the only situation in which I appreciated their help.

If it hadn't been for Silas and Levi, I would have spoken up in the dining hall when Mrs. Prince discussed women with Kincaid. Fierce anger had urged me to shove my fist down her throat to shut her up. I hadn't wanted Kincaid to think about other women. I may have to be bound and gagged when it came time for the party she'd been speaking of... for Kincaid to find a life partner.

My good mood soured and walked out the door, and I frowned down at the brownie in my hand. My stomach lurched, and the dinner I'd just eaten threatened to come up.

My attention was captured when Kincaid suddenly stood. Levi and Silas followed, and all wore grim expressions that had my heart clenching. They started for the door. "Where are we going?" I called.

Levi and Silas turned to me, but Kincaid stayed facing the door.

Silas ran a hand over his head, his upper lip pulled up in a snarl. "Practice."

I'd forgotten, which reminded me of the almost gleeful look in Mr. Prince's gaze.

Placing the brownie on the coffee table, I stood. "I'm coming."

"No," all three of them said at once.

Stopping, I placed my hands on my hips and glared. The day's events helped me stay brave. What also helped was Levi's smirk and how Silas rolled his eyes. Kincaid sighed and banged his head on the door.

He turned and stalked over to stand in front of me. "I *can* order you to stay. I *can* send you to the dungeons if you don't listen."

My brow rose, aiming for a condescending arch. "Unless the three of you take me to the dungeons and stay there with me, you know I'll fight whoever tries, and then I'll follow anyway."

Kincaid glowered. "Maybe I do need a new maid."

Thinning my lips, I crossed my arms over my chest. "You won't because you'll worry the next maid will try and kill you."

Levi let out a bark of laughter. "She's got you there."

A smile threatened my lips, but I sank my teeth down on the bottom one. I was enjoying this courage, since it seemed I had Kincaid pegged. While he didn't trust me, he'd hate allowing someone else close to their group in case they had plans to kill him.

"You don't interfere. You stand to the side of the room and never speak. Do you hear me?"

"Yes, *master*." That time when I said master, it was a

little taunting, but I didn't miss the way Kincaid's lips twitched before his eyes narrowed even more, and he turned and headed for the door again.

"It's up to the both of you to keep an eye on her. Sit on her if you have to."

The image popped into my head, and I liked it a little too much. My core clenched and the room suddenly felt too hot.

The three of them all turned at once toward me. Their noses lifted, scenting the air. Kincaid cursed, Levi bit his bottom lip, and Silas made a noise in the back of his throat.

Levi and Silas stepped toward me, but Kincaid grabbed the backs of their tops, holding them back.

"Not now." His tone sounded tight. "If I could go alone, I would."

Levi and Silas straightened. Levi blinked, and sadness reached his eyes. Silas shook himself out and he nodded, frowning. Both reactions put me on alert.

Drawing in a deep breath, I clenched my hands and pushed away any other thought than helping the three men in front of me. I didn't know what practice entailed, but it obviously wasn't good.

"I'm sorry," I offered.

Kincaid shook his head, turned, and walked out.

"It's not your fault, Amara." Levi smiled softly. He reached out my way, and I stepped forward and took his warm hand.

"She should stay here," Silas muttered. "For her own sake."

Now I was even more determined to go. Whatever

they had to go through, I would stand at their sides because... because I had a feeling I was where I was meant to be.

My chest swelled at how real that thought was. My darkness let off multiple trills, as if agreeing with me.

"I'm coming." Together, we followed Kincaid.

It wasn't until we reached double doors in a part of the basement that Levi dropped my hand after a small, quick kiss to the back of it.

Kincaid faced me. "Do not react or say a word, or it could end my life." My breath caught. "Promise me."

The words were hard to form because a need to intervene already clung to me as worry seeped in. "I promise," I whispered.

Kincaid nodded before he turned and pushed the two doors forward. Levi and Silas grabbed one each before they swung back, and I entered between them. The floor was covered in mats, and at least twenty guards, dressed only in tracksuit pants, stood around the outside of the room. The walls were lined with weapons, and Mr. Prince sat in a balcony above the room on the right.

He stood when we entered and eyed the three of us at Kincaid's side with a sneer before he called to his son, "You're late."

Kincaid waved him off as Levi led me over to the only vacant wall where no one else stood. Silas was the first to drop onto his bottom, then Levi, and I quickly sat between them.

Kincaid moved into the middle of the mats and stopped with his feet separated and his fists drawn up. Before I could blink, the guards attacked.

All.

At.

Once.

A gasp escaped me. I went to move, but Levi's arm crossed over the front of me, and Silas took hold of the back of my maid's outfit.

Levi shook his head when I turned to plead with my eyes. "Still," he ordered on a harsh whisper.

Kincaid was in the middle of all those men. He dodged, kicked, swept, punched. But there was a lot he missed because it was twenty to one. Why wasn't he using all his power? He hadn't even called forth his claws or fangs to help fight. Wasn't he allowed?

It wasn't fair.

How could his father sit back and watch this with a smile on his lips?

Guards dropped to the floor but were soon on their feet again, racing back into the fight. Sweat coated Kincaid's body. His clothes tore when they grabbed for him, but he moved gracefully out of the way like a dancer until one or two got the better of him, and he took the hits but kept going.

My pulse raced. My eyes stung, but I refused to cry.

This was practice. Did he have to do this every Wednesday night?

Levi's arm tightened over me when I shifted. My darkness ached to be set free. It had never pushed at me so much before, but it wanted out to protect what was ours.

Later, I would think about what that thought meant.

Right now, I had to try and control my disgust, my anger, and fear.

Cries, grunts, and curses echoed around the room. I cringed at the sound of their fists, legs, knees, and elbows connecting. Flesh hit flesh.

I wrapped a hand around Levi's arm and slid one behind me to grab Silas's. I held on to them tightly, but even then, I didn't feel any peace. Not like from previous touches.

Kincaid crouched and flew up and over to the left of the room. The guards watched, then screamed when they followed, and it all started again. Except, at least some of the guards were out cold on the floor, and for that, I was grateful.

But still it wasn't enough.

Kincaid bled above his eyebrow, his cheek, his neck, arms, and probably many other places I couldn't see as he moved around the mats fluidly.

My body shook and I held on to Levi and Silas tighter. My power pressed against me, but it wasn't only my darkness. *I* wanted to race onto that floor and help. I wanted to fight, to make them bleed. The hunger for their pain was strong.

The men beside me edged closer. I dropped my gaze and closed my eyes as fear thickened my throat. Not only for Kincaid but for everyone else in the room because if my darkness escaped my cage, they would all die.

"Enough." Mr. Prince's voice rang out over the noise.

Drawing in a shuddering breath, I lifted my head and opened my eyes as the fighting stopped. More guards littered the ground, but Kincaid stood with a few others and looked up at Mr. Prince. His chest heaved as he swiped at the blood on his forehead. Vampires didn't need to breathe as much as humans, but exhaustion clung to him like a shadow.

"You're lacking. Last week only three stood with you. Now there's seven. Not good enough, Kincaid."

Levi and Silas locked me down in their hold when I went to stand. I bit my bottom lip to stop myself from screaming at the man.

Kincaid glared at him yet still dipped his head slightly. "Father." He limped as he made his way across to us, and we all quickly stood. Together, we walked to the doors and out them. Once out of anyone's view, Silas and Levi took a side of Kincaid and helped him back to the bedroom. I slipped in front of them and kept an eye out for anyone about. Kincaid wouldn't want anyone to see him like this. The whole way, I ground my teeth together and grumbled under my breath about all the ways I would like Mr. Prince and those guards to pay.

"What is she doing?" Kincaid's voice sounded tired.

"Keeping an eye out." Silas's light tone seemed amused.

As soon as we were in the room and Kincaid was sitting on the couch, I placed my hands on my hips. "Why didn't you use all your strength? You would have had them beat. Do you have to do this every Wednesday night? Does your father enjoy seeing you being beaten to a pulp? They... they need to pay for this treatment. You're an alpha. You're a Prince."

The three of them stared at me.

"Well?" A blazing fire burned inside me for vengeance. I wanted to go back down there and fight them myself. I hated, absolutely despised, seeing Kincaid hurt.

Another thought that surprised me. Another one I would think about later.

Silas huffed and ran a hand over his head. "We had to hold her down or she would have run into the fight."

Levi nodded with a smirk on his lips. "If we didn't have shifter healing, we'd be bleeding from her grip on us."

My lips parted as I glanced at their arms and saw redness. Sadness dipped my stomach at the thought of hurting them.

Levi shook his head. "It's okay, sweetheart. We can take it."

"Didn't realize how strong she was, though," Silas added.

Oh... I may have used some of my power's strength to try and hold on to them, because if I had intervened, it would have gotten a lot worse.

"Is anyone going to answer my questions?" I asked, hoping to change the subject.

Kincaid rested his head back against the couch with a sigh. Blood coated his skin, though I noticed most of his wounds were healed except for a few deeper ones that were on their way to fixing themselves. Did he need to feed to gain all his strength back? Did he need help cleaning them? My hands itched to assist him.

Levi caught my gaze. "His father won't allow Kincaid to use his full power because he wants him to become stronger without having to rely on his vampiric side."

And I wanted to hurt Mr. Prince even more, as that was just ludicrous. Kincaid was strong because he was an alpha; he wouldn't be beaten even if there were forty guards.

"This is wrong. I don't mean the practice is, but that" —I pointed toward the door—"wasn't how practice should go." I let out a frustrated growl. "Can't you stand up to him and stop this?" I asked softly, not understanding why Kincaid would put up with this treatment.

His head rose, his dark gaze locking onto me. "Why hadn't I thought of that before?"

"Kincaid," Silas warned. The interjection surprised me to the point that I went to look his way, but then Kincaid let out a hiss as he stood.

In a blink, he was in front of me. "Until I become the top alpha, I have to listen to him. I swore I would and signed my allegiance in a binding document, promising to follow under his leadership until I come of age and take over." He threw an arm out toward his friends. "We all did. It keeps our leaders safe so we don't murder them. Even if we did kill them, we wouldn't be in charge until the rightful age, and we're not willing to risk another to step into *our* positions. I haven't gone through all of this to fuck it up now."

Understanding sang through me. I didn't like it, but Kincaid was doing everything by the book until it was his time to rise. Only, what type of leader would he be?

Since I felt guilty for questioning him, I sank into a curtsey and offered, "I'm sorry, master."

Kincaid snarled and spun away from me. "Don't do that."

Pressing my hands into my belly as I straightened, I asked, "What?"

He didn't reply as he sat back down.

Since I didn't think I would get an answer, I looked to Silas for one. He shrugged. Levi only held a smile as he tilted his head to the side.

Sighing, I moved off into the bathroom and grabbed a washcloth and warm water in a bowl I found under the sink. When I walked back into the living area, their talking tapered off. Rolling my eyes, I placed the bowl on the coffee table in front of Kincaid and dampened the towel. After wringing most of the water out, I shifted between his legs and went to dab at his brow when his hand snagged my wrist.

"What are you doing?" His eyes had a slight flare to them.

"Seeing how bad your wound is."

He flung my hand away. "I'll shower." Kincaid tried to stand, but I pressed my hand to his shoulder and pushed him back down.

"Just let me see."

He glared. "No."

"Yes." I moved my hand forward, but he took hold of my wrist again.

"I said no."

"And I heard, but I still want to see for myself." I needed to know if he was still healing or had healed, but I couldn't see under all the blood. I would organize a feeding if his wounds were still taking their time to heal.

His nose scrunched up. It would have been a deathly look for others, but I found it cute. "You're the maid. *You* listen to me."

It was adorable how he tried to act domineering, but

there was no harshness behind it. Add that to the confidence of knowing I no longer feared him, and a smile tugged up my lips.

"What are you smiling about?" he asked accusingly.

"Nothing." I pushed against his hand, but he held strong.

"This is quite amusing," Levi commented.

"Just let her look." Silas surprised me once again.

Kincaid pulled his upper lip back and snarled at me. My lips twitched, and his glare deepened when I didn't back down. He didn't intimidate me either. He could have thrown me across the room or demanded I leave. He hadn't—one more surprise to add to the list.

"Fine," he bit out.

His hand dropped away, and he shifted his glower to the floor as I dabbed at a wound on his brow. It was slowly knitting back together but taking its sweet time.

"Do you, um, need to feed?"

He snorted. "Are you offering?"

The room quieted, and when I didn't answer, Kincaid looked up at me. His brows drew down, which caused fresh blood to seep out of the wound.

Would I really offer up my blood?

For a man I worked for. A man who was my master. A *vampire* who could have been more brutish in his role but wasn't.

"Yes."

It was the first time I'd seen Kincaid gape.

Suddenly shy, I straightened and stepped back. "I... um, that is, if you feel you need it. I'm not trying to trick you or anything by offering."

Feet shuffled behind me, and I heard a door open, but I couldn't look away from Kincaid's stare.

Why wasn't he saying anything?

"I'm sorry. I shouldn't have offered. I'll call for a donor—" A yip fell from my mouth when Kincaid flashed in front of me, picked me up over his shoulder, and in the next blink, we were in his room, and I was laid out on the bed.

"Are you sure?" Kincaid hovered over me, and heat rose to my cheeks.

There was something behind that question. I had a feeling Kincaid was asking if I trusted him for this.

Did I?

I searched inside myself for the answer, and it sang out to me. Yes, I did trust Kincaid. He could have sold me off or hurt me many times, but he hadn't. He'd been mean and snappish, but I knew that was from the experiences he'd had with servants. He didn't trust me, and I could understand that. He was only trying to keep himself and the people around him safe.

What I didn't exactly understand was the position he'd placed me in. Wouldn't he want to take from my wrist?

"Yes, I'm sure." *I trust you.*

Kincaid studied me for a moment and sat back on his knees. He sighed and snapped his hand out, and next, Levi's wrist was at Kincaid's mouth. His fangs popped free before he sank them into Levi's flesh. Levi groaned, closing his eyes, and dropping his head back. Kincaid's throat moved as he swallowed.

My core clenched, my panties became wet, and my

nipples pebbled. I wanted to reach out to them... until I saw the cold look in Kincaid's eyes.

"Ah, fuck." Levi moaned, drawing my gaze there. "Kincaid, send me something else," he groaned, dropping forward to rest his other hand on the bed. He shuddered and panted out a breath.

Looking back to Kincaid, I found his eyes were still on me as he drank. Void of emotion. My heart fractured at the knowledge that he didn't want me. Once again.

Why had he made me think he did?

Why did he carry me to the bedroom?

Was it a game?

Quickly, I thinned my lips so he didn't see them tremble when the fracture grew into a break. Using my hands, I moved backward on the bed away from him until my back hit the headboard.

"Amara?" Silas kneeled at the side of the bed, hand reaching out to me.

Blinking tears away, I shook my head and waved a hand in front of me to ward him off. He stopped. A look of pain crossed his features as his mouth drew down in a frown. Why would he care? He hadn't last time.

I needed air.

I needed to get away from them.

Sliding to the edge of the bed, I put my feet on the ground and made a dash for the door.

"Amara," Levi called after me.

Bile rose in my throat as I kept going. I swallowed it down. I wasn't their toy. I wasn't anything to them. I—

Hands wrapped around my waist and tugged me back into a body.

"Shh, it's okay." Levi's lips touched my ear.

"You fucking fool," I heard Silas bellow. Kincaid replied, but I didn't hear the words. If I was in my right mind, I would have wondered why Silas was yelling at Kincaid, but I wasn't.

With a touch of my power, I grabbed Levi's hands and pushed him away. I bolted for my bedroom door, dashed inside my room, and slid the lock into place.

A knock sounded on the door. I stumbled back and raced to the bed, slipping under the covers. Tears rolled down my cheeks, and I detested how broken the rejection made me feel.

Weakness was one of the worst feelings, and I hated how my emotions had been on display. I breathed through my pain, calling forth my anger instead. I screamed into the pillow, releasing it all. It was either that or kicking Kincaid in the balls.

Rolling over, I ignored the hollow feeling in my stomach and chest. Instead, I sent a middle finger to the wall that connected to Kincaid's room.

How naïve I had been.

How pathetic.

No more.

No. I wouldn't fall for his tricks again. Time and time again, Kincaid made it clear I wasn't anything to him. To them. I didn't know what Levi and Silas were playing at, either, but I couldn't continue believing I was something to them. I wasn't.

Forever, and only, a slave.

I had to remember that.

If necessary, I would burn that thought into my mind

so I would remember that their charming, sweet words meant nothing in the end.

Really, it was foolish to think I could be something to men like them. Alphas.

This world we lived in was cruel. My position had been set the day I was born. I knew better—power or not.

For now, I would stay in my room until tomorrow. Screw my job until then.

Screw them too.

My chest ached as if I was missing a part of something. A part of me. Tears threatened, but I wiped them away. I was sick of crying, sick of acting like a lovesick pup starved for attention.

I had to find a way to get them to leave me alone.

Fourteen

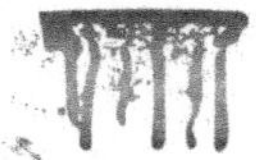

KINCAID

TO SAY I got reprimanded after the maid ran from the room would be an understatement. Silas had a turnabout of his feelings and was now ready to take on the maid as our mate, and hearing him defend her pissed me off, even knowing I deserved his anger.

When she'd lain on my bed and I'd hovered over her, I was ready to take her blood. Take *her*. I had wanted it. The gift of her giving me blood was a show of her trust. Until I realized that feeding off her would lead to more; it would seal the bond... *if* she was my mate.

I couldn't risk it, not until I knew everything about her. Not until she completely trusted us and told us what she was hiding.

There was a chance I could have handled the situation better. I could have told her what was going through my mind, but instead, I'd taken Levi's wrist, needing to sate the hunger when I'd watched her lying down on my bed. How her chest rose and fell, how her eyes held warmth, how the dress had risen up her divine legs.

The hunger had got the better of me because it wanted her, and it had been an effort when I didn't give in.

There was definitely an attraction. I couldn't deny it.

She was appealing. Everything I tried to pass off as plain and boring wasn't.

Levi and Silas had stormed out after trying to get the maid out of her room for a good half hour. They didn't hate me, they understood my reasons, but it didn't stop them from being pissed off.

The maid had taken my actions the wrong way before I could explain. I could still scent her sorrow when she thought I'd rejected her. Actually, that was wrong. I *had* rejected her, but I hadn't meant for her to become hurt or for her to blame Silas and Levi in any way.

Sighing, I scrubbed a hand over my face, weary from lack of sleep. I headed for my bedroom door, opened it, and strode across the living room to bang on her door. If Bennett or my parents saw me without a servant trailing behind me, questions would be asked. I didn't want that to happen.

Guilt twisted me inside, but I brushed the emotion aside.

Why did I need to feel guilty? It was her fault for running off without waiting for an explanation.

The door opened. The maid... she looked like hell. "Sorry to keep you waiting. What is it I can help you with?"

Her hair was still braided, but it appeared as if she'd slept in it like that from the way stray strands stuck out here, there, and everywhere. Her uniform was crinkled, and I was sure she'd slept in it also. It was her red eyes and the bags under them that told me she hadn't gotten much sleep, if any.

The guilt was back, along with shame for my own actions. They merged in my stomach and chest, repeatedly stabbing me.

"Master?" At least she was looking me in the eyes and didn't seem timid. However, I could also see the coldness in her gaze.

Why did I despise when she called me master? It had never felt right, but I wouldn't believe it was because she was my equal, meant to stand at my side instead of behind me, which her position dictated.

I clenched my hands in anger, reminding myself that she still kept something from us.

Until I knew everything, I couldn't allow the thought of her as mine to form.

"Follow." My tone was a little harsh, but the reminder of her secret had my shoulders tensing in annoyance. I didn't wait to see if she listened. Instead, I made my way to the door and through it. I heard it close, so I guessed she was behind me.

I was kidding myself.

I *knew* she was there. Her scent seemed to live inside my nose.

A scowl overtook my face, and I glanced over my shoulder at the woman responsible. She was busy trying to fix her hair and straighten out her dress.

"What time is it?"

I quickly faced forward and answered, "Six."

"Six," I heard her mutter. "Are college classes back on?"

"No." I entered the library and turned to her. "Stay by the door. I'll be doing some reading."

As soon as she nodded, I walked off toward the back of the room to a corner that was hardly used. A smile tugged at my lips when I saw the person waiting.

Samuel stood and bowed. "Hi, Master Kincaid." The boy was thirteen and worked in the gardens with his parents. A while back, I'd witnessed him sneaking into the library early one morning and heard him trying to form words from books too advanced for him. When he saw me the first time, he'd nearly wet himself and thought I would beat him senseless. I wasn't my father. It took a while for him to calm down. Then, after a couple of weeks of meeting with him to help with his reading, he finally relaxed and knew to keep these meetings secret from anyone except his parents, who were good people.

"Samuel, what have I said about bowing and calling me master?"

"Um, you see...." Samuel scuffed a foot into the floor before glancing to the side. Half hidden behind a shelf stood another young boy. I stiffened. "Master, I promise Elliot is a good guy. He and his dad work outside with me and my parents. They're really nice. He won't say anything to anyone. I promise. I wouldn't have brought him, but he told me he didn't know how to read or write, and since you've been super amazing to teach me... well, I thought you wouldn't mind another student." His gaze went to the floor. "I'm sorry, master, if I was wrong. I just didn't want him scared of you like the others when I knew how cool you really are."

Sighing, I placed a hand on his shoulder in reassurance. "Samuel, next time ask me before you bring anyone."

His gaze lifted and a bright smile shone on his face. "I will. Promise." He waved at the other boy. "Come on, Elliot. It's okay. I told you not to listen to the others and that the master wouldn't eat your face off."

Jesus, people were saying that about me?

Stepping closer to the table, I pulled out a seat and sat down to try and look less intimidating. Elliot hadn't moved yet, but I caught Samuel waving at him again.

"Samuel, how about we start and see if Elliot is interested in learning?"

Samuel brightened at that idea, though he was already a pretty cheerful boy. He tugged the chair out next to me and sat. The books we'd been working on were already spread out on the table.

"What do you want to work on first?"

He grinned. "Math!" Samuel had a knack for numbers; it was a pleasant surprise, since he struggled a lot with reading. I'd always hated how humans were treated. It was something I would change when I became alpha. At least I could change it in my area, and I knew Levi and Silas were on board as well. Of course, we expected a lot of defiance with other alphas because not a lot of them saw things the way we did.

We were prepared for the fight, though, even against others of our own kind.

Eventually, Elliot drifted out from behind the shelf and sat in a chair opposite Samuel, watching and listening to everything. They were just children. They should have been allowed to attend school and have a choice if they wanted to work for a leading family or not, rather than being forced into servitude. They needed protection, and I was more than willing to step up and make that happen. It was why I didn't care so much about the rumors of me being a killer or a tyrant. The more people feared me, the more they wouldn't question my actions.

One could hope anyway.

A mara

The floor was looking good for me to sleep on. I should have gotten more rest, and I would have if I'd known I'd be awake so early. Though, I doubted it since sleep evaded me because my body longed to be held like I had the previous night with Levi. My stupid body wanted things I couldn't have.

Groaning inwardly, I rubbed at my brow and pinched the bridge of my nose. I sounded like a broken record moaning about the same thing over and over.

Enough. I'd seriously had enough of my inner thoughts and the "woe is me" attitude. Straightening my shoulders, I reminded myself of the me I was before I came here. The strength of the woman I had grown into.

Men, human or other, were nothing but trouble. I didn't need them.

My heart clenched painfully in my chest, so I rubbed at it. The silly organ didn't believe me; it wanted the men to surround me, to take me, claim me. Those thoughts of claiming were dangerous. They were for shifters and vampires. Even I knew it was rare to find a true mate. Mr. Langley had told me all about it because he had found his. I wasn't, and never would be, a mate to anyone.

Shaking my head, I glanced at the books on all the shelves. Reading them would be a dream, but if I picked up a book, sleep would take me under. It always happened when I was tired and tried to read. I'd be fast asleep within seconds with a book pressed to my face. Mr. Langley had found me like that many times.

Thinking of him brought a smile to my lips. I missed him every day.

Shifting on my feet, I peeked around some shelves again in search of Kincaid. Could he have fallen asleep and forgotten I was there? Why were we even there in the first place, and why so early?

I jumped when the door next to me opened, and I spun in that direction. A frazzled-looking Charlotte slipped in, her lips pressed tightly together.

"There you are. I heard you were back." She took my arm in a hold. "Come on, we have to get out of here."

Tugging my arm free, I asked in a harsh whisper, "What are you talking about?"

"I can't be here any longer." She waved her hands in my face. "My hands can't take the hard work. My back has never ached so much. We need to leave before I'm worked to an early grave."

Beyond shocked, my mouth dropped open as I stared at her. "You... you want to leave because your hands and back are sore?" Even I knew that would have dire consequences. It wasn't like we were here by choice.

Charlotte glowered. "You don't understand with your cushy little job, you selfish little tramp." Her nails dug into my arm as she shook me. "You probably spread your legs for that beast. You were always a whore."

A breeze swept my hair back. Kincaid stood in front of me, his hand wrapped tightly around Charlotte's wrist. "Drop her, now." His voice was vicious, hard.

Charlotte's hand slipped away. "Master Kincaid, please forgive me. I only needed to speak with my daughter."

A snort escaped me. I had no idea why she'd bothered to seek me out in the first place. Why would she want me to come with her? Didn't she realize we'd have a bounty on our heads for running from the Prince family?

"Master, please, let me take care of this." I didn't need him to intervene with anything concerning me, but especially not *this* woman.

Kincaid looked over his shoulder to me, brows low. When I just stared up at him, I saw his jaw clench before he stepped back. He stayed right there, though. Unsurprisingly, he didn't give us privacy. Though, Charlotte looked like her jaw was going to hit the floor as she gaped from Kincaid to me and back again. Kincaid crossed his arms over his chest and nodded toward Charlotte, as if to say, "Get on with it."

Licking my suddenly dry lips, I faced Charlotte again. "Why do you want me to come with you when you run?"

Charlotte gave off a nervous laugh as she looked back at Kincaid. She shook her head. "What are you talking about, silly? I didn't say anything like that."

Of course she would lie in front of Kincaid.

"Master, did you hear her words?"

"It was something along the lines of 'Come on, we have to get out of here.' Then it was all complaining and calling you names." The last words were hard.

Charlotte dropped to her knees. "Please forgive me, Master Kincaid. I meant no disrespect."

Kincaid sneered. "Then tell her why you wanted her to leave with you, and I may look past this."

Charlotte paled and shook her head.

"Tell her, and know that I can scent a lie."

A whimper fell from her lips. "Please, Master Kincaid, don't ask this."

Whatever her reasoning was, it was bad. It certainly had me interested, and I couldn't help but feel a small amount of gratitude that Kincaid was here. If he wasn't, I doubt Charlotte would have told me.

Sudden anger took over Charlotte's features. Her face screwed as she stared at me. "I was going to use her as a bargaining chip to get into another family who is looking for young women to whore out." My eyes widened, then stretched impossibly wide when she bounced to her feet and charged at me. I took her hands in mine before she could rake her nails over my face. "I hate you. I *hate* you," she screamed in my face. "You've always been more than I could ever be. Your dad loved you more. That old man loved you more. Everyone loves you. But *I* hate you, and I will take everything you love, like I did that old man."

Dread coursed through me as I still fought her hands. "What are you talking about?"

A sinister smile lifted her lips. "I killed him slowly with poison, which made it look like a heart attack."

Fury like I hadn't felt before consumed me, burned me, and I wanted to let it out. My hold slackened when it dawned on me. "You killed Mr. Langley."

"Yes," she hissed in my face, right before she raised her hand to slap me.

She had ruined so much in my life. She was toxic, and I would deal with her no longer.

Letting the fury go was freeing.

When I swiped her hand to the side, she stumbled, but I grabbed her by the back of the hair and smacked her face into the wall. She cried out in pain, but I pressed her there and whispered, "You'll no longer tarnish my life. I should kill you slowly and painfully for what you did to a good man, but I won't. Your heart is too blackened to live another day."

Without a thought to the repercussions, I pulled a throwing star free from my bra. The blade cut into my skin as I gripped it and slid it across her throat. She screamed, but the sound broke off into a gurgle as her blood sprayed, then ran free.

Shifting back, I watched her drop to the floor, clutching her neck, gasping for breath... until she couldn't breathe any longer and her panic-filled eyes stared up at me lifelessly.

My chest heaved as I took another step back and stared down at her.

She'd been my mother, the one who'd brought me into the world, and I had just taken her out of it. Wasn't I supposed to feel bad or even remorse? Instead, I didn't feel anything. Except for peace over the action, since she'd taken from me a man I cared for. A man who had meant so much to me.

She'd poisoned Mr. Langley.

Killed him.

She deserved to die.

She *did*.

"M-Master Kincaid?"

I spun, throwing star still in hand, ready to let it fly until arms wrapped around me and bound mine to my body.

"Samuel, take Elliot and go get your parents."

A young blond boy nodded as his gaze went to the floor, to me, and back to the floor.

"Samuel. Now, please, and neither of you tell anyone."

Samuel nodded and ran off through the library. Would they come back this way? I needed to move the body so no one else saw. My stomach churned over the thought of the boy already seeing. How long had he been there? Was he a witness to me killing? What would that mean for Kincaid? What would Kincaid do to me after all this? Shrugging out of Kincaid's hold, I moved over to the body.

"Leave it."

Stilling at his words, I straightened and turned to him, tipping my chin up. "I understand I'll be punished for this, but I won't say I'm sorry for doing it." I glanced down at the body. "She was never a good mother, but the worst thing she could have ever done was take the life of someone like Mr. Langley."

"You'll not be punished."

Thinning my lips, I shook my head slightly. "I should be."

"No one will find out about this."

I threw a hand in the direction the boy had gone. "The boy saw."

"He won't say anything, and neither will his parents when they come here to take the body. I'll message Levi and Silas to have their men assist them in getting rid of the body. They'll send someone else to clean this area. No one will know."

My brows dipped as confusion rolled through me. "Why? Why would you hide this? Taking her life wasn't the right thing to do. I don't regret it, but I should be punished. She works here. What will you say when people start to ask?"

"That she came to you, hoping to run away. You turned her down, but she must have taken off." He stepped closer to me. His gaze ran over me, taking in the blood. Did it bother him? His eyes hadn't changed, though. "In the short time I was around her, I've already gathered that she wasn't a good person. She took the life of a man who not only you cared for, but Silas, Levi, and I did too. He trained us at a young age. We may have drifted apart over time, but he will always be in our hearts."

My bottom lip trembled, but I sucked it into my mouth and bit down. I nodded. It was all I could do because emotions again clogged my throat over losing Mr. Langley.

Sniffing, I looked up at him again. "Who was that boy?" Did we need to worry about him?

A soft smile I'd never seen before crossed Kincaid's lips. He pulled his phone free and started typing into it as he explained, "Samuel works the grounds around here. I've been teaching him to read, write, and do math."

Shock had my body shaking. Kincaid Prince was teaching school subjects to a human? "Why?" My tone sounded a little accusing.

"Because we may come across as monsters, but not all of us are. We see the injustice to humans, and we hope to do something about it when we become alphas."

Another wave of shock slammed into me, and I took a step back. I pressed my hand over my heart as it soared outward as if it wanted to reach for the man in front of me and hug him. I locked my body down and looked away. My gaze landed on Charlotte again just when I heard rushing footsteps coming our way from a different direction to the door near us. Quickly, I drew out a dagger in my other hand since I still held a throwing star.

"Calm," Kincaid murmured as a man and a woman rounded a corner. "We can trust them."

As they drew closer, they slowed and took in the scene. No power emanated from them, so I knew they were human, and I glanced at Kincaid again to see another smile.

Who was this man?

"Sire." The man bowed and the woman dipped into a curtsey. When they straightened, the man grinned.

"Samuel said a gorgeous woman took out an old hag, but we weren't sure to believe him. I can see we were wrong."

My cheeks heated.

"There's a little more to it, but for now, that will do. Silas and Levi will be here soon with some men. Are you able to help them get this cleaned up?"

"Of course," the woman said just before the man nodded. They trusted him. Of course they did, or else they wouldn't have allowed their son to be around Kincaid unguarded.

More footsteps pounded, and I was surprised none of the employees had appeared, wondering what was going on. I hoped they stayed away.

"Amara," Levi said with slight panic in his voice. The couple parted to allow him and Silas through. Their gazes ran over me. I knew I was in a state with blood covering me, but they didn't seem to care as both men stopped at my sides.

"Where are you hurt?" Silas ran his hands over me.

Levi rested a hand on my lower back. "Are you okay?"

Nodding, I said, "I'm... fine."

"It's not her blood." Kincaid moved off to speak with the men who'd arrived with Silas and Levi. I caught the couple watching me. Both had a soft smile on their lips and warm eyes. I didn't understand their expression, since a body lay at my feet and blood coated my uniform. How could they smile at me when I'd just killed?

"Who is the woman and what did she do?" Silas asked.

With blank eyes, I glanced back down at Charlotte. "My mother, and she killed Mr. Langley."

Low growls rolled out from the alphas next to me.

"Silas, Levi, take her back to her room. She needs to get clean." Kincaid briefly looked at me before turning back to the others, and the couple moved over to his side.

"Come on, sweetheart." Levi placed an arm around my waist.

"But... what if people see me and scent the blood?" The door she'd come through hadn't opened again since she'd entered, but the scent was strong in the air and could waft out into the hall.

"Don't worry, the crew will have it covered." Silas took my hand and drew it up. He uncurled my fingers from around the throwing star and winced when he saw it had dug into my skin. He then used the star to slice his own hand open.

"Silas," I cried and reached for it, but he pulled his hand away.

His other hand cupped my cheek, and I stilled as his warmth seeped into my cold body. I already knew he was acting differently before he winked. "It's fine. I'll heal soon, but it'll be a distraction to your scent. Shifter blood is always more overpowering to a vampire than the blood of others."

With a gentle push to my lower back from Levi, we moved to the door. I didn't bother looking down at the woman on the floor; she no longer existed for me.

Fifteen

LEVI

MY LION still paced inside of me from when we'd first seen Amara covered in blood. Silas wasn't faring well either. He hadn't stopped growling under his breath after Amara went to shower. For the tenth time, he ran his hand over his head before he spun my way where I sat on the edge of her bed.

"We need to tell her."

My head jerked back in shock. "What?"

"Tell her she's our mate, and then maybe, just fucking maybe, if Kincaid hasn't screwed this up for us, we can comfort her. Her own goddamn mother killing someone she cared about.... Someone *we* cared about." He threw out a hand. "Hell, maybe comforting goes both ways. That cunt killed Wayland. Fucking Langley."

Nodding, I scrubbed a hand over my face. A stab of sorrow hit my chest. "I know. But I don't know how

Amara will react to the news of being our mate after last night."

"Goddamn Kincaid."

"We know why he did it, but she doesn't, and she only saw it as another rejection."

"It would be good to tell her Kincaid acted that way because he's a stupid, scared dickhead for worrying about whatever she's keeping from us."

Snorting, I nodded. "He's all those."

"Her holding something back isn't going to stop me from acknowledging her as our mate. She's stood at our sides in a fight and came to us to begin with. She's proven herself."

"Says the man who only nights ago wasn't ready to listen to me either."

Silas rumbled with a growl. "I was stupid."

"What changed?" Shock had me barking out a laugh when I saw his cheeks heat. I stood. "Wait, something did happen between you two in the bedroom?"

Silas turned and stalked to the window. "Just a simple kiss, and yet it was...."

"Everything?"

His head dropped. "Yeah. If I hadn't taken her to your room, I would have gone too far with her, and neither of us were ready."

"You felt the impulse to claim her?"

"Christ, yes. It showed me you were right to call her our mate. There'd been a small connection when our gazes first met, but that kiss told me the truth."

Walking over to the window, I leaned against the

frame and caught the silly smile on his lips. Yes, he was ready to accept her. "I worry it's too soon to tell her."

Silas grunted. "Do you care that she's hiding something still?"

"No. I already trust her, and I have a feeling what she's hiding has everything to do with herself and nothing that's meant to harm us."

Silas nodded. "I want to rush into that bathroom, take her into my damn arms, and hold her."

My lion and I were in agreement. "I know the feeling." I ignored my half-hard cock when it throbbed at the thought of Amara naked under the spray of water. "However, I'm not sure if rushing into this is good. She knows about mates from Langley having lost his. But I doubt she would ever think she could be that for not only one, but three men."

"I'm not sure I can hold off on claiming her for much longer. I almost ripped that fucker's throat out when I saw him talking with her."

A snarl rolled out of me. "Talking? He was *flirting,* and I would have been at your side, helping."

"We're fucked."

I huffed out a breath. "We are."

"When will be the best time to tell her?"

"Tell me what?"

We both spun to face Amara standing in the doorway with loose wet hair, a bandage around her hand, and dressed in—

A growl sounded from Silas when he saw her in one of his T-shirts. She looked cute. Too cute, since it was large on her and exposed one shoulder.

Her eyes widened when Silas growled, and she bit her bottom lip when he went to go to her. He only stopped when I reached out and grabbed onto his top.

Amara licked her lips, and I thinned mine so I didn't moan. I wanted my lips on hers while she did that.

"Silas," I warned when he tried to move toward her again.

Amara noticed Silas's eyes were trained on the T-shirt. "I-I hope it was okay to put this on. My dress.... Well, it was a mess, and I didn't feel like getting back into a uniform just yet."

A soft smile lifted my lips. "It's fine, sweetheart."

Her gaze shifted to Silas and back to me. Her brows rose. She didn't believe me, since I was still holding Silas back, and he'd turned from growling to chuffing slightly. He, like me, no doubt wanted to be buried deep inside her. But since she was dressed in his clothes and his scent covered her, I expected his desire rode him harder.

"I'm not sure it is." She worried her bottom lip with her top teeth.

Shit. We were going to have to tell her, as Silas was finding it hard to rein himself in. His dragon was close to the surface, pushing his impulse to claim her, since she'd accepted wearing his scent.

"Look—ah, hell. We, ah, need to tell you something, and we're not sure how you'll take it."

Her hands lifted to grip the tee at her chest. "What?" Her voice was a whisper.

"You're our mate," Silas blurted roughly.

Lifting my free hand, I slapped the back of his head.

He flinched and finally locked his body down. "Fuck, Levi." He rubbed at his head.

"You didn't have to blurt it like that." I shoved him aside, or at least tried to, and looked back at Amara. Her face had slackened with shock, or was it fear? My lion roared inside me; he didn't want our mate to fear us just as much as I didn't.

"I... I can't be.... I don't understand."

I stepped toward her. When she backed up once, I stilled. My hands fisted at my sides, and worry seeped into my body.

"From the first time we looked at each other, a connection started. It's... it's why you react in... certain ways."

Her hands released and clenched her top again as she shook her head. "Not possible. I'm a... nobody—"

Silas snarled and broke if off to say, "You're someone to us."

She shook her head again. Her eyes narrowed and nostrils flared. "How can you say that? You hate me."

Silas winced. "I've never hated you. I was reluctant for Kincaid to have another servant after they all tried to kill him in some way." He ran a hand over the top of his hair. "I acted like a dick, yeah, because it's hard to be around new people who have an ulterior motive." He looked away from her. "At first, I fought this... connection, but now I don't want to."

"Why?" We both looked back at her when we heard her broken tone to see tears in her eyes.

Silas sucked in a breath. "Because I knew, after the kiss we shared, that I didn't want to miss out on the opportunity of a future with you in it." His voice was raw with honesty.

Amara glanced at me. "You.... Did you accept the bond from the start?"

"I did." Though, I felt I had to add: "The other two are stubborn when it comes to new things, but I knew they—" Fuck, I snapped my lips closed, knowing I'd messed up when I saw the puzzled dip to her brows.

"The other two?"

It was Silas's time to hit me in the back of the head.

Her hands slid down to press against her stomach. She paled. "Silas and who?"

My lion raked his claws against my insides, and I flinched. "Amara, sweetheart, please know there was no rejection involved in the last few days. It was only fear of what-ifs and trust issues, which you can understand, right?"

Her bottom lip trembled, until she clenched her jaw. "Kincaid."

Reaching out to her, I fisted my hands and dropped them to my sides.

Silas groaned as if in pain and took a step forward. "We never meant you any pain, Amara, and I'm so fucking sorry you have felt some by our hands."

She didn't say anything, only stared down at the floor, lost in thought, but I saw her tears falling. It burned my chest.

I moved up beside Silas, then took another step toward her. Silas did also. I glared at him. He scowled back. We stepped closer once more.

"Sweetheart?"

Her sniff had my lion snarling and Silas's dragon growling. It wasn't at her but at our own actions.

Lifting her gaze, her eyes widened when she saw we only stood a couple of steps away from her. She shook her head and shrugged, glancing around the room. "I... I don't know what to say." She looked back at us with sadness in her eyes, and my pulse raced.

Would she reject us?

Reject the thought of something with me because of Kincaid?

I couldn't blame her, not after what she'd been through. At least she now understood why her body reacted to us. However, acid churned in my gut as I waited for some type of sign of which way she would go.

Unless she didn't have an answer. We couldn't expect her to be open to us being her mates after everything. It was hard to unhinge my lips to speak, since I really didn't want to give her an out, but I would be selfish if I didn't.

"You don't have to say anything now. You can take time to think about it. To get used to the idea, since... since it's new and a lot to take in."

Silas shot me a look, but then he sighed and nodded, glancing back at Amara.

Amara cocked her head to the side, her eyes still shining with unshed tears. "Maybe you're both wrong. Maybe I'm not your... not who you think I am."

A growl sounded from Silas. "You are. You've felt it, right? Something between us." His jaw clenched. "I can never say I'm sorry enough for how you were treated—"

She waved a hand in the air. "I understand why." She drew in a deep breath and glanced away. In a soft voice, she added, "I would have felt the same way you did when all the servants before me were against you all."

She understood that, at least.

It was then I realized, even in the short time we'd been around each other, I didn't know if she could even care for shifters.

My heart ached at the thought of our mate not accepting both our forms. It could happen, though; I had seen it when an outsider didn't want anything to do with a member of the pride because they shifted into an animal. They rejected the bond, and it near killed the shifter that had been cast aside as if they were nothing. Only with time and a lot of support from their alpha could the shifter deal with the loss.

She cleared her throat. "But shouldn't your mate be a shifter?"

"Not always. Intermixed races have been known to bond. It's not against the law or anything. Though, some factions discourage it. We don't." Did it mean she was considering accepting us? Could she see herself with shifters?

She dragged her top teeth over her plump bottom lip and nodded.

What did that nod mean?

Silas voiced my concern. "Are you against shifters as a mate?"

She quickly shook her head, and the tension surrounding my heart lessened. "Only, I've never thought I could be someone's mate, so I'm unsure if I'll make a good one."

My lion huffed inside me. We already knew she would be the perfect little mate.

Smiling, I gently said, "I think you will be perfect."

A blush coated her cheeks.

"You've surprised me in many ways. I can see you'll fit well with us." Silas's own cheeks pinked. He wasn't used to being sweet.

Amara's lips parted. "How...." She shrugged. "I don't know. I don't know what to say or do."

She looked tired and unsure of herself. I needed to touch her, comfort her. "It's been a rough morning. Will you let me hug you?"

Her gaze snapped to mine. "I-I.... Shouldn't you both be with Kincaid? Protecting him?"

Silas shook his head. "Some of our team are with him. He's safe."

Her heart was big, and even though she was annoyed with and still probably hurt by Kincaid, she was making sure he would be okay. He was an idiot.

Stepping closer, I softly called her name, "Amara?"

Her brows dipped and new tears threatened. "I don't know."

"Sweetheart, you're our mate. We want to comfort you after what you've been through, what you found out. Can you let us do that?"

"Us?" Her tone wavered.

Silas grunted. "Levi and me."

Her eyes widened on Silas. "You want to?"

"Yeah, Amara. I do." His dragon would be pushing him, like my lion, but it was also the human side of us that wanted the contact.

She shrugged. "Um, okay?"

That was enough.

I swept forward and picked her up bridal style in my arms. She let out a cute, quick yip before I walked her back into her room with Silas following. Elation filled my body. Unable to wipe the smile off my face, I hid it against her hair when I pressed my nose there, dragging in her scent.

Mine.

Lying on the bed, I brought Amara in the middle as Silas climbed on the other side and settled beside her. I knew he would hear how fast her heart raced, which was why he started chuffing into her hair as he lay on his side, facing her. I curled onto my side as well and picked up her hand, taking it in both of mine.

"Such small hands," I teased. Amara huffed and went to pull away but stopped when I pressed a kiss to her fingers. "I like them."

She blinked slowly at me, relaxing from Silas's chuffing—he had used the same tactic on me and Kincaid many times when we'd been upset or pissed over something. She mustn't have gotten much sleep the previous night. Not that I could blame her, since she thought we didn't want her.

Leaning in, I kissed her temple, and her sweet perfume of arousal hit the room. Silas's chuff changed to a growl. She tensed, and Silas quickly switched back.

"Are you sure I'm—"

"We're sure, sweetheart." I brushed my nose against her cheek.

Silas rested a hand over her waist and dragged her

closer into him. Her face heated, and I grinned, though I was also annoyed he thought he could have more of her. I quickly wiggled closer, which brought a smile to Amara's lips before a giggle escaped and she slapped a hand over her mouth. Her nose scrunched up and her eyes dulled a little. After the morning she'd had, she probably thought she wasn't supposed to enjoy the attention.

Silas glanced at me over her head. He touched his lips to her temple. "It might not be something you want to hear, but I'm glad you did what you did in that library. I would have done the same. Wayland was a good man."

A whimper escaped her. Suddenly she moved to face me, burying her face into my neck, but I didn't miss how she'd grabbed Silas's arm and dragged it over her, tugging him in close.

Nodding my appreciation to Silas, I kissed her forehead, and together we comforted our mate until she fell asleep.

Soon after, with contentment ringing through me, I followed her into slumber.

Sixteen

SILAS

SHE WAS WARM AGAINST ME. At some point as we all slept, she had rolled over, and now her head was on my chest, her leg thrown over mine, and I could feel the extra weight of Levi at her back. I glanced down at her hand in mine, only to realize it wasn't her hand but Levi's.

Jesus. Dropping it, I placed my palm on her arm and smiled approvingly when she burrowed into me.

I had my mate in my arms.

Amara.

Never had I felt this type of satisfaction before. My dragon was even curled up lazily inside me. He didn't care about anything but the mate at our side.

The door opened, and I stilled until Kincaid stepped in. He paused, taking in the sight, and frowned. Lifting my hand slowly, I pressed a finger to my lips. I didn't want Amara to wake, because she had looked exhausted earlier.

Kincaid shifted closer to the bed. His jaw clenched. In a soft tone, he asked, "How is she?"

He cared. Levi and I knew he did, or else he wouldn't have sent us back with Amara. In that situation, he could have done things differently, but he hadn't.

"Okay."

"How did you manage this?" He nodded at the bed. Meaning how'd we end up in bed with her.

"She knows about us being mates."

Kincaid's eyes flashed wide as he dragged them from her to me.

"We explained why we were hesitant. She said she understands. Look, I'll be honest—I don't think she's over your rejection of her or maybe mine either." I lifted a hand before he could talk. "*I* know you weren't rejecting her intentionally but trying to make sure the bond didn't take until you know everything about her. *She* doesn't know that."

Until now maybe, since I felt her tense a little against me. Not that I'd tell him that.

"Also, I'm not sure she believes us about her being our mate."

Kincaid grunted, his gaze shifting back to her. "She probably thinks she's not worthy."

My brows reached for my hairline, and even my dragon perked his head up. "You think she is?" Kincaid's usual scowl was back. When he didn't answer, I teased, "You like her."

Kincaid turned. "I'll be in my rooms, going over a few things."

And I thought I was stubborn.

"You can join us. I'll even let you cuddle into Levi's back."

Kincaid shot me the middle finger over his shoulder, making me chuckle. When he was out of the room with the door closed—softly I might add—I kissed the top of Amara's head.

"How long are you going to pretend to sleep?"

"For a while longer." Her voice was soft and husky. She tipped her chin up to look at me. A blush spread across her cheeks. "I would move, but it seems Levi is stuck to my back."

Grinning, I brushed hair from her eyes. They closed, and a shaky breath dropped from her lips. I was a fucking fool for thinking she wasn't mine.

"Is what Kincaid said true?"

Her eyes opened, lips thinning. "What?"

"That you think you're not worthy to be ours?"

Since she was still plastered against me, I felt her tense. Her palm slid up my chest quickly, and she went to shift away. I took her hand in mine, and she stilled.

"Amara, you're more worthy than any of us. Shit, I'm not usually nice, but being around you brings it out because I want to be a better person. You already are worthy."

Tears clouded her eyes as she shook her head. "I'm not."

"You are. Believe that you're in the right place, and learn to trust we're the right men for you to live a happy life with."

Her eyes widened as her body pushed into me before

Levi's head popped up behind her. "It's hard for me to admit, but he's right, sweetheart. It was luck our paths crossed, but this is where you're supposed to be, and we'll make sure you'll see you're appreciated and adored by us." He kissed her shoulder.

"Levi," she uttered before grazing her bottom lip with her top teeth. Her blush deepened.

Nodding, I added, "I'll make up for being a dickhead in the beginning."

Amara dropped her head, her forehead hitting my shoulder. "I don't know if I can take a nice Silas."

My dragon and I grinned together. He was happy at her words, and so was I. Laughing, I ran a hand over the back of her hair. "You'll get used to it."

Levi nipped at Amara's shoulder. "Take it, sweetheart, but be prepared, he'll be an ass to everyone else still."

A giggle escaped her, only it stopped as soon as Levi slowly ran a hand up her side. "Should we get some lunch or rest some more?"

Amara lifted her head, a mild scent of arousal rose, and even her eyes were a little dazed from Levi's attention. "L-Lunch," she breathed.

"Lunch then." I nodded. Though it was the last thing in my thoughts. Before I moved off the bed, though, I couldn't resist her slightly parted lips. I dipped in and pressed my mouth to hers.

It was meant to be a quick, innocent kiss.

But I couldn't pull away.

Our eyes were open and on each other, both wide-eyed and frozen with our lips touching. Levi must have done something because, in the next second, she gasped. Her hips jutted forward, and her eyes closed. A growl slipped out of me as I gripped the back of her head and closed my eyes to deepen the kiss.

Holy fuck toy, Batman.

My body ignited as she gripped my shoulders when our tongues slid, twisted, and rubbed against each other's. My dragon chuffed over and over, happy with the development.

She broke the kiss to pant out some breaths. If I stayed here, there was a chance I wouldn't be able to stop. Slowly I pulled my body up the bed until my back rested against the headboard. I choked on a breath when I took in Levi rutting against Amara's sweet ass, and kissing, licking, and nipping at her bare shoulder. Her hand was on my thigh, rubbing up and down, and her delicious scent of arousal bloomed higher in the room.

Instantly, my cock hardened more than it already was. My mate needed attention, and it was ready to deliver.

Fuck, maybe I should have stayed lying down.

"Levi," Amara whispered.

"What do you need, sweetheart? More or less?"

Her hand tightened on my thigh. "M-More."

Levi growled, "Anything for you."

Amara gasped when Levi lifted her and sat her on my lap, facing me. Her legs surrounded my hips.

"Ah, hey," I lamely said.

She snorted and cackled, dropping her head to my forehead. I gripped her to me when hands wound around my ankles, and Levi dragged me down the bed a little.

"What the fuck, Levi! I could have dropped her."

Levi snorted as he climbed up the bed straddling my thighs to get behind Amara. He tsked. "See, sweetheart? Grumpy with everyone but you."

The smile Amara gifted me took my breath away. Chuffing sounded in my chest, as my dragon and I was pleased to see her happy. I rested my hands on her waist as Levi pressed into her back and looked over her shoulder. His lion shone in his gaze. He nipped at her naked skin.

"Sweetheart, I need you to understand something."

"Yes?" Her tone was soft, almost shy.

"Know that we want you not because you're our mate. We want you as the strong, protective woman that you are. It's not the bond forcing our desire for you, but you... as you are."

Leaning in, I kissed her temple. "He's right."

When she nodded, Levi placed a hand on her shoulder and pressed down. She gasped as her panties-covered pussy brushed over my hard cock, her eyes hooding with want. I ground my teeth together to keep the groan inside. Even so, my throat still vibrated from all the chuffing my dragon was doing.

"Do you still want more?" Levi asked, placing his forehead on her shoulder.

My hands tightened on her waist when she licked her lips and hummed under her breath.

"Words, sweetheart. I need to hear them."

"Yes, please."

Cupping her cheek, I told her, "Baby, you don't need to say please. We'll give you anything." Her eyes warmed, and to my utter shock, she made the first move and leaned forward to kiss me.

Levi hummed. "That's it, sweetheart, take what you need."

Stars, that was all I saw when she ground down over me, drawing a moan from her lips into mine. I sucked down the sound and wrapped an arm around her waist, holding her close. Her hips moved over me, a little faster than before, and she tore her mouth from mine to whimper, "Levi. Silas."

"Hmm, sweetheart, feels good, yes?" He rocked behind her, and I knew he'd have his cock snuggly pressed between her ass cheeks, thrusting.

"Good" was all she said before dropping her cheek to my shoulder. I flicked her hair away from her neck to lick and taste her.

"Fuck," I groaned.

Amara whimpered between us as Levi reached over me to grip the top of the headboard while he kept pushing his cock up and down against her ass. I wished we didn't have clothes between us. I wanted to feel her wet pussy surrounding me as I thrust up inside her. Thinking of it had my balls drawing up. She rubbed herself over me in all the right ways, and I couldn't believe I was about to lose a load just from grinding with my mate.

Gripping the back of her hair, I tugged her head back so I could have her hooded eyes. "Holy hell, Amara, you feel good."

She hummed, eyelids falling closed, panting through breaths. Her reaction to our attention was heaven. Levi nuzzled her neck, her shoulder, and then nibbled on her ear. She moaned, reaching back for Levi.

"Oh, oh, I'm.... Levi, Silas."

Levi groaned, his head falling back, eyes closing. "Yes, sweetheart, come for us."

We held her as her rhythm picked up, driving me even more crazy. I kissed her chin, the corner of her mouth, and then she fused our lips together, sending me over the edge. My cock throbbed and pulsed. I growled into her mouth as cum filled my boxers.

"N-Now," Amara cried, still griding up and down over me, sending shock wave after shock wave through me. Her moan was loud and long as I kissed her neck.

"Christ yes," came from Levi, and he rocked against her over and over from behind. Levi dropped to the bed with a small, satisfied laugh. I curled both arms around Amara and tugged her body down so she rested all her weight on me. She didn't put up a fight, still sated from her release.

As I rubbed my palms up and down her back, Levi reached up and took her hand in his, pulling it down to kiss the tips of her fingers. "Are you all right, sweetheart?"

She snorted and I grinned, as did Levi. Amara flopped her head to the other side so she could look down at Levi. "I'm all right."

Levi's gaze heated. "Good."

Sliding my fingers through her hair, I massaged her scalp. A sigh slipped past her lips. "That was unexpected, but damn fun."

Her cheek brushed over my chest as she nodded. "Uh-huh."

Our grins grew. Levi got to his elbow and kissed her nose. "No regrets?"

The side of her face I could see turned red. I touched her. "What's this for?"

"Um, well, no regrets, just...." On a whisper, she quickly said, "Fewer clothes next time." Hiding, she buried her burning cheeks back into my chest. Levi and I shared a satisfied look. She'd enjoyed what had happened between the three of us and wanted to do more next time. My dragon started chuffing while Levi made a noise in the back of his throat as he kissed her shoulder.

"We can make that happen." He bounced off the bed, and Amara lifted her head to watch him. He winked. "I'm going to freshen up and get us some food."

My gut damn fluttered at the thought of alone time with our mate. Even though I needed to clean up, I wasn't moving until I absolutely had to. When he closed the door after himself, I gently squeezed her to me. "Can I have your eyes, Amara?"

She dropped her cheek back down to my shoulder and shook her head.

Smiling, I cupped the back of her neck. "Why?"

She sighed. "It dawned on me that I probably shouldn't have done that."

"Why?" My tone held a harsh edge, so I softened the impact by massaging her neck.

"Silas." The way she whispered my name had my cock throbbing. "I'm a maid. I should be working and.... I.... Is this even real?"

Lifting my legs, I took her under the arms and dragged her body up until I had her wide eyes. I slid a hand to her cheek. "It doesn't matter that you're a maid. We can figure that out later. But know that for me, for Levi, and even for Kincaid once he gets some sense knocked into him, this is real. This is happening, as long as *you* want it."

Her lips thinned and I stilled. My heart skipped a beat.

"Do you want this, Amara?"

Fuck, did she? My dragon whimpered at the thought of her not wanting us.

Jesus, she probably needed time to think about it, and there I was, putting pressure on her. Made me feel like a dickhead again.

Stroking her cheek with my thumb, I told her, "Forget it. You don't have to answer right now. It's new and scary."

She nodded. "I never thought I could be someone's mate. Are *you* sure—" She let out a squeal as I rolled her onto her back and hovered over her.

Smiling, I nodded. "I'm completely sure. Another reason I was probably an ass was that it shocked the fuck out of me. I didn't think *I* could be so lucky to have a mate."

Her smile was warm as her fingers brushed the side of my face. My dragon chuffed in content at her petting.

"Your dragon seems happy."

Shaking my head, I laughed. "Yeah, happy is an understatement. He was pissed when I didn't get my head together right away."

Her grin made me damn giddy. "Silas."

"Yeah, baby?"

Her eyes warmed. "I *am* sure I want this, but like you

said, it's new and scary, and I don't.... Kincaid is my master. It doesn't fit or make sense."

Fuck yes. She wanted to try this. She accepted us as her mates. I dropped my head and brushed my nose against hers. "We'll figure it all out together."

"All right," she breathed before I took her mouth in a hot, claiming kiss.

SEVENTEEN

AMARA

WHAT HAPPENED WAS CRAZY. Totally and utterly crazy. I didn't know if I had done the wrong thing or not when it came to Levi and Silas because I couldn't get over the super squishy emotions bursting inside me every time I thought of them.

It was their words.

Their smiles.

The way they touched me.

Everything that had happened in my room shot a swarm of butterflies to my stomach. Logically, when we'd connected nearly a week ago, I probably should have thought about our future more, but I wanted to reassure Silas when he asked me if he and Levi were who I wanted. Panic had swirled in his eyes. Not only didn't I like his worry, but I couldn't have ignored what was happening between us. Especially since our physical connection escalated, but even before then, a part of me held them close to my chest.

Now I knew it was because we were mates.

Mates to be bonded when I was ready for the next step, which Levi had explained when we'd eaten lunch together. It had been hard to tell him I wasn't sure when that would be. I didn't know if I was waiting for Kincaid or if it was something else holding me back.

Maybe it had to do with me hiding my real self from them.

Because there was a chance they wouldn't want anything to do with me once they found out what lingered inside me.

Fear clutched my stomach, and I pressed a hand there. Silas shifted on the couch beside me. "Are you okay?"

Kincaid and Levi's gazes snapped to me. I moved my hand off my stomach, but it wasn't the action that Silas asked about. The color had drained from my face.

Should I tell them?

Could I possibly confide in them, share my secret, and trust that they wouldn't want to use me as a weapon or have me sent off to be experimented on?

Not knowing made my heart heavy.

Forcing a smile, I patted Silas's thigh as I thought better of sharing and sent a quick glance to Kincaid. "I'm fine."

Silas frowned. He didn't believe my lie but didn't push either. I could feel Kincaid's glare burning the side of my face, but I refused to look that way. Levi stood, walked around the couch I sat on with Silas, and rested his palms on my shoulders. Calm washed through me, and even more so when Silas took my hand.

"Sorry to interrupt," I offered.

Kincaid stared at us, his annoyance clear. Silas and Levi's openness with me, their touching me, grated on him. His fixed scowl was proof enough of that.

"It's fine." Levi kissed my temple just as the door to the suite opened.

Levi straightened out of my view, and I saw a gaping Mary standing in the doorway. Her eyes flicked back and forth between Levi, Silas, and me over and over. Silas had said she'd been busy with things and hadn't had a chance to get back to see me, even though she wanted to.

"I.... Wait, what's going on here?"

Kincaid sighed and scrubbed a hand over his face. "You could have at least got off the couch and pretended to be a servant."

Oh.

He was right. If it had been anyone but Mary, Silas and Levi's attention on me would have caused trouble.

Quickly, I stood.

"Too late now," Kincaid clipped, and his attitude was getting on my last nerve. Ever since Levi, Silas, and I had come from the bedroom a week ago, he'd been snapping at everyone.

I'd had enough.

"Shut it, pain in my ass." The words tumbled out before I could lock my lips. Lifting a hand, I covered my mouth and stared at him with wide eyes. Never would I have spoken like that to Kincaid before. A crippling fear of what would come from it previously prevented me. Now,

I was confident my words wouldn't bring any pain my way from my master. Besides, he hadn't harmed me for anything I'd done so far. With my courage growing, I didn't hold back as much as was sensible.

Still, I couldn't help but see the funny side of my outburst. Especially at Kincaid's shocked expression.

Snorting, a laugh left me abruptly over his wide eyes and his gaping mouth. Silas and Levi chuckled, while Mary remained frozen in the doorway.

Dropping my hand, I dipped into a patronizing curtsey. "Sorry, *master*."

Kincaid closed his mouth, then opened it, only to shut it. I was sure I saw his lips twitching a little before he said, "I'm sure you are." He shook his head and stood, moving over to the window to stare out. It seemed he liked to gaze out a window while thinking. But I wondered what he was thinking about.

"Ah... what the heck is going on?" Mary yelled.

Levi chuckled, went over to her, and pulled her through the door before closing it. He ruffled Mary's hair, then moved back to the couch.

"That doesn't explain anything." Mary stamped her foot. She pointed to Kincaid but stared at me. "You told him to shut up and he didn't do anything." She pointed to Silas and Levi. "My bosses were sitting close to you, which looks intimate. What am I missing?"

Not believing it was up to me to say anything, I glanced at Silas and Levi. They were both looking at me in a way that brought a blush to my cheeks.

"Oh my." Mary's hand fluttered up to her mouth. "Is it.... Are you all mates?" She squirmed.

"Yes." Levi winked at me. I smirked and rolled my eyes, but really, I loved it.

Who would have thought that after promising myself to keep distance from them all, I'd be where I was now? Not me. Being bonded had been the furthest thing from my thoughts when I'd panicked about our reactions to one another.

The switch felt like whiplash. The way it had flipped and changed was exhausting. Not a chance I'd worry about it now, though. The thought of spending my days with these men, my mates, overrode anything and caused my whole body to shiver in pleasure. Knowing they were mine had me smiling, and warmth bloomed within my body.

My gaze shifted to Kincaid.

Silas had known I'd been awake when Kincaid had come in that day a week ago.

Bubbles had fizzed in my belly when Kincaid had asked after me. That he hadn't argued with Silas when he said that Kincaid had fed from Levi because he didn't want the bond to finalize before he knew me still sent a jolt of surprise through me.

Only, would he ever really know me?

I still didn't have an answer to that, and I wasn't sure Kincaid could ever let down his walls until I did the same and shared everything about me with him. I couldn't say I blamed him in wanting all the information before taking the biggest jump into a long-lasting relationship.... Yet, I still wasn't sure if sharing my secret was the right thing to do.

Mary's squeal had me covering my ears. She clapped

and bounced over to me, her hands landing on my arms, where she shook me. "This is incredible!"

Laughing, I smiled happily and shrugged. It was still early and hard to tell if it would be incredible, but I did love what was growing between us—so much so, I felt lighter inside. Like a weight had been lifted from me, and it helped me float. Internally, I groaned at how cheesy I sounded.

"Mary, can you leave our mate alone?" Silas stepped up behind me and gently moved me out of Mary's reach.

"I can't believe this. No wonder Kincaid didn't bite your head off, since you're the mate to his friends."

Cue awkward silence.

Something I felt I had to fill. "Yes, that must be it."

"Mary, what do you have for us?" Silas asked, drawing her attention away.

Before she spoke about business, though, she gripped my hand in both of hers. "We're so having girl talk later."

Smiling, I shrugged. "I'll have to see if I'm free. I still have a job to do." I pulled my hand free and patted her shoulder.

Kincaid spun from the window. "Actually, we should talk about that."

"Sorry?"

Kincaid sighed and moved back to the couch opposite Silas. "Sit."

"Woof woof," I muttered.

Silas coughed, covering a laugh. Levi snorted and tapped his ears. My eyes widened. Oh. I winced, looking at Kincaid while Mary giggled like a hyena.

Once I sat, Kincaid drew a brow up. "Good puppy."

Narrowing my eyes, I fought the urge to flip him off and instead leaned into Silas, which was surprisingly easy to do. Levi jumped the couch and sat on my other side. He took my hand in his, and we shared a smile.

Bliss spread through me, and my stomach fluttered up a storm. This felt right, being beside the both of them.

"What did you want to say?"

Silas placed his hand on my thigh. A tingle spread through my lower belly. It made me think of what happened in the bedroom. My cheeks heated, and a wave of shyness came over me when I remembered I'd practically told them I wanted to do it again, but naked. My core throbbed. I wouldn't have minded doing it again now, only I wasn't sure they knew I hadn't been with anyone before. Was that something I needed to share before anything happened again? God, it would be embarrassing to tell them, but worth it in the end, if it led to us all in bed—

"Sweetheart." Levi's tone was a soft growl as he brushed his nose against the top of my ear.

"Sorry, did I miss something?"

Mary snorted. "Only the fact that you've got two guys horny as hell from your scent."

Sucking in a sharp breath, I covered my burning face with my hands.

Silas's arm curled around me, and he tugged me closer. "Don't fucking embarrass her."

"Shit, sorry, Amara. But don't stress about it. It's normal for unmated couples when they're around each other until they mate. Then again, some mated couples still give off strong scents of—and I think I'll shut up now, since both of them are staring at me like my life is on the line."

Uncovering my face, I took Silas's and Levi's hands. "Sorry, I'll try and keep, um, my thoughts from drifting to certain things."

Levi shook his head. "Don't you dare, sweetheart. I love your scent."

Mary hummed under her breath. I looked at her and found her staring from Kincaid to us and back again. I glanced at Kincaid. He had a death grip on the couch cushions and his jaw was clenched.

Mary tapped her chin. "Usually, a mate who hasn't bonded yet would become very possessive when another alpha is around. Especially when their mate produces the sexy-time scent."

Oh....

Levi threw a hand out. "We trust Kincaid."

Mary hummed under her breath.

Kincaid ran a hand over the back of his neck. "It's time we talk about the maid's job now." He stared across at us. "The best solution, for now, is to pretend she isn't anyone's mate."

"Why?" Silas demanded roughly.

"Think about it. With everything going on, with the threats to our lives, it would be better she's not connected to... anyone other than being a servant. It's safer she stays a maid. If someone finds out she's more important, she'll become a target. They'll use her to get to you."

"Isn't that a risk no matter when people find out? Even if I'm a mate, I'll still have the same job. I'll still be your servant. It's not like being a mate gives me a free pass from working."

The room quieted.

"Right?" I asked.

Levi cleared his throat. "Mates are cherished. If it came out you were ours, then things would certainly change. You would be expected to live on one of our family estates and be guarded to make sure nothing did happen to you. You wouldn't work as Kincaid's servant any longer. Even the Prince family respects mate pairings and wouldn't argue with you moving on from your position."

Irritation had me blurting, "I would be expected to be kept safe and hidden like a good little wife? What, am I to cook and clean and make sure the house is perfect for when you lot come home after work? Next you'll be telling me I'm not allowed to fight alongside you if anything were to happen."

"Well," Silas drew out.

Bouncing up from the couch, I spun toward them with my hands on my hips. "No. Don't even try to keep me from protecting any of you when I have proven I can help in a fight. I will not sit back *knitting* when trouble comes."

"What about crosswords as a hobby instead?" It surprised me that the suggestion came from Kincaid.

Glaring at him, I huffed and shook my head. "I'll stay as Kincaid's maid, but don't expect me to just roll over and play nice when it comes to all that other stuff. I am not a kept housewife. I'm a fighter." The certainty of my words took me by surprise and caught my breath.

Kincaid rolled his eyes. "You're overreacting."

I turned my narrowed gaze at him, frustration tangling my tongue when I said, "I... I... I'm going to kick you in the balls—"

"Sweetheart." Levi stood and crowded me. His hands dropped to my shoulders, and he ran his hands up and down my arms. "I do love seeing you threatening Kincaid, but how about we take a breath? Silas and I may *try* to get you to sit fights out, if one happens, but we would never stop you from doing anything you want."

Nodding, I drew in some deep breaths. The annoyance cooled within me, and I realized why I had gotten so worked up. I wasn't some weak kitten they needed to defend. I was strong, and I wanted to be a mate who stood by them through all the tough times. It wasn't like they'd listen to me if I asked them to stay out of a fight, so they better not expect it from me either.

"We're equals," I uttered, determination turning my words to steel. Accepting my men as mates may have sent me into a tailspin, but newfound resolution settled into my soul.

I needed to protect them.

While I'd been seen as nothing but a servant, it was time for them to understand I was strong. I'd have their backs and would do everything I could to protect and hold this newfound happiness they'd given me. "If this is to work, you have to accept that I'm not one to stand by and watch if the people I care for are in trouble. I'll stand beside them and help."

My words rang true. I would do anything for them, and they needed to see me as someone who wasn't to be coddled, but who had the strength to join them.

Kincaid growled and shoved Levi out of the way before standing in front of me. "You're human; at least that's what we think. In order to protect you, you will do as you're told. If we say you don't run into trouble, you don't."

"Oh shit," I heard Mary say.

Fury flared as I lifted my knee and hit him right in the balls like I said I would. He coughed, gasped, and grabbed his crotch.

"You'll no longer lord over me. We're equals." As soon as the words were between us, regret slammed into me, and tension formed low in my stomach. Kincaid wouldn't understand until he knew the power I had backing my words.

Kincaid snarled in my face before he stalked to his room and slammed the door. The room fell silent.

"I don't think I've ever seen a woman knee him in the balls." Levi grinned.

Silas snorted. "Remind me, princess, to never piss you off."

Huffing, I bit my bottom lip and glanced back at Kincaid's bedroom. Levi cupped the back of my neck, bringing my attention to him. "Don't worry. You did the right thing. He needs people to stand up to him."

"Sorry. I just get so frustrated when you're all willing to throw yourselves into danger and don't expect me to do the same."

"Preach it, sister." Mary fist pumped the air. "Though, I'm okay with hiding." She nodded.

Silas groaned. "Mary, did you catch Cassar outside to—"

"No." She blushed. "Why would I? It's not like we hang out all the time."

Levi and I shared a smile. "Someone is protesting a little too much."

Mary rolled her eyes, snorted, and picked up her bag, which I hadn't seen her enter with, before plopping herself down on the couch. She opened her bag and pulled out an iPad. "Right, let's get down to business."

Actually, girl time sounded good, then I could question Mary about Cassar. I knew I had seen interest from both sides. Levi took my hand and led me back to the couch. I sat back down between the two guys and cuddled in. Mary gave me a soft smile, which I offered back.

It was good to feel happy.

Eighteen

AMARA

ANGER PULSED through my veins as I paced Kincaid's suite the following Wednesday at the Prince estate. They'd locked me in since Kincaid didn't want me at "practice" with his father in case I tried to intervene. Silas and Levi had agreed because they hated to see me struggle through watching Kincaid getting his butt kicked to satisfy his sick and twisted father.

They'd been gone an hour. Surely they'd come back soon, and when they did, I would give them a piece of my mind. At least now I was comfortable enough to tell them they were goddamn fools for locking me in. They could've let me watch, since for the last week, I'd been the good little actress at college by playing Kincaid's servant. No one had even seen when Silas and Levi snuck kisses or touches when they could. They also slept in my bed every night since they'd moved me up onto their floor, not wanting to risk other

229

servants trying to persuade me to kill Kincaid. Of course, my shifters didn't listen to me when I said that it could be a good idea for me to play undercover agent with the servants.

Nothing untoward had happened since we'd stopped the previous headmaster. It made me think maybe he was the only one behind it all, but although their employees were turning up no new evidence, which clearly frustrated all of them, the guys were still certain there was someone else leading the sabotage.

But, if that was the case, wouldn't it have been more important for me to stay with the servants so I could see what happened? However, when I'd suggested that, it'd been a no from all of them, even Kincaid.

They were pigheaded, annoying, and stubborn, but eventually, I'd get them to see I was always right. I snorted to myself and shook my head. I wasn't *always* right, just close to it. With time they'd see I didn't need to be hidden away and protected.

Though, once they realized the power I had, I could lose them.

My stomach plummeted down to my feet, and I stopped pacing to press my hands against my belly. Every time I thought about how they would react, tension coiled inside me. My darkness wasn't a simple or small thing that I'd kept from them.

I was still confused about continuing not to say anything. I just wished I could be sure if everything would be okay if I told them my secret. However, if I did, there was a high risk of Kincaid never accepting me and even Silas and Levi rejecting me.

All of it was a catch-22, really. If any of them found out, it was likely they would reject our bond.

The thought of losing them crippled me to the point that it felt like my lungs stopped working and I couldn't breathe. I rubbed at my chest and sucked in some deep breaths.

And even though Kincaid frustrated me, and I wanted to kick him most of the time, I still felt that need. That want for him. It was like he was missing even though he wasn't far away.

Groaning, I went over to the table and picked up some hair ties. Maybe I did need a hobby to quiet my confused and troublesome thoughts.

The door unlocked, and I marched toward it when it swung open to reveal Kincaid surrounded by my shifters and gripping his ribs.

Stilling, I pressed my fingers to my lips. "What happened?" He looked worse than last time.

Silas thinned his lips for a moment. "There were more guards this time." They guided Kincaid over to his bedroom. I raced ahead to open the door. Gently, they helped him sit on the edge of the bed.

A phone rang. Levi answered it and walked back out into the living room.

"Do you need a donor?" I asked. "I can call for one."

He shook his head. "I'll take a shower."

"Kincaid, you probably have internal damage."

"And it'll heal with time."

Throwing my hands up, I growled under my breath. "While you wait, you'll be in unnecessary pain."

He scowled, leaning back on the one hand and holding his side with the other. "It'll be fine."

"I have a feeling you need to protect your balls." Silas smirked.

Kincaid snorted but stopped to groan. "It's already feeling better."

"You stubborn—"

"Silas, there's a breach," Levi announced as he came back into the room. "We have to go. You two stay inside, and I'll send Cassar up when I can."

Taking a step toward Levi, I said, "Let me come."

His brows dipped, but he managed a smile. "Stay, sweetheart. Kincaid will need help."

"I don't need any damn help." His tone was harsh and snappish, but then he glanced at me, and added more softly, "But she can stay."

I bit my bottom lip as conflict filled me and tightened my throat. Kincaid did need me, but Silas and Levi were walking into trouble.

Silas stepped close, cupped the back of my head, and kissed my temple. "Stay, princess. We'll be safe and back soon."

Gripping his tee in both hands, I looked up at him. "You better be safe, or I'll hurt you."

He grinned and planted another kiss on me before walking to the door. I followed and wrapped my arms around Levi. "Please, no matter what's going on out there, you come back here if it's too much."

My dinner threatened to come up from the worry twisting inside me.

Our lips met in a quick, hard kiss. "*You* be safe, and scold Kincaid up if he doesn't listen."

"I will." I watched them until they disappeared out of the suite. My hands shook as I raced to the window to peer outside. Only there wasn't anything to see. I wished they'd told me what type of breach it had been.

"They'll be fine."

Turning, I nodded. "Right then. You go shower, and I'll organize a donor." I started toward the phone on his bedside table, but I paused. Kincaid hadn't moved. "Do you need help with the shower?"

"No," he clipped and stood. I noticed his wince, though. At the door to the bathroom, he stopped. "Don't call for a donor."

"Why?" Was he being just stubborn?

Even from his side profile, I caught his jaw clench. "Because I can't drink from them."

I jerked my head back in shock. "Why?" My tone was higher than necessary. I moved closer, trying to see more of his face, but he turned it toward the bathroom.

He growled under his breath. "Because it seems my body only wants my mate's blood."

Oh.

Ohhhh....

Ah, where did I go with that information? If I offered up my blood, he would reject it like he had before, and I didn't like the thought of hearing him say no again.

Suddenly, he spun around, head cocked to the side.

"Kincaid?"

"Silence," he snarled quickly.

I'd taken some steps toward him but froze at his word.

I waited, staring at his scowl, and listened. I heard nothing out of the ordinary.

"Fuck," Kincaid bit out before he flashed toward me, picked me up, and threw me onto the bed. I bounced and backed up to hit the headboard.

"Kincaid?"

Glass shattered as the door smashed open, and figures dressed in black from head to toe appeared. Some floated in from the window, while others stormed into the room from the living room.

More and more kept coming.

"Surrender to us and no one will get hurt." A man raised a gun and pointed it at me.

Kincaid snarled at him.

"Surrender now," the same man said.

Kincaid glanced over his shoulder at me. He mouthed, "Run," before he turned back and forced a dark, humorless laugh. "Do you know what I find funny?"

"I'm sure you'll tell us." I didn't recognize the man's voice, but it didn't mean it wasn't someone Kincaid knew. The others around us moved, and some of them held flaming fireballs, while others held water. One had a crossbow. Several had their claws out.

There were too many.

Kincaid was still healing, so he didn't have all his strength.

We were screwed.

They'd take Kincaid away, or worse, kill him.

"That you think you'll get away with this." Kincaid straightened, unleashing his own claws.

The man snorted. "What's also funny is that you

didn't think this wasn't planned for when you were at your weakest."

Someone from inside these walls told them about his training days. Possibly one of the guards Kincaid had bested.

"Now, this is your last chance to surrender," the same man added.

Kincaid's body tensed, and I knew he was about to throw himself into the fight.

A gun fired.

Pain bloomed in my shoulder as I cried out. Kincaid hissed and turned to me.

"Kincaid, no," I tried, but his eyes bled to red, and his fangs lengthened longer than I had ever seen them.

While we were strong, we were outnumbered. I wasn't stupid enough to believe we could get through this. Without help, we wouldn't.

"Kincaid." His eyes met mine, and they changed back to normal. I sucked in a shuddering breath when I saw the sadness there.

He knew as well.

We would lose each other.

Levi and Silas would lose us.

Shaking my head, I jutted my chin up and stood from the bed, ignoring the pain radiating in my shoulder.

"Don't move," the man shouted, but I didn't listen.

I made my way to Kincaid's side and cupped his cheek. "I'm sorry." My bottom lip trembled.

What I didn't say was that I was sorry this would be the last time I would see them.

I was sorry it had come to this.

I was sorry the happiness we could have had would end on this night.

"Amara," Kincaid whispered.

My eyes closed for a brief moment to cherish the way my name sounded from his lips without the title in front of it. Like I was his. Opening them, I dropped my hand and faced the others.

"You don't know me. You don't know what *I'm* capable of. *Please*, for your sake, tell us who's in charge and then leave so you'll live another day."

Some started laughing, even the man who shot me, before he said, "You've got some balls, servant. I know who you are. I know you're nothing. But to them, you're something. I've seen it in the way they look at you."

"Then you know I'll also do everything I can to keep them safe."

He waved his other hand around. "Look around you, girly. You're outnumbered."

Laughter continued.

We *were* outnumbered.

However, we wouldn't be if I let my darkness free. It was already pushing against its restraints.

Sadness twisted through me at the knowledge that they wouldn't back down, no matter what I said.

"Are *you* the one in charge?" I asked. I needed to know if someone else was backing them from the shadows before I took control.

The man snorted. "We're just some of many who seek to do what our master asks us."

That was all I needed to know.

"Amara." Kincaid took my hand, but I shook his hold

off and took a step back before I dropped my head, chin to my chest.

Closing my eyes, I begged, "Please, don't do this."

"I've had enough of this shit. Take Kincaid and kill her—"

It was my turn to laugh, which caused them all to halt and stare at me. I could *feel* their gazes, *sense* their apprehension. Some were even smart enough to back up at the little trickle of power I let free.

"You've made a mistake coming here tonight. Your last mistake."

I unlocked the cage surrounding my darkness and set it free.

My back arched.

My head shot back as the darkness soared out of me— through my fingertips, my eyes, and my mouth. It attacked, it killed, and it soaked up the fear and turned it into more power.

Screams started. So many.

Drawing out my daggers, I threw myself into the fight, knowing my darkness wouldn't get to all of them in time.

Most. But not all.

A cry of pain at my back had me turning to see Kincaid fighting. He snapped the neck of an enchanter and met my gaze. His eyes were wide and wild at seeing my true self for the first time.

And I knew what he would see. Mr. Langley had shown me.

Midnight eyes, sharp black teeth, and raven veins that ran over both sides of my face and down my arms.

I turned away before I saw Kincaid's disgust and flew

at an enchanter who was trying to get to the window that my darkness had blocked. I ran my blades through their back, and as they fell to the floor, I moved onto the next.

Happiness pulsed from my darkness. As if I witnessed it from a third eye, I watched how and who it killed. How it protected Kincaid from someone sneaking up on him.

Kill. Kill. Protect.

Kill everything.

Until there were no more left alive.

Panting, I turned around and around. Now standing in the living room, I peered at the ground that was littered with bodies. Noise at the doorway to the bedroom had me lifting my dagger, ready to throw.

Kincaid appeared. Bloodier than before, also panting.

He stepped toward me but stopped when I backed up and called my darkness to me. It didn't want to retreat. It liked being out and killing. Worse, it wanted to rub all over Kincaid as if it were a cat.

In fact, as my power swept by him, it twisted around his body. Over his face, his neck, shoulders, chest, legs, and he let out a surprised grunt when it slipped between his legs, running over his groin before it swept across the bloody floor and back inside me.

A roar sounded from outside. I gasped as the living room window broke and the nose of a dragon appeared. Tension rolled off me. There was only one dragon who would want to be close. It huffed, which quickly turned into a chuffing sound right as a lion appeared in the broken living room doorway. The lion stopped and looked around before slicing through a body with its claws and a snarl.

In the next blink, a naked Levi stood where the lion had been.

If I wasn't full of fear from head to toe, I would have appreciated the view. He started to move toward me, but I held my hands up, shaking my head.

"Amara, sweetheart, what happened to your shoulder?"

Sorrow stabbed me in the chest. He was worried about *me*. I didn't deserve him. Any of them.

"She was shot." Kincaid ignored my glare. "But am I right to say it's healed?"

He was. My darkness had fixed it even before I pushed my power toward the wound to heal it. Just like my hand when I'd killed Charlotte with the throwing knife.

Nodding, I pushed the tattered maid outfit aside and showed them.

Levi glanced back and forth between us a few times. "What's going on?"

Tears clouded my eyes.

The darkness would always be a part of me, and if anyone escaped these rooms with the knowledge of what I could do, I would be hunted and used. I also didn't know what Kincaid would do with me, and that had my stomach clenching.

My mates were my light. My happiness. A guide through the darkness.

But I should have realized that within the darkness, there wasn't supposed to be a light.

"I'm sorry," I whispered.

Levi chuckled, only it was a hesitant one. "Sorry? What for?"

My bottom lip trembled as I looked from Silas to him. "I've never been happier than I have this last week."

His brows dipped and panic crossed through his eyes. "Amara, what are you talking about? We can still be happy." He shifted his gaze to his friend. "Kincaid?"

Kincaid groaned. "Whatever you're thinking, Amara, don't."

I bit my bottom lip, as it wouldn't quit trembling. Wiping tears away with the back of my hand, I shook my head. He'd used my name again.

"All of you deserve better."

Kincaid growled under his breath. "You're scared. It's fine to be scared."

"What the fuck is going on?" Levi yelled, and Silas roared outside.

"What are you thinking?" Kincaid demanded. "Leaving? After what happened? Don't you think questions will be asked?"

"That's what I'm afraid of."

"You have nothing to fear," Kincaid snarled. He was trying to get his point across, but I couldn't believe what he was saying when all I heard from Mr. Langley was that I would be used.

Levi snapped, "Kincaid—"

"No." Kincaid shook his head. "You're not running, and that's final."

"Running?" Levi whispered. "Sweetheart, why would you think of running?"

Silas roared again, and it nearly broke my heart at how mournful it sounded.

Tears fell as I met Levi's unsettled gaze. "Because you

all deserve better. I'll only ever be a problem."

"A problem? Christ, Amara, you took out most of these." Kincaid flung a hand around before he pointed at Levi. "Are you just going to leave your mates unprotected?"

I would never. "I-I'll keep an eye out."

Levi took another step my way, and I backed up again, which had him frowning. "Sweetheart, please tell me what this is about. We can fix it."

Smiling sadly, I shook my head. "It can't be fixed."

My darkness glided out of me at my call, and I caught the shock on Levi's face. He took it all in as I surrounded my lower half with my power. It wanted to reach out to Levi and Silas like it had Kincaid and sulked when I wouldn't give it free rein.

"Amara, don't," Kincaid warned.

"I really am sorry. I'll cherish the days we had forever."

Silas's roar rang out into the night, and just as Levi and Kincaid started for me, I swept my darkness over my body and stepped through it.

I dropped to my knees on the cold wooden floor in Mr. Langley's deserted, run-down cottage. A sob caught. I gasped and cried as pain sliced at my chest. Anguish choked me and had me shaking as I fell onto my side and curled up in a ball.

They were better without me. Without my darkness destroying their lives. They would try to protect me when others came for me once they'd learned the truth of me having this ability.

I couldn't risk them.

Not my only light within the darkness.

Nineteen

AMARA

As I LAY on the floor, I allowed the anguish to burn and twist inside me for leaving them. My darkness surrounded me, even petted my back as my voice cracked, my soul bled, and my heart tore.

I had a chance at happiness, and it was gone because I feared too many things.

Feared I would be used.

That I would be hunted.

Worst of all, that if knowledge of my power leaked, my mates would be caught up in any danger I would bring into their world.

My darkness prodded me in the side.

"Sweetheart?"

A broken noise dropped from my lips before my eyes widened and I got to my knees, wiping at my face, trying to see through the darkness.

Had I heard wrong?

I reached for my power and called the darkness back into me within the dim room. It reluctantly swirled around two forms before floating to me.

Levi's lips curled into a smile when he stalked toward me and dropped to his knees, pulling me onto his lap.

"W-What...?" A mewed sound caught in my throat. "I-I left you."

"Which was a stupid idea." Kincaid's rough tone had me snapping my eyes over to where he stood.

"How?" Even my voice sounded wrecked, and fresh tears filled my eyes. How was I supposed to push them away again? The first time had wrecked me enough.

"Whatever your power is snapped out and dragged us with you," Kincaid explained as he crossed his arms over his chest and scowled down at me. "If Silas wasn't in dragon form, I'm sure it would have taken him as well."

Why would the darkness have done that?

"Your, ah, power seems to like us." Levi kissed my shoulder. "I've never been caressed so much from, ah, smoke?"

My face heated. I wiped away more tears as I snorted.

My darkness had a mind of its own. When it had first manifested, it had waved at me before chasing butterflies until I called it back. It still had a compulsion to kill and torment—not that it had ever acted on it before—but there was another side to it.

A side where it liked my mates.

A side where it understood my feelings and acted on its own without me controlling it. Did that mean it would kill without me as well?

Fear thickened my throat until the darkness brushed reassuringly within me. Really, that had been a foolish thought; it wasn't like I couldn't trust it. It had never acted violently on its own before. Not until protecting or connecting with my mates.

Was it protecting me from heartache?

Shaking my head, I admitted, "I don't know what to say." My bottom lip trembled. "But I'm still certain you'd all be better off without me."

"Sweetheart, please don't say that." Levi tucked my hair behind my ear. "You having this power doesn't change how we feel about you."

Thinning my lips, I dropped my gaze to my lap. "Mr. Langley warned me not to show anyone what I could do for fear that I'd be used or experimented on. But there's also the fact that the darkness could bring danger to your doorstep."

Levi hummed under his breath. "Don't you think that even without you there, danger would be in our lives anyway because of our roles? Hell, it already is."

That was true, but I would just add to it.

More tears threatened, and I wanted to kick myself for being weak, but I couldn't bottle these emotions even if I tried. They were important because they had to do with protecting Levi, Silas, and even Kincaid.

"I don't know what having this darkness inside of me means for everyone. What happens if—"

Kincaid groaned. "You're annoying me."

Grinding my teeth together, I glared up at him. "I can't be unfeeling like you. It wrecked me to make the choice to leave. It broke me leaving... you all, but I did it because it was the best decision for *your* future."

"Bullshit," Kincaid clipped.

"Kincaid," Levi growled, his arms tensing around me.

Kincaid waved a hand in front of him. "I'm not saying your thoughts are wrong. But take a damn breath after a battle and consider everything before making snap decisions for *all of us*." His hard tone boomed around the room. Running a hand through his hair, he shook his head and sighed. "Did you think about what your mates would be like without you? Their pain? You didn't think we would take on anything to keep you at our side? Or what about other battles that they would face without you? No, you thought of no one and nothing but your own choices."

Stunned, I gaped at him.

He wasn't wrong. I didn't take their reactions into account. I still couldn't stop thinking they'd be safer without me, though. While it was true that we hadn't completed the bond, how would they have reacted to losing me?

Levi pressed his lips to my neck, and he whispered, "Losing you would have been like taking away a part of myself that I needed to keep living."

Tears welled. My heart ached. "I'm sorry."

His fingers tangled through my hair. "We'll figure everything out together."

"There's nothing else you're keeping from us?" Kincaid's brow rose in a patronizing way.

"Isn't having a power that can kill enough?"

He rolled his eyes. "It's nothing to be ashamed of."

"I'm not ashamed."

Kincaid's gaze narrowed. "Then you must have hidden it because of a man who was paranoid over everything."

When I pushed to my feet, Levi grunted, but I was too busy getting in Kincaid's face. "Mr. Langley was the nicest man I've ever known. He was also a part of the paranormal community, so why wouldn't I take his word for what it was when I saw the fear in his eyes after he found me using my power?"

Kincaid's upper lip rose, fangs showing. "Did you ever consider that his fear was over his own feelings for you? He would have seen you as his daughter, and he would have protected you in such ways as well. Do you think he would want his daughter to fight? To go against alphas like us? No, he wouldn't have. He would have drilled the same fear he felt for you into your own mind, which is why you hid your power all this time. You're not human, Amara. It's time you start acting like one of us, since your power makes you a high-ranking alpha."

Stunned once more, I took a step back, my mind awhirl with thoughts. Could he be right? Mr. Langley had always treated me with kindness. He'd given me so much and taught me well.

He *would* have been scared for me.

How stupid had I been for not seeing it.

Kincaid sighed. "It's not your fault. You wouldn't have guessed his motive. He was all you've known. He was someone you trusted even over the family you had left. But now, it's time to think clearly and to take *all* matters around you into account."

Gripping my dress, I glared at him. "I really hate it when you make sense."

An abrupt laugh escaped him before he covered it with a scowl. "Get used to it."

Snorting, I turned my back on him and found Levi standing close. His smile warmed my chilled body. It didn't go unnoticed that he was still naked. Also, Kincaid and I were still bloodied from the fight.

Levi reached for me. "Will you take us back to the estate?"

The only thing on my mind was that I needed time to figure out what the right thing to do was, but I guessed I could do that back home with my mates.

Moving to him, I took his hand and nodded. "Yes, of course. Besides, Silas is probably going crazy right now." Guilt gripped my chest that I'd reacted so quickly, racing to escape without a thought to the consequences.

Levi grinned. "He will be." He brought me into his body, his arms circling me. The calmness of being close to him, knowing I wasn't going to lose him, had me drawing in a shuddering breath.

A flutter of nerves twisted my insides at the realization that I was once again about to reveal my other form. Glancing down at Levi's chest, I scraped my top teeth over my bottom lip.

"What's wrong?" Levi asked softly, kissing my temple.

Stupid insecurities. That was all they were. Both Kincaid and Levi had seen me already and had accepted how I'd looked. I was worried for nothing.

Shaking my head, I lifted my gaze to his and smiled. "Nothing."

"Can we move already?" Kincaid clipped from behind me.

His snappy tone had me wanting to bark back, but I didn't. All of us had been nothing but stressed these last few hours.

Inhaling, I called my darkness.

Nothing happened.

"Amara?" Levi inquired, feeling me tense.

"I-It won't come out."

"Why?" Kincaid demanded.

"If I knew, I'd tell you," I snapped back, and then drew in a steady breath. I tried again. It slithered out from me, where I felt the change alter my features. But it didn't take us back. Instead, it curled around Levi and me and squished us together. My face heated.

Levi chuckled. "I mean, I don't mind this even a little, but is it trying to tell us something?"

"It wants her linked to someone before we go back," Kincaid said.

"Linked?" I asked.

It was the first time I saw Kincaid's cheeks heat a little. He looked at the wall for a moment before glaring over at me. "Bonded. As in, to complete the bond with a sexual act and exchange of blood."

My body heated.

"Oh" was all I managed to say as my darkness swirled around Kincaid, ruffling his hair before gliding over to me and going inside my body. My features morphed back. Apparently, my darkness was excited that he understood.

But then I remembered Kincaid and his thirst. Everything that had happened had been in such a short amount of time that I'd forgotten it had all been after Kincaid's lesson. Even now I could see the tightness around his eyes and the way he held his body stiff.

Levi nudged his nose against my cheek gently. My gaze shot back to him, and my body warmed even more. He was still naked, and pressed against me.

"Levi," I whispered.

"Sweetheart," he murmured against my lips before placing a chaste kiss there. His lips trailed toward my ear, where he said, "He hungers, Amara."

Swallowing, I made a noise in the back of my throat.

"He needs your blood. You know this."

I did.

"I can hear you," Kincaid complained roughly. "Send *me* back."

Turning in Levi's arms, I rested against his chest while he wrapped his arms around my waist and we both looked at Kincaid.

"Why?" I asked.

He ground his teeth together.

Drawing in a steady breath, I said, "Before everything happened, you told me you couldn't drink from anyone but your mate."

His gaze darkened. "And?"

"Meaning me?" *Just admit it, please.*

He glanced to the side again, his jaw clenching over and over.

He couldn't or didn't want to admit I was his mate. Would he ever? And then, if he did, would it be because I was his blood supply, since a part of him now refused others?

Sadness gripped my heart.

He didn't really want me.

He just needed my blood.

Clearing my emotion-filled throat, I asked quietly, "Would you be able to feed off Levi or Silas after I've bonded with them?"

His red filled eyes flashed to me. "You don't want me?"

Anger swarmed me. I straightened from Levi's chest and glared. "I don't know if I want an egotistical asshole who can't even admit I'm his mate. Who doesn't want *me* to begin with. Why would *I* have to admit I want you when *you* can't seem to stand the thought of me as yours." I threw out a hand. "I'm just a lowly maid who's beneath—"

"Enough," he roared, stepping closer.

"No!" I shouted. "I've put up with you for weeks, and I want *you* to tell me to my face that you can't stand me. I want *you* to tell me Fate was wrong to put us together and the thought of accepting me makes you sick, but your stupid sexy body won't let you have anyone's blood but mine." I snorted. "And in the end, that's all I'd be to you. Just a blood bag for you to—"

"You're wrong," he snarled.

I laughed humorlessly. "Wrong? Me? You're unbelievable. You—" I snapped my mouth closed and thinned my lips when my bottom lip trembled. I tore my gaze away from him. I didn't want to hurt him any more. It never had been my intention.

"Amara," Levi whispered, his hands rubbing up and down on my waist.

Lifting my arm, I held out my wrist, and softly said, "I'm offering you my blood as a peace offering. I understand you don't want me, but you need my blood, and...." I dropped my arm because of another thought. Closing my eyes, I tucked my chin down and opened my eyes to the floor. "Unless you're concerned about a bond being formed from drinking mine." I shrugged. "I guess we'll have to figure something else out because I would never force anything on you that you don't want."

And he didn't want me.

He never had.

"How can you want me to drink from you when I've been nothing but cold toward you?"

His gentle question had me snapping my gaze up to his. Though his eyes were hard, I could see the worry in them after they bled back to their normal color.

"You didn't trust me," I pointed out the obvious.

"No."

I shrugged. "I understand why. If I was in the same situation, after dealing with so many who wanted me dead, I would have acted the same way. Detached to save myself from believing someone could be different."

"And yet, when I knew you were different from the rest, I still didn't change."

"I'd still been keeping a secret." *Yet now he knows everything.*

His jaw clenched again. "It was never a question about me not wanting you."

Tensing, I allowed my heart to take that extra needed beat.

"What?" I breathed.

Levi chuckled at my back, his lips pressed to my neck. The tension melted away from his warmth surrounding me. My belly fluttered and nipples pebbled at the reminder of how naked Levi was, especially when he pressed his erection into me. "Hmm, I believe, sweetheart, that Kincaid has always been attracted to you."

I scoffed. "No, he hasn't."

Kincaid scowled. "Now you're going to try and tell me if I'm attracted to you or not."

Levi's hand slid to my stomach, and he pressed me back into him. A need so strong had me wanting to push that hand between my legs.

Instead, I cleared my throat. "Y-Yes." Levi nipped at my shoulder. I wanted him to do it harder. "Um, a-at least you know if I'm..." My whole body flushed. "You know, ah, aroused, because you can smell it. With you, I have no idea."

Levi glided his nose down my neck. "Speaking of arousal." A purr started in his chest, and I pushed my ass back into him, rubbing against his stiffness. "Sweetheart," he growled.

Warmth at my front had me lifting my gaze again, and it widened seeing Kincaid inches away from me.

A mew left my lips when he cupped my cheek and pulled me close. "Your secret is out of the way now," he stated roughly.

Gulping, I whispered, "Yes."

"Do you fear me?"

Hadn't I proved I didn't? "No."

"Do you want me as you do Levi and Silas?"

Licking my suddenly dry lips, I opened my mouth to

answer that I did, even though he annoyed me, but he said more.

"I'm not speaking about a matter of sex." Because he already knew I was attracted to him. I wanted him. "I mean as your mate."

I did. I wanted all three of them. I didn't care that my connection to the three of them was because of the magic from the Fates. It was soul deep, and I couldn't imagine my life without them. I'd done it for a moment, and the pain had taken me to the floor. I didn't want to go through that again.

"Would you want me?" I challenged.

His gaze narrowed. "You're stubborn—"

"Have you looked in the mirror?"

He let out a hiss. "Disrespectful, bossy, but also..." I made a noise in the back of my throat when his eyes transformed from hard to soft, even though his hand slid from my cheek to my neck and tightened when he added, "...the sweetest woman I have ever laid eyes upon. It would be an honor to have you as my mate."

Levi cleared his throat.

"*Our* mate," Kincaid clipped.

"Yes," tumbled out of me. I slid a hand down to cover Levi's at my waist and gripped it.

"Yes what?" Kincaid demanded.

"Yes, I want you the same as I do Levi and Silas."

His hand around my neck convulsed. "You'll want forever with us? You'll want to bed us? Together or alone? You'll want to take me between your legs so I can slide my cock into your tight heat?"

"Jesus," Levi muttered behind me, rutting his dick

against my backside. It seemed I wasn't the only one affected by Kincaid's words.

Panting, I hummed.

"Tell me, Amara," he ordered darkly, dipping closer to suck my bottom lip between his teeth where he nipped enough that I could feel his fangs.

"Please," I managed.

Kincaid licked over my lips as Levi started kissing my neck, drawing my head to the side by his fisted hand in my hair.

"We'll need a bed, Kincaid," Levi said.

My darkness pushed from the inside. I allowed it out, and the men stopped to watch it shoot from the room and down the hall. Next, we all heard the crashes and bangs until the darkness tugged the single bed into the room.

I jumped when the wooden frame landed on all fours. My face burned when my cheeky, yet helpful, power drew into me.

Kincaid was the first to huff in amusement while Levi pulled me back against him, also laughing heartily.

"I do love your power, sweetheart." Levi smirked.

My darkness buzzed inside me.

"Speaking of, do you know where your ability came from?" Kincaid asked. "It's something I've never seen before. I would—"

"No," Levi clipped, pointing over my shoulder at Kincaid. "Fuck no. We are not getting distracted now."

A small laugh escaped me.

Levi waved to the bed. "Sit on the bed, Kincaid. Back to the headboard."

I hid my next laugh behind my hand when Kincaid

scowled at his friend. Even though nerves bubbled inside me, I watched as Kincaid stomped over to the bed and sat where he'd been told.

A yip slipped out of my mouth when Levi spun me and picked me up. There was no choice but to wrap my arms and legs around him. "And you, my sweet angel—I have plans for you."

"Yeah?"

His gaze flashed from amber and back. "Yes," he growled low. He walked us to the bed with his heated gaze on me.

"Wait," Kincaid ordered.

Levi placed me on my feet, and we looked at the door Kincaid was glowering at. A thump sounded outside just as the ground shook.

"Levi," I cried, gripping his wrist as his other arm wound around my waist. I glanced at Kincaid. He rolled his eyes and leaned against the headboard again. Levi snorted behind me.

"What's going on?" I asked. Why weren't they worried?

"It's fine, sweetheart. He—"

The door shattered, exploding inward. Through the rubble and dust, I caught a silhouette of someone.

"Are you fucking kidding me?" Silas roared, stepping into the room in a pair of loose shorts. He crossed his arms over his chest, glaring.

"Silas," I breathed, stunned he was here. How had he found us? "What.... I...."

"You all take off in a fucking blink of an eye, and I

have to fly all over the damn place, scenting, and scenting. I nearly lost a damn bird up my nose."

An abrupt laugh escaped me. I slapped my hand to my mouth when his gaze sliced to me, and it turned into a snort slash cough.

Levi chuckled for a beat, and then said, "I'll catch you up quickly then. Our darling Amara was going to leave us after revealing her secret. After fighting to save all of us once again. At the time, she didn't understand we still wanted her as ours, even after seeing her other form. She didn't know we would protect her and her secrets with our lives. We finally have her understanding, and were about to move on to finalizing the bond between us."

"Levi!" I snapped and pushed his hand away from my waist to step closer to Silas. "You don't have to agree with them. If this isn't something you—" I clamped my lips closed once again when Silas's chest rumbled with a growl as he stalked my way. "Silas?"

He stopped just before me to cup my face and stare down at me with such intensity, my pulse spiked. "You. Are. Ours," his roughened tone bit out.

"Um...." I licked my lips, and his gaze darkened as it followed the movement. My stomach tumbled. "Okay," I whispered.

Silas grunted. "Good." He straightened to look over my shoulder. "What's the plan?"

Twenty

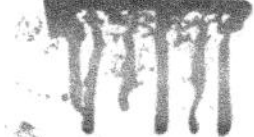

KINCAID

I WATCHED as Levi slowly and wickedly grinned at Amara's third mate. Silas chuckled and shared a quick worried glance with me. I shook my head slightly. His beast was probably telling him I was a threat, but even as the hunger dried out my throat and sent stabbing pains to my stomach, I would continue waiting to feed until she was comfortable.

"Back to me, sweetheart. I need a taste before I tell Silas what I have planned for this beautiful body of yours." Levi drew Amara in for a deep kiss, distracting her.

Silas slipped close and softly, so she wouldn't hear, and asked, "I can feel your hunger. Will it be safe for her first time?"

"Yes," I hissed through clenched teeth. "I can control it when it comes to her."

His hand landed on my shoulder and squeezed. "That I believe."

I nodded once. When my gaze went back to Amara, Levi picked her up, turned, and I spread my legs in time for Levi to lay her between them so her back rested against my chest. Her heart fluttered faster and faster as Levi removed her shoes and socks.

Amara tilted her head to the side and up, concern flashing in her eyes. Was she worried I didn't want her close? She didn't need to be. I'd fought with myself for so long, and now I had the chance to feel her, to cherish her.

Slowly, I traced my thumb over her bottom lip. "You are where you're meant to be," I told her as her chest rose and fell rapidly.

She licked her lips, her tongue touching my thumb, and my digit followed it back into her mouth where she sucked on it. My aching cock throbbed.

"Christ," Silas bit out.

"Sweetheart." Levi caught her attention, and my thumb slipped from her mouth when she turned his way. Her pulse drummed under her skin, calling to me. But I'd ignore it for now. This was about our mate. Levi climbed onto the end of the bed to kneel. "Are you all right if we remove this?" He lifted the edge of her torn and tattered dress.

We all heard her heart skip a beat as a gorgeous blush filled her cheeks, spreading down to her neck. My mouth suddenly watered when my gaze snagged on the beating vein once again, but I was quickly distracted when Amara nodded.

"Good girl," Silas rumbled out.

Levi lifted it up in one hand, and unsheathed his claws on the other. With one finger, he sliced down the front of her dress, causing her to gasp. He pushed the two parts aside. My fangs popped free and dug into my bottom lip as desire gripped my body.

She lay before us in panties and a bra, plus those straps on her thighs where her daggers were attached. My attention caught an edge of something peeking out of her bra. I pinched the edge and tugged it free.

Silas grinned. Levi chuckled, and I said, "Now I know where you hide them."

Her smile up at me had my heart clenching.

I needed her.

I had to have a taste.

I had to.... Fuck, my soul clawed at me to reach out to her.

"Levi," I clipped roughly before I dropped the star to the floor. Amara's eyes widened for a moment from my tone until I gripped her throat and pulled her higher to claim her mouth.

She moaned against me, opening up to me. I controlled the kiss, but I knew, like it was burned into me, that she didn't mind at all. She wanted me. Our tongues danced, our lips moved, and her teeth nipped.

I couldn't risk returning the action, not when my fangs ached to be embedded in her smooth skin.

"Lift, angel," Silas said.

A growl left me. I didn't want to lose her mouth. But it was only her chest that lifted off me for a moment.

Amara surprised me once more when her tongue

traced around a fang. Groaning, I pulled back, breathing heavily.

"Drink," she murmured through her kissed-red lips. She arched, slamming her eyes closed, and moved her head to face forward.

"Fuck," I gritted as her fingers threaded through Levi's hair to hold his head against where it was buried between her legs. She used her other hand to curl over Silas's back while he feasted on her breasts.

They'd been busy while I'd been lost with her mouth. My fangs extended even more—lust, hunger, and the need to claim her making them tingle.

"Kincaid, please," she whispered before she let go of Levi's hair to press the back of her hand to her mouth as she whimpered. Her eyes widened.

Had she never?

"Oh... Levi," she cried. Her legs shook. Her arm tightened around Silas, who trailed his lips over her chest. Her other hand covered her face. "God," she murmured. I took her wrist and moved it away from her flushed face.

Levi lifted his head, grinning. "Delicious, sweetheart."

She made a noise and slapped at his shoulder. She tried to roll away, until Silas caught her and lifted enough to tell me, "Close your legs under her." He rested her ass down on my upper thighs. The move brought her neck closer to my mouth. It also had her perfect ass right near my cock.

Silas hooked a hand under her inner thigh. "Spread them, princess. Levi isn't done."

"W-What?"

Silas dipped in to kiss her. She melted into it, and I wasn't even sure she was aware of Levi assisting Silas in widening her legs. Levi with his knees on either side of my legs, scooted closer.

He mimicked biting and then made a lewd gesture with his hands. I knew what he meant, though. He wanted me to drink when he entered our mate, hoping my feeding would distract her from the pain. Not only from losing her virginity, but because Levi had to bite her. Blood and sex sealed the mate bond.

For a quick beat, I didn't want him to enter her or bite her because of the pain, but he was right. *My* bite would help from the emotions I could send her way. I could help her relax... or become more aroused. If my compulsion worked on her in *this* type of situation. Still, it was worth trying.

Nodding, I watched Levi shift close. He took his cock in one hand and placed the other on the bed beside Silas, who knelt on the floor beside Amara's upper body.

Trailing my fingers down her arm, I dipped my head and looked up at Levi. He slowly edged inside her while I sank my fangs in.

On the first drag, when I sent her desire, she tore her mouth from Silas's and cried out in pleasure. Levi thrust the rest of the way inside her, and a new scent of blood filled the air. Levi ducked his head and latched his sharpened teeth into the top of her breast.

A growl rumbled out of me as I took another sip of her sweet, intoxicating blood. I curled an arm over her stomach, bringing her close while her body rocked against mine with Levi's thrusts as he fucked and marked her. He lifted his head, licking his lips. I saw Silas moving back for Levi to bend and offer Amara his shoulder.

"Bite him, angel," Silas ordered. A shiver raked over all of us when her power shot forward. Her features changed, her teeth lengthening before they dug into Levi's skin.

He shuddered before they stilled for only a beat, letting the bond, the link, lock into place. Next, she was grabbing at all of us as Levi moved over her, in and out of her faster.

I heard her lick over his neck before her teeth shifted and she begged, "Please.... God. More."

My cock leaked in my pants as her ass rubbed up and over it.

"Amara. Sweetheart—fuck, you're beautiful. Stunning. So tight, wet, hot. Jesus. *Mine*." He snarled the last word, possessiveness from the link driving him.

I took one last pull of her blood, feeling better than I ever had. Our link wasn't complete, not until I took her and she bit me. I couldn't wait, though.

I wanted it now.

She was beyond what I had imagined for a mate. Even if she hadn't forgiven me fully—not that I could blame her—she still wanted me in her life. Her soul was the kindest I'd ever felt. I wouldn't be in the position I was in if that wasn't true.

She'd kept me.

Wanted me.

"Levi," she cried, slamming her eyes closed as one hand clutched my arm over her stomach and the other blindly reached out until Silas took it.

"Fuck." Levi's hips stuttered, then sped up as he groaned. The scent of his cum spilled out as he filled her. It was lucky she wasn't at a fertile stage because we hadn't even considered her conceiving before we'd begun. At least we all knew none of us could carry human diseases. Our mate had also been pure.

Levi slowed his thrusts until he completely stopped and moved back. As soon as he was out of the way, Silas picked her up and planted her feet on the floor before turning her to face the bed and pushing her upper body over me where I sat. His shorts were already down when he plunged into her wetness.

She threw her head back and moaned, "Silas."

"Mate," Silas chuffed low, his dragon present. When I went to reach for her, Silas growled.

From where Levi sat with a smug grin and a purr in his chest, he said, "Dragons are more territorial when mating than lions. It's best we don't touch her for their first time."

I grunted and clenched my jaw in annoyance. Although, I could understand the dragon's need, since they were overprotective of their treasures, and their mate was the best fortune to be found.

At least I could still have my eyes on our mate, watch her pleasure, see the way her breasts swayed with each thrust and the way she clawed at the blankets. What spiked my desire even more was her blissed-out look as she took a cock inside her.

She loved it.

"Silas," she whimpered. He ran a hand up her back and reached around her, offering his mate his forearm.

"Bite, mate," he ordered.

Her teeth lengthened once again, and just as she latched on to Silas's arm, he took her shoulder in his mouth. They both groaned when the link slipped into place before she dropped his arm and pushed her ass back against him.

"More," she said softly.

Demanding little thing, and I fucking love it.

Silas chuffed, licking at her shoulder proudly. He straightened, gripped her hips, and thrust back into her. She cried out and then whimpered. Her sweet scent of climax reached my nose before Silas's overpowered it as he emptied into her.

Silas eased out and helped her up, turning her in his arms to rub his face over the top of her head again and again while his dragon chuffed, low and contentedly. With her cheek rested against his chest and her face twisted my way, I saw her gentle smile as she wrapped her arms around his waist.

"Mine."

She tipped her head back. "Yes."

He ran his nose up and down hers.

I unclenched my jaw and was about to tell him her attention was all mine now, but sweet Amara got there first.

She patted Silas's chest and said, "I have another mate to bond with. I promise more of this soon."

Silas's chuffing stopped as he growled. Levi suddenly appeared at Silas's side. "Come on, dragon. You can scent our mate on me. Let's cuddle while we watch the show." He hooked an arm through Silas's and dragged him toward the floor where a blanket had been thrown down. I wasn't even sure when Levi went to get one; I'd been too busy watching her.

With my mate on my mind, I glanced back at where she stood beside the bed, watching me.

I held my hand out to her. "Come here, Amara."

Her skin pebbled with goose bumps as she shivered. I could look at her nakedness all day long and never get bored. I no longer had to lie to myself about my attraction to her.

I had her.

She was about to be mine.

I didn't care what my parents' thought of us being bonded. All that mattered was Amara's happiness. I already knew, even before this day, that I'd do anything for her. Now I didn't need to hide my need to protect her.

The first day she'd arrived in my room, she'd lit something inside me. She was my soul, my light… my everything.

When her hand slid into mine, I gave it a squeeze. "What is it you want right now?"

She licked her lips and squirmed under the weight of my heated gaze as it ran down her body. My dick jerked under my pants. I wanted to bury it between her legs where she was already leaking my friends' cum.

"You," she whispered.

Lifting my eyes, I cocked a brow. "Are you sure?" I still couldn't understand how she could give me this gift of herself after the way I'd treated her. But if she agreed now, I wouldn't stop until she was mine completely.

She nodded once. "I'm sure."

I drew her hand up to my mouth and pressed a kiss against it. "Then I'll do anything to make sure you live your days happy." Leaning forward, I removed my top and then popped the button of my pants, sliding down the zipper. I preened as she glued her gaze to my hand when I reached in and pulled myself free.

My sweet, seductive mate scraped her top teeth over her bottom lip at seeing my hard length. She smirked, and suddenly her power was out enough to morph her features, sharpen her teeth, change her eyes, and bring forth the black veins.

For a moment, I stilled when she said tauntingly, "Are you just going to sit there, vampire?"

Laughter sounded from the corner of the room, but I didn't look there. I shifted to rest my feet on the floor but stayed sitting on the bed. "Are you sure you want to tease me, mate?"

Her head cocked to the side. "I gave my blood freely before, but now you have to fight me for my body."

She smiled wickedly when my eyes changed, my fangs dropped, and claws sprang free.

The dragon growled off to the side somewhere, but I didn't take my attention from my prize. "You challenge me?"

"I do, vampire. Prove you want me. Prove you have the strength to own me. My other mates redeemed themselves way before this point, but you... not so much."

I was more than willing to prove myself, but I reveled in the idea of playing with our mate before fucking her into submission.

Standing, she took a step back.

"Run if you like, mate, but I'll be buried inside you within seconds."

Her smile grew. She turned and ran toward the door.

In a blink, I blocked her exit before she'd even come to a stop. I wrapped my arm around her waist and spun us until her back was to the wall.

"Too easy," I clipped low.

Humor lit her eyes, which should have warned me. In the next second, I was thrown across the room. I landed in a crouch not far from—I did a double take when I saw Levi's hand wrapped around Silas's cock, jerking. Silas glared up at me, but kept Levi gripped tightly to him with his nose buried against Levi's neck where Amara had bitten.

He'd found comfort in Levi because he didn't like Amara and me playing a little roughly. Though, neither of them seemed to mind what was happening between the two of them.

Levi winked and nodded to the other side of the room. "Heads up."

A body smashed into mine, and teeth dug into my neck. I snarled yet lifted her so she wound an arm around my neck, opposite to the side she drank from. I dug my hands into her thighs and lifted so they wrapped around my waist. I shoved my cock inside her while I buried my fangs into her other shoulder, holding her tightly to the wall.

My hips slowed when the link connecting us started to form. It felt as if my chest opened and accepted something new, something foreign inside it. A beat later, it fit, and the rightness that ran through me settled into my bloodstream.

She was mine.

Finally.

I tore my fangs from her and gripped the back of her hair to pull her off me so I could claim her mouth just as she morphed back. Blood dripped between us from our mouths. We tasted each other in a searing kiss of teeth, tongues, and lips.

Her arms wrapped tighter around my shoulders as I thrust harder and deeper into her. Losing control, but knowing, by the power in her blood, that she could take it.

She did, and she moaned her pleasure down my throat while scraping her nails over my back.

She tightened even more around me and ripped her mouth from mine, dropping her head back against the wall.

"Oh God, hell, Kincaid. Please... there."

She was stunning. So fucking beautiful.

Mine.

Someone hissed near us, and even while I still fucked her, we both glanced down to see Silas coming over Levi's hand.

"G-Guys," Amara whimpered, her pussy clenching around me.

"You like seeing that," I stated.

A shaky "Yes" escaped her. Her breaths were short, and her limbs suddenly squeezed around me. My mate was as close as I was.

"Amara." I licked over her lips as she opened her eyes to meet mine. With a nip to her bottom lip, I heard and felt her whimper as she came over my cock, which slid in and out. Her tightness had me spilling over with a groan.

Cupping her jaw, I tipped her chin up to capture her eyes, and the smile she blessed me with clenched my heart.

Mine.

Pressing my lips to hers, I said, "You've made me a very happy man, love. Thank you for the gift of accepting me."

Tears brimmed in her eyes. "Kincaid."

"Our lives begin only now, and I'll prove to you my worth as your mate. You've honored me, Amara."

Her jaw clenched and she sniffed. "I-I don't want to cry after feeling so much from you all."

When I grinned, she sucked in a breath and traced a finger over my lips. "You'll do that more often?"

"Anything for you." And I meant those words. I would redeem my actions and harsh tones.

"Sorry to be the bearer of bad news, but we should get back," Levi said as he stood.

Sighing, I nodded once before I rested my forehead against Amara's. She shivered as I withdrew from her, and the urge to slip back into her warmth once again was strong.

With a final kiss, I went over to where my shirt lay. It was torn and bloodied, but it would work. Turning back, I saw that Levi and Silas had crowded her. Jealousy would never come between us. Silas could get possessive, but he knew we were all hers as well. It would hurt her if he ever got angry enough to injure us. Just like Levi and I knew this to be true; together we were stronger for her.

Amara laughed at something Levi whispered into her ear. She beamed up at him and placed a soft kiss on his chest. "Not only was it hot, but I'm happy you're willing to help, since there's only one of me."

He winked. "There's nothing wrong with a handy or a bj among friends."

Silas snorted. "Shit, I wouldn't say no. Not when watching our mate get pleasure turns me on."

Rolling my eyes, I walked over and helped our mate into my shirt. "I'll let you know *if* I need a hand." The thought of Levi's hands on me didn't concern me. I'd never considered it before, but things could get enthusiastic between us for sure.

My gut suddenly twisted at the thought of leaving here. I sensed things were about to get worse before they got better. But we needed to end whoever was behind the assassination attempts in order to protect our mate. There was also the fact that we'd need to talk about our next moves.

Amara looked at each of us. "Ready?" she asked with a sad smile.

"We'll come back here," Levi offered. "We can make it our own little place of privacy."

"That sounds wonderful, but I'm not sure it'll stay empty for much longer."

Levi and Silas turned to me.

"I own it, love."

She gaped for a moment before she made a noise in the back of her throat. I wasn't sure if she was speechless that I'd bought Wayland's property, or over the endearment I'd used again.

Silas tapped under her chin, all of us amused by her.

"Why?" she asked me.

"I know he meant a great deal to you." It was something I could finally admit to myself too. Knowing she had fond memories here had driven me to buy the place.

Tears welled. "Thank you."

I tipped my chin down and shrugged. A wave of bashfulness washed over me. I'd never felt bashful before in my life.

Amara cleared her throat and glanced down at our bodies. "Um, where should I place us on the property?"

"The guys should have the rooms cleared. So, Kincaid's bedroom," Silas said.

Amara nodded. She seemed hesitant to let her darkness, as she'd called it, out as she bit on her bottom lip.

"We accept you as you are, Amara," I told her. "Never doubt that from us. You are beautiful in both forms."

Her bottom lip trembled. "Maybe you need to go back to being demanding. I'm not sure I can take this side of you." While we laughed, Amara called out her power, and as the darkness caressed me in places I wasn't sure were appropriate, we disappeared in a blink.

AMARA

HESITATION TIGHTENED MY SHOULDERS. Someone could be waiting in Kincaid's room. Someone could see me.

Thankfully, when I called my darkness in, and it reluctantly withdrew after rubbing its scent over the guys, we saw that the room was cleared and cleaned. Levi moved first, quickly stealing some of Kincaid's boxers for himself and Silas while I glanced around in shock.

"Who would have done all this?" The room should have been in ruins.

Silas curled an arm around me and drew me in. His touch and the gesture were normal, natural.

"Before I left, I told the team to clean and spread the word we were off investigating the situation."

Smiling, I slid my hands to his chest. "Smart," I told him, and he chuffed low.

His body vibrated with it, and I blinked at my hands on his smooth skin.

It all dawned on me then.

I loved that I could touch all three of them freely, and they wanted it. Welcomed it.

All *three* of them.

They were mine. My mates. My husbands. My future.

Never would I have ever pictured myself in this situation, and yet, here I was in Kincaid's room, without any secrets between us and bonded to them.

Bonded. Me. The servant with three alphas. It was still mind-boggling.

New tears welled as euphoria filled me. Glancing up, I brushed some hair from my eyes before I said, "This is real."

Silas grunted. "Yes. We're all bonded. Even the stubborn dick over there." He nodded toward Kincaid who snorted.

Smiling, I told Silas, "There were always barriers between us all. I also remember someone else being stubborn."

"Not me," Levi pointed out.

Laughing lightly, I curled my lips in a warm smile. "No."

Silas tucked his nose behind my ear and drew in a breath. "I'll regret—"

My grip on his arm tightened, silencing him. He pulled back, and I said, "We don't need to go back. We don't need to remember. We're where we are meant to be. Together."

He grunted with a nod. "We are."

Suddenly, the door burst open. Silas spun me and held me close to his back. I didn't see who entered from where I was hidden by my shifters and vampire. A low rumble dropped from Levi, a deep growl from Silas, and a sharp snarl from Kincaid.

"Where have you all been?" I recognized Mary's voice straightaway. "Whoa, what's going on?"

Silas growled again, until I pinched his side. He let out a yelp and jumped. I shoved myself between Silas and Kincaid. I scowled up at them. "It's just Mary."

Only, when I glanced over with a smile, it died, because it wasn't just Mary, who stared gaping at us. Cassar and two other men also stood just inside the doorway.

"Did she just pinch Silas?" one of the men I didn't know muttered. The other stranger nodded.

A new growl rumbled out of Silas.

"What's she wearing?" the first asked.

"Is that Kincaid's?" the second asked, and then I had a blanket wrapped around me, and I was being ushered away.

I tried to fight the material, but whoever held it was strong. When I heard a door click shut, the blanket dropped, and I glared up at Levi as we stood in the en suite.

His hands landed on my shoulders. "Believe me when I say this, that was for your own good."

"M-My own good?"

He nodded and stared at me with a serious face. "If I didn't get you away from them, they would be dead. Not that I care, but you would've been upset."

"What?" I breathed.

"Amara, sweetheart. The way they were looking at you —" A growl dropped from his lips as he turned enough to scowl at the door, but then shook his head. "—we could tell they liked what they saw." Another growl rumbled out of him just as there was a smash out in the room. "If you were there longer, they would have scented you were claimed, and maybe pissed themselves in fear once they caught all of our scents over you...." He glanced back to the door in thought. "Maybe we should test that theory."

When he reached for me, I swatted at his hands. Thankfully, there was a light tap on the door. Levi's chest vibrated as he spun to face it, backing me into a corner.

"It's Mary. I have clothes."

Why were they acting this way?

I poked Levi in the side. "It's only Mary."

Levi took a deep breath and nodded before he went to collect the clothes by opening the door a crack and shutting it again.

"Hey," Mary yelled.

Crossing my arms over my chest, I gave Levi a questioning look. At least he winced and shot me an apologetic smile. "I've heard that for a couple of days after bonding, the male mates can be a little dramatic when other men are near."

Gasping, I shook my head. "A couple of days?"

"Yes." He nodded and, after placing a new maid's outfit on the sink, he started unbuttoning the shirt. I went to take over, but he gently slapped *my* hands away. Then he froze for a beat before he met my gaze. "We're also attentive and will want to do many things for you." He licked his lips and blew out a breath. "I've heard of that a few times, but most mates who have bonded are locked away for at least a week, enjoying the new connection. Which also gives time for the fiercer needs to settle."

"Will they settle?" I asked.

"Somewhat." He glanced to the side in thought. "Though, my father did kill a man when he flirted with Mother and wouldn't listen to her telling him she wasn't interested. I've also heard Mother yell at Father for not letting her do certain things."

What was in store for me with all three of them?

Oh shit.

Three.

Not *one*. I had *three* mates to deal with when it came to possessiveness and fawning.

"What about the women? Will I get crazy when other women are around? Well, crazier, since I was about ready to kill those other—" My darkness shot out of me at the thought of those vampire women wanting Kincaid. Were Levi and Silas constantly hit on or being set up at their estates? Did they have women throwing themselves at them?

I snaked my darkness around Levi and drew him close.

"Are there women waiting for you at your estate?"

The only part of him showing from beneath my darkness was his head. When his lips twitched, I narrowed my gaze on them until he opened his mouth and said, "No, sweetheart. There isn't, and my family won't arrange someone for me. Neither will Silas's. They might suggest—"

My lips pulled back in a silent snarl and my teeth lengthened.

"But they won't force us, and if push came to shove with Kincaid's parents, he *will* tell them to back off. He's only placating them for now. He'd never have chosen someone they'd suggested, even before he discovered you were his fated mate."

The change swept away when I called the darkness back inside me. Hell, this was going to be a yo-yo game with the way my darkness was zipping in and out of me. Levi wrapped his arms around my waist, pulling me close.

"How was I so calm with you all around Mary, and yet at the thought of... those others, I want to kill them?"

He shrugged. "Maybe because you already know Mary. Know that she's only our friend and employee. Or your subconscious sees the attraction between Mary and Cassar, so you're not worried."

Groaning, I dropped my forehead against his chest. "How will we deal with this? We can't hide away for a week."

His hand slid up my back and cupped my neck. "I wish we could, but you're right. We'll have to talk to the others about it."

I lifted my head, searching his face. "Maybe my darkness was wrong to complete the bond so soon."

"No," he stated quickly. "The bond that connects us will make us stronger for the storm that's still brewing. We're now linked, so we'll know if any of us are in danger and where to find each other."

With my worry suddenly drifting away, warmth filled

me at the realization that I could go to them when they needed me.

"Okay," I whispered, tipping my head back just before his lips met mine in a hard, needy kiss. His hands gripped my butt, and I jumped a little to lock my legs around his waist as he took us a step back to lean me up against the wall. His erection pressed against me in the best way and nearly had me clawing at his back and shoulders, wanting him closer, yet I knew he was as close as he could be.

Did we have time for him to fill me? The only barrier between us was Kincaid's shirt and his boxers.

I broke the kiss and panted. "Levi, please."

He groaned, rocking into me as he kissed down my neck. "Fuck, sweetheart, you smell like the best dessert. Like home. Like mine."

"Yes. Yours."

"But we can't right now."

Whimpering, I gripped the back of his hair and pulled his head up. "Please."

We heard someone roar, "Out" from the other room.

Levi went to turn his head, but I cupped his cheek and drew his gaze to mine. "Need you."

His jaw clenched, but at least he slipped a hand between us. "It doesn't bode well for me that I can't say no to you, Amara." I hid my smile against his shoulder until he filled me with one thrust.

I rolled my head back, moaning. "Yes," I breathed. Even though I was slightly sore, the gripping need to have him inside me overrode anything else.

He lifted me a little higher, and his fingers dug into my skin as he held me up to fuck me senseless.

"Christ, sweetheart. Such a sweet, tight pussy. All mine. *Ours*. Fucking delicious and warm."

"God," I moaned, drawing his lips back to mine. If he kept talking, I would lose myself too quickly. "Levi," I whimpered against his lips before he speared my mouth with his tongue, which I sucked on while he thrust faster and faster inside me.

When the door opened, I broke the kiss to glance over. Levi didn't stop pounding into me, so he must have known it was Kincaid and Silas entering.

Kincaid's gaze swirled to red as he made his way over to the shower to turn it on.

As I sucked on Levi's shoulder, causing him to groan and shudder, I stared at Silas, who leaned against the wall with a heated gaze.

Wetness coated me within, and Levi's seed seeped out and down my legs. Moaning, I pushed my head back against the wall, tightening my legs around Levi as my belly tingled. I slammed my eyes closed at the sudden onslaught of pleasure filling my body. My pussy clamped tight around Levi, and I held him close, with my body locked, riding out the orgasm.

"Amara," Levi clipped on a groan, his hips stuttering for a beat, but then he drilled into me faster as he continued to fill me. While we were still catching our breaths, Levi stepped back, slipping from me and leaving a mess behind.

Silas stepped in and picked me up in his arms.

When he'd gotten naked, I didn't know, but I was grateful to feel his skin. I felt his broad and strong chest chuff under the hand I lay over it. He moved us into the shower where a naked Kincaid waited with an affectionate smile that had my pulse racing. Seeing him looking at me like that was still so new. All of this was, but now that I'd had a taste of them, I wasn't sure I'd ever get enough.

Silas placed me on my feet and tugged me around so I had my back to his chest. His hands stayed clasped around my upper arms as he dipped his head, and in a raspier, deeper tone, he asked, "You ever sucked a cock before, princess?"

"No." I ran my gaze over Kincaid's body. He was already hard and slowly stroking himself as he watched us. "But I want to."

Silas's hands glided over my breasts, pinching at my nipples, making me gasp. "Yeah? You want to take Kincaid in your mouth? Suck on him while he fucks your mouth and I bury my cock in your cum-filled pussy?"

Panting, I nodded. "Yes."

His other arm curled over my chest, holding me against him while he ran his palm down over my stomach, cupping my mound before he slid one finger just inside. Silas brushed his nose against my neck, drawing in a breath. "Fuck, I can smell how much you want this." He pressed on my clit, circling it with his finger. My legs shook as pleasure rolled through me.

"Silas, please."

"You want to be filled, both ends?"

Moaning, I nodded. I did. I wanted it so much.

He removed his arm from my chest and pushed at my head gently. "Bend over. Kincaid will hold you up. Just open your mouth for him."

My legs shook some more, but I managed to bend at

the waist. Kincaid held out his hands. I placed my forearms in them and licked at his tip. On my second lick, Silas's dick brushed against my opening, and I glanced over my shoulder to see him watching me.

He tipped his chin up. "Suck him, princess. Just no teeth."

Biting my bottom lip, I nodded and faced the cock in front of me. Releasing my lip, I licked over the tip once more and came away with a salty, bitter, yet sweet taste.

I needed more of it.

As Silas pressed in, I opened my mouth and sucked Kincaid in, licking down and around the edges of his cock.

Kincaid drew in a sharp breath, and bit out, "Fuck yes."

Silas slid deeper into me, causing me to moan and tighten my lips around Kincaid, breathing through my nose.

As Kincaid gripped me, Silas slowly glided out of me, but he thrust back in, causing Kincaid to hit the back of my throat, and I gagged. My vampire pulled free, and I coughed.

"Guys, find a rhythm," Levi ordered from where he stood outside the shower, watching. My belly tingled, knowing he was there, seeing everything we did.

"Kincaid, you hold still," Silas said. His cock brushed over my hole again before he slipped back in.

"Silas," I breathed, loving the feeling of him, of any of them, when they filled me.

"Don't worry, princess. We'll have you coming soon."

I wasn't worried. I did enjoy the process of it all, though.

Licking over Kincaid again, I opened for him and bobbed up and down. Silas curled over me a little and fucked me in a slow, teasing motion that drove me insane. With the feel of Kincaid in my mouth and the sounds they both made, it didn't take long for a climax to threaten.

Saliva dribbled out of my mouth and dropped onto the tiles where the water swept it away. I pulled an arm free to wind it around Kincaid's thigh, dragging him closer. I wanted him deeper, like Silas was filling me all the way.

Kincaid cursed and snarled in between giving me praises. He tangled his fingers into my hair, gripping.

"Christ," Silas yelled. "Tell me you're close, baby."

I hummed around Kincaid, which set him off. He groaned as he exploded into my mouth, giving me a better taste of him as I drank it all down. Silas hooked his arm over my chest and pulled me up. He cupped my throat and fucked me harder, rubbing me in a spot that had me slamming my eyes closed and crying out his name as I released over his cock while he unloaded his cum inside me.

He stepped back and turned me in his arms as Kincaid crowded my back. Silas cupped my cheek. "Are you all right? We didn't hurt you?"

Shaking my head, I kissed his chest. "I'm fine."

"Move over. I'm coming in," Levi said, opening the shower door.

Kincaid snorted. "It's good I had the largest shower installed."

Levi nodded. "It is. You two shower down that end. I want to wash Amara's hair."

"I want to wash her hair," Kincaid gritted.

Silas shook his head. "No. I'll do it."

Shit.

"How about we all wash each other?" Besides the fact that it would be sweet, I couldn't deny the heat I'd felt when Levi took care of Silas's erection back at the cottage. I'd love to see more of it, but I'd settle for helping each other so we could finish the shower and eat before we had some much-needed sleep.

The guys stared at one another.

"The faster we do this, the quicker we get food and then sleep." They still didn't move. "I'm hungry and tired, guys."

That got them moving.

Silas drew me under the water while Levi grabbed the soap and shoved Kincaid under the spray of water at the other end. Levi threw another bar of soap to Silas, who assisted me while Kincaid and Levi helped each other.

I had to press my thighs together a few times over it. With a quick glance skyward, I thanked the gods and goddesses for this good fortune and also for the confidence I felt when I was naked around them.

Without a doubt, I would kill anyone and anything to keep what we'd formed. A bonded circle of love, respect, and happiness.

Honestly, I would put up with all the awfulness in my life again if it led me here.

Twenty-Two

SILAS

AFTER WE WERE SHOWERED and dressed—which was good, since our mate's body was pure temptation—we convened in the living area of Kincaid's room to wait on the food Levi had ordered. I'd just pulled Amara down to my lap when the door rocked open, and Mary stepped through.

I thought she'd say something about what she'd witnessed earlier, but when she didn't tease us in any way, I tensed.

"Kincaid, your mother would like a moment please." She closed the door behind her and gave us wide eyes.

Kincaid clenched his jaw, annoyed at the interruption. Besides needing sleep, we also needed time to sort shit out before seeing anyone.

"When?" he asked, leaning back on the couch opposite Amara and me to place his arm along the back of it.

Mary's lips pinched. "Now. She's right outside." No wonder she was in professional mode.

All our gazes widened. If Mrs. Prince entered, she'd scent our bond.

I stood with Amara in my arms, ready to make a run for it. Mary whistled low, and I caught what she threw at me as I lowered Amara to her feet.

"From the scent earlier, I had a feeling you guys would need this. A friend owed me a favor. It'll hide the bond, but reapply after every shower."

"Really, the best thing to do would be to tell people. I don't want to hide our relationship," Kincaid stated.

While I agreed, I couldn't stop the niggling feeling that this wasn't the time.

Levi shook his head. "Not yet. It's not the right time." My brows furrowed at his words that were almost a copy of my thoughts.

"I agree," Amara said.

"Quickly then," Kincaid said with a wave of his hand our way. I took off the lid and sprayed Amara, Levi, and then myself before passing it on to Kincaid.

"Mary, get the window and then open the door to her," Levi ordered.

By the time Mary was back at the door, Amara was standing behind Kincaid as he rested on the couch with a book in hand. Levi and I stayed on the opposite couch.

Mrs. Prince glided into the room with a concerned gaze that she ran over her son. "Kincaid, I heard about the attack on the way home, and I needed to see for myself you were all right."

"I'm fine, Mother. Nothing I haven't been through

before."

She stopped just inside the door and clasped her hands over her chest. "This is happening too often. I still don't understand why someone would want to harm you."

"We're searching for the answer also, Mrs. Prince," Levi said.

Her gaze slid to him. "How confident are you that the attacks aren't because of you both being here? Maybe my husband is right in saying that the only guards our son needs are *ours*."

Levi smirked. "We can't be certain it's not us they're coming for, but either way, it's better we work together to defeat them."

"They aren't leaving, Mother."

"Kincaid—"

"No. Levi and Silas stay."

A tick started in her forehead. Why was she suddenly listening to Mr. Prince in the first place?

"Of course, but I'm sure soon they'll be too busy taking care of their own estates once they start to lead."

Kincaid placed his book on the couch as he twisted to place his feet on the floor. "You needn't worry yourself about their futures, Mother."

Things regarding Levi's and my own future were something we needed to decide on, and soon. For a long time now, we'd been playing around with the idea of declining the roles of future leaders. It wasn't the norm to refuse, but it had been done by some. My father was one of them, leaving his brother, my uncle, in charge of our area. The precedent he set made me believe they'd accept my choice as well. Levi and I often talked about how content we were with the business and our positions guarding Kincaid.

Now, thinking of Amara, the likely option was to act on our desires and decline the leading roles in order to work alongside Kincaid and his mission to change the imbalance in society. In the background, we could help to obtain a better world for all kinds.

Our siblings weren't stupid. We'd often talked to them about what was lacking in living peacefully with humans. None of us thought it was fair that the lower-class humans and others of our species were kept in servitude. Their choices were taken away decades ago, and we wanted to see that changed.

Could it happen?

We weren't sure, but the younger generation knew the future would be calmer if all species, no matter their wealth or status, were equals.

It may be naïve to believe we could make this change, but we had a lot of time to try.

"I look forward to seeing how all your futures unfold. Speaking of, Kincaid, it might be best to bring forward the party in hopes that you find your life partner soon." Oh fuck. My gaze swung up to Amara in time to see her grip the back of the couch as Mrs. Prince went on, "I would hate for you to move on to the next step in life alone. I was there—Kincaid, what is your maid doing?"

"Mary, take her to the bathroom," Kincaid ordered smoothly.

Mary raced over and curled her arm around Amara's waist and tried to pull her away, but our mate wouldn't move.

Christ. My dragon tensed inside me, raising its head to peer through my eyes, not liking that our mate was upset.

"Kincaid, I do think it might be good for you to find another servant. Especially after what happened with her mother."

Just as I was about to snarl, Levi gripped my leg, thankfully cutting me off.

"No," Kincaid stated in a bored-sounding tone. "I've already trained this one."

Amara's hold on the couch finally lessened, and Mary guided her out the room.

Mrs. Prince had better listen to Kincaid on this or else.... Fucked if I knew, but none of us would be happy.

Levi squeezed my thigh once again before he released it, and shit, I wanted his hand back. The contact relaxed me enough to not forcibly kick Kincaid's mother out.

"Really, Kincaid, she doesn't seem like she's learned anything. She didn't even bow when I entered."

You stupid fucking bitch. She's more worthy than you'll ever be; she doesn't need to bow. My dragon huffed inside me. We wanted to burn this woman for speaking about our mate like that.

Levi made a noise next to me. I glanced over, and it was my turn to grab hold of him. His claws had unleashed.

"Mother, we'll speak of this another time. For now, I want to leave the party as already scheduled for a couple of weeks from now. I'm in no rush to find a life partner."

Because he had a bonded mate, and I couldn't wait to see their faces when they found out they couldn't control Kincaid through this part of his life. Not that he would listen. So far, the women they'd pushed him to meet weren't his type, and he'd confessed to us that he'd seen the disgust in their gazes when seeing his scars.

"At least think on it for a couple of days. I often recall the time when your father stepped into his leadership role, and how I was by his side, supporting him. He's even said it was easier, knowing I was with him."

Kincaid's jaw clenched. "I'll think on it."

She smiled. "That's all I ask. I do worry about you, my dear."

"Thank you."

"I'll leave you to it. Please advise us if you hear any information about the attack."

"We will," Kincaid said.

Levi patted my hand over his other one. I hadn't realized I still held it. Crossing my arms over my chest, I could feel my face heating.

Levi and I had always been close. Thoughts of him taking the edge off and making me come wouldn't leave me, though.

It blew my mind. We were close, but never that close.

I didn't know what it meant for the future, but I wasn't opposed to it happening again.

When Mrs. Prince started for the door, I stood and made my way over to Kincaid's bedroom where the en suite and my mate were. I watched the witch leave, and then opened the door.

Amara was already there and out first, wrapping her arms around my waist.

"I'm sorry," she offered.

"Princess, you have nothing to be sorry about."

"I know, but—"

"Love, if I could have predicted what she was going to say, I wouldn't have asked you to stand through that," Kincaid said as he approached, and I gently removed her arms from around me and guided her into Kincaid's. He cupped the back of her head as she rested it against his chest.

"Can they make you take a life mate?"

"No." Kincaid met my gaze and then Levi's. "It's time we step up our hunt to find who's behind this."

Levi nodded. His sharp eyes locked with mine. "We make the decision today."

I nodded and told him, "I'd prefer to stay as we are."

Levi grinned. "Agreed."

Amara turned in Kincaid's arms. "What's this?"

"Did everyone forget I was even here?" Mary demanded and moved between us all, throwing up her hands. "Is this how it's going to be now? You all in your bonded bubble? I mean, don't get me wrong, I think it's fantastic, but whatever decision you guys are making, you need to tell me. It's my job to run interference if I need to."

"Mary, dear. Did Cassar not put out last night?" Levi teased.

She whirled on him and scowled. "If you didn't pay my wage, I would beat the shit out of you."

"I'd take that as a no," I muttered.

Mary spun to me and opened her mouth to yell, but then tears welled, and she covered her face, bursting into tears.

I took a step back, wide-eyed. "What do we do?"

"Does she need chocolate? Do we have chocolate?" Levi demanded.

"Amara, do something," Kincaid said, and thrust Amara toward Mary with his hands on her shoulders.

"Seriously, you guys?" Amara shook her head as she gave us disapproving looks and approached Mary. We all tensed when Amara curled an arm around her shoulders, but thankfully Mary didn't react and hurt our mate. Instead, Mary allowed Amara to lead her back into Kincaid's bedroom, closing the door after them. A sigh dropped from my mouth.

"I didn't scent blood," Kincaid said as he scrubbed at the back of his neck.

"Should we get her chocolate anyway, just in case?" Levi asked.

I shrugged. But it could come in handy. "Probably."

Levi sucked in a sharp breath. "We didn't forget her birthday, did we?"

Tensing, I shook my head. "I can't remember when it is." Fuck, this wasn't good. The last time we'd forgotten, she'd glued all our socks shut.

"It's not," Kincaid said. "Besides, with everything going on, I doubt Mary would be upset this time around if we did."

Levi waved a hand around. "I'm sure Amara will have it handled."

I grunted. "She will."

"You're right." Kincaid nodded.

I glanced at Levi and smirked. "How much shit are we going to give him for—"

"You're not," Kincaid clipped.

Levi snorted. "Bullshit we're not. At least tell me I was right all along."

Kincaid made his way back over to the couch. "Am I right to guess that earlier you were both speaking of your positions?"

"Nice distraction tactic, but it is a good idea to talk about this," I said, taking my spot on the opposite couch again. Levi sat next to me.

"Later, we'll get back to you telling me I was right. But you're correct about the other thing. We've been leaning more toward declining, and now with Amara as our mate, it's best that we all stick together."

I tipped my chin up. "Makes the idea of us all moving in together easier for people to understand and accept. As soon as they know we're all bonded, no one can question it. The laws for bonded couples or circles trump any others."

Kincaid leaned forward, hunching a little to rest his elbows on his knees, then steepling his fingers to place his chin on top of them.

He looked regal. Like a ruler already. Levi and I had spoken many times about how Kincaid, out of all of us, would be the best to stand in front and take charge.

"The question is, when would be the best time to tell the world of our bond? If we do it now, while someone or a lot of someones are still wanting to see our downfall, then we paint a target on Amara's back."

As Levi's lion shone through to let out a growl, my dragon raked its claws inside me, and a snarl escaped my lips.

Kincaid eyed us both. "My thoughts exactly. But how

will we handle these new desires and wants around other people? I can't up and leave college. I have one year left because, as you know, the courses are a prerequisite to stepping into my alpha leader role, and I'm supposed to go back tomorrow. What will we do then? The concoction Mary gave us obviously works or else Mother would have scented the bond already, but one of us could slip up and forget—"

"We won't," I stated. "We can't afford to because it would mean the cat's out of the bag before we can end the lives of the people coming for us. Until that threat is neutralized, we guard our bond like our lives depend on it. No, like our mate's life depends on it, because it does."

"I agree." Levi nodded.

"As do I," Kincaid said.

"You're right, but I'm only agreeing to this because I know you three idiots would exhaust yourselves in keeping me safer than your own bodies," Amara declared from the bedroom doorway with her arms crossed over her chest. Mary glared at us over Amara's shoulder. "What I'd love more would be for all of us to go into hiding. But I know that's not possible because none of you, myself included, would abandon the humans and the others under your protection."

Kincaid stood. "I'm glad you understand, love. I'd also like to ban you from—" He glanced at Mary and back at Amara again. "—doing *that* thing in front of people, even friends, so no one learns—"

"No," she cut in with a snappish tone as she planted her hands on her hips. Hell, even I knew Kincaid had fucked up using the word "ban." Amara huffed in amusement, only without the humor behind it. "You do not get to *ban* me from anything. It was you who talked me out of running. You who got me to see sense."

"I understand, but you were right. There is a worry of people using you or—"

"No one will use me or experiment on me because I know none of you will allow that to happen. And I'll fight anyone who tries. Also know that if any of you are in trouble, I'll show the world what I can do if it means saving you three idiots. I'm not stupid, though. I won't reveal it to just anyone. Only people I already trust. But if it comes down to protecting someone and keeping it hidden, I'll bring it out." She took a slow breath. "What you don't understand is that since the three of you accepted me, truly so, I've come to terms with the fact that I'm not human."

"Princess, the banning part was Kincaid's idea. We knew nothing of it."

Her gaze swung to me as she scoffed. "I'm sure you thought it as well."

Shit. I had. I would wrap her up and take her away to somewhere hidden just to protect her.

"Am I forgotten again?" Mary asked. "What are you all talking about?"

"Nothing," Levi said.

"Not for you to know," Kincaid stated.

Amara huffed and, in the blink of an eye, she'd morphed, and her darkness surrounded her. Slowly, she turned to Mary, who had a look of pure shock on her face.

"I'm sorry for showing you this way. Since my darkness manifested, I've been scared of it. Not for my own sake, but for the sake of others, and how I could be forced to use it." She drew in a shaky breath, and we all watched as her darkness swept around the room, running over us. It even leisurely reached out to Mary's palm and caressed it.

Mary lifted her hand, blinking over and over.

"I'm tired of keeping this secret from the people close to me," Amara admitted. She laughed lightly. "I may never have realized how challenging hiding this has been if it wasn't for those lugheads." She drew her darkness back within her. "But when they found out, when they accepted me... the weight lifted from me was freeing." Her smile shook, her gaze turning watery. She sniffed slightly. "The world's not ready to know just yet, but I don't want to keep this from you, Mary."

Mary stayed silent, and I fucking begged her to say something.

She opened her mouth and closed it again.

Shit. Amara's shoulders slumped and she nodded to herself. Levi and I stood at the same time, but Kincaid was already striding toward our mate.

Only, we froze when Mary lifted a hand and punched Amara in the shoulder. "It's good to see my new friend isn't just a human, that she's a little special like me."

The tension was swept away, and I dropped my gaze to the ground, smiling.

"Can you show me again? What can you do exactly? Do you know why you have this power? What does it mean? How long—"

With a laugh, Amara threw her arms around Mary, hugging her close.

"I don't know why or what my darkness is, but it's a part of me, and I hope we can all learn together why I have it and what exactly it is."

Levi and I would task Mary to see if she could, discreetly, find any information from the archives of a power like Amara's. Our mate wanted answers, and we'd find them for her.

But for now, she needed to rest.

"Mary, that might be something you could look into. For now, our mate needs to eat as soon as the food arrives and then rest."

"Try our library here at the estate," Kincaid added quickly. "There's another room in the basement with mountains of books."

"Sounds thrilling," Mary deadpanned.

"Mate. Food. Rest," I reminded her, hoping she'd take the hint to leave.

"Or... rest then food." When Amara turned to me with a sweet smile and heat in her eyes, my cock fattened. My dragon chuffed, excited by our mate's interest.

Growling low, I stalked toward her.

"Seriously, is this how it's going to be?" Mary complained.

She'd understand when she found her bonded.

Amara let out a squeal when I picked her up and flung her over my shoulder. Kincaid wouldn't care if we went to his room. Besides, no doubt they would follow. None of us could resist Amara's sweet, arousing scent when it filled the room.

Twenty-Three

LEVI

A WEEK later I was walking down the hallway of the college, thinking over how hard it had been since returning to school. Kincaid, Silas, and I had nearly taken many lives since classes resumed. Many. It seemed the male population on campus finally took notice of the beauty Amara was. We'd lost count of the number of times people approached us to buy her.

"Master Grayson," a servant called, and I turned. He bowed low. "Master Danton is seeking for you to pass on an offer to Master Prince—"

"No." I about-faced and started walking.

I heard his skuttling feet behind me. "B-But, Master Grayson, you haven't heard the offer."

"If it's about Kincaid's maid, the answer is and will always be no. Tell anyone you wish to."

"What makes her so important?"

I spun toward the new voice and placed a fake smile on my face to cover my annoyance. "Jasmine, lovely to see you. But what are you doing here?"

"Mrs. Prince suggested I take a few minor classes on supporting a leader." She shot a sultry smile at me before her gaze switched to the servant and she flicked her hand. "Leave."

The servant bowed and quickly left.

Jasmine stepped out of the classroom I'd been about to pass. She had two servants in tow. "Please let Kincaid know I'm around. It would be wonderful to get to know him away from the estate and his meddlesome parents. I'm sure I can make him relax more." She licked her lips.

I looked at my fingernails and gave her a thin-lipped smile that hopefully hid my irritation. "I'll let him know."

She shifted closer, running a finger down my chest. Great, I'd have to have another shower. It was sad to see her pushing herself on those who she thought were available alphas the way she had been. Deep down, I doubted she wanted to. It would be her parents in her ear, encouraging her to gain status among us.

She leaned in. "I've heard you like to watch, Levi. I wouldn't mind if Kincaid didn't." Then again, there were a few who just wanted the fame even without their parents' instructions. Women weren't the only ones either. Men were the same when they saw women in power and wanted an easy life. Thankfully, they were only a small percentage compared to those who wanted a real bond or life partner.

Don't stab her. Don't stab her.

I hated that I had to pretend so she didn't suspect anything.

Smirking, I winked. "I'll also bring that idea up with Kincaid."

Her smile grew. "You do that." With an air kiss, she went on her way.

Just as I turned the corner, I slammed into a hard chest as hands gripped my elbows. "Our mate wouldn't want that female touching you," Silas growled in my face. "She's already upset enough. Do you want to make her more so?"

True. Amara hadn't left Kincaid's side after we'd returned to the estate for his "training" the previous night.

Reaching out with my lion's sense of hearing, I noted no one else was nearby. I stepped closer to Silas to get in his face. "What would you have me do, Silas? I'm tired of this pretending as much as you, but for her safety, I'll put up with it a little longer until the world knows she is ours."

He snarled in my face and turned us until my back was against the wall.

For a beat, I was shocked. Until I realized the other reason he was cranky. Then I smiled smugly. "It was you."

"What?" he bit out.

"You were jealous of her touching me. Silas, I didn't know you cared that much."

He gnashed his teeth at me, which had me smiling brighter as my heart pounded in my chest, and my dick thickened.

"Do you need me to reassure you that I only need the

touch of our mate... and you? Maybe Kincaid also, if he wanted it."

"No," he clipped.

I arched a brow. "No? Why? Are you worried what our mate would think?" I chuckled low before I licked my lips. His gaze followed my tongue. "Wasn't it her begging me to suck your dick in bed two nights ago while she watched and Kincaid fucked her from behind?"

His chest rose and fell rapidly.

"Then the night before, after I'd been inside our mate, wasn't it you who licked her juices off my dick?" I slid my hands up his chest. "If our mate is busy with Kincaid, I'm sure she won't mind me... helping you out." His grip on my arms lessened as I pressed forward and nipped at his chin. "But we better be quick, since we have to go soon."

Silas let out a huff, and was that his dragon chuffing in his chest? He grabbed my wrist and dragged me into the closest vacant room before shutting the door and locking it.

I dropped to my knees, eager to have his cock fill my mouth. I fumbled a little with his button and zipper but then got them down and pulled him free. I dove onto his erection, sucking at the base while I gagged a little, wetness springing to my eyes.

"Fuck," Silas whispered harshly.

I bobbed up and down on his length while I frantically undid my own pants to pull myself free to jerk off. I loved sex and got off on pleasing others. I groaned around his cock, drawing out a curse from him. I squeezed my dick. My release was already too close.

Silas tangled his fingers in my hair. He held my head

still and when I looked up, I met his gaze, then he started to *fuck* my mouth.

His jaw clenched, but the passion burned brightly in his eyes as I allowed him to have my mouth. To use it in any way he wanted. The need to gag was heady. I got off on the feel of it right at the back of my throat, cutting off my air.

"Levi," he bit out before he exploded onto my tongue and shoved his dick to the back of my throat. I drank it down as my own cum landed on the floor.

When he slipped free of my mouth, I panted for a couple of breaths before I sucked in a deeper one.

"Jesus Christ." Silas's hands went under my arms, and he pulled me to my feet. He cupped my cheeks and stared at me in what looked like awe. "Jesus Christ," he uttered again. His gaze dipped to the ground and then skimmed up to meet mine as I wiped at my face. "You liked that."

Grinning, I said, "We'll work Amara up to taking you like that, but for now, you can use my mouth."

My eyes widened for a moment before they closed when Silas kissed me. It wasn't sweet. His tongue invaded my mouth, and I fucking loved it. He was rougher and harder than Amara. I wanted it both ways.

He broke the kiss, still cupping my face and still staring at me. "Jesus Christ."

I squeezed his waist. "Are you moving past those words any time soon? Because we really need to collect the other two and head off."

With another quick, rough kiss, Silas fixed my clothes before he straightened his own and took my wrist to drag me to our suite.

As soon as we entered, I saw Kincaid and Amara walking from Kincaid's room in each other's arms. Amara was laughing about something while Kincaid stared down at her fondly.

She noticed us first and paused what she was saying as she eyed Silas. "What's wrong?"

Snorting, I rolled my eyes. "I sucked his brains from his dick, and now he might be concerned you won't like that I did it."

Kincaid chuckled.

"As long as his brains are actually still in his bigger head, he should know I love the idea of you two pleasing each other when I'm otherwise occupied with my other mate."

I knocked my shoulder into Silas. "Told you. Now, let's get out of here."

"Are you sure I should come along?" Amara asked.

Smiling, I made my way over to her. I couldn't resist pulling her into my arms for a hug and kissing the top of her head. "Since we're going to our families' estates to see our parents and let them know we're no longer taking over because we're bonded to a wonderful woman, then yes."

We'd decided that since Silas and I were older than Kincaid and closer to the appointed time for taking over, we needed to inform our leaders we were passing on the position and that they needed to start to train our siblings for the role. Amara had made us promise her this was what we honestly wanted, and we both told her it was. I'd never been excited about leading our species. Running our security company and protecting our clients was different and more thrilling. We'd grown our business for years.

While our families had been skeptical, we'd proven them wrong.

The deadline to move things along had also shortened as we'd found the perfect place to move in together. Something that was close to college, so we didn't have to stay here, and we could return home to be ourselves among people we trusted.

Kincaid's parents wouldn't like the move. They could even fight against it, since he still had a few years to go, but he would do everything in his power to make them understand the importance of independence when he had such a huge role coming up. We just had to pray it worked. Besides, it was becoming increasingly obvious that we needed them to see less of Amara. They were starting to pay more attention to her than we liked. Even his father had questioned Kincaid about her, wanting to know if it would be best to replace Amara, since her mother had betrayed them by running off. Kincaid declined, but the more he refused, the more it would seem out of place, since he usually didn't care what happened to his servants.

At least Silas and I trusted our parents. They'd never harmed us. They showered us with trust and love. We knew, if asked, they wouldn't share our news until the time was right. Which was what we'd be doing that day.

Amara's body trembled slightly against mine, and when she looked up at me with worry in her gaze, my heart clenched. On a whisper, she asked, "What happens if they don't accept me?"

Kincaid crowded her, giving me a pinched look, and I heard Silas approach, but I slipped a hand to the side of her neck and gripped. "They'll love you because we do. They'll accept you because you're everything to us."

Silas grunted at our sides. "He's right."

Rolling my eyes, I smirked down at her. "If only they listened when I tell them things."

She laughed lightly, and I felt her relax somewhat. "Okay. I can do this. I just wish it wasn't while I'm wearing a maid's outfit."

"Mary placed clothes in the car. You can change before we arrive at my pride first."

She tipped her chin up and met my lips in a soft, sweet kiss. Pulling back, she said, "I can do this."

"You can, and we'll be right there with you."

Her smile shot a canon of butterflies into my gut. How'd we get so lucky?

~

With Amara's hand in mine, we climbed out of the car and stepped to the side to wait for Silas and Kincaid. She was now dressed in black jeans and a dark blue cashmere sweater with her usual combat boots. It'd been a difficult time to keep my hands to myself as she'd changed in the back of the car, and I was sure I wasn't the only one who had the same problem.

Kincaid had nearly ground his teeth down, while Silas nearly ripped the seat.

We made our way up the front stairs to the door, which opened as soon as we reached it.

Our main servant, Basil, bowed. "Alpha Levi, it's a pleasure to have you home." He swept a hand into the house. "Your parents are in the library, and there are refreshments for you all."

I patted his upper arm. "Thanks, Basil. I hope the better half is doing well."

He beamed, like any other time I spoke of his wife. "She is, sir."

"Good to hear."

He tipped his head down, and I didn't miss him looking at Amara, but until things were out in the open, I wouldn't introduce her. Not that I didn't trust Basil, but I couldn't risk anything.

"Alpha Kincaid, Alpha Silas," Basil greeted. My family and I had always preferred our servants to greet us with our first names instead of our last. It felt too impersonal otherwise, and they were around every day, helping us.

When Kincaid and Silas had finished with pleasantries, I tugged Amara down the hall to the left and into the library. Silas closed the door behind them.

"Son," Dad boomed. His wide grin set off my own. He made his way over and dragged me into a tight hug.

"Dad, it's good to see you," I said, patting his back with my free hand.

Dad pulled back, and with his hands on my shoulders, he shook me a little. "Shit, boy, you've grown taller."

Rolling my eyes, I snorted. "It's just your eyesight. I'm the same."

"Levi." Mom's soft tone brought my attention to her where she was standing at Dad's side.

"Mom." I drew her into a hug as tears shone in her eyes.

"I've missed you."

"Of course you have. I'm the better child out of all my siblings."

Her laugh was like a cute little pixie's. When she moved back, Dad curled an arm around her waist, and she leaned into him. "Kincaid, Silas. Good to see you both."

They both dipped their heads. Not that they needed to, but it was nice they wanted to show respect.

"And who do we have here?" Dad asked, shifting his gaze to Amara.

Letting go of her hand, I placed my arm around her shoulders. "I'd like you to meet Amara Kenna, our bonded mate."

Mom gasped as more tears filled her eyes, and she lifted a shaky hand to press against her lips.

They both stared at Amara in wonderment. Our mate flushed, a beautiful pink filling her cheeks, and she shifted on her feet awkwardly while my parents gaped at her.

Silas moved up to Amara's other side, taking her hand. Kincaid stepped close to Amara's back.

"Wait... all of you?" Dad asked.

I nodded. "Yes. We're a bonded circle."

Mom burst into tears, covering her face, but then she threw her arms wide and grabbed Amara, dragging her into an embrace.

"My son. A bonded mate. Oh my God, this is beautiful." She stared up, since she was shorter, at Amara, cupping her face. "You're stunning." Another sob broke free and she hugged Amara once again.

"Joey, darling. How about you quit scaring the girl." Dad tried to pull her back, but she held on strong to our mate.

"I'm not scared," Amara said quietly as she rubbed Mom's back.

My lion paced its confines, worried Amara would be starved of oxygen from the way she was being held.

"Mom," I clipped roughly, my lion riding my tone.

Dad smacked me in the back of the head. "Don't growl at your mother."

"Mrs. Grayson, can you please let go of our mate before you break her," Kincaid asked nicely, only I could hear the small edge to it.

Mom sniffed, but she did release Amara, who we quickly drew away from my emotional mother.

"Leon, our son has a bonded mate."

Dad tightened his hold on her in case she was about to grab Amara again. "I see that, dear."

"What?!" someone screeched from a corner. The far door had been thrown open and my youngest sister, Danny, ran in. Following her were my five other sisters and three brothers. "Is this real? Someone got stuck with you?"

While Amara laughed, I left her in between Silas and Kincaid while I went over and wrestled Danny into a headlock. "Yes, pain. It's real."

"Our condolences," Lennon said with a smirk. He was the second oldest, the one who would take over my role, if he chose to. Though, I expected he would. He had a thirst for control, knowledge, and was more diplomatic than I ever was.

"Thanks." Amara grinned.

"S-S-She's real pretty," Lineal stuttered; he was the second youngest brother.

Kincaid's eyes swirled red while Silas glared. My lion wasn't too happy about my brother's comment.

"Lineal, what have we told you about bonded couples?"

"That they're crazy possessive and we could get killed if we look too long or say admiring things... oh. Oops." His hands shot up and he took a step back, half hiding behind Dad. "Don't kill me."

As I passed him, I ruffled his hair. "You're safe for now. Just be careful."

He nodded. "I will."

"Do all of you sleep together?" Jess, the third oldest, asked.

"Jessica," Mom snapped.

She shrugged.

"Can I tell the girls at school? They keep asking about you, brother," Luis asked.

"No," I clipped.

"Son?" Dad turned his concerned gaze on me.

Sighing, I ran a hand over my head. "Sorry, kid, didn't mean to snap. But for now, we all need to keep this just between the family. It's complicated, but I need you all to swear to me, you won't say a word to anyone."

"Kids, now," Dad barked.

They all promised, and I knew they'd keep their word, especially since it was Dad, our alpha, backing me up.

"All right, rascals," Mom called. "We'll talk more later. For now, leave us. We'll call you in for afternoon tea soon."

"Lennon, I need you to stay, please," I called to my brother.

His brows shot high. Silently, he moved to the couch to sit down. After we said goodbye to the rest of the pride, Kincaid, Silas, Amara, and I took a seat on the couch opposite where Lennon, and now my parents, sat.

Amara looked squished, but before I could pull her onto my lap, Silas did. That was more than okay as he shifted closer to me with her.

"What's going on?" Dad asked.

"The attempts on our lives are still happening."

Mom sucked in a sharp breath, and Dad cursed while he curled her in close to him.

"Though, we think they're mainly targeting Kincaid. We're still searching for answers, but whoever is behind this is covering their tracks well. Until this ends, we'd like to keep the information about our bond quiet."

Dad nodded. "Understandable. Let me know and I'll speak with Dash about giving you more men." Dash was Dad's second-in-command.

Shaking my head, I glanced at the others beside me for a beat before saying, "We have plenty. Thanks, though. However, there is something else. Having become a circle, you'll understand we'll want to stay close to one another." Standing, I dropped to my knees and bowed my head while I placed my hand over my heart. "It has been an honor to be in line to lead for our pride, but now I must decline my position, and I wish to pass the title on to Lennon."

Dad's hand landed on my shoulder. "Raise your head, son." When I did, he went on, and what he said had my throat thickening with emotion. "Your path leads you in a different direction now, Levi. An honorable one that has you standing by your mate and bonded brothers. We're proud, my son."

"Thank you," I managed to get out, and Dad dragged me into a hug when we stood. Smiling, I looked at my brother. "I know you'll do well for the pride, Lennon. But also the people."

"I will, brother."

I mock punched him on the arm. "Besides, it's not like you'll get rid of me. I'll be at Kincaid's side when it comes to anything political."

Lennon groaned. "And here I thought I was clear of seeing your ugly mug."

Snorting, I shook my head. "We all know I'm the good-looking one." Turning to Amara, I asked, "Isn't that right, sweetheart?"

She shrugged. "Your brother can give you a run for the title."

My lion snarled in offense, but I knew she was only teasing.

Lennon's chest puffed out. Dad chuckled, gripping the back of his neck. "Looks like I'll have some extra years before I give up my position."

I winced. "Yeah, sorry about that."

Mom scoffed. "Like he cares. Levi, you know your father would've been in your ear, trying to lead behind you until he grew tired of it... if he ever did at all."

"True, he's always nosey."

Dad huffed, crossed his arms over his chest, and scowled at us. "I can't help that I like working."

"He talked about statistics the other night in his sleep."

"Now, Joey—"

She waved him off as she stood. "Amara, come have some refreshments while these brutes speak or before the others come back in and eat everything."

"I'd love to," Amara said, moving over to the corner where everything had been set out in anticipation of our arrival.

Silas and Kincaid joined our huddle as Dad asked, "Why can't I scent the bond?"

"We're blocking it by magic. I don't trust my father enough to share this news as yet," Kincaid offered. Dad knew all about Mr. Prince and what a fucking prick he was. Kincaid had always had my family's support as well as the support of Silas's family.

"Sorry you can't share this grand news with your family. I thank you for your trust in us."

"You've always had it," Kincaid replied.

Dad nodded once, his gaze warm. "Keep her close, boys. She's human, yes?"

I shared a glance with Kincaid and Silas. "Not exactly."

"Share when you're ready. But she has strength to face any upheaval over this bond? Because tying together three powerful alphas could be seen as a threat, even by the council."

"Her strength is beyond anything we've seen. The power shared between us all will be unbeatable."

"I pray you're correct, son. I do."

"You'll have the pride's support," Lennon said.

I swung my arm around his neck. "Aww, look at you, stepping up even before I leave."

Lennon rolled his eyes and shoved me. "Shut up, idiot."

"Come on. Let's get some food, and I want to get to know your bonded. Before you leave, we'll see to you signing the documents to abdicate."

"Thank you, Father."

He clasped me on the shoulder and shook me a little. "I can't argue about your choice. I know I would do anything for my bonded. You have more to consider, and I believe you're making the right decision."

"I know I am."

Walking over to the table, I bent and pressed a kiss to Amara's neck. She smiled up at me, taking my hand in hers. I would do anything for her, for our circle. But it was good to be reassured that I had my family's support.

AMARA

As we drove away from Levi's family's estate, I couldn't help but think that it had gone well. His family was amazing. His dad reminded me of Mr. Langley at first. It'd hurt to listen to him, but I pushed that aside and enjoyed our time together. The other siblings had drifted back in for afternoon tea and teased Levi relentlessly.

"Sweetheart, I think my family loves you more than me now."

Silas snorted. "Anyone would."

Smiling, I reached out and took Levi's hand before resting back into Kincaid's chest. "They're all very charming." Laughing, I shook my head. "I can still picture the look of shock on their faces when you told them I was Kincaid's servant."

Kincaid's chest moved at my back as he chuckled with Levi and Silas. Luis had nearly fallen off his chair.

And yet, they'd still accepted me. They waved off the announcement of my lowly status like it was nothing, which made me fall for all of them that much more.

Kincaid slid his arm across my waist. It still surprised me how affectionate he was with me. Who was I kidding? Shock lived inside me constantly while I got used to the idea that I was bonded to three men.

But now... now they were mine.

I threaded my free fingers through Kincaid's at my waist while I held Levi's hand and rested my legs on Silas's lap.

Mine. Mine. Mine.

The darkness trilled inside me on a spin. It loved knowing I had them. Knowing I was claimed. It spun in time with my belly's butterflies.

Would I ever get used to this? As in... us being an *us*. Connected.

Maybe.

What I wouldn't get used to was the fury that shot high when I noticed all the women, and even men, yearning for their attention. None of them knew they were taken, and I'd lost count of the times Mary had to talk me down from going on a killing spree, but at least I managed to keep my bloody thoughts as only that —thoughts.

Thinking of Mary, I smiled. I loved how we'd become fast friends. It was good to have another woman around all the testosterone. When she'd explained why she'd burst out in tears the week before, my heart had gone out to her. She was such a sweet soul and had been outside, caught in the attack at Kincaid's estate when it'd started.

If it hadn't been for Cassar, she would have been hurt, possibly killed. On top of all the shock of that, the tears had come because she'd been terribly worried for all of us.

Though, when Levi and Silas sent her chocolate later, she told me she felt a whole lot better.

When I'd seen her the day after we returned to classes, her spirits were high. Later, she'd dragged me to the side and told me that Cassar had gone to her father for his permission to take her on a date. Which would happen this weekend. I'd been thrilled right along with her, certain they'd be good for each other. While I didn't know Cassar too well, I could easily read his interest, and if he was willing to seek her father out just for a date, that said a lot more.

Could they be bonded mates? I wasn't sure and hadn't asked. Mary would tell me if she wanted to. I hoped they were. If not, they could pick one another for life partners, but I was getting ahead of myself. I'd see how their first date went before I imagined them walking down the aisle together.

A phone chiming brought me from my thoughts, and Silas pulled his cell free.

He groaned.

I tensed. "Is something wrong?"

"Fuck yes."

Straightening, I asked, "What?"

"It's my father telling me my grandfather will be at dinner."

Kincaid's foot shot up and kicked Silas in the shin. "You worried her for nothing."

"Shit, man." He rubbed at his leg. "It's not nothing. You know what he's like."

"Is he mean?" I asked, brows drawing together in confusion.

Kincaid drew me back against his chest. "No, he's not." I relaxed a little from his words.

Levi chuckled. "He's just eccentric."

Silas scoffed. "He's batshit crazy."

Tensing again, I didn't know who to listen to, but was Silas worried what I'd think about his grandfather? He needn't be.

"You don't need to worry. I'm sure he's nowhere as bad as my mother was."

He sighed, reaching out to pull me onto his lap from Kincaid's. I went easily. "Princess, no one can be as bad as her."

Kincaid cleared his throat.

"Besides Kincaid's father, the old dragon just drives me crazy. He's loud. He can be rude and annoying. Don't take to heart anything he says. Hell, I'll try and get uncle to kick him out." He reached for his phone again, but I grabbed his arm.

"Don't. I'm sure I can handle it."

He studied me for a moment before nodding once. "You've got your throwing stars on you?"

"Yes," I said hesitantly.

"Feel free to use them on him to shut him up."

Levi found that funny.

Shocked, I smacked his chest. "I'm not injuring your grandfather."

He huffed, wrapping me tighter into a hug. "Pity. Kiss

me for courage because we're nearly there."

I gave him a quick peck on the lips.

"Amara," he growled.

Laughing lightly, I curled my arms around his shoulders, slanting my mouth over his in a deeper, hotter kiss that curled my toes.

When the car pulled to a stop, I broke the kiss, and Silas cursed against my mouth. "Maybe kissing right before I have to climb out wasn't a good idea. They're going to give me hell."

Kincaid snorted. "Take a moment."

"Sweetheart, come here." Levi patted his thigh, and I crawled over to him.

The door opened, and Kincaid called out, "Give us five." It was quickly shut again as Silas sucked in a deep breath and rested his head back.

"You smell too damn good, princess," Silas said. His eyes opened and landed on me. "I want to spread your legs and drink you down." His chest rumbled.

"Silas," I breathed, loving the idea of it.

"Fuck," Kincaid clipped. He slapped a hand down on Silas's leg, who jolted. "Now is not the time for this."

"Shit. You're right." He nodded, and I felt a little guilty for getting aroused and knowing they could scent it. Which could explain why Levi had his nose buried into the crook of my shoulder and neck. Though, he loved doing that, as did Silas. Maybe it was a shifter thing.

"How about I get out for a while?"

Silas shook his head. "Levi first, then you, Kincaid, and I'll be fine by then."

Levi scooped me up and sat me on the long seat in the

back of the limousine. He pushed the door open, climbing out. I quickly followed and Kincaid stepped out slowly. I heard Silas take a deep breath and then he was out of the car. The driver shut the door a second later. Like at Levi's home, the guards stayed near the vehicles while we climbed the stairs to the front door.

"Do your parents live here also, or is it only for the alpha?" The estate appeared similar to any alpha's place —massive.

Silas grunted. "My parents, siblings, uncle, and his family. Others are out the back in their own homes on the one-hundred-acre property." He took my hand at the front door, just as it opened to reveal—

"Jim," I cried with a thrilled smile. I couldn't resist moving to him and hugging him close while ignoring the three men at my back and their noises of complaint. Still, for their sake—and Jim's—I stepped back quickly.

"Miss Amara, it's so good to see you."

I gripped his hand in both of mine. "You too. How are you? Do you like it here?"

He laughed but nodded. "I love it, miss. They're so kind here. I get to eat all the time, and I've never seen my mom smile so much. They're even teaching me school stuff."

"This is the best news, Jim. I'm really happy for you."

His head cocked to the side. "Then why do you have tears in your eyes?"

An abrupt laugh left me. I sniffed, wiping at my face. "Happy tears. I promise." Releasing his hand, I turned to Silas and threw my arms around him. "You're an amazing man," I told him.

His body shook from his chuckle. "I couldn't stand to see the hurt in your eyes, princess. I had to do something."

My heart swelled. "Even back then?"

His fingers threaded through my hair, and he tugged my head back, our gazes locking. "Even back then."

"Whoa, you hugged our alpha-in-training," Jim exclaimed from behind us.

Grinning, I faced the young boy again and straightened out my clothes.

"I did. He made me very happy to see you enjoying it here."

Jim blushed. "Thanks, miss."

"Jim, please tell me you've greeted the people properly," someone called from inside.

Jim winced. He pushed the door wider and bowed. "Alpha Silas, Alpha Levi, and Alpha Kincaid, welcome back." He stood tall. "And you, miss, welcome—but...." He glanced from my clothes to Kincaid and back to me. In a whisper, he asked, "Weren't you his servant?"

"I still am, but it's, um, my day off."

"Cool, you get a day off." He looked behind him. "Do I?"

"One day, after you've learned everything," a man said from where he stood behind the door.

Jim dropped his head back and groaned. "I'll never get a day off."

There was a sigh and Jim was ushered out of the doorway. A man who appeared to be in his early fifties took Jim's place and bowed. "Welcome home, Master Silas. Greetings, Master Levi, Master Kincaid. The family awaits you in the dining room." His gaze switched to me. "Miss."

"Hi," I offered with a friendly smile.

"Thanks, Otis." Silas stepped in, leading me with his hand on my lower back. "Please tell me my grandfather got lost or he forgot where the dining room is."

Jim chuckled while Otis's lips twitched. "He did not, master." Levi reached out and squeezed Otis's arm in greeting, while Kincaid tipped his chin down and smiled. Seeing them acknowledge the servants warmed my heart.

"Damn it." Silas nodded, rolled his shoulders, and took a deep breath. "All right, let's do this."

"Bye, miss," Jim called.

"Bye, Jim. I hope to see you again."

"Me too," he called before being shushed by Otis.

My gaze took in what it could while we walked through. When we stopped outside two large swinging doors, Silas drew in another deep breath, as if he needed to brace himself. Honestly, the grandfather couldn't be that bad, right?

"I can hear him breathin' out there like some weirdo. Get your ass in here, boy. I'm starvin'."

I pressed my fist against my mouth to keep from laughing while Silas ground his teeth together. Levi didn't hesitate, though. He chuckled and pushed through the doors first. Kincaid went after him but held one open for Silas and me.

"Ah, shit, he brought guests. We got enough food, Finley?"

"There's always enough food, Gus."

"Good."

Before I got to see the grandfather, a couple moved in

front of us and hugged Silas warmly. They must be his parents.

"Great to have you here, Silas," the dad said with a soft smile.

The mother smacked Silas upside the head after the hug. "You never call. I nearly fainted when your father told me you were coming to dinner."

Silas rolled his eyes. "Mom."

She waved him off. "Now, why did you want dinner to be only us and your uncle, plus Finley?"

"Stop chattering near the door. Let the boy in. The quicker he talks, the faster I get fed."

"No one asked you to come, Dad," a large man at the table said. If I was to guess, he must be Silas's uncle, the alpha to the Peril Weyr family and area.

"Bah, when I overheard the phone call, and Silas said he had somethin' important to say, I had to come. That shithead always has good gossip."

I didn't miss the gazes of Silas's parents. I hoped my genuine smile was enough to get them to like me. My stomach already churned with nerves, but now my pulse raced so fast, it nearly had me light-headed.

"Who the fuck is she?" Gus yelled. I froze and my heart skipped a beat when his gaze suddenly widened, and he stood so abruptly, his chair fell to the floor with a bang. "Motherfuck. Holy motherfucking fuck."

"Dad," Alpha Peril clipped.

Gus walked around the table and straight up to me, shoving Silas out of the way to grip my upper arms. Silas let out a rumble from deep in his chest. Levi started growling, while Kincaid's eyes bled to red.

"Get your hands off her," Kincaid ordered.

"I can see it," Gus whispered.

We all stilled. I focused on the older man in front of me.

"Dad, close this area down, now. No one is to come near us," Silas ordered, and someone ran off.

I didn't look away from Gus's searching gaze.

"What?" I asked on a breath, heart hammering behind my ribs. My darkness pushed against me, wanting out.

Did it mean we were in danger?

"Step back from her, Gus," Levi demanded.

I was okay. My mates surrounded me. We'd be all right.

Gus shook his head, almost like he couldn't believe what he was seeing. "I can see it swirling inside you."

"Dad, she's human," the alpha said from somewhere close, and I heard him drawing in a deep breath, taking in my scent again. "Human."

"Back off, uncle," Silas's roughened, deeper tone warned.

I jolted when the doors banged open. "Area cleared."

"Silas, who is she?" his mom asked, and out the corner of my eye, I saw her and another woman standing close.

"Let it out." My gaze flew back to Gus and his command.

"I'll rip your fucking hands off if you don't let go," Kincaid warned.

The alpha's dragon woke and started growling. "You won't touch him, vampire."

Gus ignored everything and grinned. Finally, his hands lifted off me, and he took a step back. A wonderous laugh dropped from his mouth when he eyed Kincaid, Silas, and Levi, who all surrounded me close, like a second skin. "Bonded. To the three of them." Another sharp laugh. "This is fuckin' brilliant."

"What. Is. Going. On?" the alpha demanded harshly.

Gus held up a hand at him for a moment but stayed staring at me once more. "Shit. My damn grandson. Yeah, he might be a shithead sometimes, but the Fates chose well for you. Three alphas." He shook his head. "Never in my years did I think I'd get the chance to see you reborn. I'd heard stories, many stories, but I'd thought it a myth... until now."

A gasp fell from my lips when he bowed in front of me.

"It's a true honor."

"What is, Gus?" Silas's mom asked.

Gus straightened and waved a hand toward the table. "Please, come sit and we'll talk." His brow rose. "Unless you'd honor me more by showing us your other side."

"Other side?" the alpha muttered, his frustration blending with his confusion.

"Dad, have you finally lost your marbles?" Silas's father asked.

"Gus, we can all scent her as human," my mate's mother said.

"You're all bloody idiots then. Although, maybe this sight comes with age. Call that old bat in here."

Finley, who must be the alpha's wife, sighed. "My mother is not an old bat, Gus." Still, she walked out of the room, doing as he'd asked.

"Are you all right?" Kincaid whispered in my ear.

Relaxing into the three of them, I nodded.

"Just give me the word and I'll kick the old coot's ass," Silas offered.

Gus scoffed. "Like you could take me on, loser."

Silas puffed up. "I will if Amara wishes it."

"I won't," I quickly said. "Um, no one needs to hurt anyone. I'm just very, ah, confused by this."

"We all are," the alpha said.

Gus made a noise in the back of his throat, his wide gaze on me. "Even you don't know?"

"Know what?" I asked.

"How... what... fuck." He shook his head, scrubbing a hand over his face. "Amara, was it?"

"Yes."

"You're—"

The doors swung open, and all of us turned to see Finley return with a woman who seemed a little older than Gus. She glanced around the room, passing over me until her gaze widened as she swung it back for another look.

A half gasp or cry escaped her as she slowly bent at her waist with Finley's help. "Goddess."

Gus hooted and laughed. "Yep, gotta be an age thing. Finley, get the old bat to rise before she falls on her ass. Amara, please come and sit. We'll talk."

She'd said "goddess." To me. Right?

Maybe it was a good idea to sit down.

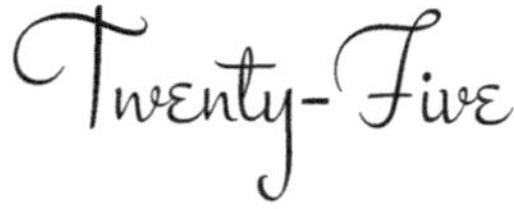

Twenty-Five

AMARA

SILAS TOOK my hand and led me over to the table. I quickly sat and my dragon shifter took the seat on my left. Kincaid was on my right, while Levi settled next to Silas. Opposite us, Gus picked up his chair and dragged it along on the other side of the table so he could sit exactly across from me. He even moved Silas's father out of the way.

Besides the alpha who was at the end of the table, the others sat wherever they could.

"First of all," the alpha started, "before my father gets long-winded about things, what did you, Silas, want this dinner for?"

Silas's arm rested along the back of my seat, and we exchanged small smiles.

"Wait!" his mother cried, making me jump. She pointed at us, including Levi and Kincaid. "You mean Gus was telling the truth? You're bonded? A circle? A true bonded circle?"

"Is this true?" his father asked.

"Yes. Amara has bonded us all together."

His mom dropped her head back, and said to the ceiling, "Oh sweet gods and goddesses." She faced us again. "A bonded couple is lucky, but to have a circle is rare and a godsend." She then clasped her hands in front of her chest, over her heart. "Praise the majestic first dragon. This is wonderful news." She reached over and shoved her husband. "Did you hear that, Camden? Our son is bonded. Bonded in a circle!"

Camden chuckled, but his eyes gleamed with pride. "I heard, Monique."

She started to stand, saying, "Just wait until I tell—"

"Mom, hold on," Silas called. Slowly, she dropped back into her seat. "That's another thing we have to tell you. For now, we're keeping this a secret. Amara came to us as Kincaid's servant."

"What the fuck?" Gus yelled.

"We have to pretend she still is, because her life could be at risk. The threats to our lives are ongoing. While they're mainly concentrating on Kincaid, with Amara being so close, we don't want more attention drawn to her as our bonded."

"Not that I'm worried about my life—" My men made noises of complaint, and I rolled my eyes. "—but I know it's better to go with this plan because they'd be too occupied with worrying about me rather than their own lives."

The alpha snorted. "Reminds me of you, Fin."

Finley and I shared a look as she smirked. "Men can be overprotective fools sometimes."

"Finley," the alpha warned, but she just shook her head at him.

I gave her an appreciative smile.

"We understand why this must stay among us," the alpha said. "I'm also predicting that you don't want to take over my position. You'll want to stay close with your bonded circle."

Silas nodded once. "Correct, uncle. I appreciate everything you've done for me, and—"

He waved Silas off. "Please, I've hardly done anything. You've grown to be a strong businessman, and I already expected this day would come because you enjoy working security so much." He grinned. "Which is why I've been training your brother on the side."

I glanced up to see Silas's gaze widen. "You have?"

"Yes. We'll get the documents organized and signed tonight."

Silas gave his uncle a grateful smile and tipped his drink up to him.

Gus snorted. "I doubt he came to the conclusion on his own."

"Father," the alpha gritted, his dragon flashing in his gaze.

"Sorry, Conrad. But I'm keen to move on to other matters."

He sighed, seeming frustrated. Until he stared at me. "Actually, I'd also love to know why Silas's mate scents like a human, but my father thinks she's not."

Unease rolled my stomach. Levi hadn't told his family

everything about me, but since Gus could apparently see my darkness, my secret would be laid bare. However, I had to ignore the nerves and worry because it was obvious Gus had more information about me than I did. I wanted to hear what he had to say more than I needed to listen to my own fear about revealing the news to people I hardly knew.

So really, knowledge outweighed anything else.

Looking at Gus, I asked, "What is it you see?"

"The darkness. The power."

Silas and Kincaid took my hands in theirs.

"How can you see it?" Levi questioned.

"So... he's right?" Camden, Silas's father, asked.

I sunk my top teeth into my bottom lip and nodded. "When this... darkness manifested, I never knew why or what I was. I, um—I've kept this a secret from fear of being used or experimented on." I peeked at my men. "Until these three."

Silas grunted.

Kincaid raised our joined hands and kissed the back of mine. Levi glanced around Silas and grinned cheekily. "It was a shock to see her power, but we accepted it quickly. Not only did she help save my life, but we're all different in one way or another, and the fear of losing her was too much. She'd been so scared about revealing her other form that she tried to run from us."

"I wanted to protect you all, even from myself," I put in defensively.

Kincaid's fingers grazed against my cheek. "Thankfully her darkness brought us with her."

Smiling softly, I nodded. It had been lucky that my

darkness ignored my feelings. "They were the first to see me. Well, except for one other. He'd been like a father to me, but, as I learned, he'd also instilled fear in me about what I could do. It was why I didn't imagine I'd ever be accepted, even knowing we were mates." I shifted my gaze to Finley's mother. "You called me a goddess?"

She nodded. "The Goddess of Darkness."

My darkness trilled inside me, caused my body to hum, and I couldn't help but smile. Right about now, maybe I should have been panicking or scoffing at the ridiculousness. But my darkness's reaction stopped that in its tracks.

Finally, I knew what I was. The only detail missing was how I came to have this power gifted to me.

"How do you know?" I asked.

"Thousands of years ago, on the darkest night of any before, it was said the first dragon was born with the help of the Goddess of Darkness. And since that night, there has been a link with the dragons and whomever carries the darkness. However, the only ones able to see the true one are the oldest of dragons. They are wiser and careful to keep the goddess's identity safe."

Everyone turned to Gus.

He flushed and rubbed at the back of his neck. "My ma must have skipped that part."

"But... why me?" I asked softly. I shook my head, gazing at all the people around me. "How did I become a goddess? My parents are human. We've always been servants. I... just don't understand."

"There's a myth saying you're born a goddess, but it's not true. You're chosen by a higher power, and the darkness combined with you from a young age. The reason is unknown. It could be the Fates had always planned to set you with three powerful alpha mates. It could be that they saw something in you and knew you were worthy. Whatever the reason, it's a gift to be blessed with the darkness."

I'd known it was, even when I feared people finding out. The darkness had always been there, trying to reassure me. I hadn't always listened—something I regretted—but maybe this was what the Fates intended.

That I was exactly where I was meant to be.

My darkness brushed up inside me, comforting and warm.

You really are a gift.

"Can we see it?" Gus blurted gruffly.

My darkness trilled, wanting out to show off. Who was I to deny it? We were obviously around people we could trust. People who knew more about my power than I did. But also, I'd denied it on many occasions.

Yet nerves gripped my stomach.

Kincaid picked up my hand and kissed the back of it again as he leaned in. "Don't feel you have to. It's your choice."

"Exactly," Silas said, and I caught him glaring at Gus. "You don't need to listen to the old coot. No one wants you to do anything you don't want."

Levi leaned forward to wink at me. "We can leave if you want." He was worried for me. They all were.

But wasn't it time to embrace this?

Closing my eyes, I took a steadying breath. With a thought, I unlocked the tight grip I had on the darkness, and it soared out of me. My features morphed as the darkness connected with my human form.

Gasps sounded and a chair screeched back. I opened my eyes to see the alpha, Conrad, on his feet. Fear tightened his eyes and mouth. He reached out to Finley to pull her up, but she swatted his hand away.

Unhurriedly, so I didn't scare him further, I stood and backed up a few steps. My mates moved with me.

"Stand down, son," Gus said.

"She... the power I feel... I can't."

My mates made noises of protection. "It's okay," I told them with my gaze to the floor. I nodded more to myself than anyone. I couldn't feel what the alpha was when he felt my power level, so I didn't understand his reaction to it. Yet, I hadn't even let the darkness explore like it wanted to; instead, it brushed only over my mates and the floor around us.

The doors suddenly burst open. I spun and extended my darkness to hold whoever entered.

"No!" the alpha yelled.

But already my darkness and I saw no threat by the four bodies it held. Through my mind's eye, I saw that they were only children. Harmless.

Set them gently down.

My darkness trilled and swept over the floor to place the kids in front of the alpha. The youngest, a little girl, giggled when it tickled her. She waved her hands through the darkness until it manifested like a hand and tickled her again. The girl thought it was hilarious.

I met the alpha's eyes. "The only times it's harmed anyone is when I've been in danger, or my mates have."

He nodded once, drawing the older children close while the youngest still played with my darkness.

"W-What is she?" the oldest daughter asked.

"Someone who's owed respect," Gus said.

"Silas, why are you over there?" the same girl questioned.

"Because this is my bonded mate and I stand by her."

"Silas got hutched?" another asked on a gasp.

"Hitched, sweetie," Finley told her. She smiled down at her daughter before turning to her husband and whispering low.

"She ain't that pretty," the little boy said.

And even when Silas roared at him, I laughed. The hand my darkness had manifested clenched and swept over to wave in his face before it returned to entertain the little girl.

Levi curled his arms around my waist and drew me back against him. "She's beautiful."

"She's powerful," Gus stated, awe in his gaze. "I can honestly die a happy man, having seen and met you, goddess."

Upon hearing this, my darkness split off from the little girl and glided over to him to cup his cheeks. He closed his eyes, and shock rippled through me when a tear dropped free.

He let out a shaky breath. "You're back to protect all of us."

"What do you mean?" Levi asked.

Gus locked gazes with me. "We might be part of the cause, but we never meant for this to happen. The world has gone to shit since the humans found out about us. We might've been living in the dark, but we'd been happy. The humans and lesser shifters, vampires, and enchanters are rising up. A war is coming. I can feel it in my bones. You can stop this."

My throat thickened as I tensed.

"You can set things right. You were born a human, but the darkness chose you. You've lived in both worlds. Now is your time to stand up for what's right. Get the humans back some rights. Stop those who want to control and rule for the wrong reasons."

"Bring peace to all," Finley's mother added, and Gus nodded.

I'd always wanted to help, but my old fear had overridden everything.

Panic was still present, though. If I could help, how would that be possible without bringing any harm to me and mine?

A tightness grabbed at my lungs. I took a step back, and Levi moved with me.

Gus expected too much. I'd only just come to terms with my darkness, and now he wanted me to lead a fight so that eventually there'd be peace?

My darkness patted at my shoulders, arms, and legs, trying to settle me.

"Amara, sweetheart, breathe."

"Love, you don't have to listen to him. It's not falling on your shoulders. You don't have to help."

"Kincaid's right, princess. You don't have to listen to the old fool. I told you he's crazy."

Shaking my head, I sucked in a lungful.

"Good, that's it. Just relax," Levi said, taking Silas's place.

"You can't just throw shit like that at her. You don't know what she's already been through. You don't know the fear she's lived in," Silas yelled.

And seeing him upset on my behalf was enough to calm me down to take another deep breath. The thought of what Gus was asking overwhelmed me.

I wanted to yell that I wasn't strong and that I couldn't handle it. Running also crossed my mind. Only, I wasn't the person I'd been when I first showed up at Kincaid's estate.

The situations I'd faced proved I *was* strong. I *was* powerful. I also had support. Something I'd never had before. Mr. Langley protected me like a father would a daughter, but my mates would stand beside me through whatever I had to face.

Looking at all of them, I noticed I already had Levi and Kincaid's attention while Silas still yelled at his grandfather.

Together we were powerful.

Together we could do so much for so many.

While I didn't know what it would entail, a small burning part of me wanted to find out.

Drawing my darkness within, I took Kincaid and Levi's hands, making sure I didn't slice them as I transformed back to my human form.

I heard the kids' shock through gasps, cries of surprise, and a "Holy shit. Now she's cute."

"Daniel, you've been around your grandfather too much," Finley scolded.

Silas turned and strode toward me. He cupped my cheeks. "We can leave. We don't have to stay here or listen to his bullshit."

"It's not bullshit," Gus said.

Wrapping my hands around Silas's wrists, I squeezed them. "From the very start, I've always wanted things to change. I hate how the world is and the way we are treated all because we don't have the money or strength to stand up and be seen or heard. If I can do something about it, I want to try. I won't claim that what needs to be done doesn't scare me, but I'm not on my own anymore."

"Damn right," he stated roughly.

"Together," Kincaid said.

I glanced at him and smiled. "Together, we have the hope to make a difference."

"You'll have the support of the pride," Levi offered.

"As well as the dragons of the Peril Weyr family and warriors," someone said from across the room. Silas shifted to the side, and I was surprised, and warmed, that it came from the alpha.

"I'm sorry for how I acted, but I didn't understand the power you held. If you need assistance from us on this journey to make the world better for all, then you have it." He tipped his head my way.

Pressing my hand to my chest, I said, "Thank you." Then I turned to look at Gus. "Is it possible to prevail in this change?"

"You're stronger than you even realize. People will listen to you."

"I remembered something my father once said," Finley's mother said, speaking up. Our attention went to her. "When the Goddess of Darkness arises again, it will be at a time of need. A time to lead. A time to protect those who can't help themselves. She will be victorious. But there is always a risk of pain and death."

Well... shit.

Gus huffed. "Don't worry about the last part the old bat said. Let's relax and eat. It's not like anything needs to be done this instant."

"Gus, if you call me 'old bat' one more time, I'll burn your balls off."

The kids tittered. Yet, my stomach churned. The fight was closer than we thought. An urgent pulse drummed through me with the need to stop whoever wanted Kincaid dead. Maybe instead of waiting for information to come to us, we could be more proactive. Not that my mates weren't already; they did have their employees working on this constantly. I understood why my mates didn't put themselves right into the mix of things, instead wanting to act like nothing was amiss. But it couldn't hurt to expand our circle so we could bring this person down before any of my mates got hurt.

It was something to talk about at least.

AMARA

"Silas, you're taking up all of the room," Kincaid complained as we lay in bed that night in the dorm rooms. It was a tight fit, with me and Levi in the middle, Kincaid behind me on the edge, and Silas behind Levi. It was the first time we were trying to sleep all together. In the past week, we'd been taking turns with whose bed I went to after some, ah, nightly activities. But after the day I'd had, and all the information bombarding my mind, I wanted all my mates close, and they'd quickly agreed.

Silas got up onto his elbow and smirked over Levi at Kincaid. "I'm *really* comfortable, though."

"Move over," Kincaid clipped, and then muttered, "We need a bigger bed."

Laughing, Silas eased back, pulling Levi with him. I thought it was cute that Silas didn't care about having

Levi up against him. Though, from the wide eyes Levi gave me, he seemed shocked, only to settle seconds later when Silas's arm rested over his waist. A small purr started in his throat. I loved that sound. I'd fallen asleep to it, as well as to Silas's chuffing.

Kincaid curled into my back as I rolled onto my side, facing Levi. He clasped my hand in both of his.

"Are you all right?" he asked softly.

"I'm... I don't know. Numb in a way. I don't know what I'm expecting or what I have to do to start making a change." I shrugged.

"We'll work it out. You're not alone, Amara. We'll keep you safe."

Smiling, I told him, "And I'll keep all of you safe."

"I know you will."

Silas's hand slid up and grabbed both of ours. "Whatever comes, we're all here for one another."

"Always," Kincaid added.

"I know, and I'm very grateful for it," I told them.

"Did you ever think you would be here?" Levi asked me.

"In bed with the three of you?"

They all chuckled, but Levi shook his head. "No, well yes, but also bonded to three men and reaching for a future outside of servitude?"

I shifted closer, and hid my grin against our hands. Kincaid followed as he tucked his arm around my waist.

"Never. I thought I'd die working." I peeked over my shoulder when Kincaid got up onto his elbow to stare down at me. "But I didn't think it would be with the

Prince family. I was sure you were going to get rid of me. I'm surprised you kept me around."

His gaze warmed and he kissed my temple. "How could I not? You fascinated me the moment I saw you. Even with the bruised cheek, you lifted your gaze when I ordered you to, and my lungs seized. I'd thought you were beautiful when you were standing in that room next to that woman, but up close, you're stunning. I never thought I'd be grateful to my father, but I was that day when he gave you to me."

"Kincaid," I whispered, reaching up to tug him down for a soft and sweet kiss.

Silas snorted. "Why do you think I bought a servant because of her? I couldn't resist."

"And yet, they were the most stubborn. However, *I* wasn't," Levi commented smugly. "I knew right away you were important and that I'd do just about anything for time alone with you."

A blush warmed my cheeks. Levi noticed and kissed me there. "I nearly swallowed my tongue when I saw you getting dressed that first time, though."

"You what?" Silas near shouted.

Levi patted his arm. "Relax, I didn't take advantage. She was hard to resist, though."

"Levi," I admonished.

Another chuckle fell from his lips. "Hey, I didn't. But I did manage to con you into letting me brush your hair. I loved that moment and will always cherish it. You let your guard down for a short time."

"Until Mary walked in."

He wiggled his hand and Silas moved his away, then

Levi moved in close. "Yes. And what had I been about to do?"

"Kiss me," I whispered. My gaze searched his heated one. I wanted his lips on mine. He was gorgeous. Reaching up, I brushed hair from his eyes.

"I was, sweetheart." He pressed his mouth against mine, then pulled away. "Back then, would you have let me?"

"Yes."

"Would you now?"

In reply, I tilted up to touch our lips together. He never needed to ask. Against them, I said, "Whenever you want."

A purr rattled within his chest before he slanted his mouth over mine. I opened up to his tongue and tangled mine with his in a seductive dance, moaning when he dragged me close. Sliding his hand down and cupping my bottom, he squeezed before he glided it down to the back of my thigh and pulled it up and over his hip.

My hips jutted forward, wanting more, needing friction at my aching and throbbing core. Breaking the kiss, I breathed hard against his lips and uttered, "Levi."

Tracing fingers over the side of my face, he smiled softly. "You need me, sweetheart?"

I nodded.

"Then you have me."

A gasp escaped me when I was suddenly pulled up and over Levi. I sat back to straddle his hips. Biting my bottom lip, I rocked over his erection. He groaned, placing his hands low on my waist. Dropping my hands to the bed near his head, I rocked over him again. His hardness pressed against my clit, and pleasure spiked higher.

Soon I'd soak through my panties and leave a wet spot over his sleep pants, but hopefully before that happened, he'd be inside me.

I glanced to the side where Silas lay as he rubbed his hand up and down my calf, and he smirked up at me. Like always, having all my mates here while being intimate had my heart beating in excitement.

Kincaid's hand snaked up to my breast, and he gently massaged it in his palm. Levi lifted his hips a little, grinding up against me.

"I need... clothes."

His brows shot high. "You need clothes? Right now?"

Silas chuckled. "You idiot. She wants them off." He sat, then got to his knees. "Both of you, tilt your asses." I got to my knees, and Levi tipped his butt up with me. The material of his pants slid down, and then his warm skin pressed against my inner thighs.

As I went to reach for Kincaid's shirt that I was wearing, which he liked me sleeping in, a hand touched my wrist. Kincaid was already sitting up, and when I met his gaze, he asked, "Let me?"

Nodding, I let go of the shirt and raised my arms above my head. Kincaid pulled it off me and threw it over the side of the bed. He dipped in to kiss the top of my breast.

"And now these." He traced the edge of my underwear at my hip and, in a blink, a claw sliced through the material. "Silas, get the other side."

"With pleasure."

I dropped my gaze to Levi. He was watching Silas as he pulled the material out at my side and sliced through it. As I stared at Levi, he bit the corner of his bottom lip, his gaze growing darker. Silas slid the material from between Levi and me away.

"God," Levi groaned, gripping my hips. "Your scent is headier without a barrier."

Blushing, I coated my wetness over his length as I glided my hips up and down against him. I was a little shy about knowing they could smell me like that, but I also loved how aroused it made them.

Bending, I met Levi's lips in an unhurried kiss, tangling our tongues together, tasting, playing. A hand that wasn't Levi's, as his were still at my hips, brushed over my bottom. It came from Kincaid's side. Then another hand joined—Silas's this time—and he pushed at my bottom. I lifted a little, and then Levi groaned low in my mouth when his tip brushed against my entrance. Silas helped guide Levi's cock up.

Slowly, I sank down onto him, breaking our kiss to arch my back and breathe out unevenly as Levi filled me to the brim. His purr amped up when I lifted off him and slammed back down.

"Fuck," Silas uttered next to us.

As I rode Levi's cock, my lion shifter glided his hands up to cup my breasts. I glanced down, and my core clenched when I saw Levi's leg was bent between Silas's thighs, who was grinding down on it.

"Yes," I whimpered.

It didn't matter that I'd lost one of Levi's hands, because each skim up and down on Levi's cock drove my desire to a soaring height. It increased even more when I looked down at Kincaid.

"Hell," I cried, slamming myself down over and over on Levi. Kincaid had his sleep pants pulled down to his thighs. His hand was wrapped around Levi's over his cock, and together they jerked Kincaid's leaking dick.

Levi groaned loudly. His free hand ran over my body, touching me everywhere that Kincaid and Silas weren't. "Jesus, sweetheart. So good. So fucking good."

Leaning down, I met his lips. The kiss was different from before; it was like we couldn't taste enough of each other. I wanted more of him inside me. Our movements were fast and sloppy, both of us moaning and groaning as I rode him faster.

Silas's hand slipped between us. A finger circled my clit, causing me to shatter around Levi's cock. Then suddenly, Levi snarled, turning his head to Kincaid before he broke off in a deep grunted groan as he swelled and filled me while Kincaid drank from his shoulder, his bite causing Levi to lose himself. Levi wasn't the only one coming. Kincaid's eyes flashed open. A noise grated in the back of his throat, and I glanced down to see him spill out over their hands and the sheet.

I stayed seated on Levi as he softened inside me, panting and heart racing. I turned to Silas, who was still rocking over Levi. Not wanting him to waste his cum in his pants, I licked my lips just thinking of it. I wanted to drink it down.

"Make him come like you did me," Levi bit out at Kincaid.

"Don't you fucking dare," Silas said, his hips stilling.

"Silas, can you... I want it in my mouth," I said, my face heating.

"Christ, princess," he clipped, but in the next second, he bounced up to sit next to Levi's head with his sleep shorts around his thighs. "Come here." He held a hand out, and I took it. Slowly, he tugged me until I bent over and sucked him into my mouth. His raspy, deep tone gritted, "Hell yes." The chuffing sound in his chest skipped and then shot louder. "That's it, baby. Suck on me.... Yeah, just like that. Christ, Amara."

I let go of his hand to roll his balls around gently. They sprang up against his body, and he hissed, grunted, and groaned.

"Shit, fuck." His hips jerked. His cock hit the back of my throat, and I swallowed around him as he came.

After drinking him down and lapping at his spent cock, I straightened. I wiped my mouth and met his gaze.

"Fuck, princess, look at that smile. You like sucking cock."

My face burned, but I nodded. "I like the taste too."

Kincaid groaned on my other side, and Levi's cock twitched inside me.

"But... I also want to see, um, Levi doing it again."

Levi chuckled. He reached up and curled an arm around my back to drag me down. "No arguments from me, sweetheart. I like this kinky side of you." His brow cocked. "Though, I love all sides." He sobered. "You know that, don't you, sweetheart? I've said it before, but I'm not sure you took it in."

My heart skipped a beat. "What?"

"That I love you."

My heart got all melty and warm. "Levi."

"I do, Amara. With everything in me. You have my love forever."

Sniffing, tears welled, and I ducked my head, pressing my forehead into his shoulder. "I love you too."

Levi hugged me tightly to him and kissed the side of my head.

Until I was suddenly out of his arms and planted on Kincaid's lap. My gaze widened when I started to leak.

"Kincaid—"

"Don't worry about it." He cupped my neck. "Eyes to me, love."

When I did, my belly rolled before butterflies took off from the tenderness in his gaze. Before he could make me melt even more, I blurted, "I love you too. I do. Even when you're a pain and stubborn and think you know best, I'll still love you."

His beaming smile was my reward. "The same for you, love. Until the day I stop breathing."

I lost his hand to my neck when I pressed forward and kissed him, wrapping my arms around his shoulders.

When a hand settled on my back, I pulled away from Kincaid and looked up.

Silas stood there. "My turn." Only he picked me up and flung me over his shoulder with a startled gasp from me. "You guys clean the bed. We're showering first."

Laughing at the others grumbling, Silas took me into the en suite and shut the door. He set me on my feet and went to start the shower. I tilted my head to the side when I noticed tension in his movements.

"Silas, what's wrong?"

He adjusted the water but didn't answer. I approached and rested my hand on his waist, kissing his back. "Are you all right?"

He turned and bent a little to rest his forehead against mine. His hands went to my back, dragging me close. I glanced up to see his eyes were closed. "I'm not good at talking feelings and saying sweet things. Not like those two."

My heart clenched. I ran my hands up and down his back. "You don't need to be like them, and you don't even have to say anything. I know you love me. Your actions show me that. And I love you as you are."

He grunted and pulled back, nodding once. He led me into the shower and helped wash my hair. It wasn't until after he insisted on drying me and had finished doing so that he tensed.

"Amara, never doubt you have my love."

Pressing into him, I tipped my chin up, and with a smirk, he gave me what I wanted. A slow, deep kiss.

Opening my eyes, I smiled up at him, and his gaze ran over my face. "I'd never doubt it, Silas."

"Good."

"And I've never been happier than I am with my three bonded mates."

"I'm glad we can bring that to you, because you deserve it." He shifted back, wrapping the towel around me. "Come on. Let's get some sleep." He opened the door, and Levi stood there naked with wet hair and a smirk on his lips.

"I knew you were a sweet teddy bear under all that dragon."

Silas growled, nostrils flaring, and then he was on Levi, taking him to the floor in a tackle. Levi laughed as they wrestled.

"Love, over here." Kincaid held his hand out from where he sat on the bed, which had clean sheets. He also had wet hair. They must have gone to shower in one of the other rooms.

I made my way over with a happy smile and slipped my hand into his. He pulled me close and then rolled me over so I was back in the middle of the bed.

"Just a teddy bear," Levi teased.

"Shut up, pussycat." Silas got Levi onto his stomach on the floor with his arm pulled behind him. A yawn suddenly overtook me.

"Can you two give it up already? Our mate is tired," Kincaid called.

I laughed when they both jumped to their feet. I didn't miss their half-hard cocks, though. "I didn't mind watching," I told them.

Levi winked, climbing onto the bed on the other side of me. "Next time I'll let Silas shove his cock in my mouth to shut me up."

Silas groaned. "We're supposed to be getting sleep, not getting turned on again."

Levi chuckled, shifting close to me to make room for Silas to lie down behind him. "Maybe you need to gag me."

Silas snorted. "You'd enjoy it too much."

From behind me, Kincaid nuzzled the back of my neck. "You two quit it or I'll bite you both."

"Now who's the one getting kinky," Levi said. Silas

chuckled, and Kincaid grumbled something under his breath, but we all settled down, ready to sleep.

Though I did it smiling. I really did enjoy this so much—their banter, their closeness, and their love for me and one another. It had my heart feeling light.

Twenty-Seven

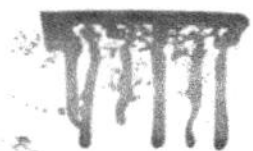

KINCAID

TWO WEEKS LATER

I'D ALWAYS DISLIKED COLLEGE, yet it was a necessary part of my alpha leadership preparation. Now, I despised it because I had to act the part of the cold master to Amara. And my mate, my beautiful, sweet mate had to silently stand behind me. I wanted to pull out a chair and have her sit. No, I wanted her on my lap with my arms around her while scowling at anyone who looked in her direction.

At least people feared me enough that when I caught them staring, they looked away after I moved into their view.

The professor announced the end of class, and I stood. Amara picked up my bag and heaved it over her shoulder. My hands itched to take it from her. Instead, I fisted them at my sides and walked ahead, knowing she was at my back with her gaze to the floor.

She was supposed to be at my side with her head held high.

She was more important and powerful than any of us, yet she had to act the role.

Silas and Levi caught my look and nodded.

The investigation into the attacks wasn't bringing up any new information. It appeared we were at an impasse. Thankfully there hadn't been another one. But still, we were tired of waiting. We were sick of treating our mate as a pariah in public.

Even if we had to place her in an impenetrable bubble, we were moving up the timeline. Soon everyone would know she was ours.

Guilt still crushed my chest when I thought about how harsh I'd been with her. If only I'd trusted my instincts more than I'd listened to my stubborn thoughts.

A hand briefly brushed my back, and softly, my mate said, "Please relax and stop overthinking. We've been over this, and I don't mind acting the devoted servant."

"I'm fine," I said through clenched teeth. Her brows rose. Rolling my eyes, I took a breath and tried to force the damning thoughts aside. Nodding, I glanced around as we walked toward the cafeteria. Since no one moved close to our group, thanks again to my attitude and Silas and Levi's dark looks, I asked Silas, "Have you heard from Mary yet?"

He shook his head. "Nothing."

I thinned my lips. Usually she checked in, and she liked to have lunch with Amara since she couldn't sit with us for lunch.

Levi pulled out his phone. "I'll try again." We stepped through the doors, and I clenched my jaw. Our mate had to carry my bag, get my food, and then sit on her own.

I didn't like this.

Not in the slightest.

"Maid Amara, sit with us today," I ordered.

Her gaze swung up to me. "But... um, master, I'm not supposed to."

I didn't give a fuck about the rules. Unease spread through me, and my gut twisted.

Was my worry over Amara sitting on her own, or was it something else?

Glancing around, I listened to Levi when he said, "Still no answer."

Silas, Levi, and I only trusted Mary with Amara when we had to leave her side.

Our mate shifted close. "I'll be fine," she whispered.

Fuck. What was the right choice? Would it be best to force her to eat with us or let her sit on her own? If she was on her own, then there was a possibility she'd be approached. They wouldn't usually, knowing Mary worked for us, but there could be others who could try to sway her to kill me.

Was I overthinking this? Possibly, but risking our mate wasn't worth it.

Shaking my head, I glared down at her. "No. Sit with—"

"I'll get your food, master."

And she quickly scuttled away. Did it mean she was going to listen to me? Probably not.

"We can't exactly tie her to us or a chair at our table," Levi said for our ears only.

"I'd do it," Silas muttered. "And we'll have to when the world finds out we're bonded."

"Fuck," I uttered, running a hand over my head before I made my way over to our usual table.

Jasmine stepped into my path and tried for a sultry smile. "Kincaid—"

"No," I clipped low. Levi covered his mouth and coughed through a laugh. Silas snorted.

"I don't think your mother would appreciate you speaking to me in such a way."

I stopped in front of her and looked down. "My mother isn't here."

"You do know of her wish for us to be—"

"Nothing. We'll never be anything. Now move." It probably wasn't best to take my anger out on this woman, but frustration ate at me.

"Kincaid, why are you acting this way?"

Sighing, I changed tactics. With a touch to her forearm, I put the charm on that I used only when I had to. If she went complaining to my mother, there was a chance my parents would take a closer look at what was going on in my life. I didn't want that just yet, not until we made our own announcements. "Jasmine, as you can see, I'm not in the best of moods. Please leave me be, and we'll speak another time."

She stepped closer, studied my face for a moment, then looked over my shoulder before she took my other hand in hers. "Is there anything I can do for you to put you in a better mood?"

Jesus Christ. I should have stuck to getting rid of her in any way necessary, consequences be damned.

"Master, I have your food."

Shit. Turning, I noted the tight grip Amara had on the tray. She was probably thinking of smashing me upside the head with it for having a woman close. Then again, maybe Jasmine was at more risk than I was.

"Maid Amara, place it on the table for your master," Levi dictated smoothly, but I didn't miss the tightness around his eyes.

This was getting to all of us, and I was nearing the point of breaking and telling everyone about the bond. Luckily, we'd moved up the date to announce it.

Silas walked Amara over to the table, and I caught him whispering something to her. She shook her head and walked away.

"Kincaid, are you paying attention to me?"

Something wasn't right.

Silas watched Amara make her way to the lunch line again. Levi glanced around us, his hands clenching and unclenching at his sides.

Did they feel it too?

"Kincaid, you really aren't listening to me."

"What?" I snapped, looking back at Jasmine.

She crossed her arms over her chest, pushing up her breasts that were nearly popping out of her dress already. "I would like to have dinner with you."

"No," I stated.

"Kincaid." Silas stopped at our sides. "I've got a weird feeling."

"You can't just say no to me like that without even thinking about it," Jasmine said in the background.

"So do I," Levi admitted.

We all looked at our mate; she'd just turned from the counter with her tray and met our stares. She stopped, and her brows dipped low in confusion.

"Go to her," I ordered.

I heard Jasmine stomp her foot. "Kincaid!"

Silas and Levi were halfway across the cafeteria when I saw someone jump the lunch counter from behind it.

"No!" I roared.

Silas and Levi were still too far away.

The man wrapped an arm around Amara's chest, and in a blink, he whispered something before she fell to the ground. A body jumped on my back, and I tried to grab for it, but I was distracted when I saw Silas and Levi being attacked.

People screamed.

Reaching behind me, I gripped material and snarled, trying to pull them off.

"Nighty night, lover boy." *Jasmine.*

Something stabbed into my neck, but I managed to get a better hold on Jasmine and threw her across the room, snarling at the other people approaching. My gaze turned hazy, but I could see others making a run for it. They didn't understand what was going on. Neither did I, but I had to get to Amara.

There was a roar. Levi.

I blinked slowly and saw him crouched near Silas as he tried to pull him across the floor to Amara.

Mate.

With my head growing weary, I still tried to reach her. Tried to help her, but my limbs weren't working.

Where were our people?

Where was our help?

Amara was my final thought as I dropped to the ground.

"Kincaid" was yelled close by, jolting me awake. Groaning, I blinked at the bright light above me. I went to pull my hand up to shield my eyes, but it wouldn't move. Panic flooded my system. I fought against the bindings around my wrists and feet, but I couldn't get them free.

"Kincaid" was barked again.

I glanced to my left. Levi was there, still unconscious. To my right, Silas scowled at something in front of us.

My father stood with his arms crossed over his chest. A boom sounded outside, and the walls around us groaned. My father tipped his chin toward Silas. "That's their people. Employees and family trying to get in. Someone tattled about the attack."

"Where's the maid?" I demanded.

He ignored my question. "They might have arrived to help, but really you made it too easy to take you all in the first place. You thought you were safe at college. Look at how wrong you were."

Fuck. It was true, and I wanted to hurt myself for letting our guard down all because we'd been in our own contented circle of happiness.

Fucking foolish really. After everything, we should have been more alert.

"Where's the maid?" I asked again.

Father sighed and shook his head. "You shouldn't have bonded."

"Where. Is. Amara?" Silas bit out.

"Amara?" Levi groggily said. His head rolled to the side, and he slowly opened his eyes, stilling. "What the fuck?"

"Father, I swear if you've done something to her—"

"You shouldn't have bonded." He started to pace. "After everything. This is what it comes down to."

The chains rattled when I tried to lunge forward. "Where is she?"

He turned to me and tsked. "Those bindings won't break."

Bringing my strength forward, I pulled at the restraints, raising my upper lip as I strained.

His gaze widened when they groaned.

Silas and Levi half shifted and tested their own. Again, the bindings groaned.

"Not possible," he muttered.

One restraint snapped. I reached for him, but in a flash, he was gone from the spot.

"You're stronger." He started pacing again. Something was different about him. Erratic. Unhinged. Where were his guards? Why was he in here on his own? "The bond?" he muttered. "But how? She's human.... Unless being in a circle can bring more strength. It could happen. They're both alpha shifters."

I stilled when something occurred to me. "Who told you about the bond?"

He didn't answer, just kept pacing and muttering.

Using my free arm, I pulled and tugged at the other one that was still bound. If I could just get it free, I'd be able to find Amara. Surely, they held her somewhere close by.

Please keep her safe.

Another boom rocked the room.

My father stopped and looked at the small window. I did the same. It was then I realized where we were—in one of the rooms of the basement on our estate. Outside the window, the sun was setting, which meant we'd been unconscious for half the day.

"They're trying very hard to get to you all. But they won't get through, and we have more people."

"Get through what? Why are you doing this? Why do you want your own son dead?" Levi snarled.

Father didn't get to answer. The chains around Silas's arms snapped. His gaze lifted and locked onto my father. His dragon shone in his eyes. "Take me to our mate."

"I wouldn't bother escaping. Do as I tell you and I'll let you see her."

Did we trust him? No.

"If Silas gets his feet free, we'll be out of here—"

He pointed up at the corner where a red light flashed. We were being watched. "If you don't comply, she'll be killed."

Fuck.

"We could make it to her before they did anything," Levi whispered.

Did that mean...? Closing my eyes, I reached inside myself. The link shone like a beacon. I followed it through my mind's eye, and it stopped on the other side of our estate.

She *was* close, but could we risk it?

"No," Silas growled. "They'll be too close to her."

Father grinned. "Exactly."

Was she still unconscious? I knew our mate, and if she was awake, she would have released her darkness, engulfing everything and anyone looking for us.

From the sounds of it, Father remained clueless about who she was.

"What do you want?" I asked, slumping into the seat.

"The council is here. They'll be our witness, and they have the best enchanters to do what we need."

"What?" Silas clipped.

"To sever the bond of course. Our son can't stay connected to the help when he's to marry Jasmine."

I wanted to laugh, to be surprised that he'd orchestrated this just so he could control who I married, but really, I wasn't. It explained why Jasmine started college to get close to me. "Why Jasmine?"

"She's a young, vibrant, upstanding woman and vampire in our community. Her father also happens to be on the council."

He'd always wanted an in with the council, and this was obviously his way.

"Bonds can't be broken," Levi said.

"It's a long process and it'll hurt, but they can be. Now, you'll all come willingly, won't you? Or else the servant will be harmed in a very unpleasant way."

Christ, I wanted us to save our mate, but we couldn't risk acting out and hurting Amara while unconscious. We didn't know what they would do to her.

He really was clueless about what was in store for him when Amara woke. I couldn't wait to see his surprise before I ended him for touching her in the first place. Even if he hadn't placed a finger on her, that was semantics; he'd been the one to organize it all.

He was behind everything.

"Why risk trying to kill me if all you wanted was an in with the council?"

"Your morals are a hindrance to our vision for the future. It didn't go unnoticed that you're intending to try and change our relationship with the humans. We can't allow it. Still, when the murder attempts seemed futile, since you foiled every one of them, this is the alternate plan."

We.

Not him. But we.

He wasn't working alone.

"You're going to keep Amara as a bargaining chip so Kincaid will do what you want," Levi stated coldly.

He grinned. "Yes. Now, play nice and we'll go and see your little doll."

We'd play nice until Amara was with us, and then we'd make sure they all paid.

<h1 style="text-align:center">Twenty-Eight</h1>

SILAS

My dragon hadn't stopped pushing at me to change forms since I woke. But I couldn't. We needed answers first. We had to make sure our mate was safe before we swooped in to save her.

But I had a feeling that wasn't going to happen, and she'd be the one to save us. My dragon grumbled. Yeah, I was on board with him; we wanted to do the saving. We wanted to make sure our mate was safe, and then we wanted the blood of everyone who'd touched her.

Kincaid's father, Kane, stepped up to the door and opened it. "They'll be good boys now," he said to someone in the hall.

He took a step back, and at least ten guards entered. They undid our chains, and I didn't miss the surprise on their faces when they noticed mine were broken.

My strength had grown since bonding. I hadn't realized how much until the metal broke.

Which was good because it would make me unstoppable in dragon form.

I unsheathed my claws as I stood and stretched. What I really wanted to do was to bury them in the guards' guts and spill their intestines everywhere. I wouldn't be the only one wanting to deliver death. Levi and Kincaid followed the guards' every move with punishing gazes.

We couldn't act yet, though.

Still, a growl rumbled out of me, and smoke billowed from my nose. The guards stepped back.

"Don't fear them," Kane yelled.

Mate.

Yes, we'd have our eyes on her soon, and we'd make sure she was unharmed, *then* we'd play.

The guard closest to me shoved me toward the door, causing me to stumble. It seemed he wanted to act tough in front of his boss. I'd let him, for now.

Another one pushed Levi so hard, he flew across the room. Thank fuck for his catlike reflexes because he landed in a crouch. With a low growl, he turned slowly to eye the guard. I smirked when the guard swallowed thickly.

"Touch me and I break every bone in your body," Kincaid warned when a guard got too close. "I wasn't allowed to use my full strength in training, but I don't seem to care about that now."

"Move," the guard snapped.

Kincaid squared up until I called his name.

He met my gaze, nodded, and started for the door.

Kane was in the lead, then five guards, us, and five more behind. Ten guards for the three of us were nothing. We could have taken them, but again, the risk outweighed the reward until we had eyes on Amara.

They took us up some stairs that opened into the kitchen. The maids were running around in a titter.

Kane barked, "Relax, none of them can get through." They all froze to dip into a curtsey while we kept going and moved out of the kitchen into a hall.

What did he mean, they couldn't get through?

When we entered another room, I glanced out the window. "What the fuck?" I muttered.

The line stopped, and Kane turned. "As you can see, your rescue attempt is failing."

There was a border of shimmering blue surrounding the estate, and on the outside of that were our employees, my family, and Levi's all trying to break through.

Levi made a noise in the back of his throat. "But the house shook...."

"That was their first attempt just before we erected the barrier. Now, they won't penetrate it."

Which meant it would be up to our mate and us to fight. I knew how many men Kane had employed. It was eight hundred. Honestly, I still believed we could take them all. My dragon huffed in agreement.

"How is the council standing by all this? They'll see our families trying to break in," Levi said. He brushed up against me to get a better look outside. His lips thinned. Was he worried about destroying the barrier? He needn't be. I was sure our mate's power would have the means to get it down. If not, we would take out whoever created it to get it to fall.

Levi glanced at me, and I wanted to reach out to him. To reassure him that everything would be all right. We'd get to Amara, take out the bad guys, and make sure not one of our friends and family members would be hurt.

Fuck. I prayed it went that way.

"Onward," Kane called.

We walked out into the foyer. More guards stood around the walls. Some sneered, others looked away, but what I didn't understand were the ones who scented scared.

Why were they working for him if they didn't want to?

"One stop first before we get this matter sorted," Kane called over his shoulder as he headed toward his office door. He opened it and stepped out of the way. The guards in front of us moved off to the side.

Kincaid went through first, then Levi, and finally me.

I stilled while Kincaid and Levi rushed forward. On the floor in the corner was Mary's beaten body.

"Mary," Levi called. "Mary, come on, honey. Come on." He lightly tapped her cheek, but she was still, too still.

"She's breathing... for now," Kincaid solemnly said.

Anger pulsed through me. My chest vibrated as I slowly turned to Kane. "Did you do this?"

He warned, "Remember what will happen if you don't behave."

Grinding my teeth together, I spun back around. "They've treated her like a beaten dog thrown in the corner. Lay her on the couch, and let's get this shit sorted."

"Not sure what you think you'll sort," Kane commented. I ignored him.

Levi's eyes were shining all lion as he carefully placed Mary's limp body on the couch. I grabbed a pillow and gently lifted Mary's head to put it under. We all hovered around her, burning with fury.

She'd get her revenge. Only we'd be the ones inflicting it.

Kincaid brushed hair from her face. "Get her a healer," he ordered coldly.

"No," Kane replied blandly.

"She needs help to heal from what you fucking cunts did to her," Levi roared, swinging around to face him.

Kane straightened from the doorway and held up his hand to ward off the guards who suddenly appeared behind him. "Then this is an extra incentive to behave for the next part."

I curled an arm around Levi's chest when he took a step closer to Kane. "Think of Amara," I whispered roughly, even though I wanted to rip them all apart myself.

He took some deep breaths, staring Kane down while his lion's growl rumbled in his chest. Suddenly, he threw my arm off him and turned back to Mary. Bending, he picked up her hand. "Be strong, Mary. Please, hold on."

"Follow," Kane clipped, and he turned, walking away from the doorway.

"They'll suffer. We'll make sure of it," Kincaid said, his

tone roughened with emotions. Fury and fear sounding close to the surface.

"We'll be back as soon as we can," Levi told Mary, and I hoped she heard. He straightened and faced us. "It's obvious they questioned her about our bond."

I nodded. "She should have told them right away."

Levi dropped his head back, glaring at the ceiling, but I didn't miss the tear that spilled. "Let's get our mate. Get her safe. She... she might be able to help Mary."

"Or Cassar will," Kincaid added.

I winced. "I want to say I feel sorry for the people who did this when Cassar or our mate finds out, but I'm not."

"They deserve it," Levi said.

"Come," Kane called, annoyance clear in his arrogant tone.

Together, we made our way out into the foyer. I was surprised that Kane stood by the opened front door. Why would he want us outside? Unless he got off on having an audience when they tried to sever our bond.

It wouldn't work, though. It couldn't.

Guards stepped further away when my dragon growled in response to my thoughts.

That's right. We wouldn't let anyone take our mate from us.

Once down the stairs, Kane strode out onto the grassy area, stopped, and turned to face the house.

Was he waiting for the council?

Where was our mate, though? I glanced around, unable to see her. I reached into the bond and felt the connection, knowing she was close. Was she awake?

Off to the right side, outside the barrier, lions paced

and dragons flew. Our families were ready to help once we could get them in. To the left, our men and women were waiting, some in shifted forms, while others chose to stay in their human appearances. Even the enchanters we had on the payroll were there, powers at the ready.

We could do this. We could—

Kane let out a shrill whistle, and I braced myself. As did Levi and Kincaid.

Pounding footsteps sounded, and more guards marched from around both sides of the house. They kept coming and coming. About 10 percent were already transformed into their animals, and I could see red shining in the eyes of another 10 percent. Vampires. The rest were either humans or enchanters. All up, there stood over a thousand. More than I expected.

Turmoil filled my gut, but I forced it down. No matter how many there were, we wouldn't give up.

Our mate was at risk, and we'd fight them all to get to her.

"I can feel the nerves rising," Kane commented. Guards that were closest chuckled.

Our families and friends on the outside roared, snarled, and yelled.

I glanced over and caught my father's gaze. Fear had his eyes glistening as he held my mother close. Three flying dragons let out a stream of fire from above.

The alpha was readying our army, along with Gus and my brother.

Even if we broke the barrier, would we have enough fighting power?

My dragon snarled at me from inside as he pushed

forward an image of our mate in her other form. I'd caught a glimpse of her that night she protected Kincaid.

Yes, with Amara, we would have enough. Certainty had me grinning.

"What are you smiling about?" Kane questioned sharply.

"Nothing."

Kane turned to me. "You still think you have a chance? You can't stop this. No one can." He glanced at Kincaid, and for a beat, I thought I saw remorse before he blinked and the emotion disappeared. "You shouldn't have bonded. If you act out, the servant will be harmed."

Was that.... It couldn't be a twisted type of warning.

He *was* behind this.

Right?

"I tried," Kane said quietly, staring at his son.

"Tried what?" Kincaid asked, lowering his arms from across his chest and clenching his fists at his sides.

Was this a part of the plan?

"I couldn't do it. I couldn't—" he cried out and fell to his knees.

"Now, now, Kane. You're not telling them all my secrets, are you?"

Slowly, I pulled my wide gaze up to the top of the steps where Kincaid's mother, Crista, stood.

"What...?" Kincaid was as confused as Levi and I were.

She threw her head back and laughed. "Did you seriously think your father could plan all this?"

What the fuck?

Seriously, what the fuck?

Why?

Kincaid's head jerked back. "You?"

She beamed. "Of course."

Kincaid looked at his father on the ground, jaw clenching, then back up at Crista. "All along, I thought he was behind everything."

"I know."

"Kane, get up and come to me," Crista ordered.

Kane groaned but got to his feet and shuffled the whole way up to stand beside his wife. She turned to him and patted his cheek. "You were always a fool, weren't you?"

"Yes, dear."

Her hand slid to pinch his cheeks together. "Pathetic," she spat. "I wasn't blind to the ways you helped him. The training, hoping you could make him strong enough for this moment. The real reason you scarred him was so no female I picked would look at him or want him because you didn't want that woman to be in his ear like I've been in yours." She grinned maniacally. "None of it worked, though. I've found him the perfect partner, and his training won't help him tonight. Not when I have many devoted followers who want the world to stay the way it should be."

Suddenly, she punched her arm right through Kane's stomach. Blood sprayed from his mouth as he coughed out. I caught movement and grabbed Kincaid, as did Levi.

"Right now, there's nothing you can do," I whispered through clenched teeth.

All along, Kane had been trying to help his son in the best way he could. Why the fuck hadn't he just told Kincaid?

Crista pulled her arm free, and Kane dropped to the ground. She shook her arm out. Blood and guts went flying.

"I'm surprised you even made a move to assist him, Kincaid. After everything he's done to you."

Kincaid stilled and we dropped our hands. "I'm surprised as well, Mother."

She cackled. "You were always a soft soul with a hard exterior. But I was never fooled. Not when you snuck off to help the humans around the estate." She tsked and shook her head. "Such weakness." She straightened out her dress. "I always knew you wouldn't rule the same way I had your father doing. The young are so softhearted, but the world doesn't need to change, Kincaid. It's perfect the way it is—until I convince the council of my new vision, that is."

"How did you get him to do as you asked?" Kincaid asked.

Her smile grew, and her lips moved silently. She looked over her shoulder as she held her hand up and it started to glow.

Magic.

She wasn't just a vampire, but an enchanter as well.

Doors crashed opened and guards filed out onto the upper stairs. But then, fuck me, I saw Amara floating across the ground, head hanging low, still unconscious.

Crista laid Amara at her feet.

"Poor little thing hasn't woken yet." She landed a kick to Amara's leg.

A growl rolled out of me as I took on my half form,

and Levi snarled as he shifted into his. Kincaid's hands clamped around our wrists.

"Boys, act civilly. I haven't harmed her… yet. But that can change if any of you even take a step."

"What do you want?" Kincaid called.

"I'm sure your father explained everything. After we've killed the bond, you'll marry Jasmine." Her gaze shone. "That girl is easily manipulated with status and power. Takes after her father."

Fuck, did that mean we'd have trouble from her father who was on the council?

Something to think about another time.

"However, for now, I need something else." Her lips moved as she clicked her fingers.

Something bound my hands and feet together. I fell to the ground with a grunt. I wasn't the only one. Levi landed close to me.

"What the fuck?" I yelled. The dragons and lions were going crazy on the outside of the barrier. I tried to break the invisible bounds by stretching and pulling, but they weren't budging. They weren't like the ones Kane had us in.

"Mother, what are you doing?"

I stilled as guards moved closer. Kincaid bent, grabbing my arm and Levi's to drag us closer to him. He hissed out at the guards closing in.

"Stop," he ordered, gaze swirling red. "What are you doing, Mother?"

"I was informed that some paperwork had been filed. They're stepping down as leaders. It means I won't need them. I'll only need you alive, Kincaid."

Kincaid's hand tightened around my arm. "If you want me to be cooperative, you won't harm them. After this, let them leave."

She kicked out at Amara again. "I think you'll listen if I keep this thing around. That is, if you want her to live."

Kincaid stood. "All I'll ask is for you to leave these three alone, and I promise I'll do anything you want."

"Anything?"

"Yes."

"Hmm, I don't actually believe you."

Kincaid waved a hand out. "Are you actually thinking things through here? If you kill Silas and Levi, the dragons and lions will come for your blood."

She laughed. "That doesn't scare me. As you can see, I have many." Her gaze moved off to the side. "As sympathizers, they all need to be destroyed anyway. The lion first."

Fear slammed into me. Levi's family roared. I strained and fought the magic holding me. Kicking my legs up, I rolled to the side and tried to slide toward Levi, who was fighting as much as I was. Kincaid took a few guards down when they tried to approach.

"Stop," Crista called. She held a sword in her hand. The tip rested against Amara's throat.

"It's okay," Levi whispered.

Kincaid and I looked at him. I clenched my jaw and shook my head. Tears threatened.

Levi gave us a watery smile. "For Amara."

"Levi," Kincaid choked.

"It's all right. Keep her safe and happy."

"Do it," Crista snapped.

"No!" I snarled.

"Silas, don't," Levi begged. His bottom lip trembled, and my heart shattered. Kincaid made an anguished noise in the back of his throat and froze where he was.

I shook my head. "She can't live without you. None of us can."

"You can. With her, anything is possible."

Anything was.

A guard dragged Levi to his feet. Another one pulled a sword free and swept his arm back, ready to take his head.

My throat closed over when Levi's gaze met mine.

Baby, princess, please, wake up. We need you.

Twenty-Nine

AMARA

GROANING, I tried to lift my head, but my body was sluggish. Where was I? What happened? My darkness brushed against me. The urge to set it free was present, but why did I want to? I had no idea why it wanted to come out.

Licking my dry lips, I pushed myself up into a seated position and lifted my head, my neck aching from stiffness.

"Wait" was yelled close by.

Wait? For what?

"Maybe we could use this moment to get her to comply."

Who was speaking so loudly? Who to comply to what?

"Love, open your eyes."

Kincaid.

I struggled to open them, but they weren't obeying. My darkness smashed against me, making me gasp. It'd never done that before.

"Amara, come on, princess. You need to see."

Silas.

I rubbed at my eyes with my palms. My darkness slammed against me again, and I slapped my hands down behind me when my back arched. I opened my eyes wide as my pulse beat so fast, it rang in my ears, and under my hand, I suddenly felt something wet.

Turning, I gaped and blinked down at Mr. Prince. Lifting my palm, I looked at his blood coating it.

Who did this?

Then images filled my head. The cafeteria. The panic in my mates' eyes. The pain stabbing in my back. The person's words: *"It's a sedative, you'll be all right."* And then nothing.

Scrambling to my feet, I stepped back and away from Mr. Prince's still body.

Hands grabbed my arms, and I looked left and right. Guards were everywhere.

What was going on?

My darkness pushed against its cage again. But I needed to assess the situation first.

"It's good to see you finally awake, dear."

I lifted my gaze and locked on to Mrs. Prince. Blood coated her front. Had she killed her husband? Had she done it to help her son?

"W-What is this?" I asked.

She sneered at me. "Do as I say and I won't hurt anyone."

"What?"

"Amara." At Silas's voice, I swung my gaze down the staircase and out onto the grass where I saw my mates. Silas lay on the ground as if bound, and Kincaid stood beside him, but what had me gasping, what made my eyes widen and sent fear shooting through my veins, was seeing Levi being held as a guard pointed a sword at him.

"No," I uttered.

"Yes," Mrs. Prince stated. "If you don't do as you're told, I will kill the shifters."

My gaze snapped back to her before I took in Mr. Prince again. Fury spiked, causing my skin to prickle, and my darkness pushed once more.

Soon, I promised it.

It was his mother all along. *What the hell is up with mothers these days?*

She'd been trying to kill her son. I didn't understand the reasoning, but the present threat was real. She wanted Kincaid alive to manipulate him. She wanted *my* shifters dead because they were of no use and probably harder to control.

But no one would harm them.

Not while I was around.

"You shouldn't have done this," I whispered, my gaze dropping to the ground.

Mrs. Prince scoffed.

Actually, she didn't deserve her title. She didn't deserve my respect. She would only be Crista. And she'd soon learn she'd made a mistake by touching what was mine.

"And why is that, human? You're a lowly maid. *I* have

the advantage. *I* have the collateral. This is my party, servant. I will always get what I want. For too long I've sat back, but now, when my son thinks he can change the world and have us work alongside the humans and lower species, I won't tolerate it. No one has stopped me so far. Not when I'm a vampire filled with magic, so why do you think you can?"

I shook my head. It didn't matter that she held magic. My darkness was immune. Could that be why whoever had taken me and promised I'd be all right had injected me with a sedative instead of using magic? Maybe. But who it had been, I didn't know. I hoped he'd escaped before this madness started. It seemed to me that he really hadn't wanted to follow orders.

Lifting my gaze, I stared at her coldly. "You *really* shouldn't have done this," I said again.

She cocked her brow, oblivious to what lay in store for her. "And why is that?"

Laughter rang out. I knew who it was coming from.

Crista spun to glare down the stairs. "What are you laughing at, Kincaid?"

I glanced down at him and found him smiling. "For anyone who wishes to leave, now is the time," he called out. I glanced beyond the barrier to where dragons roared and lions snarled. Some even pawed at the barrier. They knew what was coming; they were ready for the fight, and I prayed that my darkness could allow them entrance. It trilled inside me, spreading hope through my veins.

Silas snorted. "It'd be a really good idea to listen to him because once we're free, we'll be getting payback."

No one moved.

"They're loyal to me," Crista smugly called.

"I promise you this. We *will* be free. We will win. If you don't wish to die this night, leave," Kincaid said, sounding deadly serious.

It seemed there were some smart people among them; they started walking off around the side of the house.

"Don't move," Crista screeched, like a schoolgirl not getting her way.

They didn't listen.

"You will not win. You will not be free." In a blink, she was in front of me with her hand around my neck, lifting me off my feet. I grabbed at her wrists. "Kincaid, she'll die. I'll kill her. Stand down, say no more, and do as you're told."

"No, Mother, because it seems you have all the information—except for one thing."

Her hand tightened. "What?"

"Mother, meet Amara. She's the center of our circle. She's everything you are not because she has the softest of souls and kindest of hearts I've ever seen."

"I care not for her, but to win," she declared roughly and snapped my neck.

My body was flung to the ground.

But I'd already let my darkness free, and it filled me in a rush, healing my neck by stitching the broken bone back together and mending my muscles and veins while keeping my heart beating and brain working.

"Do you see what you made me do!" Crista screamed.

My darkness swept slowly out of me, peeking around us while I played dead. It wanted to cause pain. It wanted to drain them all of power and life.

And we would.

"Why aren't you in pain? The bond broke. You should be in agony." She stared down at them.

My men shared a look, smiling. God, I loved them for having faith in me.

"Hunger for power will never get you anywhere in life," Kincaid announced. "You will soon see that those who push to have it all will be punished. It is time for change. It's time we treat all with respect. We can live together peacefully."

"Your dream is nothing but that," his mother yelled.

More people walked off.

"Stop," she shrieked, shaking her fists out. "Don't listen to him." She shook her head before gripping her long locks. "I don't understand. I killed her. I killed your bonded."

"Did you?" Kincaid asked.

Fully healed, I floated up to stand behind her with the help of my darkness. Power thrummed through me, dancing across my skin. I unsheathed my daggers that they foolishly hadn't searched me for. When people started to murmur and gasp, Crista slowly turned. People began to scream. Not that I could blame them. I knew I would be a sight to behold with my teeth, claws, black eyes, and veins. The darkness swayed behind me like I had four tails.

Crista took a step back, wariness in her gaze. "What are you?"

"The one who will set the world right."

"Kill them all!" she bellowed.

My darkness shot out into the night as I attacked Crista. I flew right into her, daggers raised. She expected me, though, and twisted us enough to throw my momentum off. I sailed to the side and landed in a crouch.

Standing, I smiled, all sharp teeth. *See, I have more than you.* "You've been the one trying to have him killed."

"I wished they'd succeeded," she snapped, her upper lip rising, fangs flashing.

I flicked out my hand, sending the dagger straight to her heart, but it missed by inches. It didn't stop her cry of pain. As she pulled it free, I smirked when she gasped and cursed.

"You may have power, but I have more." Her lips moved and she lifted a hand. Sparks of gold touched her fingers. She sent it my way, laughing. The sound faded when I stayed where I was and let the magic wash over me.

From her screech of fury, it obviously wasn't what she wanted to happen.

My darkness caught my attention when it sent a pulse of frustration. I glanced down to see my men fighting against many others. My darkness helped where it could, while also trying to break through the barrier.

Kincaid fought gracefully with his vampiric power. Silas and Levi were in their half forms, clawing, biting, and breaking anyone who got close. While they could take on a lot, there were too many.

They needed backup.

A smile lifted my lips when Crista obviously thought I wouldn't notice that she was advancing. The darkness made it possible that I could look in multiple places at once.

She lunged. I stepped aside and turned to her. "I'll be back to play soon."

Her head jerked back, and her mouth dropped open when I suddenly lifted off the ground and flew to the barrier.

My mates' employees stood on the other side, watching me, some in horror, some in awe, and the rest wore determined, excited expressions. I caught the lion shifters moving closer to where I was, and then the moonlight was blocked out by two dragons. They roared together.

I placed my hands on the barrier and opened my mouth. More darkness spilled out of me, coating the wall, spreading out. More came from the tips of my fingers to glide along the sides and spread down to the bottom.

And then I pushed.

It cracked.

The dragons let out a conjoined puff of fire along the top. The men, women, and shifters pressed from their side, all species helping.

With a cry, I pulled more of my darkness away from fighting and shoved it into the barrier.

It splintered from the bottom all the way up to the top.

People screamed in pain in the distance, and I knew it was the enchanters who created this.

The splinters widened, expanded, and slid down the sides. I didn't know how they managed to use their magic to create this barrier that my darkness couldn't easily brush away. Still, it soon wouldn't matter.

With one final push, it shattered.

At once, everyone raced in and joined the fight. A dragon landed beside me and chuffed in my face. Somehow, I knew it was Gus. I ran my hand up the side of his face. "Help your grandson," I told him. He huffed and walked off, crushing people who tried to come at him with weapons, claws, or magic.

The darkness released an excited trill and swept over the earth to kill and drain those who were against us. My darkness showed me my mates fighting.

Kincaid ripped a head clear off a body. He turned to a shifter and a vampire who were close by and demanded, "Make sure the humans are safe. Check the barn and outer cottages." They nodded and raced off. My mate then threw himself into another fight, helping others who worked for Silas and Levi.

Silas had fully shifted into his dragon and sprayed fire at a group getting close to Kincaid. Levi was running in his lion form. He leaped and slashed at someone's back. The person spun, red eyes glowing, and dropped Levi's mother, who was in her half form. Blood dripped from the vampire's mouth; he'd been trying to drain Levi's mother.

Levi snarled, dodged an attack, and latched his jaw and sharp teeth over the vampire's head until it snapped off. Levi spat the head out and rubbed his head against his mother's side.

I needed to get back to Crista.

I needed to end this.

Take out the general, and the rest would stop.

Looking at the stairs, I saw Crista up there, throwing balls of power at the dragons above. Guards surrounded her, blocking the dragons' fire when they tried to burn her.

Gliding along the ground, I made my way toward Crista.

She saw me coming, and I smiled when she paled. After everything she'd done, I thrived on her fear.

"Amara." Cassar landed heavily in front of me, his wings still a flutter, but his wide, crazy eyes sent worry throughout me. "Please, please come with me. Mary.... She... she needs help." Tears fell from his eyes, and my blood turned cold.

"Where is she? What did they do?"

"The house, please. Dear God, please. I can't heal her. She's.... I can't heal her."

"Where is she?"

"The office, this way—"

"Wait," I ordered. My darkness was already on the move, searching for her.

"We can't wait!" Cassar yelled.

I took a step toward him but watched through the darkness. Reaching out, I gripped his arm when he went to move.

"Please, Amara. Please," he choked.

My throat closed over and I whimpered when I saw her. "What did they do to her?" I whispered, staring with black eyes up at Cassar.

"Y-You see her?"

"Yes." Gently, my darkness picked her up and carried her out to me. She flew over everyone, cradled in my power. I crouched when she was placed on the ground, and the darkness receded.

"Mary," I uttered. Reaching out, I felt for her pulse, but I couldn't feel one. "No. No, no, no."

Not Mary. Please don't take her. Please.

My darkness urged me to lay my hands over her, so I did. Once more, power surrounded her, but again I had to withdraw from the fight. I poured it over Mary's lifeless form and prayed for it to do something to help.

Finley's mother's words rang through my mind: *There is always a risk of pain and death.*

A lion bellowed in torment. Someone screamed in anguish. A dragon whined in agony.

No, no, no!

A scream tore out of me. More darkness spilled free and stretched into Mary, while across the ground, fighting, killing, drinking, and draining continued. There was so much. My darkness took, it fought, and it protected. Even if I had to use everything inside me, I would.

No one would die this night.

Except maybe me.

And I could deal with that if it meant everyone else stayed safe and alive.

I lifted my gaze and, through the darkness, touched each of my mates. "I'm sorry," I uttered before another scream broke free, and I pushed harder.

Thirty

LEVI

When Amara's scream echoed through the night, I turned and roared. I could feel her draining herself. I could sense her pushing everything out.

Darkness surrounded everything now. Bodies dropped, one after another. Those who attacked us and our people all fell to the ground as the darkness threaded through their bodies.

On the run, I shifted, letting the darkness guide me through it.

It opened up to Amara laying over Mary. Eyes closed. My heart lodged into my throat and my gut dropped. Cassar shook Amara's shoulder, calling her name.

Just as I skidded to a stop, Kincaid and Silas dropped to my sides. I picked up our mate, sitting back on my ass and holding her in my lap.

She was limp in my hold. With her arms hanging

down at her side, her eyes stayed closed, and her breaths became shallower.

Silas brushed hair from Amara's face, crowding us as much as Kincaid was doing on my other side as he picked up her hand and pressed it against his cheek.

"Amara, listen to me. Pull the darkness back. Please, sweetheart, pull it back." *Save yourself.* I could feel her fading.

"Love, come on. Listen to our lion."

"You got them all, princess. Everything's stopped."

A cough sounded behind us. Cassar held Mary in the same position I did Amara. She was alive, gasping for breath and crying, but alive.

Palming my mate's cheek, I rested her head against my chest. "Please, sweetheart. We can't lose you."

"Amara. Drag the darkness back. Now," Kincaid clipped. Fear rode his harsh tone.

"Don't leave us alone," Silas whispered as he moved to rest his head on her lap while he begged her not to leave.

Tears filled my eyes and dropped. Kincaid pressed her hand to his forehead and closed his eyes, his body locked full of tension, fear, and worry.

I sniffed and looked to the sky, swallowing thickly. Dipping my head, I kissed our mate's forehead, her temple. "Come on, sweetheart. Pull it back. You don't need to fight anymore. We're safe. Take our strength. If the darkness needs more to help you, we have it. Take ours. Just stay with us. Please, sweetheart."

Something caressed over my back, and I opened my eyes to see the hands of the darkness. It brushed against Silas and Kincaid.

"Please," I begged it. "If you need our strength, take it. Just make her okay."

Another caress before it receded into Amara—through her nose, under her eyelids, her fingertips, and lips.

Until there was no more, and she was back in her human form.

I lifted my gaze when Gus said, "Give her to me."

"No," Kincaid snarled, flashing up to stand in front of us, arms stretched out.

Silas growled low and got to his feet when his grandfather took another step closer. "Now's not the time—"

"She'll be okay," Gus reassured with a soft smile. "She's just exhausted. There were so many left. She got to them all. However, there's something you all need to deal with."

I couldn't see beyond the people surrounding us. Our family and friends were here to check if our mate was okay. My heart clenched. Slowly, I climbed to my feet with our mate in my arms. The only thing keeping me from going crazy was seeing and feeling her chest rise and fall.

"Son, give her to Gus. Look." My father nodded toward the house.

Turning, I sucked in a sharp breath.

"What the fuck?" Silas breathed.

"Amara," Kincaid said, with awe and shock.

Besides the ground being littered with lifeless bodies, there were also many who were alive but bound with... some had curtains wrapped around them, others with bedsheets, clothes, or ropes. I presumed it was anything her darkness could find to hold them still.

They weren't our people; they'd been Crista's. But why they weren't slaughtered was something we'd have to ask Amara.

"She saw innocence within them," Kincaid announced.

I swung my gaze to him. "You think so?"

He nodded. "I saw a few of them slinking around, trying to hide, not wanting to be involved in the fight."

"Guys," Silas clipped. When we glanced at him, he nodded toward the stairs.

Crista stood atop them, smiling smugly with her hands on her hips, but she wasn't the only one. The council stood with her.

"Gus" was all I said, and he stepped forward. With a kiss to her temple, I gently passed our mate over to someone we knew would protect her with his life. "Get her away if this gets ugly."

He nodded. "Got it."

"Son." My father passed me and Silas some pants. We quickly slipped into them, and then with Kincaid, we made our way toward the bottom of the stairs. I took a quick glance at Mary, who clung to Cassar, shaking, with her head buried against his neck as he held on to her tightly while whispering something in her ear.

Drawing in a deep breath, I puffed it out when we stopped at the bottom.

"You may speak now, Alpha Crista," Councilman Thomas, a bear shifter, ordered.

"I feared for my life. Their bonded mate is something I've never seen. Look at the destruction around you. So many lives lost." Crista wiped at her eyes when the fake tears fell. "It's a tragedy. She needs to be locked up or sentenced to death."

Both my animal and Silas's hissed out of us at the idea of a death sentence. We agreed with their anger. We'd kill them if they tried.

"Do we not have a voice against these lies?" Kincaid called. The council stared down at us. "You could get an award for your acting, Mother, but there are many witnesses who will back our version."

"Those people fear her. Of course they'll say anything to agree with you all. She's your bonded. The shifters' bonded. They'll protect her over our kind, my son."

"Which is it, Alpha Crista; they fear her, or will protect her?" Councilwoman Rodriguez asked. She was a wolf shifter.

Crista faltered a little, opening and closing her mouth.

"Council members, you've heard about the attempts on my life. I'd always wondered why no one could find information about who was behind these attacks. At first, I thought it was my father. I hadn't suspected my own mother would want me dead."

"I would never!" Crista yelled, taking a step back.

"Do not move, Alpha Crista," warned Councilman Anderson, an enchanter.

Crista pointed down at Kincaid. "What fabrication! These are all lies in hope to protect his bonded's life. *She* was the monster. She attacked me and my people. It's she who needs to be punished. Dragon, bring her here."

"Stay where you are," Councilman Moore snapped. His gaze swirled red and back again. "Alpha Kincaid, finish."

Kincaid dipped his head. "Everything came to light today. We, along with our bonded, Amara, were kidnapped and brought here where we were threatened to comply or else they'd hurt our bonded, whom they'd taken somewhere else."

"Why wasn't your circle bond reported? Why have you been keeping it a secret when a power like hers can be only seen as a threat?" The councilman who spoke was another vampire and also Jasmine's father. "I recommend we terminate their bond and lock her up."

My lion snarled, and I balled my hands into fists even though I wanted to wrap them around the pompous cunt's neck and wring it. No doubt I wasn't the only one imagining his death. I could hear Silas's heavy breaths and Kincaid's quiet, harsh cursing.

"Yes!" Crista cried.

"It's lucky you're not ruling on your own, Councilman Blake," Councilwoman Green, another enchanter, stated.

"Fellow council members," Councilman Blake took a step forward. "It is ridiculous to even listen to this young boy when his concerns are only for his bonded woman. Who, let me remind you, is a servant."

"Exactly," Crista said. "Isn't there a law about bonding with the help?"

The enchanter known as Councilwoman Wright laughed. "I'm sure you wished there were."

Councilman Blake moved forward a step. "My daughter was promised Kincaid's hand in marriage. She is better than a servant. She will—"

"Enough," Councilman Nelson roared. His tiger

shone in his eyes for a moment and then it was gone. "We'll get back to what you were promised, Blake, but *after* Kincaid shares his side of the events."

Kincaid dipped his head once again. "When we woke, my father told us the plan of breaking our bond so I could marry Jasmine. If I didn't comply, they would harm our bonded. We were taken outside here where the Grayson Pride and Peril Weyr family were barred from this area by a barrier because they were here to help us. Mother appeared, killed my father—"

"I did not kill him. She did. I would never hurt my husband. I loved him," Crista screamed.

Kincaid went on, ignoring her outburst, "She told us of her plans for my future. If I didn't comply to her orders or Jasmine's, our mate's life was at risk. She was in the process of slaughtering Alpha Silas and Alpha Levi, since they were of no use to her because they've stepped down as leaders, when our mate, Amara, woke. As did her power. If needed, I could go into more details."

"*Lies*. It's all lies. How can you listen to this?" Crista glanced frantically around.

"A shifter told me you allowed anyone who listened to leave and save their lives," Councilman Thomas said and then added, "Is this correct, Alpha Kincaid?"

"Yes."

"Alpha Crista Prince, did you murder your husband, Alpha Kane Prince?"

She laughed crazily and waved her hands around. "I didn't. Do you see his body here?"

Where did it go?

"Council members, if I may, please?" Mary curtseyed at my side.

"No. They don't hear from underlings. She's nothing but a—"

"A shifter of our community," Councilwoman Rodriguez stated with a growl. "Speak, Mary."

"It was Alpha Crista Prince who tortured me for information about Maid Amara. I would be dead now if it weren't for Amara and her power."

Crista swung a hand down at Mary. "She works for them. She'll say anything."

Crista knew she was failing. She knew they weren't listening. I hated to see what she'd do when they believed Kincaid over her.

No matter. We would be prepared.

Councilwoman Turner shook her head. "Mary's words and Alpha Kincaid's are backed by another who witnessed everything."

"Who?" Crista demanded.

"Step out."

We couldn't see the doors from down here, but we heard them open, and then Kane appeared. His shirt was soaked in blood, but he was completely healed.

His wife gaped at her husband.

"What's the meaning of this? I didn't hear his side of the story. He could be placing all the blame on his wife," Councilman Blake yelled. Crista nodded, stepping closer to him, and she took his arm while whimpering like a scared woman.

"It's true. He planned all this. I had to. He would have hurt me otherwise. I—"

Councilman Anderson snorted. "Save it." He waved his hand. Crista and Blake were separated and bound. "I saw your lips move, Crista. We know about your dual nature. Something you hadn't informed the council of." His glare shot to Blake. "We'll be having a word after all this about your involvement since you happened to slip out of the room, which was how you missed the arrival of Alpha Kane Prince." He glanced at Kane. "Though, for now, Alpha Kane, can you please let everyone know, how did you survive?"

"When my *wife*," he snarled, "punched a fist through me, I felt the magic she'd infused with it. A spell that turned me immobile while liquid fire burned slowly around my heart. The pain was agonizing until it suddenly stopped. I was dragged inside by darkness. It melded with my body, healing me, and the spell dissipated, which sparked my own healing ability."

Amara had saved him.

Our mate had saved Kane.

I glanced at Kincaid to see the shock on his face. Reaching out, I gripped his wrist and squeezed. Kincaid dropped his head and nodded while taking a deep breath. She'd seen good inside of Kane. It was the only explanation for letting him live.

The council members suddenly tensed and looked over at us.

"I saved you because you didn't deserve to die when you tried everything you could to stop this."

We spun around to see Amara walking toward us. She gave us a tired smile, and as soon as she was close, we pulled her into us, surrounding her. I pressed a kiss to the top of her head, Silas to her neck, and Kincaid to her temple.

"Sweetheart," I whispered, drawing in her scent. Relief settled the beating of my heart. She was okay.

"Love, you scared us," Kincaid said.

"Don't do it again," Silas ordered. Amara tipped her head back and glared at him, but it didn't last. She leaned in and kissed his chest.

"Let me in," Mary demanded, pushing at my back.

I stepped away and she barreled into Amara, hugging her tightly and crying, "Thank you, thank you, thank you."

Our mate's eyes glistened as she sniffed. "I'm so happy to see you're okay."

"All thanks to you."

A throat cleared. We faced the council members. Mary returned to Cassar, who dragged her close and wrapped his arms around her. Kincaid placed Amara in front of him while Silas and I stood at her sides, taking her hands.

"Amara Kenna, servant to Kincaid Prince," one of them called.

"Yes," Amara stated.

"We'd like for you to tell us your side, but start from the—"

"She does not get to speak. She is a meager servant. I won't have my world, my vision taken from me because of a human servant!" Crista spewed.

Her bindings broke from a word whispered by her. Next, she held Blake with a dagger to his neck.

"I'll kill him. Let me leave and I'll let him live." Hysteria chased her words.

"Stop!" was screamed, and Jasmine ran out from the house. "What are you doing? You promised you'd win, and I could have Kincaid. I got him here like you asked. I drugged him. I want him. You promised you'd kill those shifters—"

"Shut up, you stupid girl," her father snarled.

A few of the council members laughed, and Jasmine paled. She backed up again and again, only stopping when two guards took her arms. "No, please. I-I didn't mean what I said. It's all that servant's fault."

"I'm growing weary of this," Councilwoman Wright complained. With a spell from her lips and a wave of her hand, Jasmine was muted. "Fellow enchanters on the council, please join me in removing Crista's powers."

Crista dug the dagger into Blake's neck. "I'll kill him. I will."

Councilman Moore waved his hand in a circle. "By all means, do it. We're not blind or foolish enough to think Blake hasn't assisted you. He'll be removed from the—"

"What, no! I haven't done anything untoward," Blake tried, his pleas falling on deaf ears.

"Can we please move this along?" Councilwoman Turner demanded. "Alpha Wright, Alpha Nelson, and Alpha Anderson, please contain these three and lock them away. We'll deal with them later. Guards, help the ones who are bound and take them into a vacant room. We'll want their testimonies." Guards glided down the stairs to help the others. The vampire councilwoman turned to us. "Meet us in the dining room. We'll have your story, Amara, and some answers."

Amara curtseyed before turning into our arms as they

left with Kane, dragging Crista, Blake, and Jasmine with them.

Our mate was safe. We had won.

But now we had to deal with the council when all I wanted to do was go to Wayland's cottage and have our mate rest.

"Just a little longer," Kincaid said, cupping the back of Amara's neck.

Amara looked up, sinking her teeth into her bottom lip before she blew out a breath. "Will they make me leave you?"

"We won't let them," Silas growled.

"Hear them out before you jump to any conclusions," my father said as our family and friends crowded us.

Amara nodded. "I will, I just—"

"It's understandable to expect the worst," Alpha Conrad said. "But know that all of you will have our support." He dropped to his knees, and I felt Amara tense from the shock.

"You have the Grayson pride also," my father added, and they, along with our friends, fell to their knees in a bow. "Thank you, Goddess of Darkness, for saving us all."

Those who were still bound but hadn't yet been led away also kneeled.

Kincaid stepped forward. "We thank you for your support. All we wish is to help lead in the right direction. We believe change is coming, but it'll be for the better." He turned and went to Amara's side with an intense gaze that had her blushing.

People started to roar. Excitement, adrenaline, and happiness rode them all.

As I turned, I caught my father's pride-filled gaze, and he tipped his chin up. I glanced behind him up at the stairs.

The council members had returned and stood up top, watching everyone.

Good. Take it in. Know they believe and trust in our mate.

Thirty-One

AMARA

WHEN I WALKED into the dining room to meet the council members, nerves churned inside me—even more so when I noticed they weren't yet there. The waiting only allowed my mind time to doubt all the choices I made during the battle. Had I done the right thing? Did I do something to upset them? Would they believe anything Crista said?

The door banged open as they entered. I jolted and then watched them walk to the table. Before they sat opposite my mates and me, they bowed.

They *bowed*. Right there, in front of me.

"If you please, Goddess, we would like to convene with you in a relaxed manner. Would you allow us to call you Amara?" Councilman Nelson asked.

Staring like a fish out of water, I opened my mouth

and a sound dropped out. Blushing, I pressed a hand over my rapidly beating heart. "I would prefer it that way."

"Thank you. Can you tell us of your past up to today?" Councilman Anderson said once he'd sat down.

Wonderment clutched my chest at their reaction to me. I licked my dry lips and cleared my throat. Levi squeezed my hand, as did Kincaid on my shoulders from where he stood behind me. Silas ran his palm up and down my thigh, all three of them encouraging me.

With a deep breath, I told them everything. How I'd come to have my darkness, my life with Mr. Langley, and moving into Kincaid's estate.

Kincaid then picked that moment to inform the council of the headmaster's demise and of the other attacks.

All was laid out for them.

The silence after we stopped talking scared me the most. Silas gripped my knee, which I didn't realize I'd been bouncing.

"All I ask," I started softly, looking at my hands on my lap where I was clutching Levi's, "is for no one to take my mates from me."

"That was never an option, Amara," Councilman Thomas stated. "Bonded couples or circles are cherished among our kind. You have nothing to fear from us about losing your mates."

Closing my eyes, I let the tension roll off my shoulders and thinned my lips to stop their tremble. Losing my mates had been my main worry.

I opened my eyes when someone cleared their throat. Councilwoman Wright smiled softly before she said, "The dragons aren't the only ones who've heard about the Goddess of Darkness. Change has been a long time coming, and we've been in deliberation about said changes for quite a while. But I'm afraid that when we shared our thoughts to the area leaders about altering the laws for *all* species, it was what set Crista off."

"We knew there'd be some against our plans, but we didn't know to what extent," Councilman Moore explained. "Crista hasn't been the only one who started a movement to overthrow any alterations we made. Yet, we never suspected Crista of anything. We never knew she'd been trying to have her own son killed because he, like us, saw the wrongdoing of all species."

Reaching up, I took Kincaid's hand in mine.

"What pisses me the fuck off is that none of us saw this coming," Councilman Thomas boomed. The table under his hands groaned. "Shock after shock with shit we should have seen coming."

"How could we, Alpha Thomas?" Councilwoman Rodriguez barked. "We've been watching the wrong person all along."

"You've been watching who?" Silas demanded.

The other council members shot Rodriguez a sharp look. She waved it off. "They'll find out eventually." She leaned forward in her chair and looked behind me. "As I'm guessing, you suspected your father?"

Kincaid replied with a grunt.

"We've had our eyes on him because he approached the council a long while ago, demanding to know why we were wanting change to begin with. Told us it would never work. That we were foolish to even think it. When nothing else came from it, we brushed it off but kept watch from afar."

"We never suspected Crista was pulling his strings with her magic," Councilwoman Turner said with distaste. "She hid her magic well and for a very long time."

"It wasn't until a human came to us yesterday with new information that we realized," Councilwoman Green said.

"A human? Who?" Levi asked.

"Enter," Green called.

The doors opened and a man I'd seen before walked in. Behind him was Kincaid's father. But what shocked me more was seeing their hands clasped together. Kincaid squeezed my shoulder. He released it quickly to slide his hand closer to my neck as he made a noise in the back of his throat.

"Lyall. He works the grounds around this estate," Kincaid said.

Yes. I remembered Lyall was there the day I started. He and his son Elliot.

"Lyall, please, let Amara and her mates know what you heard."

Kane watched Lyall as he nodded. "Recently, I overheard Mrs. Prince talking to Alpha Blake outside. She planned to get the council here under false pretenses. Her aim was to trap and kill them while placing the blame on her son. But this was only after she'd compelled the council to rid Kincaid of his bond so he would be free to marry Alpha Blake's daughter. In the end, she wanted to appear as the savior by stopping her son's plan, and then create her own council to rule however she wanted."

The room hummed with anger on all sides.

Lyall cleared his throat and rubbed at the back of his neck. "I, ah, well.... I told Mr. Prince...." He looked at Kane.

Kincaid's father gave him a soft hum of reassurance. "Lyall and I have been talking since he arrived and have gotten close."

Silas snorted.

Kane dropped his gaze to the floor for a beat before pulling it up to his son. "He figured out I couldn't speak freely because I'd been magically bound to keep silent about all matters regarding *her*. He went to the council for me and told them of her plans. Son, I've wanted to tell you everything, but I couldn't. All I can do is beg for forgiveness—"

"We'll speak of this another time," Kincaid clipped.

Kane's jaw clenched but he nodded. He shifted his sorrow-filled gaze to me. "Wayland Langley was an honorable man." I sucked in a sharp breath, and Kincaid's grip on me pulsed. "Many years ago, Wayland and I were friends. While he was away traveling, I met... her, and by the time he returned, I was already under her spell and had cut off all ties, fearing she would harm him. With Wayland being well known among our community for his teachings, I knew if I displayed a hatred of shifters, she would push Kincaid at them out of spite. It was a shock that it worked and she sent our son to Wayland." He glanced off to the side and back. "And I knew Kincaid to be stubborn enough to want to keep them around if I continued my act of despising them. That decision was the best I've ever made, because Wayland was the gentle father figure I could never be, and he helped shape my son into the man I never was. A strong, kind-hearted, respectable man."

He didn't share this for me to hear, but for Kincaid. He had tried to help in any way he could.

My throat thickened and my chest tightened as I realized how much Kane had been through, even risking the relationship with his son.

A tear escaped and trailed down his cheek. "I'm grateful that you were able to spend most of your life with Wayland," he said to me, "but more so that he sent you to our family in his will."

I straightened. "He... he did?"

Kane nodded. "I made it look like we bought your contract so as not to raise suspicion, but Wayland sent you here. At first, I didn't know why he would, as he'd known I'd changed. He knew...." He shook his head. "Now, though, I understand. He sent you to Kincaid, which was why I made you his maid to begin with."

Blood rushed to my ears. I reached up and grabbed Kincaid's hand as he leaned in and rested his forehead against my shoulder.

"Alpha Kane, Lyall. Thank you for your time, but please excuse us for a moment," Councilman Anderson said.

When they left, Councilwoman Green said, "Kincaid, your mother isn't yet aware that we know of her plan. But she will be informed and charged with intent to murder. With everything else, it isn't looking good for her."

"She's no mother of mine. For all I care, she can rot in hell," Kincaid snarled.

I turned my head to press a kiss to his hand and felt some of his tension roll away.

Councilwoman Green nodded. "As you can see, there is a lot we missed. A lot we need to think about. And a lot we still need to understand. For now, do you have any questions?"

My pulse raced as I nodded. "Where are things going from here? For us? For the world?"

Councilwoman Rodriguez shifted in her seat, gaining our attention. "The knowledge of the Goddess of Darkness arising once again will run like wildfire through the people. Footage from the attack tonight is already going live all over the place. We've had our people set the story straight with the correct information about Crista being behind an uprising. People are already starting to see you, Goddess, as our hope for change."

She glanced around at her fellow council members before continuing. "We spoke before we arrived here in this room, and we have a few suggestions, but of course, you don't have to agree to anything. We will be altering the laws and regulations for all kinds. We would love it if Kincaid would consider stepping in as a councilman after he completes college. Unless he prefers to stay as the clan leader of this area. If he does, we'll find another suitable candidate for it, since Kane wishes to step away. The council would also be honored if you, Goddess, would work with us on the changes and help with situations that could need your attention. Your guidance would be appreciated in all matters we're unable to agree upon."

My heart filled with hope.

Could it be this easy?

Councilman Anderson tapped a knuckle on the table. "Over the next few days, we'd like to publicly announce your circle and let the people know of the new laws coming."

"Of course, this is if you, Goddess, agree with the new laws. As well as you, Kincaid." Councilwoman Wright grinned.

Looking behind me, I glanced up at Kincaid. He squeezed my shoulders. "May we have time to think on things?"

Councilman Nelson chuckled. "Smart, Alpha Kincaid. Take your time. For now, we'll go and deal with our prisoners."

They stood, glancing at each other before they turned back to me and bowed. My darkness hummed with happiness inside of me.

Councilman Moore said, "Alpha Amara." The new title he used gave me goose bumps. "Goddess of Darkness, thank you for controlling the situation tonight, and for the leniency you gave to those who were coerced. They will be questioned and dealt with."

Standing, I curtseyed.

"Please, Goddess, do not curtsey to us," Councilwoman Green said softly.

Straightening, I nodded. "I...." I blew out a breath and laughed a little uncomfortably. "It's I who am thankful for your understanding in everything that's happened."

Councilwoman Rodriguez grinned. "Humble as well. We'll speak soon."

~

In a way, we were all still in a daze when we arrived at Mr. Langley's—no, Kincaid's—cottage later that night after we'd showered and changed clothes at his family's estate. My body ached a little, and weariness tugged at my limbs, but when I opened the door, my throat thickened. Someone had done up the cottage. It was now clean and filled with furniture. A cute little six-seater table had been placed not far from the kitchen we stood in. My heart beat so fast, I gripped at my chest as I walked into the living room.

Turning, I asked, "Who did this?"

Levi shrugged. "Kincaid said he wanted the place tidied up, so I had someone come out and decorate it after doing some renovations."

"It's beautiful. Perfect. Stunning," I told him.

Levi grinned as he walked my way. I let out a breath when he picked me up and took me to the couch. He pulled me into his lap when he sat down. "I'm glad you love it, sweetheart. But I want to know how you're really doing."

Leaning into him, I sighed. "Honestly, I don't know." I shrugged as Silas sat down and hitched my legs up over his thighs.

Kincaid kneeled on the floor, facing us. He held my hand to his chest. "After everything that's happened, we're just happy to see you safe."

Tears welled. "We're all safe now."

Levi kissed my temple. "We are."

I drew in an unsteady breath. "I... I like what they're proposing. But I... I think I want to try a few courses at college before... well, before our lives get hectic with everything else."

"Do it then," Kincaid said. "There's nothing stopping you from trying anything now, love. You're no longer a maid, a servant. You're a free woman."

"But for now, how about we get some rest?" Silas suggested.

Smiling, I nodded. "I'd like that. All of us together."

Levi hummed. "It's good I bought the biggest bed there was. At least Kincaid's complaining should stop."

Kincaid glared as he stood. "I never complain."

Levi laughed while Silas snorted. Kincaid grumbled under his breath as he stole me from Levi's lap.

And even though the bed was huge, my mates still crowded close around me, and I fell asleep with a smile on my lips and a heart so full, it felt like it expanded my chest.

Happy. Safe.

And looking forward to a new start.

Only, it was sometime later when I woke to lips trailing up and down my neck and my dragon rutting against my ass.

Reaching back, I gripped his shoulder and breathed out, "Silas." He shifted back a little, and I fell onto him so I could take his mouth with my own. At first taste, I moaned into the kiss. His tongue slowly glided along and tangled with mine as he slid a hand into my panties and cupped my pussy. I pushed my ass back against his hardness and his dragon woke, chuffing from deep within his chest.

"Please." I whimpered into the kiss.

"I've got you, princess." He hooked his thumb into

the waistband of my panties, and I lifted a little as he slid them down. Spreading my legs, Silas tapped a finger against my clit. A shiver of lust raked over me. I bit down on my bottom lip and hummed in the back of my throat.

"Knees," Silas ordered gruffly.

Eagerly, I twisted around and got onto my knees. Silas shifted to kneel behind me. His fingers entered me first, and I gasped as he pumped them in and out.

"Fuck, princess, you're drenched."

"Yes," I whispered, nodding against the pillow. I jutted my ass back, and he sped up his finger fucking. Moaning, I turned my head to see Kincaid up on his elbow behind Levi, who was next to me, both watching with dark desire in their gazes.

Suddenly, I lost my dragon's fingers and let out a mew of complaint until Silas fisted my hair and dragged me up while he slid his cock inside me.

Moaning again, I reached back and gripped his hip. He locked an arm around my chest and slowly pulled out before he pushed back in just as leisurely.

"More, please," I begged.

"Soon," Silas bit out. He glided a hand over my breasts, down my stomach, and stopped to cup my pussy. I glanced to the side. Levi was palming his dick, watching Silas's hand. Kincaid's gaze was locked on my face.

Silas spread my pussy lips. "Lick, Levi," he ordered.

Levi dove forward and tongued at my clit. I cried out his name and held his head close while I watched him. He glided his tongue up, over, and around my clit before dipping low to lick over where Silas thrust in and out.

Silas grunted behind me, and his chuffing rose while

Levi purred between my legs. Kincaid suddenly stood and stepped in front of me. I opened my mouth, sticking my tongue out, and he slapped his cock against it, over and over.

I went to close my mouth around him, but I looked up in time to see him shake his head. He wiped his wet tip over my cheeks, my tongue, and neck, marking me with his scent.

"Fuck," Silas gritted out. He held me tightly in place by my hips while he pumped in and out. Levi slipped a hand between my legs, feeling Silas's cock entering me.

My body coiled tight at the oncoming orgasm while I cupped the back of Levi's head as he sucked, nipped, and licked at my clit. My other palm coasted up Kincaid's leg to play with his tight balls when he finally let me lock my lips around his cock. Gripping my hair, he held me still and fucked my mouth with a silent snarl on his face. His fangs peeked out, and hell, did I love that look on him.

"Jesus," Silas yelled. He kissed and nipped at my neck while he grunted and groaned as he filled me with his cum.

Silas slowed his thrusts. I tugged on Levi's hair when his tongue and lips helped drive me overboard. I pulled off Kincaid's cock to cry out. My body shook from the intensity.

Warmth splashed over my face and chest. I opened my eyes to see the last spurts of Kincaid's cum spilling out to land over me.

Panting, I reached up and ran my fingers over my chest before I stuck them in my mouth to lick him clean. Kincaid swore under his breath, and I shivered as Silas slipped out of me and moved back. Kincaid was shoved to the side next, and Levi was in front of me, between my legs on his knees.

He lapped at my chest, taking Kincaid's seed in while sucking on my nipple. He kissed and licked his way up until he had my mouth, sharing Kincaid's cum with me. Levi then guided me onto my back, and I spread my legs to accommodate his weight while he filled me with his cock.

"Fuck. Warm, wet, and still full of cum. Love it." Levi grinned down at me until his face pinched. "Shit, I'm not going to last."

"Give it to me then," I told him.

"Sweetheart, you've got to come first."

Laughing lightly, I shook my head. "I already did."

"Again," he said against my lips. "Kincaid."

My hand was lifted from Levi's back, and I sucked in a breath when Kincaid pierced my skin at my wrist with his fangs.

More pleasure spiked through me as Levi lifted himself onto his palm beside me so he could drive in and out, slapping our skin together.

Another pull from Kincaid's mouth and I crashed over into a second orgasm.

"Thank fuck," Levi groaned. His hips stuttered and then slowed as he pumped the last of his cum inside me.

Epilogue

AMARA

Five Years Later

"Sweetheart, come back to bed," Levi called from the other room. I hadn't long crawled out and showered, but my lion was always frisky. All right, I'd admit that all my men were.

"Later. We have food to prepare."

An arm wrapped around my waist, and a nose was pressed against my neck. Wet hair tickled my cheek. "Let me help. I'll make a dessert. We know what a sweet tooth you are." Silas kissed me before he went to the refrigerator to grab some eggs. "What would you like, cookies or muffins?"

I grinned and faced him for a moment. "Cookies, please." He caught my gaze and smirked. He read me so well. He stepped up and cupped my cheeks, kissing me again.

A groan sounded from down the hallway.

Silas pulled back and snorted. "Looks like Levi found someone to entertain him."

We both laughed when we heard Kincaid cursing, "Fuck yes. Lick it like that again."

I was glad Levi was busy; he was a disaster in the kitchen and often distracted me, and I couldn't have that now when I knew our guests would be on the way. "Do you think steak and salad will be enough?" I asked when he went back to gathering the ingredients. The steak was on the counter, warming to room temperature while I sliced up some tomatoes. I'd already made a potato salad and had moved on to a Greek one.

"It should be, since we know Mary will bring something."

"True." I beamed over at him. Silas loved to help me cook when we stayed at the cottage. Being here was different than being at our estate. There we had employees who did our cooking and were paid a proper wage and actually wanted to work for us. It helped so much, since our days were always busy.

For Kincaid's final year at college, I'd gone with him and had stood beside him and my shifters in the halls as an equal. We'd only separated when I went to my own classes. Still, I'd had one of my shifters with me at all times.

And I found I needed them often in the first year after revealing myself. They supported me through the stares.

The judgment. The... fans. Which was something I never expected to happen in my life. But I now had people who admired me and my darkness.

The attention was strange, but I would take all of the admirers over the ones who hated me and my power. I'd expected there to be a risk of malice and fear, but I never anticipated the death threats.

Slowly, they'd eased up and were now far and few compared to the early days. Still, I wouldn't change anything. If I hadn't revealed my true self, I would have lost my world, my mates.

Our lives were understandably different, and really, there were more good days than bad.

The world had also definitely changed since the night of the attack when Crista tried to destroy our bond and my shifter mates.

To this day, I still couldn't believe how lucky we'd been that night and still were now with the changes in place.

Humans were once again free from their servitude. Though, some stayed in their positions—with an added bonus and a real wage—because their employer had always treated them with respect.

The biggest change the council made was to appoint a few humans as area leaders. One area was for humans who'd been traumatized by the other species, where they could live peacefully without the fear of the paranormal. That area was controlled by the army and navy, and my mates and I stepped in as needed when people tried to take away what we'd built for those who still suffered from nightmares from their time as servants.

We also assisted with other situations when the council needed us to. They'd been right when they'd said not everyone would agree with change. To this day, there were still those who tried to stand against us, seeking control, power, and money.

And we took them down every time.

A kiss to my neck dragged me from my thoughts. "You all right, love?"

Dropping the knife, I turned in Kincaid's arms. "I am. Just thinking how fortunate we've been."

He snarled low. "Except when the nonbelievers try to test you."

Reaching up, I curled an arm around his neck and kissed him. "Nothing we can't all handle together."

"Damn right," Silas agreed.

"It just infuriates me that there are people who think your power is all smoke and mirrors," Kincaid complained roughly.

I shrugged. "If they have to see it for themselves by trying to bring me down, then so be it."

His jaw clenched, and Silas growled off to the side. They hated it when someone questioned my darkness even when there was enough proof online or from the stories told about that night. Still, I'd always thought that if nonbelievers were stupid enough to try and come at us, we'd show them that we couldn't be contended with. No matter how many they brought with them.

A knock sounded on the cottage door. Kincaid kissed me quickly and walked over to answer it. He opened the door, nodded, and stepped back. "Father."

Kincaid stilled when Kane hesitantly hugged his son.

Kane stepped back and dipped his head my way. "Hello, Alpha Amara."

I smiled. "Remember, Kane. Here it's just Amara."

"Amara." He smiled gently.

"Where are Lyall and Elliot?" I asked. We shouldn't have been surprised when Kane announced he was in a relationship with his former gardener, but we had been. Still, the man had definitely changed from the vampire he used to be.

Kincaid was slowly accepting his father into his life again. It was hard to forgive the pain Kincaid had been put through. But it was coming. My vampire had a soft heart.

What helped was the way Kane treated me. A few days after the events five years previous, Kane had approached me and broken down over his part in what had happened. He'd also been so very thankful to me for saving his life. I never told him it'd been a hard decision because of the heartache he'd caused Kincaid, but deep down, I'd felt he'd tried everything he could to prepare his son, even if he went about it all wrong.

"Much to Elliot's displeasure, they had to be elsewhere. They promised to come next time."

"They'll be missed."

He gave me another tender smile. "I'll let them know." He turned to my dragon shifter. "Silas."

"Kane," Silas greeted.

"Is there anything I can do to help?" Kane asked.

Smiling gratefully, I nodded toward the stack of knives and forks. "Could you and Kincaid set the table outside?"

"Of course." He nodded and grabbed the items before walking outside.

Kincaid slid up to me and nipped at my bottom lip. "I know what you're doing."

I gave him an innocent look. "I don't know what you're talking about."

A gasp escaped me when his fangs pierced my neck. I clutched his shoulders as my core throbbed. "Not fair," I whined. Not that I minded at all.

Kincaid licked over the spot and pulled back, smirking. "I don't know what you're talking about." He turned me, gave my butt a slap, and walked out after gathering up the placemats and plates.

Silas stood chuckling while he rolled the dough into balls and placed them on a baking tray. I glared and he grinned wide.

A lion appeared in the kitchen and stalked up to me, rubbing his face over my hips, nearly knocking me to the side.

I ran my hands through his mane, loving the softness. "They'll be here soon." Just as I spoke, the door swung open.

"The party people have arrived," Mary announced with a beaming smile. Only next she was dodging the rascals that followed her into the house. They squealed and ran for Levi. He jumped out of the way and raced outside with Mary's horde following.

As I laughed, Mary rolled her eyes and set down the trays she carried before hugging me tightly.

"Hey, honey." Mary smiled.

"Hi, it's good to see you."

The squeals outside grew louder after we heard a roar. Mary snorted. "Levi needs a tribe of his own to play with."

I shrugged. "One day." If my mates had anything to say about it, I'd be pregnant the next time I was fertile. What they didn't know was that I was on board with the idea. I loved seeing my men with Mary's kids. My ovaries exploded every time. I was ready for the next stage in our lives.

Mary turned to her boss. "Silas, good to see you barefoot and in the kitchen."

"Mary, where's your better half?"

She mock glared. "Talking to Kincaid and Kane outside."

"We're nearly done here," I told her, and together we finished cooking before taking it all outside.

"Cassar." I smiled as I put some food on the table.

"Amara, lovely to see you." He held his arms out for a hug, but Kincaid spun me back out of his reach.

"Come sit, relax, and eat," Kincaid said. Cassar snorted and rolled his eyes. Even though Cassar and Mary had been married for over three years, my men were still possessive when other men were near. Though, I was the same about women.

We settled at the table and sat around eating and talking. Usually, we had Levi's and Silas's families with us, but they were busy.

I could never have guessed where my life would lead me after my first day at Kincaid's estate. Glancing around, my chest swelled with how right this felt. How contented I was.

I leaned over and kissed Silas when he looked at me. Then I winked at Levi on Silas's other side as he bounced one of Mary's toddlers on his knee. Turning to find

Kincaid, I saw he was already there, waiting for my gaze with a smirk and soft eyes.

God, I loved them. They made my life so much better. Complete.

No longer did I fear where my life would lead. No longer did I live in worry.

I smiled down at my plate as my darkness buzzed inside me.

Who would have guessed that by accepting myself within the darkness, I would find love and be at peace with the world that was becoming a beautiful one.

Read on for a look inside:
Infinite Bond
A m/m/m/m stand-alone fantasy romance

INFINITE BOND

L. ROSE

Chapter One

MICAH

As I PICKED up the dirty dishes from a table, I couldn't help but overhear the waitress, Tanika, serving a new group sitting in a booth close by.

"Welcome to Danny's. Can I start anyone with drinks?"

"Can you tell me why your boss would hire a freak like that?"

Already, I knew they were talking about me. The guy's voice sounded familiar, one I probably pushed to the back of my mind from my high school days of being bullied. I didn't need this crap on top of the fact I was feeling like hell.

My head throbbed, and a headache wouldn't be far away.

Tanika harrumphed. "Sorry, who are you talking about?"

"Can't remember his name, but he used to slink around high school like a loser. I see he still dyes his hair that weird color. What a fucking loser."

I had always liked my dyed light blue hair. At first, I dyed it to try and get people to notice me, as I was tired of feeling alone. It failed. But now I did it because *I* liked it, and it made me feel different from others. Something special.

"I'm guessing you're talking about Micah." From Tanika's tone, I could tell she was pissed. From the first day we'd worked together two years ago, Tanika had been protective of me. Even though we were twenty-one, she'd taken me under her wing, accepting my quiet nature.

A tornado of worry formed in my gut.

Tanika and I hadn't gone to the same school. She didn't know I'd been the loner. The kid who lived in a trailer park with a drugged-out mother. The kid who got beat on for just being around. The kid who was nothing and no one to anyone.

God, I sounded pathetic.

I reminded myself that I got out of that trailer. Got away from her. It didn't matter that I was in my own trailer on the other side of town. It was still all *mine.*

Who cared that people didn't like me because I was quiet, and that made me seem strange? Or because I was timid—thanks to my mother—and book smart?

Only, I wasn't smart enough to gain a scholarship and go to a college far away. Instead, I was stuck in this hellish town, working three jobs just to keep my head above water in case Mom's debt collector paid me a visit when Mom didn't have the funds needed to pay off her gambling debts. It had happened before, quite a few times, and the reminder of my fear from the first time, when Lax, her debt collector, held me at knifepoint as he screamed at Mom to pay, had me setting aside what I could as a "just in case." I'd only been seven then, but it'd been embedded in my mind since.

Really, I didn't even have time for community college.

Would Tanika think differently of me from the guy's words?

"Yeah, that's the one. Shit, he was such a—"

Tanika threw her notepad in the guy's face. A woman beside him yelled in complaint, but Tanika ignored everyone while she pressed her hands to the table and leaned into his face.

Happiness floated through me from Tanika's actions, but I had to stop this. Usually, I wouldn't involve myself in confrontations. I hated fighting or talking, really. But this was Tanika. A friend. My only friend.

"Take your fucking foul mouth and ugly face out of this diner before I kick your ass."

The guy smirked with a glare. "You're getting defensive over *that* guy?"

"He's more of a man than you'll ever be." The warmth from her words had me straightening and flicking my light blue hair from my eyes. Tanika swung her arm back, and I moved quickly over to her, taking her elbow in hand and spinning her around until she was at my back.

"Leave," I told the guy. I still couldn't remember his name or face, just his voice as one of many who taunted me.

He smirked. "Are you going to make me?"

Fiery anger spread through me—a feeling I wasn't used to. But I was older, and I *didn't* have to put up with his words.

"I will if I have to." It may have been fake bravery, but I honestly thought that if push came to shove, I would stand up to him now because I had someone at my back I cared about, and I didn't want Tanika to think she was alone in her fight to have my back. I'd be by her side, as she was the first person to *want* to know me.

I clenched my shaking hands, wishing he'd just disappear from in front of me. I wanted him gone. I wanted him... to hurt. My gaze flicked to the salt and pepper shakers on the table before I moved my glare back to him.

I stumbled back into Tanika's hands. Blinking rapidly, I watched as the guy rubbed his forehead and throat.

The shakers had forcibly flown across the table and smacked into the guy before shattering, leaving salt and pepper, plus glass, all over him.

"Oi, what the fuck is going on over here?" Ivan, the owner of the diner, strode over and stopped beside Tanika and me, throwing his hands onto his large waist.

Tanika gently shoved me aside. "They were saying shit about Micah, and the table tipped when he went to stand, spraying salt and pepper over him."

That didn't happen.

Did it?

It did.

Right?

Glancing at the other couple, I saw they stared dumbfounded at their friend. The shock on their faces told me I couldn't point the weirdness in their direction. They hadn't done anything.

How did the shakers move?

Pressing my fingers to my lips, I hid my snort under my breath. I was overthinking it. There was nothing strange or special about what just happened.

"Get out, now." Ivan pointed toward the door.

"That's not what happened," the guy yelled. As he stood, salt and pepper rained down all over the floor from his body.

Ivan crossed his arms over his chest. "Yeah? Then tell me what happened." I caught Tanika poke Ivan in the side.

"*He* did this." The guy threw a hand my way.

Tanika mimicked Ivan's stance and snorted. "He wasn't even close to the salt and pepper."

The woman climbed out of the booth, as did the others. "Jon's right. He made them move across the table."

Tanika and Ivan laughed loudly. Tanika even bent at the waist to slap her thigh. She straightened, wiped under her eyes, and shook her head. "Did you hear that, Ivan?"

Ivan chuckled again. "I did."

My head throbbed again, and a new pain burned in my stomach, which had me gripping it.

"You think he used his mind to move things across the table?" Tanika shook her head. "You're crazy."

"Are you on drugs?" Ivan demanded. "I don't allow junkies in my diner. You need to get the fuck out of here."

Jon went red in the face. "I'm not on drugs or a damn junkie. It's that freak you have working for you."

"Sure," Ivan drew out. "Look, take your shit magic

trick and work it on someone else. You ain't getting my worker in trouble for something you did."

"I didn't—"

The woman beside Jon touched his arm. She shook her head. "It's not worth it."

Jon clenched his jaw before he dropped a sigh and started for the door. As he went by me, he gave me a new look. This one held fear, and I wasn't sure why. I hadn't done anything, and he was wrong if he thought I'd somehow moved those shakers.

"Thanks, guys," I said, facing Tanika and Ivan, who were both staring at me. I tucked the long strands of hair behind my ear. I needed to cut the front of it. Though, it was good to have it longer to hide behind. Yeah, I would probably leave it.

Why was I thinking of my hair?

To distract myself, maybe? To stop focusing on the pulsating behind my eyes and the way my stomach wanted to revolt?

"Are you feeling okay, Micah?" Tanika asked with a furrowed brow. Her mirth had quickly changed to worry.

How had she read me so quickly? Besides my body acting up, I felt like Ivan had turned the heat up in the diner.

Wiping at my brow, I nodded. My hair dropped forward into my eyes again. "Yeah, I'm fine." I gestured toward the door where Jon and his friends had just walked through. "Sorry about that situation."

Ivan slapped a hand on my shoulder. "Don't stress, kid. I know you wouldn't cause trouble." He smiled, but it was a little strained. "You sure you're good, though?"

"Yes. I only have an hour left anyway." My head pulsed again. Maybe I was coming down with something.

"All right. Let me know if you want to shoot off early. Tanika, keep an eye on him."

"You got it, boss." She saluted Ivan's back as he made his way into the kitchen, then bumped into my hip. "You know Ivan won't care if you need to get out of here. Or I can call in Jassy early."

"No, really, it's just a headache." Their kindness nearly brought tears to my eyes.

She grabbed my arm and gave it a squeeze. "Let me know if you need anything."

Nodding, I moved back to clear the table and take the dishes to the kitchen. Maybe when I said I only had Tanika as a friend, I was wrong. Ivan was also one. He took a chance on hiring me and had also stuck up for me before.

It just annoyed me that my past couldn't stay in the past where it belonged.

I'd been lucky enough in the last two years that no one else who'd haunted my days in high school had come into the diner. It had been bound to happen. I just wished it hadn't been tonight. I was already freaking out about seeing Lax, the debt collector, since the scene of Mom coming into the diner earlier was still fresh.

The door opened, and I happened to glance that way. Mom spotted me and stalked right up to shove my shoulder.

"I need money." She scratched at her arm and glanced around in jerky motions.

My heart beat franticly as I told her softly, "I won't have anything until after my shift."

The panic in her eyes set my pulse to race. But in a blink, she changed and scowled up at me. "You useless piece of trash." She itched at her arm again, at the scabs. "Why the fuck did I give birth to you? I should have aborted such a waste of space. Hopefully, *they'll* take care of you for me." And with that final note, she stormed from the diner.

I wanted to stand up to her, or more so to Lax like I had Jon, but Lax worked for someone with a worse reputation in town, which made him scarier than anyone I knew.

Hate pumped through my veins over how weak I sounded and acted. I ground my teeth together as I walked back out into the diner. My head hammered again, but it wasn't the worst pain I'd had. I'd put up with beating after beating whenever Mom had a boyfriend over with a violent streak. There were also the times I got my ass handed to me at school, usually after I'd found enough courage to smart back with a comment.

Those beatings had worn me down to a point where I didn't see a reason to fight back or say anything. When I did, they only got worse.

Sighing, I picked up another set of dirty dishes and forced those depressing thoughts from my mind.

I had survived.

I was surviving on my own two feet and away from her.

One day I would get away from here. One day I would

think back to these situations and laugh at them because I'd be rich, smarter, and worth something.

My future *would* be better.

My stomach twisted and my lunch threatened to show up. I placed the bucket down on the table I'd been cleaning and sucked in some deep breaths. I flicked my hair away from my eyes and glanced at the clock on the wall. There were still another twenty minutes to go. I had to make it for the money.

Sucking in another deep breath, I picked up the bucket, cringing when my stomach clenched.

"Hey," Tanika said from my side so suddenly, I jumped. She smiled apologetically. "Sorry. Look, I think you should get going. It's not long until your shift ends, and I'm sure Ivan will still pay you for it."

Shaking my head, I rubbed at my stomach. "Then I feel like I'm cheating him." My head picked that moment to throb painfully. I closed my eyes and sucked in a sharp breath.

"That's it." She took my arm in one hand and the bucket in the other. My gaze flared at her strength. How could she carry it with one hand, especially since I'd found it so heavy with dishes?

Tanika marched me out into the kitchen, where Ivan was laughing at something with his wife, Flora. Once they saw us, they stopped.

"Micah's leaving a little early," Tanika announced.

"Micah, are you all right? You do look a little green." Flora approached and rested her hand against my forehead. "And clammy."

Taking her hand from my skin, I patted it to show my

appreciation for her concern before letting go. Flora was a sweet soul, but I wasn't close to her as I was Tanika, and I didn't enjoy people touching me. I'd only grown used to it with Tanika, as she was super affectionate, and over the years, she'd gotten me used to it.

"It's just a headache and a slightly twisted stomach. Nothing I can't handle. I can still finish my shift."

They all shared a look. Flora's lips thinned in worry while Ivan's brows dropped in confusion. About what, I didn't know.

"Tanika will walk you home."

No!

"No, I'll be fine." Quickly, I undid the apron, pulled it over my head, and stalked to the cubby where I stashed it before I grabbed my wallet and keys.

If Tanika accompanied me home, and Lax showed, he would see her and somehow drag her into something horrid. I didn't have a doubt about it at all. I couldn't let that happen.

"I'll get going. See you all tomorrow night." I opened the back door.

"Micah, wait. I'll come." Tanika tried pulling her own apron off but got stuck in it.

"No, stay. No one's here to take both our shifts. Bye." I waved lamely and quickly stepped out, shutting the door behind me.

In a rush, I started my walk home. I kept glancing over my shoulder to check Tanika wasn't there. Thankfully, she hadn't followed. It wasn't until I neared the trailer park that I realized I'd forgotten to pick up my pay.

"Shit," I muttered.

A whistle sounded, startling me. "That's a naughty word for a guy like you, Micah."

Stuff me in the ass with knives.

Anything would be better than facing Lax when he realized I didn't have any money for him.

Turning slowly, I caught Lax moving out of the shadows and into the light of the streetlight. Four other guys followed him. Usually, he had about ten guys with him. Maybe he noticed I didn't put up a fight and told the others to go deal with someone else.

God, I'm weak.

"Lax...." My head throbbed as I wiped my sweaty palms on my pants. "I, ah, wasn't feeling well at work. I left early and forgot to get my pay. Can I give what Mom owes your boss tomorrow?"

Lax laughed. The others quickly joined in when he shot them a look.

Tension tightened my shoulders as I drooped them more, trying to make myself invisible but knowing it wouldn't work.

My stomach clenched and my head pulsated.

Slowly, I rubbed at my temples.

"Aw, look, guys. Poor little Micah has a headache."

More laughter rang out.

My stomach warmed in anger. I was sick of this. Sick of going from one messed-up situation to another. Sick of being weak. Sick of all the self-loathing, and the "I wishes," and the "I should haves."

"Hey, I'm talking to you." My shoulder got shoved. I stumbled back, lifting my gaze to Lax. "You go back to work and get me the goddamn money." He looked down at his hand. "Why the fuck you wet?"

I knew I'd been sweating from the pain, but I hadn't realized how much.

"Jesus." He wiped his hand on his jeans. "Just go back and get the money."

"No." My tone was soft but snappish. It even surprised me. If my head wasn't crying out for aspirin, I would have patted myself on the back.

Lax crossed his arms over his chest. "No?"

Nodding, I rubbed at my forehead.

"You're not listening again," Lax yelled, and I flinched, snapping my gaze up to his livid red face.

"Lax, please. I'm not well."

He leaned in and snarled in my face, "I don't give a fuck."

My head rocked back from the force of his punch that followed. Blood sprayed from my nose. Covering it, I stepped back.

"Go back to work and get your money. Last fucking time I tell you, or else I'm sending the boys into your trailer."

They would take everything.

Pain stabbed at my temples and stomach. I took another step back.

Lax's jaw clenched. "Right, guys, teach him a fucking lesson, and I want his keys."

"No," I cried out, moving back further. The trailer was all I had. "No!" I yelled, throwing my hands out in front of me.

His people suddenly flew back from where they'd

been standing and landed on their asses; groans filled the area.

Lax wasn't the only one with wide eyes. Slowly, he looked at me. "What did you do?"

"N-nothing."

He started for me. I backed up over and over and didn't stop until a new voice, a voice I knew, said, "Stop right there."

Ivan and Tanika moved out from within the trees. Lax looked to them and back at me before he ran at me.

"Stop." I threw my hand out to the side, and Lax shot the same way my hand moved.

Dumbfounded, I looked down at my hand as I heard Lax drop to the ground with his own groan. It was then I noticed the pain in my head and stomach had vanished.

"You're all right," Tanika said from right in front of me. I saw her shoes first, then lifted my gaze to hers. She smiled softly. "Hey, it'll be fine now."

"Did... did I do that?"

She patted my shoulder and nodded. "Yep. Bit of a late bloomer, but that was all you."

"What? How.... I...." I shook my head and looked over to Ivan, who helped Lax to his feet. I called out quickly, "He's armed. He's always armed."

Tanika curled her arm around my shoulders and steered me toward the trailer park. "Don't worry about him. Ivan will have it covered."

It was fine to say don't worry, but fear still formed a pit in my gut.

I looked over my shoulder to see Ivan leading Lax over to his guys. Surprise shot through meLax moved willingly.

He didn't put up a fight, didn't say anything, just walked beside Ivan like I hadn't just thrown him across the ground.

But I had.

Somehow, I'd moved him. I just didn't know how.

Facing forward and with my heart in my throat, I stared down at my hands again. I swallowed thickly.

Excitement and fear churned inside me.

Glancing at Tanika, I wondered why she wasn't freaked out. "Did you see what happened?"

"I did." She stopped at my trailer.

Wait, how did she know where I lived?

When she looked my way, she laughed. "Don't worry, I'm not a stalker. Open up, and I'll give you some answers while you pack."

My head jerked back in shock. "Pack?"

"Well, yeah. There's a place where you can learn how to use your powers."

"Powers?" I whispered.

"Yep. I don't know if you'll have more, but it looks like you have telekinesis."

As I tripped up the steps, all I could think was that I didn't want to face-plant. I put my hands out to stop my fall but found myself flying backward into Tanika. She grunted before I was suddenly weightless again and my butt hit the ground.

Tanika stood beside the door, grinning.

I glanced to my doorway and back to her. "How... you were behind me."

She knelt beside me and placed her hand on my shoulder. "There's a lot you need to learn, young grasshopper."

Also by L. Rose

The Hidden Kingdom Trilogy

(why choose)

A Torn Paige

A Lost Paige

A Final Paige

Standalones

Infinite Bond (m/m/m/m)

Within the Darkness (m/m/f/m)

Titles under Lila Rose

Hawks MC: Ballarat Charter

Holding Out (Free)

Outplayed (standalone related to the Hawks MC)

Climbing Out

Finding Out (novella)

Black Out

No Way Out

Coming Out (m/m novella)

Out to Find Freedom (standalone related to the Hawks MC)

Hawks MC: Caroline Springs Charter

The Secret's Out

Hiding Out

Down and Out

Living Without

Walkout (novella)

Hear Me Out (m/m)

Break Out (novella)

Fallout

Hawks MC: next generation

Coyote

Ruin (m/m)

Texas

Standalones related to the Hawks MC

Out of the Blue

Out Gamed (novella)

Romantic Comedies

Making Changes

Making Sense

Fumbled Love

Bumbled Love

Polished P & P series (m/m romance)

Wreck Me Forever

Never a Saint

Working Out West

Diamond MC

Country

State

Trinity Love

Left to Chance

(Includes bonus novella of Love of Liberty)